GAIA II

OUR FIRST VOYAGE TO THE STARS

BOOK 1

JACK R. WOODS

First Edition.

First Printing, December 2017

Available for nationwide print-on-demand distribution through Ingram Content Group.

ISBN 9780692952382
LCCN 2017914502

Cover art by Hubert (Skip) Hicks.

Contact Jack at jrwoods57@gmail.com

FORWARD

First, I'd like to thank you for picking up this book to read it. A lot of time and energy has been put into researching, writing and editing, while working at a full-time job and trying not to totally neglect my family. Every star and some planets that Gaia II will visit are real places. Trying to get the science right to the best of my ability has been very important to me. In the beginning, Gaia II was going to be one large novel with five parts. It now appears that it is going to be eight books.

I've wanted to write this book for about forty years now. My motivation has been the desire to voyage to and explore other solar systems. More than likely, no one will be taking this trip in my lifetime, so I am taking a "voyage of the imagination". This phrase, of course, was coined by Carl Sagan for his classic series "Cosmos". I believe Sagan wrote "Contact" for the same reason. He came to realize that it was looking pretty bleak that SETI was going to find intelligent alien life while he was still with us on the planet.

There are several reasons why I am finally following through on my lifelong dream. So much information is available at our fingertips now. I am making a promise here that, if I make any money from this series of books, that I will make a healthy donation to "Wikipedia". There is also a wonderful resource called ADS (Astrophysical Data System) http://adswww.harvard.edu/ and a motivational on-line magazine put out by NASA called Astrobiology Magazine http://www.astrobio.net/. What has mostly inspired me is the revolution in the discovery of new planets around other stars. As of May 19, 2017 there are 3610 *confirmed* exoplanets (http://exoplanet.eu/) with still many more candidates from the Kepler mission awaiting confirmation. With the coming of extremely large, new technology, ground based telescopes, aided by an amazing system called "adaptive optics", this generation is privileged to be living through a "Golden Age of Exoplanet Discovery and Classification". We have always suspected they would be there, but to actually detect them and get information like mass estimates and orbital radii is unbelievable.

Non-fiction classics such as "The High Frontier" by Gerard K. O'Neill, the Gaia series of books by James Lovelock, "Leaving the Earth by Space Elevator" by Bradley Edwards and Phillip Ragan and "Physics of the Future" by Michio Kaku have so inspired me over the years that I wanted to incorporate these ideas into a science fiction novel. One of my favorite books is a very thorough compilation entitled "Exoplanets", edited by Sara Seager. This book will be used extensively in my future writings. Never would I have dreamed, when I was in college, that a book about alien planets at this level would exist in my lifetime.

There are numerous other internet sites and other information sources that I relied on. For instance, a website called "futuretimeline" http://www.futuretimeline.net/ , is the basis for my own "Abbreviated History of the 21st Century" (events that effect Gaia II's voyage). There is a full listing of website sources along with fictional and non-fictional books and video resources in my appendix.

Also, in the appendix, there is a glossary of terminology used in this writing. Again, I need to thank Wikipedia for the accuracy of my definitions. The asterisk marked terms and names are ones that I created for this novel. Others seem like I made them up, but are real concepts being developed today (such as catoms).

A list of the stars and "planets of interest" that Gaia II will visit is provided in a Mission Itinerary in the appendix. A star map illustration uses galactic coordinates, because this is the best way to visualize star locations in relation to the sun. This first book only travels to one star and its red dwarf companion. There are seventeen more to go not counting the companions.

I had a particularly fun time designing space hotels as part of space elevator systems and would love to see a talented architect tackle the project with three dimensional models. Along the same vein, I tried to convey my fascination with the O'Neill cylinder in my descriptions of the Living Areas of Gaia II. Future books in the series will get more in depth into examining the Life Support Cylinder. There will also be new Living Regions created.

As with most books, this has not been a totally solo effort. Ideas have come from family and friends on numerous occasions. My wife came up with the maglev ring as a means to board the rotating ship and a buddy at work helped me decide on what my crisis would be near the end of the book. My daughter actually came up with the "Phoenix" constellation that Ali Zamani draws while contemplating the sun from Gliese 250. I couldn't believe that someone, Bruce Mills, actually figured out how the stars would be arranged when looking back from this system. See this site: (http://www.bdm.id.au/localspace/systems/250.html).

Several people have read my drafts before a final version was submitted. They offered suggestions from a reader's point of view and I tried to listen and do what I could. Unfortunately, being a first time author, I had a very difficult time finding experts with whom to discuss the "science" of Gaia II. A graduate student, in the University of Washington Astrobiology program, Brett Morris, did clue me in on "serpentization". My daughter has a biology degree with a computer science minor and has been constantly correcting my false thinking in these fields.

I have tremendous respect for the greats of hard sci-fi. Isaac Asimov, Arthur C. Clarke, Carl Sagan and others kept me fascinated as a youth and younger adult. More recently, Kim Stanley Robinson has become my favorite (this book was completed before *Aurora* came out). As I write more, my story telling and literary skills will improve. I doubt that I will ever reach the level of those mentioned above, but I hope that there is a select audience *out there* who will enjoy this series.

In closing, I would like to thank my wife and daughter for putting up with my obsession.

FOUR THINGS THAT MAN MAY NEVER BE ABLE TO DO

1) Cause there to be negative entropy in a closed system or prevent positive entropy.

2) Cause any object* to have a velocity vector, in space-time, greater than the speed of light.

3) Create matter/energy from nothing

4) Create complex life from inorganic matter

  *larger that 10^{-15} meters

CONSEQUENCES OF THE ABOVE:

A) Can't travel backwards in time
                (same as first part of 1)

B) Can't travel faster than light in 3 dimensions
                (consequence of 2 and A)

C) Teleportation of living organisms not possible
                (same as 4)

D) Cryogenics for long periods of time not possible
                (consequence of second part of 1)

If man can ever accomplish 1 through 4 he can truly call himself God.

cc www.scientific-american.com/2100/Jan/pg36

ABBREVIATED 21ST CENTURY TIMELINE*

Late 20th Century

1969	Man steps on the moon (first visit to an extraterrestrial body)
1976	Viking probes land on Mars (first man-made object to land on another planet)
1989	Fall of Berlin Wall symbolizes end of the "cold war", beginning of a new dangerous age
1990	Hubble Space Telescope launched (revolutionizes astronomy)
1991	Carbon nanotubes discovered by Sumio Iijima working for Nippon Electric Company
1995	First exoplanet orbiting sun-like star discovered by Michel Mayor etal. (51 Pegasi b)
1996-2007	Smart phone developed (voted #1 technology that changed humanity)

21st Century

2000	Worldwide celebration welcomes the new millennium
2001	Attack on World Trade Center towers symbolizes the new destructive power of the few
2001	Wikipedia's first year on the internet
2003	Mapping of all of the genes of the human genome completed
2004	Beginning of the testing of "BrainGate™" technology at Brown University
2004	Breakthrough with graphene will revolutionize many industries
2005	You Tube's first year

2009	3D Scanning hits the market
2009	Launch of Kepler Telescope ignites an explosion of exoplanet discovery
2010	Solar sail technology is successfully demonstrated
2012	First 100 Year Starship Symposium held (outlines the hurdles to overcome)
2012	Voyager probe is the first man-made object to leave the solar system
2012	Higgs boson discovered at CERN (completes Standard Model of Particle Physics)
2012-2013	Planetary Resources and Deep Space Industries founded (later to be mega-industries)
2013	Gaia astrometry mission launched (finds first planets using this method)
2016	First observation of gravitational waves announced (a new "window" of astronomy)
2017	"Googles" released to mass market (first "smart glasses")
2019	James Webb Space Telescope launched (replaces legendary Hubble Space Telescope)
2019	First molecular computer sold commercially (Moore's Law extended)
2019	Last new gasoline powered cars manufactured
2020	New Decade Symposium: "space junk" declared an international crisis
2021	First HHM (Home Health Monitoring) devices mass produced
2022	"Comm-goggles" surpass smart phones in sales
2023	Particle discovery at CERN may prove that dark matter is a family of heavy particles
2026	Breakthrough in Japan allows production of unlimited length carbon nanotube ribbons

2029	First Space Elevator at Tsiolkosky Station in the Pacific Ocean is completed
2029	Can purchase your own full genetic code on digital media
2030	New Decade Symposium: Decade long "space junk" clean up successful (90%)
2030	State of the Earth Accords foresees dire consequences of global warming soon to come
2032	5 Year Southern Planetary Survey completed by CODEX at E-ELT (out to 200 LY)
2032	Launch of NGIRI (New Generation Infrared Interferometer) long awaited planet finder
2033	Privately funded craft to Europa successfully penetrates to subsurface ocean (no life)
2034	Once in a century solar flare detected. Worldwide grid shutdown prevents disaster
2035	Major clash in Southern Europe highlights global warming refugee crisis
2036	Russia overtakes US in food production (regains a "superpower" status)
2037	First nano-medicines ("smart bombs") are used
2039	Ocean acidification peaks (coral reefs and many species have been lost)
2039	The last of the three Earth space elevators, base stations and geostations completed
2040	New Decade Symposium: Project initiated to launch "nanocraft" to stars in ten years
2041	First solar energy satellite beams energy to Earth
2042	First "space habitats" being built (resorts for the wealthy)
2044	First permanent moon base established (Lunar South Pole, by Shackleton Crater)

2045	Secret study of "fountain of youth" technology results in international ban
2047	Triad of far side lunar observatories and connecting rails completed and operational
2048	Special UN meeting decides to create an isolated "tech city" in Antarctica
2049	First lunar mine in full operation supplying materials to space construction
2050	New Decade Symposium: Decision to establish a permanent manned station on Mars
2051	Increase in internet bandwidth to allow "holovision"
2052	First fusion reactor with 10X power output secretly operational in Antarctica
2050-2055	Crossroads for Humanity: world population peaks (can technology save us from itself)
2050-2055	Nanocraft Project sends tiny probes to twenty stars using laser light-sail propulsion
2055	"Tech City" in West Antarctica complete (name sticks)/ First families move in
2056	Apollo Space Telescope in L2 location is first with mirrors made on the moon
2058	"Catoms" (programmable matter) are commercially produced
2058	Mars Research Station completed in Sagan Crater
2060	UN Emergency Meeting: Governments adopt "neosocialism" to share resources
2060	Many first world coastal cities have "floating districts" now due to water level rise
2065	Mars Research Station finds layer deep below permafrost with fossilized microbiology (evidence of a second genesis)

2066	Nanocraft data returns from Alpha Centauri (first images from another star system)
2066	Mars Space Elevator completed (allows research station to be manned permanently)
2067	Egyptian CELSS project attempts long term isolation (Seker Fayed)
2068	Nano-fabricators hit the market (products created from basic components)
2069	Climate change report: Not reversed, but reaches an equilibrium
2070	State of the World Report announces that fusion energy now supplies most of Earth
2070-2075	Second Generation Nanocraft Project sends probes to 85 stars
2072	Minerals and volatiles supplied by the moon and asteroids surpasses that from Earth
2074	Metamaterial developed that can partially protect from radiation and cosmic rays in space
2080	Global Warming Report: 4 degree centigrade rise this century / 80% of rain forest gone
2083	Recyclers mass produced that can break down waste into atoms and molecules
2085	"BrainGate™" technology now ready for widespread commercial use (controversial)
2088	Breakthrough research allows the harnessing of "vacuum energy" to propel spacecraft
2090	New Decade Symposium: Due to a new understanding of Earth's vulnerability and breakthrough technology, decision made to build an interstellar craft (launch est. 2112)
2090	Third generation nanocraft project postponed to start in 1995 in order to use Petr Romanov's

"vacuum energy" propulsion. Will now be able to slow down at destination

2091   First QFT (Quantum Fluctuation Temporizing) interplanetary craft is successful

2092   Fusion energy plant at Sagan Crater Research Center and success of Seker Fayed's CELSS allows the creation of a fully self sufficient biosphere on Mars

2095   First "BrainGate™" video games released after a decade of controversy. This marks the beginning of the "computerized/ Cyborg brain" as foreseen by Arthur C. Clarke

2099   After a century of research the Quantum Computer is finally ready for mass production due to efforts of Gerhardt Straub and others at CERN in Geneva, Switzerland

2100   SETI meeting: After more than a century still a null result. (Are we alone???)

* Events relevant to this writing/ inspired by futuretimeline website

The dark, gray alien land has mountains, hills and valleys, but looks nothing like home. This lifeless place has no plate tectonics to push up sections of the crust. Volcanic activity ended billions of years ago. Every surface feature here was created by violent bombardment during the creation of the solar system.

The field of view is somewhat limited due to crater rims and fallout from the impacts. This side of the moon is much more rugged than the other side. Very few flat, smooth lunar seas or maria exist in this hemisphere. Looking to the southeast, however, there is a gradual slope going downhill for as far as the eye can see. The sun is hanging low in the sky now, so shadows are very long and dark. The black airless sky is lit only by starlight.

A pair of elevated rails make a straight path down into the depression. The tracks seem totally out of place here as if they were left behind by some ancient civilization. But then, a three sectional, white, metallic worm-like object appears on the rails coming over the horizon. In no time, the object is speeding by and disappearing down the long dark gray slope. It seems to be in a hurry to get out of this desolate place.

As the train flashes by, four portals can be seen on the side of the front section making it look like some strange eight eyed creature. For a brief moment, a silhouette can be seen through one of the *eyes*.

Richard Gordon is fixated by the scenery as he cruises at 500 kilometers per hour down into the South Pole – Aitken (SPA) Depression. He thought he would be reading a book or listening to music on this long five hour journey from Mare Orientalis Station to Bose Crater. He just can't seem to stop staring out of the window. Richard is so mesmerized by the view, that he has immersed himself in the quiet solitude that this place seems to beckon.

There is something alluring about a place that looks docile, but would be quite deadly in a few short minutes to an unprotected human. Richard thinks to himself that this landscape does look much darker that the lunar soil of the near side maria. A travel brochure had mentioned that this was so because of a higher amount of iron oxide and titanium oxide in this region. The lunar dust he can see, that's not hidden in shadow, reminds him of the ashes from a charcoal grill on his deck back home in Seattle.

Richard Gordon is a professor of astronomy at the University of Washington. He is a sixty year old man, but keeps himself very fit for his age. Richard's hair is gray now and he is slightly balding. He has a rugged face showing years of hard life experiences. Even so, he has a happy and contented nature as if he has obtained some kind of inner peace. This trip has sparked a youthful enthusiasm in him that can be seen in the sparkle in his eyes.

The magnetic levitation (maglev) train carries its passenger down into the dark abyss on the far side of the moon.

As it approaches its destination, the train is now in total darkness. Only the vehicle's intensely bright spotlights illuminate the rails ahead. It is heading directly toward a rise in the landscape. As it gets closer, Richard can see a large metal door where the rails terminate at the hillside. The maglev train slows as it nears the door and it opens frustratingly slowly as if not to disturb some sleeping creature within. As the vehicle proceeds through the door and it closes behind, he grins at the thought that this reminds him of some top secret laboratory entrance in an old spy movie.

Looking out a side portal, Richard can see that the gray outer walls of the airlock he has just entered are just a few centimeters away from the outer shell of the train. An automated voice message announces, "Welcome to Bose Crater Lunar Array. When we have 100% seal, the doors will open and you may enter the crater rim station. We hope you have had a pleasant ride and enjoy your stay."

There is a mechanical moaning noise as sections of the airlock wall attach to the train. As promised, the two doors of the passenger compartment open fully. Richard picks up his carry-on tote and makes his way to the closest exit. As he steps out, Richard's first sight is a husky, middle aged man with a big white beard. With his casual clothes and ruddy appearance, the man looks as if he might have just stepped out of an old novel about life in the mountains of Tennessee.

The greeter is the first to speak. "Hi. I'm Hubert Hicks, caretaker of this remote outpost. Just about everybody calls me Skip."

Richard extends his arm for a handshake. "Richard Gordon, professor of astronomy at the University of Washington in Seattle."

"So my itinerary tells me." Skip is not rude, but surprisingly indifferent about having company considering his isolation. "Can you help me unload supplies?"

Skip has Richard put his bag on a cart and together they walk back to the supply cars. The crater rim station is large enough to handle a train twice the size of this one. The access corridor is a long sterile gray hallway. It reminds Richard of a passage, he often walks through, that connects north to south campus through the University of Washington hospital. The air in the station is cool and dry with a slight chemical smell similar to breathing from an oxygen tank.

At the first open door, accessing supplies, Richard sees that all of the freight is in cylindrical pods. Skip goes into the train and presses a button. A container is released into a position to be rolled out of the car. Across the narrow corridor, there is a semicircular bulge protruding from the floor that runs along the entire length of the hall. Skip pushes a button on the corridor wall and a section of the bulge opens showing that it is actually the top half of a conduit with the other half below floor level. He rolls the supply container into the tube. A button next to the one that opened the conduit controls its closing and the supply pod shoots off to a distant destination. Skip has Richard finish emptying the first car while he proceeds to the other car. When the supply cars are both empty, Skip joins Richard.

"Are you hungry?"

Richard had been so entranced by the lunar scenery on his five hour trip that he hadn't thought about eating anything, even though there was food and drink available on the train. "Actually, yes, I'm famished."

"Good. We're still an hour away from the research station, but when we get there I have one of my famous lasagnas hot and ready. Grab your carry on and let's go." Skip takes Richard to an elevator at the far end of the corridor.

The elevator turns out to be more like an underground cable car. It traverses the hundred meter vertical distance to the crater floor, but also an eighty meter horizontal distance. This is a strange sensation in the totally enclosed elevator room.

After an elevator ride traversing a distance comparable to the tallest skyscrapers on earth, the door opens to a small control room. With first the long elevator ride and then the small buried room, Richard gets a slight feeling of claustrophobia. On one side of the room, is a basic operations and monitoring area. On the other, there's a small transport vehicle on tracks running into the far wall.

Skip gestures toward the transport. "There's our cab. It's about 45 kilometers to the central station. Like many other places occupied by people and machinery on the moon, the entire inhabited part of the research station and transport tunnels are underground to protect from radiation. The tunnels are pressurized and breathable, but the transports are self-contained and there are double portal doors entering and exiting in case of emergency. There are also two other stations on the crater rim accessed by tunnels. One handles maglev trains coming and going from the Shackleford Crater Base at the South Pole where we also get our water and power. The other handles a train that connects us with the Daedalus Crater Lunar Array on the equator. Directly above the tunnels are radio telescope dishes spaced about 500 meters apart. Shall we go?"

"There are materials now that could protect us from radiation without having to bury everything underground. Are they planning any remodeling projects in the near future?"

"Not that I know of. It's just too costly to bring the raw materials here and build the factories to make the equipment and products needed. After all, there's not much accessible carbon on the moon."

Skip and Richard get into the transport and Skip speaks as he adjusts in his seat. "Vicki. Take us home."

To Richard's surprise, a sultry female voice answers. "Vehicle systems check, prepare for departure."

Richard smiles at Skip, "Now I see why you don't want me here. You think I'll make a move on your girlfriend." No response from Skip.

A door in the wall opens and the car on the rail enters. As the door closes, a second door opens and they are on their way to the research station. Every half a kilometer or so, agreeing with Skip's information, they pass small platforms that access the radio telescopes on the crater floor surface above.

"Better put on the coffee Skip, it's going to be a long night."

"You can stay up for two weeks if you want. I think I'll let Vicki do my watching while I sleep."

Richard Gordon is performing final calibrations and tests to make sure he doesn't miss the signal he has come all of this way to receive.

Skip grabs a bite of food on the run. "Help yourself to anything in the kitchen. I have to make a little maintenance run to one of the radio antennae this morning."

"Okay, I forgot that I'm not the only observer today. Who's using the radio telescope array?"

"There's a group from Beijing operating the telescope now. From what I understand, there is a new radio source of interest in the Small Magellanic Cloud."

"What maintenance are you needing to do?"

"The fine tuning mechanism on Antenna 33 of the southern row is having problems. Probably needs cleaning. You going to be alright without me for a couple of hours."

"Yes, thanks. I started the rotation of the liquid optical mirror about an hour ago and the secondary mirrors seem to be working fine. Sometimes I wonder why they need me here."

"I suppose they don't want to take any chances."

"Yeah, I guess. Good luck on your maintenance run."

* * *

When Skip returns, he sees Richard sitting at a monitor looking at noise signals and eating a sandwich. Shaking his head, he walks over to where Richard is sitting. "You know that the computer will subtract out all of that noise and let you know when a signal is received."

"I know. It just gives me something to look at while I'm thinking. Delta Pavonis emits quite a bit of light at our receiving wavelength."

"Do you mind if I ask you a question about something that's been bothering me?"

"Go ahead."

"I understand how nanocraft were accelerated and sent off to this star 20 light years away. I'm a little less clear on how they were decelerated. And I'm totally in the dark as to how they can join together and self assemble into a machine that can collect data and send it back to us on a laser beam."

"I hate to disappoint you, Skip, but I'm an astronomer, not a nanomachine expert. Actually, the first two nanocraft projects didn't decelerate and self assemble. These craft were accelerated by using light sails to capture light from a laser satellite. They just sped by the destination with each of thousands of tiny probes sending back a small amount of information. The capability you are talking about has only been possible since about 2090. They now use QFT propulsion like the new Mars prototype shuttles and so they don't need light sails anymore."

"About all I can tell you about the self-assembly of modern nanocraft is that each tiny ship has a very simple program that is activated at the same time as all of the others by a quantum timing mechanism. They locate each other and use solar energy to come together and connect to a specific family of compatible probes. Millions of probes are in the initial departure group to assure that some of each of the correct probes arrive at the destination. Eventually, they assemble into a solar powered satellite in orbit of the chosen planet. After taking basic observations, information is transmitted back to Earth coded in the nanosecond pulses of an optical laser beam aimed precisely in our direction."

"Sounds good in theory. I think we use the prefix "nano" a little too much."

"I have to agree with you, especially since the only use that really represents the original meaning of one billionth is *nanosecond*."

"How confident are you that we will actually get data from Delta Pavonis tonight?"

"The program has a good track record. So far all but two of the twelve completed missions have been successful. We've gotten a wealth of information about some of our nearest stellar systems."

"Any expectations this time?"

"Every mission has been a surprise. I'm sure this one will be no different. If you mean, do we think we will see lights from cities on the planet, I highly doubt it."

"Richard, unless you plan on watching that monitor for two weeks, let me show you something."

"Lead the way."

Richard gets up out of his chair, forgetting about the low gravity for a second, and leaves the ground by a couple of inches as he follows Skip out of the control center. The Bose Crater Research Station is a circular building consisting of the main control center in the middle with living quarters and kitchen/dining area in connecting cells around its circumference. The decor of the rooms is actually quite homey since the high technology is hidden in the environment. Skip takes Richard through a portal that hermetically seals behind them.

Skip's living space is small, but adequate. There is a sunken entertainment corner with very inviting plush seating and a partition hiding a kitchenette with a small island and bar stools. The sleeping area and washroom are hidden by a virtual wall that a person can walk right through. Most of the wall hangings are various sized photographs of some of the most beautiful places on Earth.

Richard looks at one photo in particular of a high mountain meadow with a glaciated peak in the background. The caption says, *North Cascades August 10, 2016*. "I've been to this peak, but it looks a lot different without glaciers. You have a nice studio, here."

"Thanks. I spend most of my time in here and eat in my kitchenette when I'm by myself."

"You must spend a lot of time in virtual reality in your cozy corner over there."

"Sometimes, but I prefer watching movies and old documentaries. If you want to join me later I'm getting a download from Earth of the new *Dune* movie."

"It still astounds me that even here we are connected to the planet. Pretty convenient that the Peak of Eternal Light at the lunar south pole can always be seen by Earth and gets year round solar energy."

"Not to mention that the deep cold of the Shackleford Crater basin has kindly preserved all the water we need among other things. I don't believe in chance. I think we were meant to come here."

"Skip, I hear that the new *Dune* movie is a prequel about *House Atreides*."

"That's right. I think it's appropriate, don't you?"

"Oh, you know about Delta Pavonis being the fictional home of the planet Caladan."

"Doesn't everybody?"

Skip pushes a remote button revealing a hidden portal to an adjacent room. "Come with me. I have something to show you."

As Richard enters the room he is astounded by what appears to be an art studio. Immediately to his right is a work area full of paints, supplies and an artist's desk with a work in progress on its inclined surface. A partitioned gallery fills the room with one area dominated by surreal nature paintings of majestic mountain peaks and lakes, temperate rain forests with trees draped by moss, pristine high altitude flora and other amazing works. Another area has a collection of captivating fantasy space art paintings. There are fantastic planetary surfaces with multiple moons or suns or even amazing nebulae filling the sky. Some have alien plants, creatures, and even intelligent lifeforms incorporated into the other worldly backdrops. Richard is amazed.

Skip reads Richard's face and grins. "When I show this room I get the same reaction every time. Nobody thinks that a hillbilly maintenance man should have artistic ability."

"I'm really sorry, Skip. I, of all people, should know you can't prejudge people."

Skip's not sure what the "I, of all people." is all about, but let's it go. He walks over to his work station. "What do you think of this?"

Richard checks out the 60 by 90 centimeter canvas on Skip's desk. The painting on the canvas looks mostly finished to his untrained eye. It's a new alien world creation. This one depicts a dry desolate place with a large red sun in the sky. Skip has ingeniously used blurry imaging to show hot air currents rising from the light gray rocks and sands. The small amount of vegetation is white with large leaves to reflect heat and collect what small traces of water vapor may still exist in the air. An alien creature in a strange looking hooded garment is walking toward a cave in the hill side. This seems to be the only place to retreat from the hot, blistering sun.

A look of realization appears on Richard's face. "I get it. This is the real Caladan. In Dune, Caladan is a beautiful earth-like world. In reality, Delta Pavonis is entering its red giant stage, so life on the planet would have to adapt to the ever increasing heat."

"Very good. When I have a visitor, I like to paint an interpretation of what they will be looking at."

"This is fantastic , Skip. Have you ever sent any of your paintings to earth? You could probably sell them for quite a bit, especially considering where they were painted."

"Not interested. All of this is too personal to me. I do this to keep my sanity during my long hours of down time."

"Don't worry, I won't tell anyone about your secret vault."

After spending a while admiring Skip's art, Richard and Skip check to see that all of the instruments are working properly, get something to eat and later watch the latest Dune movie in its three dimensional glory.

At two days, fifteen hours and twenty two minutes into the two week lunar night, a sexy female voice awakens the sleepers at the Bose Crater Lunar Observatory. "Attention Richard and Skip. Attention Richard and Skip. A signal is being received."

Both jump out of their beds, grab a robe and meet in the control center. After a short delay, that is designed into the system, an image appears on the computer display screen. The first data that the nanoprobes are programmed to gather is a spectrograph of infrared radiation emitted by the host planet after it has passed through the planet's atmosphere.

There is a spectrum materializing in front of them that is about to make Richard and Skip two of the most famous people in the history of the human race.

"Oh my god, Skip!! Look at that ozone absorption line. Do you know what that means?"

"Yeah." Skip is barely able to speak. "Photosynthesis!!"

LAUNCH

Jaswinder is sitting comfortably in his study at two o'clock in the morning. He hadn't been able to get to sleep, so had gotten out of bed an hour ago.

Jaswinder Singh is a tall, dark-haired, meticulously groomed Punjabi man. He has a rounded, young looking handsome face. Even in his pajamas in the middle of the night, he seems well dressed enough to give one of his famous biology lectures.

He pours himself a glass of Merlot and relaxes in his *smart* chair. The chair molds itself perfectly to Jaswinder's body, giving support where needed but relieving the body's pressure points. It's about as close to weightlessness as a person can get without leaving the planet.

Jaswinder then takes his *BrainGate*^{TM} helmet from the floor next to his chair and places it on his head. He relaxes and thinks "BrainGate on". The *BrainGate*^{TM} is a chip that is implanted in a strategic location just under the skull next to the cerebral cortex.(1) A link is established between the chip and the computer in the helmet allowing the user to control it with thought. The helmet totally covers Jaswinder's eyes and ears keeping out any external stimuli. It takes quite a while to master the *BrainGate*^{TM} and after a few months of practice Jaswinder is finally getting it down.

With his eyes closed he focuses and thinks, "Flying: Simulation Three". He opens his eyes and his field of vision is full of blue skies and clouds. The mental command "fly forward" sets the image in motion. He now sees the clouds as if he is flying over the top of them. To add realism, he also hears the sound of wind, but not too loud as to be bothersome.

Jaswinder thinks "left" and the image veers left. Then he thinks "dive" and he is diving into the clouds. When he emerges from the clouds, he sees a breathtaking mountain range and flies toward it. After some low flying through mountain valleys and over some pristine mountain lakes he thinks "up" and starts a vertical climb. The repeated mental command "faster" gets him climbing faster than could ever be tolerated in reality. Through the troposphere, stratosphere, ionosphere and out to the edge of space he soars. Thinking "level off", he cruises along and can see the curvature of the Earth. Jaswinder looks down at the planet below and ponders the fact that he will soon be leaving this wonderful oasis in space forever. The moon is coming up over the horizon and he thinks about it, but decides it's time to go to bed.

(1)   The name and pioneering technology of *BrainGate*™ was the "brain child" of John Donoghue at Brown University in the early 21st century. Initially the invention was meant to help people with paralysis, due to brain injury, regain control of motor activities. By the end of the century it had been perfected and released to be used in social and entertainment media. Since then, the technology has revolutionized video games.

Closing his eyes, Jaswinder thinks "BrainGate off". He takes off his helmet and sets it down by the chair. It takes a lot of effort to get up out of his *smart* chair, but he does and heads off to the bedroom.

As he climbs into bed with his wife, Leela rolls over in his direction. Leela is a young woman of 26 years (Jaswinder is 28) who has a natural beauty that only a female of Southern Indian descent could possess. Jaswinder has always felt that her dark brown eyes could see into a man's soul.

"Having a hard time sleeping my love?" Leela is only half awake when she notices Jaswinder's return.

"How can you sleep when you're getting ready to leave everything you know behind and fly off into interstellar space never to return?"

"Isn't it exciting? We will be among the first humans to see another star up close along with all of its planets and moons. I've heard that the ship, Gaia II, is amazing."

"You always have been able to hide your true feelings and stay positive for my benefit."

"I will be happy anywhere as long as it is with you."

Jaswinder settles into bed, gives Leela a gentle kiss and is finally able to fall off to sleep. Now Leela can't sleep. "The curse of being a caring wife," she thinks.

* * *

At an hour that seems way too early, Leela and Jaswinder get their *wake up call*. Leela has chosen the programming for this morning. The wall at the foot of the bed becomes a beautiful island scene from the South Pacific. The sound of tropical birds slowly fills the room. As an added touch, she has even programmed a mist spray to put a wonderful floral aroma into the room. The sun starts rising from the ocean between some palm trees. Light fills the room and they both awaken and start to stretch.

As Jaswinder slowly gets out of bed to go to the washroom, he reminds Leela, "You'd better call your mom. She'll be sitting on her couch waiting. Do you need in before I shower?"

"Go ahead. I'm okay for now. Better wait for my knock to come out." Jaswinder nods in understanding and leaves the room.

Leela touches an icon on the wall of their bedroom and a large video screen seems to magically appear on the wall. She gives the verbal command "Call mom" and a message appears on the screen, "Awaiting response".

Thousands of miles away in Bangalore, India a lovely middle aged lady in a traditional sari is pacing anxiously and doing trivial chores. Then she hears what she has been waiting for, "Call coming from Leela. Do you want to answer?"

The lady immediately replies, "Answer call." A video screen similar to Leela's appears on her living room wall. When she gets into a position where she can see and be seen, she responds to her daughter. "Where's your husband?"

"He's in the shower."

"Good, I need to talk to you without him there to cloud your judgment."

"I've already made up my mind, mom."

"It's still not too late, Leela. This is madness. You are leaving us forever to spend your whole life traveling through empty space."

"We've discussed this before. My place now is with my husband. I will miss you and papa terribly, but I am going."

"Do you even realize how dangerous space still is? They talk about it like it's a vacation trip. I've seen re-creations of what would happen to a person in the vacuum of space. Do you know that your blood would boil?"

"That's not going to happen, mom. There are risks everywhere these days, even in Bangalore. Where's papa?"

"He doesn't want to talk to you right now. Your papa and I both think you are making a terrible mistake."

Leela does her best to hold back tears. She sees that her mother's eyes are red probably from crying all night. "I will still be making regular calls to you for a while and when we are far away there will be weekly messages."

"It's not the same, Leela. You have no idea what it's like for a mother to know that she will never see her little girl again."

In spite of all of her efforts, Leela starts to cry. "I have to go now, mom. I'll call you from the space hotel."

"You tell that selfish husband of yours that we will never forgive him for this. It's just like him to hide like a coward in the bathroom."

"He's a good man and I love him. Goodbye, mom. End call." With that command the video screen disappears and Leela wipes the tears from her eyes.

Leela gives a little knock on the bathroom door and a few minutes later Jaswinder emerges. He sees that his wife has been crying and asks her if she is okay. Leela gives him a silent nod.

They are both quiet as they complete their morning rituals as if this was any other day in their condo. Finally, Jaswinder breaks the ice. "This is it, Leela, the beginning of our new life. I'm grateful that we can share this with each other."

"Me, too. I did one last look through our two crates of personal items. I'm glad they let us take a few things. There are some things that you just can't duplicate with a fabricator. I think we are ready to go."

Leela makes them both a small breakfast, but has a little trouble with the food replicator that she has used thousands of times. Jaswinder comes in to the kitchen and helps her out. After eating, they take one last look around their home of the last four years and walk out of the door.

Leela's and Jaswinder's personal crates are already attached to a *maglev* car waiting for them in the basement of their building. Together they walk for the last time through the atrium on their level to a large transparent elevator that takes them down to the magnetic levitation car staging area. Jaswinder had reserved the car that is waiting for them the day before. Nobody in Tech City owns a car and normally residents just call one when they need it, but today is different.

Jaswinder checks their crates one more time and they both climb in. When the doors are closed a voice says, "Destination, please." Jaswinder replies, "Byrd International Airport" and away they go.

* * *

Meanwhile, elsewhere in the same city, Mei Sun and Barry Donaldson are having one last breakfast at their favorite diner.

Someone gazing through the window, under an antique looking neon sign that reads "JJ's Diner", would see a very impressive couple sitting at a booth. On the left, is a tall, slender, beautiful yet very serious Chinese woman. Her short hair and attire demonstrate that she is more concerned about getting respect than admiring gazes from men. The ruggedly handsome man across from her is also tall, with dark, wavy hair and a square jaw. He has a well toned, but not bulky physique. His body language portrays great confidence, but still humility and a love for the good things in life.

JJ's specializes in breakfast and lunch and has a décor that looks just like its predecessor of over 150 years ago. A combination of Johnny Johnson's labor of love and the miracles of the modern fabricator have created a result of incredible detail, right down to the dents in the jukebox.

Mei is very quiet and picking away at her Denver omelet. She seems to have her mind in another place. Barry, however, is in "little hog heaven" with his old fashioned biscuits and gravy. A side of sourdough toast, large orange juice and coffee makes everything just about perfect. When Johnny personally comes over to their table to fill Barry's coffee and Mei's water, Barry asks him if he can sit with them for a few minutes.

Johnny makes a gesture to his cook and waitress to let them know he won't be helping for a little while and takes a seat across from the two of them. "So my friends, how are you feeling right now, being on the threshold of your great adventure?"

Barry remarks, "For starters, we're kidnapping you and taking you with us. Life's not worth living without your biscuits and gravy."

"Yeah, yeah, yeah. Well, this diner's not going to be the same without the presence of your lovely wife."

"Now I know why we decided not to bring you along."

Mei stays totally focused on her Denver omelet and for a moment wonders to herself, "Where is Denver anyway?"

Barry and Johnny make more small talk while the couple finishes their breakfast. When they are ready to leave, Barry stands up and shakes Johnny's hand. "Seriously Johnny, you've been a good friend and we're both going to miss you."

Johnny returns the handshake. "Barry, we all wish you the best of luck. Breakfast is on the house."

Barry gives him a confused look. "You know, I've been in Antarctica for so long that I forget that most of the rest of the world still revolves around an exchange of currency."

Mei Sun stands up and gives Johnny a hug. "Take care of yourself. We'll send you an e-mail from Gliese 250."

With that, Barry and Mei walk out of the diner and summon a maglev car. After helping Mei into the car and then getting in himself, the doors close and a voice asks for a destination.

Mei responds to the car's computer. "Byrd International Airport."

After the car is on its way she turns to Barry. "You know you don't have to do that sort of thing. I'm probably more physically capable than you are."

"It's called chivalry Mei and it's still alive in the 22nd century. And what's wrong with you? We are seeing friends and places for the last time and you're off in another world."

"You will never fully understand what is at stake for me. The world has spent ten years and trillions of dollars on this project. All of that depends on the success of a new propulsion system that has never been tested at this magnitude. If it doesn't work then my name will go down in history as the person responsible for destroying mankind's chance at becoming a galactic civilization."

"You put too much upon yourself, Mei. There are thousands of people and entire companies that have an equal investment in this thing working."

"Yeah, but I'm the one that will be remembered if it fails."

The rest of the ride to the airport is pretty quiet. As they near their destination a very pleasant voice in the car announces, "We are nearing Byrd International Airport. Which terminal would you like to be let out at?"

This time Barry answers. "South Pacific Terminal, Concourse B please."

The maglev car pulls up and its doors open. After the two riders get out, the doors close and the maglev car proceeds to the nearest waiting station.

Barry and Mei walk into the concourse and see the sign for outgoing baggage check. Soon they are standing in front of a three dimensional display board.

Mei speaks to the board, "Barry Donaldson and Mei Sun to check two tubes for Flight 1550."

Barry's mind is elsewhere and he comments without thinking. "It seems to me that anybody could request our personal belongings and take anything they want."

"Not with the new quantum encrypting that prevents voice imitation. You should know that Mr. Chief of Security."

Mei and Barry check their two containers that had been sent to the airport ahead of time and forward them on to be loaded upon the aircraft.

Walking toward their gate, Barry spots Jaswinder and Leela Singh in a coffee shop ahead. Barry sees that Mei notices, too. "Mei, do you know Jaswinder Singh? He and his wife Leela will be accompanying us on the flight to Tsiolkovsky Station."

"I've just met Dr. Singh professionally. He is the only astrobiologist in Tech City."

"I'm sure he has been a very busy man with the data that was received from Delta Pavonis g and Gliese 667Cd. Has he told you about any of his theories?"

"I'll let him tell you himself, Barry. We will all be on a very long plane flight together."

Mei and Barry approach the table where Jaswinder and Leela are sitting. Even sitting down, the twenty centimeters difference in their height is pronounced. Mei introduces Barry to Jaswinder. Then, Jaswinder introduces his wife to both of them.

Jaswinder takes a sip of coffee and turns to Barry. "Do you know how many others are flying with us today?"

"Only three other couples on this flight, but there are twenty-four couples from Tech City going on this voyage. That's more than from any other single location."

"Will you join my wife and I for coffee before we make our way to the gate?"

Barry glances at Mei and can tell by the look on her face that it's fine with her. "We'd love to, but I think we'll pass on the coffee. We just finished a big breakfast at JJ's."

Leela speaks for the first time. "Oh, I love that place. Their burgers and malts are to die for!"

Jaswinder looks at Leela, somewhat shocked. "When do you have burgers? I thought you preferred to eat traditional Indian dishes, trying to stay in touch with your roots."

Leela winks at Mei. "There are a lot of things that you don't know about me my dear husband."

After getting acquainted for about ten minutes, it's time to go to the plane. There are various modes of transportation available, but they all decide to walk to get a little exercise before the long plane flight.

At Gate 12A, the four travel companions walk into a clear cylindrical elevator and the door closes. A voice, this time male, says, "Names, please." All four say their names in turn and the elevator rises.

At the top of elevator is a platform supporting a sleek, aerodynamic, plasma propelled, vertical take-off jet. It is made of metamaterials of incredible strength and temperature resistance. The outer shell of the plane is essentially frictionless.

After boarding, they see four more passengers already on board and the fifth twosome comes up the elevator about five minutes later. These long flights still have a pilot and copilot to deal with malfunctions and emergency situations, so the twelve of them settle down into smart chairs and strap in.

The seating area is a large, round, open space with plush carpet and amenities. This is a typical plane flying into or out of Tech City. There is rarely a need to transport more than twenty people at a time. For security reasons, only screened personnel are allowed to come here. There is no immigration or tourism. All people moving to Tech City have been specifically selected to fill needed positions in the city.

The pilot notifies the tower, which is a sophisticated computer system, and about two minutes later (when air space is verified as clear) the plasma compression engine starts up the vertical jets. The plane rises slowly straight upward. At the selected take-off altitude, the horizontal jets kick in and the jet accelerates away from the airport. When the plane reaches a cruising altitude of 10000 meters at a velocity of 1500 kilometers per hour, the twelve riders undo their straps and try to make the best of their 8000 kilometer, six hour flight to the equatorial South Pacific.

About 3200 kilometers west of South America, in a very peaceful region of the Pacific Ocean near the equator, a very large and unusual island towers out of the ocean. It is actually more like an iceberg, because this object is a floating island with it's bulk below the surface.

Upon getting closer to the *island* it becomes obvious that this is actually five islands separated by hundreds of meters of ocean. A large central complex is surrounded by four smaller satellites. It is soon seen that all are man-made. The buildings on all five islands are cubical and colorless structures with a very militaristic appearance.

An aircraft flies in from the south. It decelerates to a hover, engages vertical jets, and slowly starts to descend toward a platform on the outer edge of the central island. Only when comparing the size of the plane to the island, can the true immensity of the structure be realized. The plane makes a perfect landing and shuts down its engines.

Ten passengers and two pilots disembark and go through the arrival check station at the edge of the platform. Security is extremely tight here even though they are in the middle of the Pacific Ocean. Personal containers are automatically transferred through a magnetic transfer system to a holding area.

Barry Donaldson, Mei Sun, Jaswinder Singh and Leela Singh are walking together and conversing casually. To an outsider, it would appear that they have been friends for years.

Leela looks up and sees something that amazes her. A powerful laser beam is firing into the sky from an enormous power plant several hundred meters away toward the center of the *island*. She hadn't noticed this before, since it is still daytime and they had been flying toward the source of the beam. Visually following the beam skyward she sees something even more breathtaking. At the terminus of the beam in the sky, there is a small metallic object that seems to be catching the light like a bottomless bucket would catch a stream of water. Very little is reflecting. Looking closely, Leela sees a faint black cable that the small object seems to be climbing. Following the cable back down to the ocean, she sees that it attaches to one of the small satellite islands that they had seen coming in on the plane.

Leela had read about and seen video of space elevators, but this is her first visit to one in person. Barry notices Leela's discovery. "That transport left Island One at 3pm. Departures are scheduled from Island's One and Three and arrivals come into Islands Two and Four. The laser accelerates and decelerates each transport on the tether for about an hour and a half. The transports are spaced so that they can focus the laser on one vehicle at a time. It's really impressive to see at night."

Barry has been to Tsiolkovsky Space Elevator Station on numerous occasions and knows the head of security here quite well. He leads the party into the Central Station Shuttle that makes a continuous loop around the perimeter.

There is tourism at Tsiolkovsky Station, but it has been curtailed for ten days. The station is operating at full capacity right now, facilitating the boarding of Gaia II. Still, an informational message, meant for tourists, begins as they ride in the shuttle.

"Welcome to Tsiolkovsky Space Elevator Station. Tsiolkovsky is one of three stations in specially selected locations around the globe. The other two are Santos-Dumont Station midway between South Africa and Brazil in the Atlantic Ocean and Clarke Island off the coast of western Australia in the Indian

Ocean. Tsiolkovsky is the largest station and the only one with four elevator tethers. It was initially established as a joint venture of Japan, the United States and Russia. The Japanese were the first to develop the technology to produce the long carbon nanotube ribbons necessary for space elevators to be possible. The United States partnered up with Japan offering the technology and experience of NASA along with military security. Finally, Russia was asked to join because of it's ground launching dominance and for political considerations."

"If you look up, you will see what it will look like when your space elevator transport approaches Noda Geostation." The ceiling of the shuttle seems to disappear as a three dimensional movie projection shows an object in a black starry sky getting closer and closer.

"Four space elevator tethers access this space station from Tsiolkovsky. They are attached to independent movable islands. Mobility of these anchoring islands is essential to dampen oscillations that occasionally build up in the tethers and also to move the cable out of the way if an object is detected to be on a collision course. Each tether extends 36000 kilometers to Noda Geostation in geosynchronous orbit and then another 64000 kilometers to the space elevator's counterweight. At the far end of the tethers, about ten kilometers from the counterweight, is a station much smaller than Noda. It is used for launching and receiving interplanetary spacecraft. This station has been named Edwards Transfer Station after one of the early proponents of space elevators." The movie on the ceiling switches to one showing a modern spacecraft arriving and docking at the transfer station.

"We are now arriving at the first shuttle stop. Any passengers getting off at the Food Court may disembark as soon as the shuttle comes to a complete stop. There will be more information and videos on other legs of this shuttle loop. Enjoy your stay at Tsiolkovsky Space Elevator Station and have a wonderful experience at the Marriott Space Hotel."

Leela isn't impressed. "This isn't exactly Disney World. They should make this place more human and fun."

Mei knows the history of Tsiolkovsky Station better than Leela. "They've done what they can. This place wasn't initially built to be a tourist destination like the other elevator stations. In fact, the first Space Elevator Hotel was the Space Hilton on the Santos-Dumont Tether."

"Well, they better have good food."

With that, the shuttle doors open and everyone inside gets out in a hurry to discover the Food Court.

The dining facility is packed with people, each one going to Gaia II. All of the new arrivals are hungry. They had lunch on the way in the plane, but after a six hour flight it's time for a real meal.

Barry and Jaswinder have been conversing for most of the flight (mostly Jaswinder answering Barry's questions). Leela and Mei have made a connection, too. The four of them decide to find a table together. Leela and Jaswinder both get a curry dish from one of the booths. Barry opts for a vegetarian Italian meal and Mei chooses a seafood pasta. They are all used to dishes made with very small amounts of real meat or seafood due to limited world supply. However, creativity and fabricated protein supplements make the dishes very palatable.

On a raised stage in a corner of the Food Court, a distinguished looking African male starts to play an engaging piano intro for the crowd. A beautiful, sultry, ebony skinned lady steps up onto the platform and starts to sing. Soon she has the room mesmerized with her voice.

Leela immediately realizes. "I recognize her. She is the famous African actress, Dakore Maredi."

Barry remarks in admiration. "It appears that she can sing as well as she can act."

Jaswinder adds what he knows. "The man at the piano is John Diallo, the head of the African Theater Company. I heard that they were recently married. It was big news on the social media, but I wonder what they are doing here."

"They are both coming with us. John and Dakore will be teaching at the Theater on Gaia II. By getting many of us involved in the performing arts, they hope to make our voyage much more enjoyable." With his newly created position of Conflict Manager on Gaia II, it has been part of Barry's job to learn as much as he can about the passengers and their backgrounds.

Barry gazes at Mei. "I imagine that one day we will be sitting in an audience watching our children perform something they have created."

Mei seems disturbed by this thought and pretends to ignore Barry's comment. "How wonderful! I thought that the whole crew was going to be a bunch of nerds like me."

Jaswinder smiles at Mei. "Mei, I suppose that Gaia II had already filled its quota of famous quantum physicists."

Barry jumps in. "Okay, okay. Don't go giving her a big head. I have to live with her for another eighty years or so."

After dinner and a drink in the lounge (Mei has ginger ale) they all go to find their sleeping quarters. The rooms are very comfortable, but not as nice as they are used to. Jaswinder doesn't care and in a very short time he is sound asleep. In the middle of the night, an alarm sounds in the distance, but with no follow up announcements or notices, he and Leela soon fall back to sleep.

September 30, 2111
Geneva, Switzerland

Gerhardt Straub is working quietly in his office. As he scratches out some final calculations on a blackboard, he is doing mental experiments to analyze the operation of the world's first commercial quantum computer. He is at CERN, the home of the particle accelerator that confirmed the Standard Model of Particle Physics by finding the first Higgs boson in 2012 and then expanded the model by finding a whole new family of heavier particles completing the Theory of Dark Matter. CERN also became a world center for the study and development of advanced computer systems in the 21st century. Molecular and DNA computers were developed here with research continuing on more exotic ideas. The quantum computer has been the "holy grail" of computer technology for over a century now, but certain impediments have kept it from being developed. Until now!

A knock on the door and in walks Dr. Straub's young brilliant assistant. Renata Toscini is a 29 year old computer scientist that was born and raised near Milan, Italy. She can be attractive if she wants to be, but dresses very casually and doesn't pay much attention to hair and make-up during her day to day life. She lives and breathes computers.

Dr. Straub's eyes light up when he sees Renata. "Renata, I've been dying to talk to you all day. I'm so excited for you. If only I could go with you."

"Who would finish the quantum computer project if you left, Gerhardt?" Both know that he is too old to be one of the Gaian crew.

"Are you ready?"

"Do you mean professionally, emotionally, mentally, physically, medically or genetically?" Renata answers partly in jest and partly in exhaustion from all of the preparation she has had to go through.

"Yes."

"As ready as I ever will be."

"Renata, I wouldn't have been able to complete this project without you. It's too bad that you won't be here for all of the hoopla when it's up and running. You know you've been like a granddaughter to me and I'm going to miss you in a big way."

Renata gets a little teary eyed (very uncharacteristically). "It's been an honor, Gerhardt. Thank you so much for taking me under your wing. I owe everything to you."

He comes out from behind his desk and Renata walks up to him and gives him a loving hug.

"I still think you should have had your wedding here. I really wanted to see you in a wedding dress."

"Well, you know Paul. He has to be the first and most dramatic with everything he does."

"When are you leaving?"

"I'm flying to England this afternoon."

With a few more pleasantries, Renata says goodbye to Gerhardt and walks out the door.

* * *

That afternoon, she turns off the lights and closes the door to her condo in the CERN residential village, then walks over to her Austin-Healey Pegasus. Her container with about 45 kilograms of personal items is attached securely to her car. Renata climbs in, puts on her safety strap and says, "Maria." This has always been her favorite name and she plans to give it to her daughter one day.

A motherly Italian voice comes from within the car. "Hello, Renata."

"Maria. Are batteries fully charged and all systems in good working order?"

"Batteries charged and all systems 100% except for an ongoing problem in the climate control system you promised me you would fix. You will not be able to adjust humidity level."

"Maria, please take the shortest time route to De Grassi Park Community Airstrip. Maria, please play Jon Holland's *Space Dance* with standard settings." It isn't necessary to say "please", but Renata always does anyway. Her close Italian family upbringing had always stressed manners.

The car starts driving away and music starts up. Renata reclines and takes a short nap.

There are a couple of other cars at the air strip when she arrives. Maria announces, "Arrival at Degrassi Park. Awaiting further instructions."

"Maria, please enter the airstrip, recheck systems, and prepare for a flight to Mildenhall, England."

"Systems ready, battery power sufficient, flight plan registered and approved. Prepare for lift-off."

When it is her turn, Maria drives the Pegasus onto the community airstrip. Coming to a temporary stop, the Austin-Healey begins to *morph* into a small airplane. Wings fold out, the tail extends, flaps adjust and the car-plane starts down the take-off runway. With the latest in lightweight materials, the car reaches take-off speed in no time and rises into the air at about a 30 degree angle.

The flight is close to the maximum range of the car's nanobatteries and airspeed is not very fast, so this is one of the longest flights that Renata has ever taken in her Pegasus. She usually drives to the coast when going to England. At an altitude of only about 1000 meters, the details of the landscape below are very discernible.

Renata's plane has side door panels with retractable protective shields so that, in flight, the driver can convert them into viewing windows equaling that of a helicopter. She decides to make the most of her last flight and retracts the shields.

It is a beautiful, sunny day in the south of France. Vineyards, small farms and villages fill Renata's aerial view. The French method of renewable terraced farming, that has kept their soil fertile for centuries, is most apparent from this vantage point. Renata thinks to herself that this is one of the most beautiful things she has ever seen. A small river winds through the valley below with cars on rural roads looking like small toys. She tells herself that she will keep this vision in her mind for as long as she lives.

In a time that seems way too short, the car-plane approaches the coast of France and flies out over open water. About ten minutes later, Renata sees the coast of Great Britain in the distance. As the Pegasus gets closer, she has a breathtaking view of the White Cliffs of Dover. Looking down in awe, Renata has the realization that she will never see anything like this again. She has spent innumerable hours closed away inside computer laboratories and it is only now that she is leaving that Renata truly appreciates what a wonderful planet she lives on.

* * *

The Austin-Healey touches down at Mildenhall Central England Public Airfield. There are still some old buildings there left from the days when an old RAF base dominated the area.

Maria taxies the plane to a halt and the Pegasus converts back to a road vehicle.

Renata has Maria drive the car to the nearest battery exchange station. She swaps out for fully charged nanobatteries and asks Maria to maintain all safety systems, but to switch to manual driving. Renata accelerates up the A1101 highway, then turns onto a back-road route to get away from the traffic. She has decided to take a country drive on her way to see her fiancee.

About an hour of driving and she turns into a long, beautiful shrub-lined drive then continues along it towards a grand manor. A system designed by the owner of the manor does a flawless security scan of the vehicle and driver and a gate automatically opens allowing her in.

A tall, blonde sophisticated man awaits Renata in front of the manor. She instructs Maria to take the car to the parking garage after stopping to let her out. Then, she runs to her welcoming gentleman and gives him a passionate kiss.

The man is Paul Drake. He is a famous man, not only in England, but worldwide. His revolutionary ideas in robotics, both on the nanoscale and macroscale, have made him a legend. Operating one of the world's largest robotics factories only a short distance from his manor, Paul Drake employs several hundred workers locally and thousands internationally. Many of his local workers live on the estate or in the manor itself. Long gone are the days of one family living alone in a hundred room mansion.

Renata and Paul seem to an outsider to be one of the most unlikely couples imaginable. Paul is tall, handsome and sophisticated with a history of being a rich, playboy bachelor. Renata, at 1.7 meters tall, barely comes up to Paul's chin. She has a very average figure and a "down to earth" demeanor. She has been taking better care of her appearance since she met Paul, but still seems to be in a different class. Renata has been somewhat of a recluse computer "geek", if you will. She lead the team that worked on the computer systems for Paul's factory. She was the first woman who had challenged Paul's intellect. Renata Toscini is not an unattractive woman, but Paul truly fell in love with Renata for her brain.

Paul escorts Renata inside. He fixes her a nice dinner and they spend the night together in the manor.

* * *

The next morning, after breakfast, Paul takes his fiancee to the stables.

"I have a little surprise for you. I thought that one last ride through the countryside to the factory might be nice. There I have my jet ready to take us to Santos-Dumont station."

Paul and Renata put on their riding gear and gallop off through the fields. She has been riding with him before and knows the estate pretty well. They are both pretty competitive and have a little race along the way. It's a slightly overcast day, but exceptionally nice for the first of October. As they trot along, Renata gazes off at the rolling fields. Hedges instead of fences still act as property lines in this part of England. In the distance, she sees a small village with a large church at its center and imagines that this view was probably not much different hundreds of years ago. Renata takes a deep breath of the fragrant country air and looks at Paul. He seems to know what she is thinking.

Renata wishes for a moment that this experience would last forever. A lump forms in her throat and she thinks, "I'm a computer scientist, I never thought that I was going to feel like this."

Arriving at the factory stable, they tie up their horses and hang up their riding gear. Paul leads Renata to a private elevator and takes her to the roof where his personal plasma jet is waiting on a platform. It has been made fully ready by Paul's friends and coworkers. Their personal affects have been loaded for them.

Paul says goodbye and shakes the hands of everybody there. The last person he talks to is his vice president, whom he asks to take good care of his company as he and Renata board the plane. Soon the plasma compression engine starts up and the vertical jets engage. At a couple hundred feet above the factory, the horizontal jets fire and they are on their way to the South Atlantic Ocean.

* * *

Paul stays in the flight control center of the plane until he feels certain he can leave the flight in the hands of the on board computer. He walks through the lounge to his office where Renata is looking at a blueprint elevation displayed on Paul's desk. She ejects a card out of the desk and inserts a different card. A new elevation appears on the desk. This one is the E level of the Computer Center on Gaia II.

"Looking at the drawings of your new home away from home, Renata?" He comes up behind her and gives her a little hug. "Once we are married I expect you to be home by five."

"Paul, can't you ever be serious? It won't be long until we will be responsible for the computer systems and manufacturing for one of the greatest endeavors ever attempted by the human race."

"Okay, you can be home for dinner by six, but no later. I've been meaning to ask you. In a couple of years we could be putting quantum computers on a ship like this. Why not wait and go then?"

"That's not for sure, Paul. There are still many tests and trials and prototypes to study. It could be a long time before we feel comfortable that we won't lose all of our data using a quantum computer. That would be a slight problem 28 light years from Earth. Maybe we can continue some of the research on board the ship."

Paul has been anxiously awaiting the quantum computer as intensely as anyone on the planet. His major contributions in the field could all be improved exponentially with this power.

On the small scale, Paul and his coworkers have finally been able to produce self-replicating nanobots that are used for the modern day nanocraft to the stars. These nanobots, sometimes called Von Neumann machines, have been the subject of many sci-fi horror movies where something goes wrong and they start to consume everything. With quantum chips in the machines, they might actually be able to communicate with each other in a very primitive way.

The greatest boon to Paul from the quantum computer would be to his large scale robotics. The focus of this part of his enterprise is producing robots that *think*. Robotics have been hidden in the environment of people's everyday lives for decades now. Paul just made them smarter.

Paul can't resist looking at the drawings for the Living Areas. "I can't wait to see what the Disney team has done with the inside of this ship. Who better to create fantasy lands?"

Renata looks up from the blueprint display of the section of Gaia II where they will be living. "I am looking forward to seeing our first home together. It will be fun to make it ours and get to know the neighbors."

"Why Miss Toscini, when did you start getting all domestic on me?"

"I guess that would be not only when you proposed to me, but also when we decided to accept the invitation to Gaia II. You do know that this means children in the near future. That's a pretty big step for a rich British playboy."

Paul instantly decides to change the subject. "Are you going to be long in here? Can I get you anything?"

"I'll come to the lounge in a few minutes. I want to look at one more level of the Computer Center." She puts a software card into the desk as Paul heads back to the lounge. He relaxes in his smart chair and pours the two of them a drink. Twenty minutes later, Renata comes into the lounge to find Paul napping.

She sits in a chair across from Paul and requests an E-book to come up on a screen in front of her. Paul feels her presence and awakens. "Hey beautiful, have you ever heard of a secret society called the *mile high club*."

Three hours later they are nearing their destination.

* * *

Santos-Dumont Station is not as big as Tsiolkovsky Station and it has a very different appearance. Tsiolkovsky was designed strictly in a utilitarian way, but Santos-Dumont has much more creativity and a European flair. Many more aesthetic architectural considerations were incorporated into its planning. The reason all of this had been financially possible was that the elevator itself, including geostation and transfer station, were a fraction of the cost, since materials could be sent up the existing elevator.

When flying into Santos-Dumont a traveler sees garden terraces with pools, a shopping mall and a transport dome of the *Buckyball* design. It is, in itself, a destination resort and not just a *bus station*.

A VTO plasma jet with the familiar logo of Drake Enterprises lands on a platform. Its two passengers disembark. An automated process unloads two containers into the station's luggage tube system and a small crew takes care of recharging and refueling the plane. When it's ready to go, Paul has programmed the jet to fly itself back to England.

Renata and Paul take a shuttle to the hotel and check into their room. Then, they decide to get something to eat and take a look at the mall.

After dinner, Paul suggests they go into a store that sells clothing designed by the most popular designers in the Soho District of London. Renata looks through the store display window. "I can't wear those modern styles, Paul. I'm a scientist not a fashion model."

"Nonsense, you are a beautiful woman. Please do this for me."

Renata reluctantly agrees so they walk into the store and see flashy signing, holograms, visual displays and a few salespeople to offer suggestions. There are no actual clothes in this store. In fact, most of the stores in the mall just sell software to put into fabricators which create products from basic components.

A clerk takes Renata into a holobooth that stores her 3D image in the store's computer system. Paul, the clerk and occasionally Renata choose several of the thousands of styles offered and the clerk inputs the software. Then, Renata, Paul and the clerk all take a seat in the viewing room.

A holographic image of Renata appears on the stage in front of them clad in a trendy modern outfit. Renata looks at Paul, rolling her eyes. "Oh my God!"

"Okay, maybe not that one." They go on to the next. After about a half an hour of groans and laughs, Renata admits that she had fun and they pick a couple of outfits for the next couple of days at the station.

Paul does the same. They also get a few basic needs such as fabricator cards for mouthwash and deodorant in a drug store.

The couple goes back to their room and stop along the way by the fabricators in the hallway on their floor. The clothing fabricator is a machine that has a main body about a meter high with cylinders of various materials rising from the top. There are a few smaller machines for other items. Renata puts in the software for one of her outfits and the nanomachines in the fabricator go to work. In a few minutes a door opens and clothing that fits perfectly is ready to wear. When Paul and Renata leave the station they will leave their clothes and other items behind to be recycled.

Renata holds up the elegant dress and looks at Paul. "If you want me to wear this, you are going to have to wine and dine me tomorrow night."

"It's a date." They finish getting the rest of their fabricated items and retire to their room. It has been a long day, so they both turn in early for the night.

The next day, Paul and Renata go through the orientation, which is required of all who take the elevator. Time frames, safety, weightlessness, space-sickness and many other topics are discussed very seriously, even though most of the passengers are already aware.

Paul makes good on his promise and takes Renata out for dinner and dancing at the nicest restaurant on Santos-Dumont station. As they sit at the table finishing off their fantastic meal, Paul can't help but notice that Renata has a far away look on her face. He gets her attention. "Are you okay?"

"Paul, this is embarrassing, but I almost cried while flying over the White Cliffs of Dover and then again while riding through the countryside yesterday. I have spent so much of my life with my nose in my work that I haven't really gotten out much. There are so many amazing places and things on Earth I have never seen. I lived in Switzerland and I've never been skiing."

"You may not believe this, Renata, but I feel exactly the same way. On our horseback ride I took in everything as if I was going to be dying tomorrow. That's why I wanted to leave that way."

"I'm glad we did. Did you see those two squirrels chasing each other up that old oak tree? There won't be any animals on Gaia II, not even pets. I feel like I am leaving behind a good friend."

"Have you called your family in Italy?"

"Yes, I called when you were out of the room this morning. We're actually doing okay. They understand how important this is to me and we will stay in touch. It was nice to have that two week visit to say goodbyes. How about you, Paul?"

"At least I know that I am taking the most important thing to me on Earth along on the adventure."

Renata leans over and gives Paul a tender kiss and Paul asks Renata if she would like to dance.

Paul Drake and Renata Toscini are up early the next morning, because their transport leaves at 7am. Cars depart Santos-Dumont at 7am, 3pm and 11pm. Since travel time to Sumio Geostationary Earth Orbit Station (Sumio Geostation) is now 40 hours, the elevator is able to handle five transports on the tether at any given time in the 36000 kilometers between stations. With one transport en-route from Sumio Geostation to Asimov Transfer Station near the end of the 100000 kilometer tether, the space elevator system is currently operating at full capacity.

Twelve people are traveling on this trip. This is at the maximum of 900 kilograms allowed for passengers, with double that amount allotted to freight.

Renata is first on board the transport at 6:30am sharp with Paul right behind her. "This is nothing like what I expected, Paul. I'm amazed that the ceiling is so high."

"You must have missed that part of orientation. They mentioned that the only restriction on transport design is weight not size. I think you'll appreciate the height after a day and a half in the car, especially when we become weightless."

In the center of the transport are fifteen *smart* chairs arranged in a fashion so as to encourage social interaction. Around the perimeter are several booths for food, entertainment and viewing. The walls are all cushioned to prevent zero-g injuries.

Paul and Renata choose a couple of chairs and other passengers come in behind them. A young Brazilian couple is in the group and they are obviously on their honeymoon. The man is very brash and athletic looking. Renata imagines that the woman spends most of her time on a beach, in a bikini. They can't keep their hands off of each other.

Renata is closest to the pair and starts up a conversation. "I'm guessing that you two have decided to spend your honeymoon at the Space Hilton."

The man nods at her. "I suppose it's pretty obvious. Actually my wife, Daniella, is the one who has been dying to do this. If she had her way we'd have had our wedding in orbit."

Daniella gives her new husband a disapproving look. "That's right, and we would have too if we could have afforded to have our parents come along."

Renata smiles and introduces herself and Paul. "I hope the two of you have a wonderful time. It looks like we are all going to be cabin mates for a couple of days."

The man introduces himself as Ronaldo and they all shake hands. "And are you two celebrating an anniversary at the Hilton?"

Paul joins the conversation. "Actually, we are getting married in space, but not at the Hilton."

Daniella, whom is much more of a space enthusiast than her new husband, has a *light bulb* moment. "I thought I recognized you two. Renata Toscini and Paul Drake. I saw your interview on the special for Gaia II on the National Geographic Web Channel. How exciting to be traveling to the stars!"

Ronaldo looks a little puzzled. "Paul Drake? That name sounds familiar to me."

"Maybe you've heard of my robotics company."

"No, that's not it." Paul leaves it at that.

When all twelve passengers are in their chairs and the cargo has been loaded in the hold beneath their floor, an automated voice makes an announcement. "Welcome aboard Transport 3. My name is Brian. If you have any questions or requests feel free to ask me at any time. This car will be hooking up to the tether in about five minutes. There will be a slight jolt when connecting. We will be raised by mechanical means until we reach a height where the laser can take over powering our ascent. Please stay in your seats for the first hour and a half while the laser accelerates the car. You all have monitors that you can fold out from the arms of your chairs for multiple uses. The ceiling and floor will be displaying 3D images taken by exterior cameras for your enjoyment. For obvious reasons, there will be no downward view until we are no longer powered by the laser below. ETA for Sumio Geostation is 11pm tomorrow. Have a pleasant ride."

Those, with their monitors in use, see the transport from the perspective of several cameras on the geodesic dome. They have icons on the screen that they can touch to access the internet to read, contact friends, listen to music or any of the endless resources available. They all feel the connection to the tether as promised and Renata notices a steady vibration as the transport starts to climb. Whatever sound is being produced by the elevating mechanism is impossible to hear through the insulated walls of the vehicle.

After about an hour and a half the laser turns off and the transport switches to solar power and electricity conducted through the tether itself. There is another slight jerk at the transition. The monitors now switch to a view looking earthward from the transport. Looking down on the Atlantic Ocean, Santos-Dumont Station is just a small speck in the middle. The space elevator tether stretches away from them in the view above and disappears into the distance.

The voice calling itself "Brian" tells them that it is okay to get out of their seats and move around the cabin now. He warns that they may still feel a little heavier than normal since the transport is still slightly accelerating. When Renata arises she notices that the floor below them is now filled with the image she has been seeing on her monitor.

Looking up she sees that the sky now appears black with stars clearly visible even though it is daytime. She beckons to Paul.

"Let's go take a look out of a side portal. I think we are high enough now to see the curvature of the Earth. Paul goes with her to one of the three viewing booths and pulls the curtain behind them to block out interior lighting. What they see out of the meter and a half diameter portal is why people have longed to travel to space for centuries. Renata leans up against Paul. "How beautiful! No video image can match this."

"Yeah, I know what you mean. I feel I could almost reach out and touch Africa."

"Look at the horizon. It's hard to believe how relatively thin the atmosphere is that keeps everything we know alive."

Paul and Renata stay in the booth for half an hour and then go back into the cabin to see how everybody else is doing. Others are taking turns in the viewing booths or interacting with their monitors. One couple is video conferencing with friends or family down below. With gravity about normal they return to their seats.

By noon, when the passengers of the transport look down, the Earth no longer fills the entire view. They can now see the blue planet in it's entirety and have a true feeling of being in space.

By morning of the next day they only weigh about half of their original weight. After breakfast and taking his turn in one of the two washrooms, Paul challenges Ronaldo to a couple of low-g games. One is a game somewhat resembling skee-ball, with balls being rolled up a ramp toward a series of concentric rings. Once adjusting they don't find the game much different than playing on Earth, maybe it would be more fun in still lower gravity. The other game they play is more of a one on one competition. The game display gives them a *trick* to do that is much easier at their lesser weight. Each has to do the trick and the challenges get progressively harder. Ronaldo beats Paul doing a trick where a player has to throw up a ball, do a back flip and catch the ball. Paul congratulates his opponent, but Ronaldo concedes. "I think I should be able to win that one. I play semi-pro football in Madras."

After dinner that evening, they are practically weightless. Renata sits in her chair and does what appears to be some form of meditation while others try to get used to moving around in zero gravity. If it wasn't for familiarity with the interior space, the passengers wouldn't be able to tell up from down.

Finally, late in the evening of their second day in the space elevator transport, an object appears on the ceiling image. Not until they are practically reaching the Sumio Geostation Depot do they realize the immensity of their destination.

As the car is pulling into the airlock, Daniella looks over to Renata. "I noticed that you spent a lot of time in your chair. Are you feeling alright?"

"I'm fine. We were trained to do a process called autogenics to ward off space sickness. You and Ronaldo were given an implant to monitor and release anti-nausea medication when needed. The medical people on Gaia II aren't allowing us to take anything during the week before arrival."

The images on the ceiling and floor fade as interior lighting shows the way to the exit portal. Paul, Renata, Ronaldo, Daniella and the others have had some practice now with their gradual change from Earth gravity to weightlessness. Of course there is still gravity here, it's just offset by the centrifugal force of the orbiting space station. They push away in a directional vector that runs through the center of their bodies to drift toward the exit.

The on board computer does the final announcement. "We hope you enjoyed your ride to Sumio Geostation and the Space Hilton Hotel. Please be careful proceeding toward the exit." After unloading passengers, the transport moves further up into the geostation to deliver its cargo.

* * *

The corridor and then the entrance to the hotel have been designed for entertainment value. Except for a handrail it's hard for the new arrivals to tell that they are in a corridor and not just floating though space. The hotel entrance looks like a Hollywood depiction of a portal in space to a different dimension. Daniella is the first one through and shouts in her excitement. "This is everything I have ever dreamed of and more!"

Looking from the entrance into the Hilton, straight ahead about twenty meters away, there is what appears to be a floating information desk. It actually is being maintained in place by tiny rockets, all computer controlled by a central gyroscope. Similarly, there are floating tables, chairs and other furniture for dining, socializing and conducting business. All, of course, have built in displays with computer access. There are side rooms with furniture on the walls and upside down on the ceiling, if there is such a thing in zero-g. There are some very interesting looking plants growing out in various directions toward light sources. The architecture and artwork is something to behold. Much of the art takes advantage of the situation. One that Renata is particularly fond of is a variation of an M. C. Escher work with water falling in various directions, all enclosed of course.

The most impressive sight is looking up at the see-through dome above. A large blue orb is suspended in space above, taking up about one third of their field of view. The sun is just now disappearing behind the Earth. Fortunately, there is a solar energy station that doubles as a shield blocking direct rays from the sun. They can, however, still see a ring of light reflecting through the Earth's atmosphere. Also, the moon must be nearly full in the Central Atlantic Ocean since the Earth is bathed in an eerie glow. The hotel keeps the lights very dim, just using directional accent lighting. The intent is to be able to have as good of a view of the planet as possible.

Renata understands the science, but is still awestruck. "Paul, I can't get used to the idea of the Earth being *up*."

"Makes for an impressive view doesn't it. I guess from this orientation you would say that the hotel is at the top of the huge space station."

"Have you ever seen the rest of the station?"

"I guess I never told you. My company upgraded the robotics in the industrial section. I got the full tour. There are research areas, facilities that support communications satellites and solar energy satellites and even a supply depot that takes care of the needs of new space habitat ventures. At the other end of the station there is a depot, larger than where we came in, for the transport that goes to Asimov Transfer Station."

"Is that where we catch the shuttle to Gaia II?"

"That's right. It's a multipurpose facility."

"Let's go find our room and clean up. It's been a long couple of days in the transport."

Renata and Paul push off and float over to one of the windows at the information desk. They find out that their room is at location 52-15-40. This is just a fun way of finding their room based on an x-y-z grid with the z-axis pointing toward the

Earth. Paul has made sure that they have one of the nicest rooms in the hotel. Their containers have been tubed to a location accessible in the room, but they will probably just leave them sealed to transport on to Gaia II.

There are special zero-g suits in the rooms for Paul and Renata that have been made to fit perfectly. These were preselected by the two of them. All basic necessities, along with special instructions, are in the washrooms.

When they open the door and enter the room, Renata blushes a little and sneers at Paul. "You've reserved the honeymoon suite."

"There are actually ten rooms like this. Do you like it?"

She looks around the room. The colors, art and lighting are all very romantic. A few large soft cushions are floating high in the middle of the room. The bed is a large cocoon-like bag attached to the wall. In a far corner of the room is a fixed chair with strap facing a computer station. On the computer display are icons for controlling temperature, lighting, music, visual wall displays, humidity, fragrance and several other environmental factors. Of course, there is one icon that accesses a different main screen for internet access and hotel information. A small vending area is in the other far lower corner of the room. It has some basic snacks and beverages and a see-through cold storage compartment with a bottle of champagne welcoming the guests. All of the consumables have been packaged for easy consumption in a weightless environment. The walls are all padded for comfort.

"It'll do." Renata yawns. "I'm going to freshen up a little, Mr. Casanova." She finds the door to the washroom and goes in. Staying with the theme of playing with zero-g, the entrance is in the floor.

Paul has a slightly disappointed look on his face as he changes into some provided nightwear. His mood does a 180, however, when Renata comes floating out of the washroom. She is wearing a very sexy red, sheer nightgown. He pushes off a wall and propels himself to the computer display. Touching an icon he had already requested when he reserved the room, the lights go out and the walls seem to disappear. The room is lit up with stars and a beautiful nebula on the ceiling. He pushes himself gently toward his fiancee and his momentum slowly pushes her back against a padded wall.

"Paul, I have no experience at this. Are you sure we shouldn't watch a video or something?"

"I thought we might just wing it." He gives her a passionate kiss and they float off into the room rotating just enough to totally lose orientation.

* * *

Renata wakes up the next morning before Paul. She is lost for a minute until she remembers she is in a cocoon with Paul on the wall of their room. The room looks just as it had the night before as neither of them had bothered to change it. She opens her side of the bag enough to slip out and pushes away in what she thinks she remembers is the direction toward the room computer. It is purposefully set up so that, with lights off, you can only see it when looking straight on. She finds it and searches the *Room Settings* options. "Yes, this is the one I want." She chooses a view of the Earth as seen from low orbit, with the sun rising in the East and a crescent moon above. Then Renata opens a door into the *South Atlantic Ocean* and enters the washroom.

After cleaning up and getting dressed in the suit supplied for her in the room, she brings Paul a coffee from the vending machine and awakens him. He pulls her close and gives her a good morning kiss. "I like what you've done to the room."

Paul and Renata have one more full day and night to enjoy the hotel. One of the most fun things that they try is a game of 3D Zero-g Laser Tag. They run into the Brazilian couple once or twice again who are looking tired, but seem quite happy. Renata comments that Ronaldo seems to be glad that he came now.

They choose to have dinner at a small restaurant that is a branch of the main lounge and so has the view of the Earth above. Both choose what to eat from an electronic menu displayed on the table. When the waiter comes over to their table he is upside down. Or are they?

Paul is curious. "Everybody here seems to have a lot of fun with weightlessness. How do you get a job in a place like this?"

The waiter can't help but show a little pride. "Hilton has customer service contests among all of their employees worldwide and the winners get to work here for two months. There is a continuous rotation due to the effects of weightlessness."

"What is the lounge like here?"

"We have two. One is a fun, lively one called the Mos Eisley Cantina Bar. The other is a more subdued, romantic spot with live music. The famous alto sax player, Scott Harrison, is playing there nightly. They will both be open until 3am to accommodate the passengers coming in on the late transport."

Renata takes a sip out of her zero-g magnetic wine goblet. "The second one sounds like the one for us. How do you get there from here?"

"Straight up about thirty meters to the bust of Isaac Newton, then go thirty degrees clockwise from the direction he is looking."

"Of course, I should have known."

Paul finally orders dinner from the waiter and it's really quite good for *space food*. Renata has broccoli and tofu in garlic sauce and Paul has the Jamaican roast stuffed pepper. After thanking the waiter, they check out the lounge, have a drink and listen to some good sax music. The couple doesn't stay for very long, because for some reason Paul is very anxious to get back to their hotel room.

The next morning they get a wake up call, because they have to get ready, eat breakfast and find their way to the far side depot to catch a 10am shuttle to Gaia II. Renata's not as tired as she thought she would be on so little sleep. Paul had mentioned that he had found it true on his previous visit that you don't seem to need as much sleep in weightlessness.

When they get to the Shuttle Port, they find out that they are the only passengers on this flight. This seems like a waste, but there have actually been numerous flights with no passengers, just taking cargo to the interstellar spaceship.

Paul and Renata board the shuttle and strap into two of the seats. When air locks are sealed and the flight is ready, the take off announcement commences. "Good morning Renata and Paul. My name is Hal. If there is anything I can answer for you about the conveniences of the cabin please ask. Our shuttle will be getting you to your destination by doing a low energy maneuver called a Hohmann orbital phase transition. Very soon we will be doing a retro velocity change of about one kilometer per second. This is commonly known as a *delta-v*. The shuttle will enter an elliptical orbit during which you will still feel weightlessness. Our closest approach to the Earth will be approximately 6500 kilometers above the surface. When we return to the apogee of the elliptical orbit, back at 35800 kilometers above the Earth, we will do an equal, but opposite delta-v burn to return to circular orbit. At this point the shuttle will have made a 180 degree phase shift in orbit and will rendezvous with Gaia II. I hope you will enjoy your trip."

Twelve hours later, on October 7, 2111, Paul and Renata see the large cylinder in space that they are going to be calling home for the rest of their lives.

August 27, 2111
Sagan Crater, Mars

A figure in a lifesuit strolls across the red, rocky surface. Even with the suit's special materials, the dust seems to cling everywhere. The lone soul in this vast desert carefully and methodically climbs up a gradually sloping hill to the top of the rim of a large crater.

The walker remembers a few other trips to this location, knowing that this will be the last and thinks, "I never get tired of this view." Looking to the west across the Martian panorama, a small sun hovers low in the sky. It's about half of the size of the same sun seen in the sky from Earth. There is still dust stirred up in the extremely thin carbon dioxide atmosphere from a dust storm a couple of days ago. This gives a hazy orange glow to the sky of tonight's Martian sunset.

Looking to the eastern horizon, the moon Phobos is setting in the opposite direction. Since it is low in the sky, Phobos is about half the apparent size of the Martian sun. Phobos is an unusual looking moon with a huge impact crater taking up about half of one side. It orbits Mars faster than the planet's rotation period. Therefore, Phobos rises in the west and sets in the east. Doing this about every eleven hours, it takes about four hours to zip across the sky.

The climber watches the sun go down, then starts to walk back down the hill right away, since it gets dark very quickly here. Once in the shadow of the crater rim, it is too dark to move safely without lighting. Having made this journey many times before, the traveler is able to find the rover with a little help from some artificial lighting and a tracking device.

The rover is activated and begins the 40 kilometer trip back to the research center. The large wheeled, high riding rover *knows* the terrain well and makes good time. A little over an hour later it drives into an underground garage with its passenger and a door closes behind it.

The rider shuts off the vehicle and climbs down from the cab. After the temperature, atmospheric pressure, air mixture, air water vapor content and a few other criteria have become tolerable, the rider takes off the lifesuit and lets her long, light auburn hair cascade down her back. In her skintight, thermal, one piece bodysuit, she hangs up the lifesuit in a storage locker. The beautiful woman dons her normal clothes, vest and jeans, and her lightweight *smart* shoes. As much as she loves her trips outside the research center, she always looks forward to getting back into comfortable attire, especially the shoes. *Smart* shoes are like *smart* chairs in the sense that they can detect a person's pressure points and automatically adjust for maximum comfort. When everything has been put away, she walks through the sealed door into the Sagan Crater Research Center.

By the 2040's, the Earth space elevators had attained full operation. In the 2050's, fusion energy reactors were becoming more common and fuel, such as deuterium from water rich asteroids and helium3 from the moon, were being mined to use for fusion power beyond the Earth. Serious plans were now being made to colonize Mars. By the end of the 2060's, a space elevator tether had been established from Sagan Crater (chosen for it's size, latitude, access to permafrost and location in the Valley Marineris floodplain, not its name) to a station 150,000 kilometers above that was named Bradford Transfer Station.

A basic research station was initially built in Sagan Crater and humans first went to live on Mars in the early 2070's. After nearly two decades of doing research there, a fusion reactor was finally established at the site and the Mars Biosphere, containing the research station, was constructed.

The shapely brunette strolls down a hallway with a confidence as if she owned the place.

"Kayla."

She hears the voice coming from a large underground greenhouse and looks to see a young African American man heading her way. He had seen her walk by the transparent doors.

Kayla comes back and opens the door to the humid room. From among the tiers of hydroponic high yield plants, the white-robed lab assistant walks out. "Did you have a nice drive?"

"Yes. That place always gives me a very spiritual, peaceful feeling. I could almost imagine what it would look like with water flowing through the Tlu Valles like it did billions of years ago." She realizes what time it is. "You're working a little late, Marcus. Aren't you going to join everybody for dinner?"

"All of our new strain of spinach is withering. Looks like it may be a genetic problem."

"No, I ran tests today. I can't find any genetic flaws. It must be something else. Why don't you come to the cafeteria with me and we can discuss it there."

"Okay, you're the boss."

Together, Kayla and Marcus walk into the dining area where the rest of the biosphere inhabitants are finishing eating. One of the diners is an average looking, small framed man in very colorful clothes. He has an olive Arabic complexion and appears much younger than his age of thirty-one.

Kayla walks over to the man and gives him a kiss. "Ali, why don't you ever come with me to the crater rim?"

"This is because I know you well Kayla, my darling. Sometimes you need the solitude to free your mind from worries."

"And I know you well, Ali. You were obsessed with some role playing game using the new *BrainGate* helmet that just came in on our last supply transport."

"Well, I did get a chip implant before we left Earth for a reason and Final Fantasy BG II (TM) is not just some role playing game."

Kayla and Marcus grab some food and sit down with the rest. Ali, as usual, is keeping everybody entertained. Kayla and Ali have totally opposite personalities, but somehow are perfect for each other.

* * *

Ali Zamani is a young biologist. He attained his doctorate as a research assistant of the legendary Seker Fayed. Fayed had perfected the CELSS (Controlled Ecological Life Support System), commonly known as a biosphere, over the previous forty years in Northern Egypt.. He had lived in his biosphere for the entire duration. His work has made the Mars Biosphere possible. Seker Fayed has always considered Ali his best student.

Ali was born in Iran and had lived there until he was twelve. Then, his family moved to Russia to work in their booming agricultural industry. He graduated from Kiev University at the top of his class. Ali had always been fascinated with Fayed's work and stayed in constant communication while attaining his Master's degree. Seker Fayed invited him to come to the Egyptian Biosphere to live and complete his PhD.

In 2109. at the age of 29, he met Kayla Novac, a beautiful, young Israeli woman. She had come to the biosphere to study food production in closed cycles. They became good friends as Ali could always make her laugh. He never imagined that they would be anything more than friends, until one night, when they were working together, she kissed him. Everything changed.

In spite of religious differences and family protest they were married in Egypt in June of 2110. Shortly thereafter, both were asked to be in charge of the life support systems and food production on Gaia II. It was an offer they couldn't refuse. To prepare, Ali and Kayla left in the fall to gain experience by replacing the lead researchers at the Mars Biosphere in Sagan Crater.

* * *

One of the men at the dinner table gets up and puts his drinking cup, plate and eating utensils into the recycler. He looks over to Ali and Kayla. "I suggest we have a little party Martian style. It's not every day you say bon voyage to someone who is going to fly off to another star."

A woman getting a beverage laughs. "Yeah, we haven't had a good Alien Bash in a long time!"

Kayla decides to play along. "No way. The last time we had one of those I woke up in the morning next to a three-eyed Alpha Centauri plant creature."

Now Ali gets a little interested. "Wait a minute. I remember that party. I was an Andromedan rock eater."

"Don't worry, Ali. Nothing happened. I don't think our parts were compatible." Kayla loves it when she can needle Ali. He is usually the instigator. "Seriously guys, I would love to, but we really need a good night's sleep for the journey tomorrow."

Ali agrees. "You heard the woman folks. It seems that we have become our parents sooner than expected."

They all know that space travel is still pretty demanding and even dangerous, so were really just kidding about the party.

Kayla and Ali do one last inspection of the labs and retire to their sleeping quarters.

* * *

In the morning, they have breakfast with the crew and get ready to meet the incoming transport. It has been traveling in their direction for over a week now. Everybody puts on a lifesuit and walks over to the space elevator station, which is separate from the biosphere.

After going through the transition room and getting out of their lifesuits, the group makes its way to where the transport will enter the station in about five minutes.

Ali is the first to say something. "It still bothers me that nobody told us who was replacing us here on Mars."

Marcus knows, but won't say. "We'll be finding out in about three minutes."

After what seems like a lot longer than three minutes, the machinery of the elevator receiving building starts up. They can hear the transport entering the upper level at the surface. It slowly comes down to the ground level of the elevator station and disengages from the tether. Then the vehicle comes into the room on tracks, where the receiving party awaits.

It's another five minutes before the door of the transport opens. When two people walk out, the second one gets instant recognition.

Ali loses it. "Seker, you're crazy. How did you get them to let you do this? You just had your seventy-fifth birthday!"

Ali's mentor laughs. "It's good to see you, Ali. I think I have earned one free ticket for my lifetime contributions. Besides, I think that this low gravity is going to be good for me."

Seker Fayed is hiding it the best he can, but the long voyage has taken quite a toll on him.

Kayla welcomes the young, attractive Hispanic woman that will be taking over her responsibilities. "You two need some good food and a lot of rest. We can take you to the biosphere and give you a tour when you're ready. Ali and I can wait for a little while before we leave."

The woman speaks for the first time. "Actually, I have done enough *resting* for a while. What I really need is some good exercise."

Marcus jumps on the opportunity. "We have a small basketball court and workout room in the biosphere. I'll challenge you to some one-on-one low-g b-ball.."

The woman grins mischeviously. "You're on."

All put on their lifesuits again and head back to the biosphere. Ali gets Seker up to speed on the life support systems and also the research projects that they have been working on. Meanwhile, the new Food Production Specialist kicks Marcus's butt at basketball.

After showering, they join the others in the lounge. Marcus looks beat. "Lucinda, why didn't you tell me you played college ball at UCLA."

"What's wrong, Marcus? You had home court advantage."

Kayla intrudes. "You two can continue your one-on-one later. Right now, I have a few things I need to let Lucinda know before we leave." Kayla and Lucinda head off to the greenhouses and computer control center. Marcus finds the nearest smart chair.

* * *

At one o'clock in the afternoon Martian time (or would that be Valley Marineris Standard time), Kayla and Ali do their hugs and handshakes and climb into the Mars Space Elevator Transport. They begin their eight day, 150000 kilometer journey to Bradford Transfer Station. About the only things of interest along the way other than a great view of Mars are a flyby of Phobos at about 6000 kilometers and an even closer approach to Deimos shortly after passing Mars synchronous orbit. With Sagan Crater at about 11 degrees north latitude, the elevator tether is at a safe distance from the moons even though the tether tends toward an equatorial position. Both Phobos and Deimos have equatorial orbits with Deimos being the more circular of the two.

Upon arriving at Bradford Transfer Station, Ali and Kayla board a Dual Propulsion Ion Thrust Ship for a 39 day trip to Asimov Transfer Station 100000 kilometers above Santos-Dumont and the South Atlantic Ocean. Then, they have a four day elevator trip to Sumio Geostation and a well deserved two days of rest and recuperation.

On October 21st, two weeks after Paul and Renata, Ali and Kayla board the same shuttle for the final leg of the voyage, a twelve hour shuttle ride to Gaia II.

January 3, 2112
Tsiolkovsky Space Elevator Station

Barry is the first up in the morning at 5am. He and Mei aren't scheduled to catch the transport on Island Three until 11am. Jaswinder and Leela have the early transport to catch on Island One at 7am. Mei is sleeping soundly so Barry throws on some clothes and a utility belt and sneaks out into the hallway.

Opening one pouch on his belt, Barry pulls out a folded up, very pliable object. When it opens up to full size, the device looks like a combination of headband and goggles. He puts it over his eyes and ears and connects both sides in the back of his head. These *goggles* are nearly invisible from Barry's point of view, but have several see-through layers that each display images. When these images are combined they visually create a three-dimensional projection in front of the viewer. Another layer displays text or attached pictures, etc. similar to e-mail. There are tiny processors, speakers and microphones on both earpieces of the apparatus.

Barry knows that Leela and Jaswinder will be up by now and gives the voice command, "AV (Audio/ Video) on" The comm-device recognizes Barry's voice. "Call Jaswinder." They had all put each other on their *friends* lists the night before last.

Jaswinder and his wife are on their way to breakfast when a little tune comes from his utility belt. He pushes a button on the belt.

Barry sees a word display that reads, "Call Pending."

Jaswinder answers his call. "This is Jaswinder."

"Good morning, this is Barry."

Leela hears this and gives Jaswinder a nod, so he takes out his *comm-goggles* and puts them on and commands, "AV on."

A message informs Barry, "Call accepted."

After a couple of seconds, small *avatars* appear in both of their goggles. As Jaswinder talks a little Jaswinder speaks in front of Barry. "You're up early."

Now, the avatar Barry, in Jaswinder's goggles replies. "Always been an early riser. Have you had breakfast, yet?"

"On our way, now."

"I won't hold you up. Since you are catching the earlier transport and we aren't getting in until 3am, I thought we might all meet for lunch at the Marriott."

"How about at 1pm at the buffet in the main lobby? Let me show you an image." He then makes the command, "Google images: Marriott Space Hotel/ main lobby/ buffet." Several images appear to Jaswinder. "Attach Image 4."

A three-dimensional view of the buffet area appears to Barry. "Okay, sounds good. We can meet you at a table on the left wall. I'll let you get to breakfast. Have a good trip."

"You, too." Jaswinder pushes a button on his belt and puts away his goggles. Barry does the same and goes back into his room.

Mei is still half asleep, but hears Barry come back in. "Did you call the Singhs?"

"Yes, I made arrangements for us to meet them for lunch at the Marriott the day after tomorrow."

"Fine. Now, I have a bone to pick with you. Come and sit down on the bed."

Barry reluctantly hobbles over to the bed and sits down. He's not sure where this is going, but knows it's not going to be good.

"Barry, I like the Singhs, too, but don't you think we are spending a little too much time with them. I need your support right now. I need more of your attention focused on me."

"Okay, I promise. Other than lunch, I'm all yours for our entire stay at the hotel."

"Don't just brush me off, Barry. I want you to take my mind off of Gaia II. Once we get to the ship, I need to focus on my job. I've got to make sure that this thing works."

"I understand. I still wish you wouldn't put all of the responsibility on yourself. You're not going to be any good to anybody if you're all stressed out."

"That's why I need you to make this next couple of days fun. Help me forget about quantum fluctuations. Let's have a mini vacation, just you and me."

"I can think of a good way to start." He quickly removes his clothes and climbs back into bed with his wife.

Mei and Barry go to breakfast at about 8:30. They catch the Central Station Shuttle back to the food court. The shuttle only goes one way so they have to go around the station to get back to the previous stop. Fortunately, the shuttle's tourist informational shows only play if there is somebody new in the vehicle.

At breakfast, Mei is thinking about the previous day's orientation. "What did you think of the couple from Hawaii that we met yesterday?"

"Seem like nice people. Did you know that Ishii Matogawa has over fifty patents? He's quite the inventor. Leilani is very approachable, too, considering her celebrity status on You Tube."

"Well, aren't you the walking, talking Wikipedia. I bet there's something you don't know." Barry takes a bite of his spinach quiche while listening. "We are going to go jogging together on Gaia II."

"That should be fun. You can start at one location and jog in one direction, but wind up right back where you started."

"You could come with us if you want."

"That's okay. Sounds like girl-time."

Mei knew what Barry's answer to that would be. She takes staying physically fit as seriously as everything else she does and Leilani telecasts her exercise classes to millions. They would leave him in the dust. She doesn't push it. "So, what is our plan for when we get to the hotel."

"I figured we would wing it when we get there, but don't worry, Mei. I promise we'll have fun."

They finish eating and get back on the shuttle to go catch the connector to Island Three.

* * *

The Island Three and Island Four tethers were added several years after the first two. By then, planners knew that most of the visitors would be tourists. They designed the Islands and the shuttles to the Islands with that in mind.

Barry and Mei are totally caught off guard when they walk out of a narrow corridor into the large open room housing their ride to the departure transport. The corridor and the room have been created to look like a natural grotto. The large cavernous room has a big pool in the middle with a submarine docked on the far side. It looks like something right out of a Hollywood set.

They walk with one other couple to the pier, where the sub is docked, and climb down a ladder into a passenger seating area below water level. There are already four people on board and the final six, including Ishii and Leilani Matogawa, arrive on the next shuttle. As they enter the sub, Ishii is talking about things he would add to this "submarine in a grotto" experience to make it even better. In his loose casual Hawaiian attire it is easy to see that he loves good food. Leilani, his wife, comes down the ladder right behind him and looks to the other passengers as if to be apologizing for her husbands loudness. She is an exceedingly well-toned, athletic native Hawaiian woman who has a very professional appearance like that of a news anchorwoman. Ishii was born in Japan, but has lived most of his life in Honolulu. Locals still mistake him for a tourist at times.

With everyone boarded, the sub automatically seals and starts its dive. It goes straight down for about fifty fathoms until it clears the immense lower structure of the *Central Island*. On the way down, they notice that beneath the water a lot of attention has been given to keeping up the illusion. There is even an octopus living in a niche of the natural looking irregular wall. Coming back up into Island Three is equally impressive.

When they all arrive and exit the sub, what they see is primarily a transport station, but there are some amenities for riders as they wait. There are vending machines, virtual reality booths and even a small Space Elevator Museum. The transport doesn't leave for forty-five minutes, so Barry and Mei check out the museum. There are numerous holographic images and hands on exhibits. Most show early construction and teach about the materials and scientific concepts that make the elevators possible. There's even a Mars exhibit.

With about a half an hour to go before departure, Mei hears a metallic connecting noise and then the whirring of a fine tuned motor. It sounds like their transport is leaving without them. Barry sees her concern and explains. "They're sending up a maintenance pod. The transport before us must have detected some damage to the tether. The pods are much lighter and faster than the transports and are totally powered by the electricity in the tether itself. They have nano-machines in them that repair the damage."

"Is there any danger to our transport?"

"No, they wouldn't send us up if there was. There are many entwined ribbons making up the tether, so there is a lot of redundancy. There has only been three times in the last year that they have had to delay a transport."

"What causes the damage?"

"Most of the time, it's microscopic meteors or atomic oxygen eating away at the carbon. There is a very thin layer of gold that protects the tether from the oxygen, but occasionally it gets breached."

"Has the tether ever broken?"

"There was quite a scare in the early elevator days, but since then the tether maintenance has been improved greatly."

"I still get the feeling that this is more dangerous than they let us believe."

As if on cue, the riders hear the official announcement. "All passengers may now board Car 34 for Noda Geostation and prepare for departure." The transport had been at the station for the entire time they had been waiting. It had been getting a cleaning and being loaded with cargo.

The twelve riders all walk through the connecting hatch into the transport and find seats. About fifteen minutes later, the hum of the elevator port motors starts and the car is raised to where the Central Station Laser Facility can take over powering the climb. The Tether Three transport, quietly and, at first, very slowly, is now on its 36000 kilometer journey to geosynchronous orbit.

The passengers of Car 34 are all experiencing weightlessness now. Many are doing autogenics to ward off space-sickness and others are practicing moving about. Barry has been to Noda before and is pretty good at maneuvering in zero-g. He has been instructing Mei and she is catching on fast. Mei is having fun and for the first time in a long time seems to not have her mind on her job.

Of the several doing autogenics, it doesn't appear to be working for one female rider. She is Nadia Kova, a young blonde Czechoslovakian woman who will be working as a technician in the Gaia II Probe Center. Her husband, Mikhail, is trying to help her any way he can. Barry goes over and assures her that even in the worst cases, the sickness only lasts for a couple of days.

Ishii Matogawa is one of the ones doing autogenics, but Leilani is doing great and is now *playing* with Mei. One of the things they do is push off each other in the center of the room and then turn at the wall like competitive swimmers. Then, they meet again, locking arms and doing a kind of do-si-do until releasing in a direction where they hope not to collide into anybody. It's a good thing there is a lot of space in the interior of transports.

As they get close, Noda Geostation comes into view on the upper wall image taken by an exterior camera. The *bottom* of the station is a huge, flat viewing window that encircles the opening for Tethers One and Two. A few lights can be seen through the window from the outside. In a concentric ring around the viewing window is a bulging, torus-like section also with large windows. Mei looks at the side closest to them and can see people barely visible at tables near the windows. Another part of the torus is completely lit up, but empty. "Where the people are looks like a lounge and that lit up room looks like a banquet facility."

Barry confirms her guess. As they climb higher they see that each level sticks out a little farther than the one *below* it. All hotel levels have windows facing the Earth.

Ishii finally looks out a side window. "We are stopping here, aren't we? It looks like we are going right past the hotel." Then, an announcement tells them to strap into their seats to prepare for arrival. They have been slowing for quite some time now, but there will still be a jolt when they stop at the station. The view of the hotel disappears as they enter the hotel arrival station and come to a stop. The floor and ceiling images fade and lights come on illuminating the exit.

"All passengers going to the Marriott Space Hotel may now exit the transport. We caution you to be very careful until you are used to weightlessness. Please check in at the welcome desk in the Main Lobby. Any passengers continuing on to the Upper Station remain seated. We hope you enjoy your stay in Earth orbit and thank you for riding in the Tsiolkovsky Space Elevator."

Mei and Barry undo their straps and push off with the others toward the exit. The airlock leads to a well lit, decorative waiting room. There are advertisements for the restaurants and game rooms that the hotel has to offer and artworks adorning the walls. Barry sees one painting that has a familiar style. "Look at this, Mei." She has already gone past him and is looking out another window. She pushes off and returns to see what Barry has found. Barry grabs one of the small handles, which are in strategic areas everywhere, and catches her.

"See this painting. Look at the signature. It's an original by Hubert Hicks." Hubert Hicks became a household name when he and Richard Gordon became the first people to witness evidence of extraterrestrial life. The Nova Website broadcasted a special called "Man on the Moon" shortly after the discovery. It was while being interviewed for this special that Hubert allowed the guest to see his hidden studio. "Hicks never sold any of his paintings making them that much more valuable. This one must have been donated."

Another pleasant voice speaks to the passengers in the room. "Please make yourself at home as preparations are made to connect to the main station. You will feel some slight movements as the Tether Three and Four Station is fine tuned into position. When the connecting duct has sealed and the hatch opens, please proceed orderly and quickly through to the waiting area on the other side. We do not like to keep the stations connected any longer than necessary."

When the hatch opens, another announcement tells them all to proceed through the duct. They are told that there is a hand rail in the duct to help them move quickly to the other side.

Nadia Kova is still feeling poorly and Mikhail tells the others to go ahead and they will be right behind them. Barry and Mei are the next to last couple to go through as Barry is making sure that Nadia is going to make it. When it comes their turn, Nadia tells Barry that she is okay and to go on across with Mei. Mei enters the duct with Barry behind her. He looks back to see that Nadia is now entering with Mikhail helping her from behind. Everything looks alright so he catches up with Mei.

The duct is transparent and Mei turns to Barry. "Barry, look at the Earth. This is fantastic. Now I know how space walkers must feel!"

When Barry and Mei are nearly to the other side an alarm sounds and there is an announcement. "Emergency! Please use the rail to evacuate the connector duct as quickly as possible. There is an object on a collision course with Tether Four. Estimated impact is fifteen minutes. You have one minute to exit the duct in either direction."

Barry looks back. Nadia and Mikhail are only about a third of the way over. Nadia has stopped and is having convulsions from her space-sickness. She tries to keep moving forward. Barry can immediately see, from his experience, that she and Mikhail aren't going to make it.

Barry shouts into the duct. "Mikhail, Nadia, listen to me! If you want to live do exactly as I say. Nadia, grab the rail and stop. When I tell you, let go immediately. Mikhail, I will get Nadia. I need for you to use the handrail to return to the transport station as fast as you can."

Mikhail is still comforting Nadia. He looks in Barry's direction with tight lips, wrinkled forehead and squinting eyes. "I will take her back!"

"You won't be able to get her out of the connector in time. I can push off hard from this side and my momentum will force her back faster. No time to debate. Go!"

Reluctantly, Mikhail returns to the transport station. He hates leaving the life of his beloved Nadia in the hands of a virtual stranger.

Barry turns to Mei. "Okay, Mei. Ball up and prepare to push me off just like you were doing with Leilani in the transport. On the count of three we will both push off as hard as we can. You will speed off into the Geostation and I will go back into the duct. One, two, three ..."

As per plan, Barry shoots back through the duct. The push off isn't perfect so he has to use the rail to straighten his trajectory and speed up. As he nears Nadia, he yells in a commanding voice. "Let go!"

Nadia follows orders and Barry collides into her. He grabs her torso and attempts to keep as much momentum as possible in the direction they need to go. Nadia vomits upon impact, but neither she nor Barry cares in the dire situation. As Barry and Nadia near the hatch, Mikhail is just making his way back into the transport station. They collide into him and all three tumble into the station. The hatch closes behind them ten seconds later.

Strangely enough, Nadia is truly feeling a little better when it's safe to go back into the duct. She is a little reluctant at first, but realizes that she really doesn't have a choice. This time, Mikhail gives her a good push like Mei did for Barry. Soon, everybody is in the arrival room of the Marriott Space Hotel.

* * *

Barry sees that Mei is a little distraught and goes to her. "Are you alright?"

"I'm good, Barry. I think I may do some autogenics though."

"Sure, I'll do it with you. Let's find a private corner." He leads the way.

When doing autogenics, a subject has to minimize sensory stimulation and relax. This is easier in weightlessness than on Earth. Mei and Barry stabilize each other and take out their special earplugs. These plugs do such a good job that they even dampen bone vibrations near the ear. They also have eye covers that block out nearly all light by automatically sealing around the edges. The new high-tech material creates a vacuum seal, but still peels off easily.

Mikhail Kova floats over to them. "Barry, how's Mei doing?"

Mei doesn't like being talked about in the third person, but cuts him some slack. "I'm just fine, thanks. We'll see you in a few minutes in the Lobby."

Mikhail shakes hands with both of them and gives sincere thanks, then joins Nadia.

After putting earplugs and eye cover in place, Mei Sun totally relaxes and holds her arms out as to not have her fingertips touch anything. There are no distracting smells to worry about. When she is ready, she begins a form of self-hypnosis that utilizes biofeedback to control systems of the body that are normally involuntary. She starts her mantra. "My right arm is heavy. My right arm is heavy. My right arm is heavy. My right arm is heavy. My right arm is heavy. My right arm is heavy. And I am very calm." She repeats this until her right arm really does start to feel heavier due to more blood being directed to it. From there, she goes to the left arm and then other parts of her body. Then, as trained, she focuses the autogenics on her stomach and, indirectly, her pituitary gland. The experts can even control heart rate and other major organ functions. When she is finished, she takes off her eye cover and removes the earplugs. Mei now feels totally calm and relaxed.

Barry finishes before Mei. He is mostly participating to give her support anyway. Together, they drift down the corridor that leads to the entrance of the hotel. There are lighted 3D scenes from the Moon and Mars on the walls of the entry hall. Near the displays are handles to grab if one wants to stop and look closer at the images. At the end of the hall there is a large door that looks like something off the set of an old Stargate movie.

When they get close, the door automatically opens. Mei and Barry are stunned by this large unusual room. From their point of view, the floor and ceiling slope to a wall about 20 meters away that is about 8 meters high. The Main Lobby Welcome Desk is attached to the wall so that they are looking at it from the top. The room is fairly dark with accent lighting here and there along with dimly lighted displays, signs and advertisements. Mei looks to the left and sees that the room is fairly long, stretching about 50 meters toward a large window that takes up the entire far wall. She sees why they keep the room dark. Through the window at the end of the Main Lobby, a familiar planet hovers in space, dominating the view. It's about 3am over the Pacific Ocean, so she mainly just sees some atmospheric reflection and some coastal lighting.

Barry notices people moving around in the big lobby. They all seem to be wearing a lighted vest and are using some sort of hand-held thrusting device to move from place to place. The entire layout of the lobby seems to be upside down. Mei says to Barry, "Do you get it? We are coming into the room through the ceiling." In their bewilderment, they have both drifted away from the entry door and have nothing to push on. Barry is getting good at this. He aims Mei at the welcome desk and pushes her that way through the center of her body so she doesn't spin. Barry moves in the opposite direction and grabs one of the many wall handles. He then pushes himself toward the desk.

As Mei arrives at the desk and works her way around to the front of it, she sees a young lady on an exercise machine. The clerk sees Mei, stops the machine and takes off her ear receivers. After turning off a little button on her utility belt, she smiles at Mei. "Hi. Welcome to the Marriott Space Hotel. My name is Cassandra."

Barry is working his way next to Mei now as Mei answers Cassandra. "Hi. I'm Mei Sun and this is Barry Donaldson. We're both new to this experience. What do we do?"

Cassandra touches a couple of locations on the screen in front of her. "Here you are. First let me tell you that there will be no need to pay for anything. Food, drink, entertainment, rentals and other needs have all been covered. You have one of our deluxe suites, Room 210, Level M."

Barry feels like a boy in an amusement park. "How do we get those lighted vests and thrusting devices?"

Cassandra reaches into a storage locker. "Here are your vests. They are *one size fits all* and you will need to fasten them around your legs as well as your torso. There are pockets on either side to store your air thrusters." She reaches into another location and gives them each two thrusters. "There are six booths next to us with instructional holo-blogs about use of the thrusters and other hotel information. We recommend that all of our newly arriving guests watch these."

Mei puts on her vest and attaches the two thrusters to the side pockets. While Barry is doing the same he has a mild urge and turns back toward the receptionist. "Thank you, Cassandra. Could I ask you if there is a restroom in the lobby?"

"The restrooms are at the high end of the lobby, which is what we call the direction away from the earth. There are also restrooms in the lounges. I'm sure you have become familiar with zero g toilets on your way up in the elevator."

"Why, yes we have." Barry won't admit that he is still pretty uncomfortable with this aspect of weightlessness. "Thanks again. I guess we'll go watch the video."

"I hope you two have a wonderful time here. We are really excited to be hosting all of the passengers of Gaia II. If there is anything I can do for you don't hesitate to ask."

Mei thanks Cassandra and they work their way over to the information booths. The other arrivals from the elevator trip are already watching their holo-blogs. There is room for two at an open booth and *seats* where Barry and Mei can clip their vests to keep them somewhat still while watching the demo. Barry touches a screen that says *Touch Anywhere* and a hologram of a familiar face appears before them.

"Hello. I am John Barrymore the Ninth. Before we proceed any farther please either use your own ear receivers or take two of our disposable ones from the lighted slot below. As a courtesy to our guests, the rest of the program will only be available through the receivers."

They both take a couple of disposable receivers and put them on. The program then continues. John Barrymore gives a much abbreviated history of the Marriott Space Hotel and then gives the following information: "You will now see an image of the hotel. As we discuss accommodations the section we are talking about will light up. The Marriott has two lobbies. The main one is called the Arrival Lobby since this is where the guests arrive and the other is on the opposite side of the station and is called the Departure Lobby. This is where the corridor to the departure elevators originates. In an emergency either corridor could be used to evacuate." As John Barrymore talks, the Arrival Lobby, then the Departure Lobby and then the arrival and departure corridors light up on the 3D image.

"Each lobby takes up one sixth of what we call the Main Hotel Ring. The other four rooms are two Atria and two Restaurant areas. The Atria have interesting art and visual displays with flora grown in weightlessness and the Restaurant areas have several different restaurants all with their unique atmospheres and food choices. At any time during this program that you need more information about any of these areas you can say *Stop Program* and get more details and schedules by touching or saying an area. When ready to continue simply say *Continue Program* and it will start up where we have left off."

"Before I tell you about the rest of the hotel you will need to know our terminology for directions here at the geostation. As you move in a direction toward the Earth we say you are going lower and away from the Earth you are going higher. The other directions can be a little more confusing. Essentially the station is a big cylinder. As you move toward the center where Elevator Tethers One and Two go through the station we say you are moving inward. Away from the center we say you are moving outward. Thus the buffet is at the lower end of the lobby and the restrooms are at the higher end. The door you entered through to the lobby when first arriving is on the outer wall of the room."

"Outward from the lower end of each lobby are lounges. For convenience there are connecting tubes to the lounges on both walls of the lower lobby. The lounge above the Arrival Lobby is called the Lunar Lounge and is a quiet place for relaxing. The Lounge above the Departure Lobby is called the Galactic Lounge and is a much more lively and fun place. Similarly, above the lower ends of the Atriums and Restaurant areas are four Banquet Halls also with connector tubes on both walls. The connector tubes from the restaurants to the Banquet Halls, however, are for staff use only." Again, as he mentions them, the appropriate room or connector tube lights up to show location.

"Our guest rooms are all in the outer hotel area and all have windows looking toward the Earth. The room levels are lettered F to M from high to low with Level M being just above the Lounge Ring. The Level F, G and H Rings have 60 Guest Rooms Each. Levels I and J Rings have 45 rooms and Levels L and M are our deluxe rooms with 30 in each Ring. There are a total of 375 Guest Rooms which at double occupancy would be a hotel capacity of 750 guests."

"This brings us to the most popular rooms at the Marriott Space Hotel. Between the higher ends of the lobby ring and the Levels F through K of the Guest Rooms are twelve very interesting, fun shaped Recreational Rooms or Rec Rooms. Well marked connector tubes near the center of the Lobbies, Restaurants and Atria on either sidewall connect to these rooms. There are also connector tubes at the high end of the lobby ring, but are used mainly by staff or guests departing from the Rec Rooms. Because of the limited number of rooms and large number of interested guests, reservations are limited to one per guest per day. Each reservation is for a one hour on the hour time slot, is first come first serve, and must be made between 24 hours and 4 hours of the reservation time. The reservation is full when four people have signed up for the time slot. Any unused or unwanted time slots are used by staff members including main station personnel. We advise that you make reservations early as the more popular rooms book early."

"Once again, more detailed information and scheduling are available by touch or voice. This is John Barrymore the Ninth and I hope you have a memorable experience at The Marriott Space Hotel."

Barry is familiar with John Barrymore. "They picked the right person to do that presentation. His family members have been Hollywood icons since the cinema began in the early 20th century."

Mei isn't very knowledgeable about the history of cinema or its present for that matter. "He certainly has the right voice and persona for it."

Barry sees an icon for thruster demonstration and touches it. A holographic lady with one of the lighted vests on appears in front of them. The lady begins her demo. "Hello. Welcome to the Marriott. One of the main concerns of our guests is how to move from place to place without spinning or bumping into other guests. I'm afraid that collisions are going to happen no matter what. I just recommend that you be watchful, courteous and remember Newton's third law. If you push off on anything or anybody that is not attached to the station, that object or person is going to move away from you just as you move away from it at a speed which depends on its size." She demonstrates this in the hologram.

"Also, we have supplied you with two hand held air thrusters that attach to pockets on either side of your lighted vest. Each one has a replaceable compressed air canister. Replacement canisters are located at many convenient locations throughout the hotel. When using thrusters always aim them in the opposite direction from which you want to go. Aim on a line through the center of your body about at the belly button area. Failure to do so could cause this to happen. She aims incorrectly causing herself to go into a slow rotation. The only way to learn is to practice so get out there, have fun and please be aware of and courteous to our other guests."

Barry can see that Mei is a little restless. "Do you want to look into anything else while we are here?"

"No, we can look later and make Rec Room reservations from our room. Let's go find our room then maybe we can have a drink in one of the lounges."

"Shall we see how to get to our room on the computer?"

"That'd be no fun." Mei nudges Barry playfully. "Come on." She pushes off, does a flip in the air and uses a short thruster burst to stop her rotation, then a longer one to send herself off across the room toward two connector tubes going up the far wall. At the tubes Mei reads a lighted digital sign that says, *To Recreation Rooms 5 and 6/ Guest Rooms 123-177 All Levels.* She then pushes off toward the tubes directly across the lobby and reads, *To Recreation Rooms 7 and 8/ Guest Rooms 183-237* All Levels. She grabs a handle and waits for Barry.

"This is it, the tubes to our room. Barry and Mei are only about ten meters away from the information booths where they had just come from."

"How did you do that?!"

"Just a hunch, the far connector tubes access two Rec Rooms and guest rooms between 120 and 180, a difference of sixty. There are twelve rec rooms so the tubes service a sixth of the hotel. Six times sixty is three hundred and sixty. So the room numbers refer to locations 0 to 360 degrees on a circle where the center of the lobby is at 180."

"How lucky of me to have wedded a theoretical physicist."

"Come on smart-alec. Let's go see what our room is like." She finds a sensor, waves her hand in front of it and a tube opens up. Barry does the same. The tubes close and a voice says, "Please keep your body straight and bring your feet in contact with the floor of the tube." When sensors detect that they are in the correct position, the floor gives them a push and up the tube they go. Barry needs to use a small handle on the inside wall of the tube along the way.

When Mei and Barry reach the top of the tube what they see is very disorienting again. Looking *downward* they see a sign above an open corridor that reads, *Level M*. Under that is a row of three more signs. One points to the left and says *Rooms 186 and 198*. The middle one says *Room 210* and the third points to the right and says *Rooms 222 and 234*. Below that are yet two more side by side signs. One pointing to the left reads *To the Lunar Lounge* and one pointing to the right reads *To Banquet Hall 3*. Barry looks down the wall to the left and sees the entrance to the Lunar Lounge, but he doesn't see any doors for guest rooms.

Mei laughs. "My poor dear. Let me show you." She really is in her element. She pushes off and goes under the sign that says *Room 210*. Barry follows. Mei points up which in geostation lingo would be outward. The doors to the Guest Rooms are in the *ceiling*. Barry is totally confused.

There was no key given to them and they didn't watch a holo-blog about this, but Mei thinks for a second and says, "Open." The room has been programmed for voice and facial recognition and so the door to their room opens and the lights come on. Together Mei and Barry enter Room 210.

The room is very spacious. The curved wall where they have entered is about 5 meters wide with washroom to the left of the entrance and a computer control center to the right. The far wall, which is about 10 meters away, is concave and is about 7 meters across. The room height is about 3-1/2 meters. There is plush, soft carpeting on the floor, ceiling and all of the walls. Large decorative cushions are floating in a corner. Barry looks up and sees sleeping pouches and exclaims, "Oh that figures, it looks like our bed is attached to the ceiling!"

Mei commands, "Lights off." and Barry sees why the sleeping pouches are where they are. *Two thirds* of the floor is transparent and when they are encased in their sleeping pouches they will be looking down on the Earth.

Barry considers the sleeping pouches. "Are you tired?"

"No. Not really." Mei knows mentally that most people require less sleep when they are in low-g conditions, but is still a little surprised considering how long they have been awake.

"How about we see if there is information on our computer about our room and the Rec Rooms then go check out the Lunar Lounge?"

"Okay, I would like to clean up a little and change clothes first. I see that they have put an outfit in a case on the wall for us."

Barry agrees that this is a good idea and Mei goes into the washroom to take a zero g shower. After a minute or two, Barry leaves his clothes floating in the room and goes in to join her. The next couple of hours are to be one of the most memorable times of their lives. Floating in zero g in the dark with the Earth below, Barry and Mei have an intense sexual encounter far beyond what they had ever imagined.

It's almost 6am when they take a second zero g shower and put on their provided outfits. Barry gives Mei another long kiss. "That was quite a physics experiment. What was that third law of Newton again that the lady in the demo was telling us about?"

"I think you experienced that numerous times my love."

"Shall we?" and they leave their room in the direction of the Lunar Lounge.

As Barry and Mei visit the Lunar Lounge, the sun is just rising at Tsiolkovsky Station in the South Pacific Ocean. At Noda Geostation, however, the sun is at a 90 degree angle from the line of sight to the center of the Earth. It's only behind the Earth for about an hour centered at midnight. If not for a large solar energy station constantly adjusting to stay between the station and the sun, it would be blinding in the late evening and early morning hours. The solar energy station not only provides power for the station, but helps protect it from dangerous radiation from the sun.

Leela awakens naturally and looks out the viewing window to see about half of the Earth bathed in sunlight and half still in darkness. She and Jaswinder were a little too preoccupied the night before to program any fancy wake up scenarios like in West Antarctica. She thinks back to the days at the Institute in Bangalore when Jaswinder was courting her. They certainly renewed a little of that spark last night.

Jaswinder stirs a little next to her in the sleeping pouch. Even though he is still sleeping she is sure that she can see a smile on his face. Leela can tell about what time it is by looking down on the Earth. She still finds it strange that the time zone they are in is the same one as her friend in Vancouver, BC. It's too early to call her friend, but it should be about seven or eight o'clock at night now in Bangalore so she decides to call her parents.

Leela opens her side of the sleeping pouch and pushes off toward the washroom. After using the facilities she puts on the outfit that the hotel has supplied. She takes her comm-goggles out of a pouch in her utility belt. Quietly Leela commands

"Audio on. Video on. Call mom." A minute or two later she sees *Call Accepted* in her lower field of vision and a 3D avatar of her mom appears in front of her.

"Hi, my little Leela. I was worried that you wouldn't call me."

"Mom, I just called you from the elevator yesterday."

"Yes, but that was a whole day ago. In a couple of weeks you will be leaving me forever."

"Mom, now don't start crying on me again. We have talked a lot about this. The mission is much bigger than our personal feelings and is of the utmost importance to Jaswinder."

"Oh yes, be a good little Indian wife and follow your husband off into the abyss."

"I love him, mom. My place is with him. We had the most wonderful time last night."

"I'm really not in the mood to hear about your zero g frolicking. Your father wants to speak to you. Conference Mahipal Reddy."

An avatar of Leela's father appears next to her mother. "Leela, you know that your mother loves you as do I. We are very proud of you. It is a terribly hard thing to say goodbye to your daughter, but all parents must someday. We will be fine. You will be in our thoughts and in our prayers."

"Dad, I love you guys. I never meant to hurt you."

"Call us again soon. You haven't left yet." The images of her parents fade. With a little cracking in her voice and a tear in her eye she says, "Audio off. Video off," and puts the comm-goggles away.

"Leela, are you okay?" Jaswinder has been listening to her the whole time. "It's still not too late to change your mind."

"Yes it is my Jaswinder. This is our life now. This is what we were meant to do."

"Oh poppycock, Leela, but I love you anyway."

"Let's go have breakfast my zero g stud."

* * *

They choose Restaurant Area 2 to have breakfast since it is inward from Recreation Room 11. Unlike Barry and Mei, Jaswinder and Leela had scoped out the Restaurant areas, Atriums, Lounges and Recreation Rooms at the information booth the night before. They had even made a reservation for Rec Room 11 at 10am the next morning. This is the way Jaswinder is. He always has liked to plan every detail of a trip or vacation before leaving. Leela is pretty sure that he actually enjoys the planning better than the trip itself. She would rather be more impulsive, but she lets him have his fun.

The breakfast and lunch place is called *Uncle Albert's Tea Room* after the character in the classic movie *Mary Poppins*. Unlike in the movie , however, you don't have to think of something funny to eat at a table floating in the air.

When it's time, Leela and Jaswinder leave their table and use their thrusters to fly over to the tubes that connect to Recreation Room 11. The game that is being played in Rec Room 11 now is zero g volleyball. They have no idea what this is going to be like, but Leela used to love volleyball at school in her teens and the time slot was available.

As they are getting out of the tubes near the entrance to the rec room, Jaswinder and Leela see two young men coming toward them from one of the higher level guest rooms. They appear to be heading toward the same rec room door. All four meet at the door.

One of the two sees Jaswinder and Leela and when close enough he calls out to them. "Hello, are you two our challengers in volleyball?"

"Hi, yes, but I'm afraid we may not be much competition. My name is Jaswinder and this is my wife Leela."

Leela interrupts. "Speak for yourself, Jas. I used to be pretty good at this."

"That's the spirit, Leela. My name is Peter and this is my husband Chris. We have a room up on Level G."

Jaswinder shakes hands with both of them. "Nice to meet you. I hope you don't mind if I ask, but I thought that the committee decided to only have couples on the mission who could have children."

"That's true." Chris answers the question not offended in the least. "I can't say that I like that rule very much, but I understand. No, we are on our way back to Earth. Peter and I have been working on Gaia II. Peter has been on Renata Toscini's team doing the final testing of the computer systems and I have been working with Ali Zamani fine tuning the life support systems."

Leela sees, through a viewing window, that the guests from the 9am slot are leaving a far exit and opens the door. "Enough small talk, boys. Let's go play so I can kick your butt."

Peter looks at Jaswinder. "Is she always this way?"

Jaswinder has a puzzled look on his face and answers Peter. "Actually, no."

Peter, Chris, Jaswinder and Leela enter. They are sort of surprised that a living, non-virtual staff member is there to greet them and teach them the game.

The room has a low ceiling where they enter. It gets higher and higher toward a far wall that is about 16 meters high. For fun, the far wall is a 3D ocean beach scene and the ceiling a sunny blue sky. There is a sandy beach in the vista with ocean waves coming in and even surfers, complete with realistic sound. There is a volleyball net in an arc from wall to wall in the middle of the room.

The guide explains the game. "This is the volleyball." He holds it up and it looks like a normal one. "When you hit this up into the air it will rise. As it goes up it automatically orients itself so that the hidden thrusters in the ball push it downward or on the ship we say inward. How high the ball goes depends on how hard you hit it just like in normal gravity. If the ball gets closer than two meters from the floor a buzzer goes off and somebody gets a point. You are only allowed three hits on your side and the same person can't hit the ball twice in a row, again just like in the normal game. I will start every point by hitting the ball in the direction of the team that lost the previous point. The first team to fifteen wins. Pick up your new compressed air thrusters here and let's get started."

Peter and Chris get on one side of the net. Jaswinder and Leela take the other side. The guide whose name is Mark asks if they are ready and says, "I always start by hitting the ball toward the Earth so get ready Leela and Jaswinder." It takes a game for all of them to start to get the hang of it. Everybody has some really good saves, but Chris and Peter kind of take it easy on the other two. Most importantly they all have a lot of fun.

As they leave, Jaswinder and Leela tell Chris, Peter and Mark that is has been really nice to meet them and it has been great fun. They head out the door then thrust toward their room.

* * *

The Singhs are the first to get to the prearranged meeting place with Barry and Mei on the left wall at the buffet in the lower main lobby. At about 1pm Barry and Mei come down the connector tubes from their room. A push and a couple of thrusts and they are heading toward Leela and Jaswinder. It is still a little dark in the lobby even with the accent lighting and a fully lit Earth in the viewing window. A little looking around and they see Jaswinder wave. "Barry, Mei, over here."

They are glad to see their new friends again and take a seat at the table. The seats and table are designed for weightlessness. The seats hold the sitter in place and the table has slots for trays from the buffet. Mei wonders what the point of sitting is, but figures it's just to connect guests with something familiar in this strange environment.

The four decide to go to get something to eat before they catch up on the past day or two's events. Leela flips up a *Table Occupied* sign and they use the thrusters to go down to the two buffet tables at the very lowest end of the lobby along the side walls ending at the viewing window. Barry sees that his air canister gauge is showing low on air and finds a station by the buffet tables to switch for a full one.

There are containers with salad, sandwiches, pizza pockets, fruit, cookies and several other choices on the buffet. The salad is in little modules and beverages that are in containers that let you drink without any liquid escaping. Barry takes a tray at the beginning of one of the tables and moves along a grab rail along the front of the table. Each food and beverage item is in a container that snaps onto the tray. He chooses a couple of sandwiches, an apple, a cookie and some iced tea. When Mei has her tray full they go back to their seats together.

Leela is still pretty hyped about the zero g volleyball experience as they chat over lunch. Jaswinder takes a bite of an apple and addresses Barry. "Which Rec Room did you two sign up for?"

"We have been spending most of the time in our room so far. What are some of the options?" Mei grins at Barry as if to thank him for being very vague with his response.

Being a man who loves his games and is also a little naïve, Jaswinder is surprised that they haven't signed up for anything yet. "Last time I looked the Laser Tag Room, Basketball Room and Volleyball Room were all booked up for the day. I believe that there are still a couple of early evening slots for the Learn How to Fly Room."

"That sounds intriguing." Mei is always looking for a new experience especially if it involves physical activity. "Do you know anything about it?

Jaswinder has watched every demo and infogram that the hotel has, much to Leela's dismay. "I did watch a little advertising demonstration for that room. From what I understand, there is an artificial air current that flows through the room away from the larger wall. The guide equips you with wings that have built-in thrusters to counteract the headwind. He teaches you and flies with you while the computer creates visual images like flying through the Grand Canyon."

Mei looks at Barry with wide eyes. "Can we?"

"Sure. Let's see if there is a slot still open." There is computer access on every table top as well as many other locations. Barry touches a few icons and brings up the schedule for Recreation Room 3. "Only two people have signed up for 6pm."

"Let's do it, Barry."

"Okay." It sounds like fun to him, too. He makes the reservation that fills the slot for 6pm.

Leela asks Barry. "Do you know how we get to the shuttle tomorrow?"

Barry is not really quite sure, but he has a basic idea. "The shuttle port is at the high end of the geostation. I saw some crew members taking an access corridor upward from the lobby. There must be a similar one that goes all of the way to the top of the station. I'm sure Cassandra will know."

Mei addresses their new friends. "What do you two plan to do now?"

Jaswinder answers Mei. "Leela wants to go and explore the atria. Somebody said that there is a wedding going on in one of them. How about you?"

"My husband has promised me a romantic evening tonight so it's up to him."

When they finish eating, the four friends shake hands and part company.

Leela and Jaswinder go through the archway opening connecting the Main Lobby and Atrium 2. It is a very beautiful, well thought-out place full of art and flora. Being grown in weightlessness, the exotic plants look very unearthly. It appears that the wedding is over, but there is still a reception area with two men dressed in white tuxes. Leela sees them first. "Look, it's Peter and Chris." They wait their turn in the well wishers line and when they get to talk to the couple Leela asks, "I thought that you introduced yourselves as *husbands* at volleyball this morning."

Chris informs Leela. "We had this ceremony to renew our vows. Sorry we didn't tell you."

Jaswinder speaks up. "Leela and I had an appointment to meet with some friends anyway, but I'm really sorry that we missed it. I bet it was beautiful."

"It was. Peter choreographed the whole thing."

"Well, we both wish you the best of luck." They move on to let the next people in line offer their congratulations.

Barry and Mei have a few hours to kill before their Rec Room appointment. Barry suggests that they go back to their room for a little while.

"Again!?" She's up to it, but is very surprised that Barry is.
He grins. "Practice makes perfect."

January 6, 2112
Marriott Space Hotel, Noda Geostation

The day has finally come. Today Leela, Mei, Barry, Jaswinder and thirty-two others including Ishii and Leilani Matogawa embark on a thirty hour shuttle trip to a generation starship called Gaia II.

Barry and Mei take their zero g showers, rinse with nano-mouthwash, get dressed in new outfits supplied by the hotel and put on their utility belts. They decide to make a couple of calls from their room before they go. Both put on their comm-goggles. Barry calls his mom in Minnesota again and Mei calls a very good friend of hers who is at Fermi Labs near Chicago.

They decide to have something light at the coffee shop for breakfast. Taking the connector tubes down to the Main Lobby, Barry asks Cassandra how to get to the shuttle. She lets him know that they can take a marked corridor at the outer, higher end of the Departure Lobby on the other side of the station. That is also where the coffee shop is. They thank her and she wishes them well.

Using their thrusters, Barry and Mei go through the arched entrance to Atrium 2, where Peter and Chris renewed their vows, then through another arch into Restaurant Area 2 and finally though a third arch into the Departure Lobby. A nice coffee shop named Tony's fills the lower end of the lobby. Barry gets a Café Americana with a danish and Mei chooses an almond latte with a croissant. Finding a little table for two they once again enjoy gazing at a glorious Earth through the viewing window. At 9am, it's time to start making their way to the shuttle.

At the high end of the Departure Lobby, on the outer wall (ceiling) there is a corridor entrance that says *To the Upper*

Station. Two slow conveyors with grab bars are on a wall and running in opposite directions. Barry and Mei each grab a bar and it takes them up the corridor. There is a sign above the conveyor reading, *Please Push Off When Reaching Your Level To Avoid Others On the Conveyor.*

The corridor is well lit and as they slowly pass the levels. Each is labeled on the wall. First, the two pass Hotel Support Levels E and D then Staff Living Quarter Levels C, B and A. They go by numerous other levels of the Main Station beginning with Cargo Receiving then Nano-tech Support, Lab Support and others. Most of the actual labs and industrial complexes are not attached to the station.

Five minutes later the conveyor brings them to the top level, signed *Noda Geostation Shuttle Port*. They let go and an automatic door senses them and opens. Mei and Barry use their thrusters to enter the port and the door closes behind them. Some have already arrived and a staff member informs them that the shuttle will be leaving on time at 10am. She lets them know that there is a vending machine on the far wall if anybody would like something during the wait.

Barry approaches the staff member. "Why does the shuttle take so long to get to the ship?" Mei knows the answer, but doesn't interrupt.

"Because of the location of Gaia II in orbit we actually let them *catch up* to us rather than the other way around. In order to do this, the shuttle will fire rockets to speed up in order to obtain a higher, slower orbit then fire again to maintain that orbit while Gaia II catches up. Then the shuttle will do the same in reverse in order to rendezvous with the ship. It is possible to get to Gaia II faster with several high energy burns, but it has been decided to use the same low energy transfers that we have been using for cargo due to the large number of passenger shuttles.

Mei knows exactly what the staff member is talking about, but Barry is still confused. "Sorry I asked."

Familiar faces start showing up at the shuttle port. Jaswinder and Leela come up the conveyor corridor five minutes later followed by Ishii and Leilani Matogawa.. Eventually all 36 passengers are present and accounted for.

The converted cargo shuttle is not nearly as accommodating as they are used to, but it's comfortable and they all enter and strap in for the long 30 hour ride to Gaia II. At 10am the shuttle pilot engages the super-efficient hybrid rocket engines and initiates what is commonly called a *delta v* for orbit transfer. The small g force is the only one the passengers have felt for the last couple of days, but after one minute they are weightless again and undo their straps.

The thirty hour shuttle ride is just about over. All passengers have monitors at their seats on which they can see what the pilot sees. Reflecting light from the sun, a small object appears in the middle of their screen.

Jaswinder holds Leela's hand. "This is so surreal. We are going to spend the rest of our lives on that little dot on the screen." Leela is speechless and just nods. They are all pretty quiet right now.

As they get closer, it gets larger to where it looks like a tin can with a huge metal suction cup on one end and a tail on the other. "Not very impressive to look at, is it?" Barry comments as they watch it get larger as they get closer.

Mei understands like nobody else what amazing technology has gone into this ship. "To me it's the most beautiful thing that man has ever made."

The pilot tells everybody to strap in for the retro *delta v* and they turn their seats the opposite direction awaiting the thrust. Again the rocket firing lasts only about a minute, but the pilot asks that they stay strapped in as they make a few minor maneuvers to prepare for rendezvous. Now on the screen they begin to be able to see just how huge the ship is. It still looks like a giant tin can with a tail and the pilot says, "I'm sorry if you were expecting something more futuristic looking, but this is a real starship not a Hollywood fabrication."

They also notice that the ship is rotating. Jaswinder checks the timing and determines that it makes one revolution approximately every minute. The shuttle approaches the tail end of the ship. Where the main body of the ship meets the *tail*, there is a recession with a ring moving around the outer edge. Actually to them the ring is stationary and the rest of the ship is rotating. The shuttle approaches slowly and with a couple of well calculated thrusts it lands and attaches to the ring. The pilot then explains that the ring is on a magnetic levitation track that will now slowly speed up to match the rotation of the ship. He tells all of the passengers to turn their seats a quarter turn so that the artificial force created by this acceleration will push them toward the back of their seats.

The sensation is actually very mild, but they do feel the rotation, even with no stationary reference, due to the anatomy of the inner ear. This makes most of the group a little queasy and autogenics are again recommended. The pilot mentions that what they are feeling is normal and will go away in a couple of days.

When the shuttle ring is in sync with the ship, the shuttle enters an airlock. The portal closes behind them and they all wait for the airlock to become habitable.

Mei does a quick, easy calculation in her head. She estimates that the diameter of the shuttle ring is about one fifth the diameter of the ship. She knows that the rotation of the ship has been chosen to give the ship about 1g (normal Earth gravity) at the outer shell. Knowing that the artificial gravity decreases linearly with decreasing radius she determines that their weight is now about one fifth of their weight on Earth.

The pilot of the shuttle instructs the passengers, "When you exit the shuttle you will notice that you are not weightless anymore. Your weight is about one-fifth that on Earth. There is a guide that will lead you to an elevator to take you to the outer edge of the ship where all Gaians live in normal 1g gravity. There is a medical facility at the bottom of the elevator where all newcomers must undergo a series of tests and procedures before being allowed to enter the living environment.

The 36 weary passengers of the shuttle exit one at a time out of the shuttle hatch. No fancy displays or even a welcome banner here, just a tall, lanky dark-haired man in white medical attire. Leela whispers to Jaswinder. "You'd think we all have the plague. Not a very warm welcome."

When they are all gathered outside the shuttle in the airlock the tall man addresses the group. "May I have everybody's attention? My name is Sergei Godunov. First, let me offer my sincere apologies that we have to greet you to Gaia II this way. We are honored to have you aboard with us. You have all been through many screening tests and procedures on Earth in the weeks leading up to your departure. With Gaia II being a small, closed environment in which we wish to flourish for numerous generations, there are certain biological entities, shall we say, that we would rather not take along for the ride. We are all going to take an elevator ride. When we reach our destination you are all going to weigh five times what you do now. I promise, no weight gain jokes. For this reason there are chairs in the elevator for everybody. Your legs are going to be a little weak from your days of weightlessness. I'm sure that some of you are already feeling a little nauseous from the rotation of the ship. The elevator ride will be very slow, which should allow you time to do autogenics which you have all been taught. We couldn't allow anti-nausea medication since that would interfere with our tests. We do highly recommend that you take a special sedative that we will supply since you will be in a transition room bed for about eight hours. Are there any questions?"

Ishii Matogawa, who is always pretty outspoken, has to ask. "What about food? I'm looking forward to being able to eat like a human off a plate with a knife and fork again."

Sergei realizes that Ishii knows the answer, but responds anyway. "I'm sorry Mr. Matogawa. You are only permitted water and a special liquid protein drink for the next eight hours. Once you get to your residence in the Living Area you have selected, you will find a well stocked cold storage cabinet and pantry."

Everybody else is too mentally weary to ask any questions so Sergei announces, "Okay, will you all follow me." He enters a code on the wall and a sealed door opens to a room with forty smart chairs. Again, it is a pretty sterile environment. Leela thinks out loud. "The first thing I am going to do here is add some color and art to our entry way."

After the door is sealed, a small crew starts to get the shuttle ready for its return trip to Noda Geostation. The elevator carrying the new arrivals and Sergei begins to descend.

It's a very strange sensation feeling increasing gravity as you descend in an elevator and many of the passengers take Sergei's advise to relax in their chair to try autogenics. The elevator ride is 800 meters and takes about a half an hour.

The last time that they all have experienced normal Earth gravity was about four days ago. As Sergei promised everybody feels a little weak getting out of their seats. Mei comments, "That was just four days. Can you imagine coming back to gravity after months in space?"

Sergei leads them all out of the elevator and down a hall toward a reception room. The hall and reception area are a little more inviting even though there are still no plants for ambiance. A nurse-receptionist opens a hermetically sealed door and lets the group into a small lobby area. She addresses them when they are all in the room and the door is closed. "Welcome to Gaia II. This medical examination is an unfortunate necessity. My name is Anna. Sergei, myself and our Chief of Staff are the only ones you will be seeing for the next eight hours. Our Chief of Staff will introduce herself to each of you once you are in your rooms. We would like to ask you now to please proceed down the hall behind me. You each have a room with your name and image on a display next to the door to your room."

Ishii realizes. "Ah, that's how Sergei knew my name."

Anna continues her instructions. "Please find your rooms, undress and climb into bed. Get comfortable and we will be in shortly."

Like a parade of senior citizens at a retirement home they all make their way down the hall and find their designated rooms. The doors to each room are also hermetically sealed. Ishii comments to all who can hear, "Welcome to CDC, Level Four."

Jaswinder's room comes before Leela's and he gives her a kiss. "I'll see you when this is over. Get some rest." He enters his room and closes the door.

The room is actually pretty pleasant other than the sophisticated medical testing devices. The bed is like the smart chairs, designed for ultimate support and adaptable to the individual. There is a screen for visual entertainment and a pad on the bed for computer access. Jaswinder settles into bed.

About twenty minutes later the door to Jaswinder's room opens and a very impressive, professional woman comes into the room in a spotlessly clean, white medical uniform. Jaswinder has been looking at some news websites to catch up on what's been happening back on the planet. The lady introduces herself. "Hi, Jaswinder. I'm Genevieve Laplace, head of the medical department here on Gaia II."

"Hello, I'm Jaswinder Singh, an astrobiologist from West Antarctica. It's nice to finally meet you. I've read about you and your husband Jacques, very impressive background."

"Thank you Mr. Singh. I'm familiar with your work also. I've read your most recent articles on the Astrophysical Journal website. Hopefully, we can discuss some of your theories at a later time. Have you decided if you would like to have a sedative?"

Eight hours in a bed when he's not that physically tired doesn't sound like much fun even with visual entertainment. He accepts her offer.

While Jaswinder is taking the sedative, Dr. Laplace gives him a rundown of what's going to happen for the next eight hours. Most of the time period is just waiting for test results. As is the case with most medical work these days most things are done externally. One test does involve drinking a solution with some specially programmed nanoprobes, but there is no discomfort at any time.

After Dr. Laplace has met all of the arrivals, they begin the tests. Sergei and Anna do the administering while she does the computer analysis and test follow up. Most people take the sedative. One of the few who doesn't is Barry, who habitually likes to stay alert because of the type of work he does. Barry spends his eight hours watching a marathon of old *Perry Mason* TV shows.

A very long eight hours later there is an announcement to all of the rooms. "Attention, new Gaia II residents. We have concluded testing. With the exception of two people, you may all put on clothes to prepare to enter your new world. Those two are Nadia Kova and Ishii Matogawa. Your partners are welcome to stay if they wish, but must stay in their current rooms. We expect to be able to let Nadia and Ishii go in about two hours. The rest of you please proceed to the waiting room at the opposite end of the hall from the room where you came in."

Jaswinder gets out of bed and stands up. He gets a little dizzy and still feels a little weak. He thinks, "Ouch, I haven't had a hangover like this since the *end of finals* parties in Bangalore." He methodically dresses in new clothes that have been provided and joins everybody in the hall.

In the waiting room, Genevieve Laplace addresses the group one more time. Four are missing as Ishii's and Nadia's partners, Leilani and Mikhail, have decided to wait. "Does everybody have the location of your new home and a map of Gaia II?" Nobody says anything, most nod. "Okay, remember that it takes a couple of days to get used to the rotation that creates our artificial gravity so you may feel a little poorly in the meantime. It is now a little after midnight Gaia II time as we are on Pacific Standard Time just like Noda and Tsiolkovsky. I'm sorry that we couldn't space the shuttles so that everybody could stay here overnight. You are all signed up for tours, if you wish to take them. They start at 10am on Monday, January 10 to give you time to settle in. There will be more information at your residences."

Genevieve opens the door to another hallway. "If you would all come this way. At the end of the hall there is a door with a control pad. Enter the code 3141 and welcome to Gaia II." She shuts the door behind them as they all walk down the hall as if in a trance.

Jaswinder is the first one to the door keypad. He knows better than any of them what to expect so he wants to be the one to open the door. He enters 3141. As the door opens, Jaswinder announces to everybody. "Welcome to Oz!"

As they walk through the door none realize that they are being video-audio recorded for posterity so they can look back someday and remember their initial expressions. All thirty-two of them are floored and absolutely speechless. Before them is a familiar scene, yet the strangest they have ever encountered. Stretching ahead is a path leading into a quaint Swiss Bavarian Alpine village. It is dark here, but enough of the lights are on in the buildings that, when illuminated by street lights and what looks like a full moon above, the whole place looks like a Christmas miniature village. Every detail has been captured. There is a lighted, Bavarian style sign with flowers at the base by the path entering the village. It reads *Welcome to Alpenhausen.* The only thing missing is the snow and a cold temperature. Also, they notice no vehicles and currently no people.

Leela looks up and is surprised to see what looks like a strip of night sky. It extends the entire distance in front of them, but only a small strip across the view above. There are images of stars and a normal size full moon on this *sky*. She estimates that the *sky* width is about twelve times the diameter of the moon. It is what she sees beyond the *sky* that holds her breathless. She knew what this was supposed to be like, but nothing could have prepared her or any of them for seeing what they were looking at.

In the distance, past the *sky*, there are lights from other villages. It's as if they were looking down on them from a very high mountain. Leela follows the curvature of the land with her eyes and sees the ground gradually get higher to where some low forested hills form a dividing barrier of some sort. The evergreen trees are slanting in her direction. Past the narrow forest the land keeps turning upward until, as it goes behind the *sky*, it is almost upside-down. They have only the light of a full moon, which somehow lights the distant landscape also, and Leela wonders what this will look like in the daylight. Then she thinks, "Daylight? But there is no sun here."

Leela then looks into the distance in front of them and is surprised to see what appear to be moonlit mountains in the distance behind the Swiss village. There is a large building on the far side of the village, but it is hard to tell where the village ends and the mountain scene begins. She turns around and sees that the door behind them has disappeared. Being this close she can tell that there is a wall, but a 3D image of a Swiss mountain scene covers the wall. Looking to the right the *Swiss valley* again rises to low forested hills, but she swears she can see the reflection of a stream with a waterfall through the trees. Once again, the landscape rises and rises on the inside of this cylindrical world to an inverted landscape that she can barely discern. Leela thinks she can make out buildings with an open Southern European style.

Jaswinder is also taking in the scene, but at the same time is enjoying watching Leela's reaction. "Can you see where we will be living?"

"Jas, according to the map, I think we are supposed to walk to that little upside-down town in the upper left."

"If you're not up to walking, my love, I believe there are some little electric carts in the village. I could go to get one and come back and pick you up if you like."

"No, I will walk to the Swiss village with you."

Jaswinder tells everybody about the electric carts and mentions that if they are going to Living Area 2, called Tropicania, just go through town to the large building on the far side and follow the signs. Most of those going to Tropicania are aware of this, but politely thank him. The entire group then starts to walk down the path toward Alpenhausen.

Leela seems to be the one to most appreciate the details of the environment that the landscapers and architects have created. In the moonlight, she sees grass and flowers reminiscent of an alpine meadow to the left and right of the path. As they approach the village she thinks that if this was on Earth it would be 19th century Earth before the automobile.

About a hundred meters down the path they reach the welcome sign. A few people get out their maps as they have chosen the Swiss village as their living choice. The rest stay with Jaswinder as he seems to know where the electric carts are. He doesn't really, but he is pretty sure that they are a little further down the road. There is a building made out to look like a stable that has a sign reading *Electric Cart Station One*.

Mei, being the analytical one thinks, "They must have somebody do nothing but drive carts back to this location during this boarding period. Either that or they are programmed to return on their own." The latter turns out to be true. Several of the people have gotten to know each other over the last few days. There are handshakes and plans exchanged for getting back together then they go their own ways.

After wishing Barry and Mei well, Jaswinder and Leela find an electric cart that is backed up into a charging station. Jaswinder says, "Ignition on." Nothing happens. Leela sees a key that has an *on* position and an *off* position and points to it. Jaswinder turns the key to the *on* position and says "Destination Wicklesby." The car just sits there.

Leela laughs at Jaswinder. "It would appear that the people who decided on this cart design were rebelling against things being a little too easy for people these days."

Jaswinder finds a lever on the dash, which is clearly marked *forward* and *reverse*. Also, he finds that there are two floor pedals, one for accelerating and one for braking. Turning the wheel in front of him alters direction. "Primitive vehicle, but it could be fun."

Jaswinder hasn't given it much thought, but the lights had come on automatically when turning on the cart. They are light sensitive and come on if it is dark enough and the car is turned on.

Leela pulls out the map and finds a little switch that turns on a reading light on the passenger side of the cart. She tells Jaswinder, "Okay, you need to continue into the village on this path," which has now widened to the size of a narrow road. "Take a left hand turn on Inverness Road and follow it out of town. They pass several really cute Swiss chalet style homes and little store fronts along the way, but see no people. There are a few people that are living here now, but it is 1am and they are sleeping.

As they leave the village on a well lit path, they wind their way through some low hills with alpine meadow fauna until coming to a forest. Leela looks to see that the buildings of Alpenhausen are all slanting in their direction. The forest only lasts for about one hundred meters before it opens up into rolling grassy hills. A very rustic little road sign reads *Wicklesby 2 Kilometers*. It's only about one kilometer away, but the road takes a long winding route to get there.

* * *

Meanwhile, Barry and Mei are making their way through the Swiss village on their cart. They have a little entourage since about half of the group is going this way. Mei has the map out and Barry is admiring the Bavarian architecture. There are many little alleyways with character. Niches in the buildings, windows with shutters and flower boxes, hanging baskets everywhere and high pitched rooftops all add to the charm. There are a few little stores mixed in among the residences, but one in particular catches Barry's eye. A very welcoming sign above a store with gridded glass display windows reads *Le Chocolatier Suisse*. He points it out to Mei. "Is it too late to change our minds about where we want to live?"

"Okay, we'll come back and try the chocolate when everything is up and running."

They come to an open park area with fountains and statues on the other side of which is a tall ten story building that has character and charm to match the village. The narrow road through the village becomes a path through the park. A large sign reading *Gaia University* is in front of a series of wide staircases leading up to an ornate entrance. They follow signs on the path to the Parking Garage.

Barry parks the cart in a charging station and they review their special instructions for residents of Living Area 2: Tropicania. Mei reads to Barry. "We need to take the elevator from the Parking Garage to Level Five, then take a long hallway to the theater, go into the theater lobby, then take another elevator back down to Level One to another Parking Garage." Along with seven other couples they head for the elevators.

The hallway to the theater is like a museum paying homage to the pursuit of knowledge. Replications of important historical documents are in ornate showcases. Shadow boxes highlighting the contributions of famous scientists, authors, industrialists, inventors, political leaders and others adorn the walls. A couple of branch-off halls lead to different departments of the university. The hall leads to a large two story high lobby area with five double-door entrances into the theater. Elevators are clearly marked on the left and right sides of the lobby. Taking an elevator down to Level One Parking Garage, they find another electric cart and follow the signs to the exit.

This time there is an exit tunnel from the parking garage. It is designed to look like a sea cave in a way that only Disney could pull off. A short ride through the cave and they come to an exit that is blocked by a wall of water that is cascading from above. A sensor on the path detects the lead electric cart and the waterfall *shuts off* allowing Mei and Barry along with the others to pass through without getting wet.

The sensation of entering Living Area 2 is equally as breathtaking as when they entered Living Area 1. Before them is a tropical scene right out of a travel brochure for the island of Kaua'i. The village is not directly in front of them as was Alpenhausen, but is off to the right. Looking farther, Barry has to blink his eyes to be sure of what he is seeing. In the reflection of the moon, or whatever it is, he sees waves white capping with water flowing onto and then receding from a white sandy beach. He notices that there is a wall blocking the view of the neighboring region of the Living Area as seen from the beach. Computer imaging on the wall attempts to give the mirage of endless ocean.

To the left are tropical hills with fairly dense foliage, but it is too dark to make out the details. The path they are on comes to a tee right after coming out from under the waterfall. There is a simple little sign with four boards nailed to a post. One points to the right and reads *Hanalei Village 0.5Km*. Another board points to the left and says *Island Trail 0.7Km*. Below that, one to the right reads *Train to Little Rio 0.1Km* and one pointing to the left *Train to Sonora 0.1Km.*

Barry and Mei are going to Hanalei Village so turn to the right. In a short distance there is an electric cart station and a small mock train station with an open air passenger train ready to depart. The train is actually only open on the side facing the living environment with artwork on the far side. The train follows the wall of the living environment to get to Little Rio. A couple of carts had taken the route to the Sonora Station and three carts park to take the train to Little Rio, so it is just Barry and Mei and one other couple continuing on to Hanalei Village. Ishii and Leilani Matogawa will be coming later.

Barry and Mei catch up to the other couple and introduce themselves. Their names are James and Cynthia Rowland and are an African American couple from California. James works in nanotech and Cynthia is going to be in charge of social events, projects and other activities in Hanalei. A polite "It's been nice to meet you" and they go on their way. It is after all about two in the morning. The two carts arrive at the sign *Hanalei Village.* Seeing and hearing the ocean waves and looking at the little bungalows with hedges and well manicured lawns, it is very easy for Barry to forget where he is. Mei is also very impressed, but is stewing on the question "How did they do this?"

Mei turns on her reading light and looks at the map of their village. "The road we are on is called Weke Road. It runs parallel to the beach through the village. Take the third beach access road to the right. It's called Hee Road. The last residences on the right, before getting to the beach, are where we are going. Look for the sign *Wailea Park Condos.*"

Residences are a little smaller and closer together than in the real town of Hanalei, Hawaii. There are some really cute unique red roof bungalows. Many are totally hidden from the road by high hedges. As they pass an inviting community center, Mei notices that the Rowlands have pulled into a little bungalow behind them. Some roads to the left appear to connect to a main thoroughfare where the shops and stores are.

Mei has a thought as they turn onto Hee Road. There is no way they transported real trees onto this ship and, even with modern genetic accomplishments, nobody has created a tree that can grow fast enough to produce the evergreens and palm trees they have seen. All of these trees must be artificial.

Finding the Wailea Park Condos, Barry drives the cart into the drive. The building is two stories high with sixteen condos. The angles in the building and foliage keep the homes private. Mei looks at her map. "We're in 108 which appears to be the last condo on the lower level."

"What do we do with the cart?"

Mei sees a little plaque on the dash with instructions. "This says that after being turned off for over five minutes and not in a charging station the cart will automatically turn back on and return to a parking station."

"I guess we had better make sure we don't leave anything in the cart."

"There does appear to be an override button if you don't want it to leave."

Anxious to see their new home, Barry parks the electric cart and takes Mei's hand to walk with her to the front door. There is a basket of flowers in front of their door with a bottle of champagne and a card attached. The envelope reads *To Barry and Mei*. Mei opens it and reads it out loud, "Welcome to Wailea Park Condos, Hanalei Village. We hope you will be very happy here."

"Shall we?" Barry tests the door to find out it's not locked. The lights are on inside the condo as they are in many of the unoccupied homes. The first thing Mei sees is their personal effects containers that have followed them the whole way. "I forgot all about these."

The condo is a very spacious three bedroom complex with modern conveniences blended in with the room. There isn't much in the way of furniture or decorations, just a couple of chairs, a wall screen, a bed and a desk with a software file. As on Earth, computer access is in all rooms and built into the desk, the wall screen, bathroom mirrors, kitchen appliances and numerous other places in the home.

Barry walks through the condo and opens a double door to a lanai. "Come look at this Mei." What they see looking out is a very inviting, private patio area with flowers, a big hammock and a little bistro size patio set. Best of all this is beach front property. There is a green lawn that extends to a white sandy beach and a nice view of the crescent bay. "I think I can get used to this."

They both go back inside and check out the kitchen. There is a cold storage island cabinet with some basic needs and a couple of premade meals. Across from that is a pantry also minimally stocked with some basics. There is a waterless dish sanitizer next to a sink. Both feed to a garbage processing unit below. Another few cabinets with some basic kitchen needs and a very versatile cooking center complete the kitchen. They notice that there is no food fabricator, but there is a computer access panel in the countertop, the pantry and the cold storage island.

There is a little card in an envelope on the counter that says "Play me". Mei takes the card and inserts it into a slot in the front side of the countertop. The display lights up and plays an informational program. The main point is that there are food stores in town and that the decision was made that these would be the only locations with food fabricators. The idea is to get people out interacting with the community. The program informs,

"There is an extensive list of food choices in the computer accessible by touch screen or voice command. If you wish to use voice command for your home computer system we have the name set right now as *Nani* , but you can choose any name or voice that you wish. The shopping list you create will transmit upon your command to the appropriate store and you can download it to your personal computer that you carry with you. There is a similar system for clothing, linens, and household needs including furniture, rugs, art and other decorative and useful household items. Smaller items are made with fabricators in the stores. Larger items are made in the nanofactory and delivered to the home."

Mei suggests to Barry. "How about if for now we go lay out on the lawn, remove our shoes and try to take this all in? Maybe we could catch a nap then stay up all day creating our new home."

"Sounds good to me, but let me take that bottle of champagne and a couple of glasses with us."

Sitting on the grass watching and listening to the waves they can see lights from Little Rio over the wall between the habitats while sipping on the champagne. It's a very comfortable 22 degrees Celsius out and they lie back together and look upward. Sonora isn't visible from where they are laying, but it is pretty dark there anyway. Their eyes follow the lights of Little Rio up the habitat to the *sky*. Mei swears she sees a shooting star as they dose off.

Today is the second day of scheduled tours of Gaia II. About half of the new arrivals are on board now adding to the fifty that have been on the ship for a couple of months making preparations. The tours all begin at the theater at the university. Electric carts are available to get to the theater, but walking has been highly recommended by the computer orientation programs. Barry, Mei, Jaswinder, Leela, Ishii, James, Cynthia, Nadia, Mikhail and the rest of their group of thirty six are slotted for 10am. Another group of 36, who arrived on the same day, are also in this tour group. It's not mandatory, but all are there.

The theater is a large, grandiose, ornate room with very comfortably spaced smart chair seating designed to hold three thousand people. There is a main floor, a mezzanine and a balcony level. It rivals any theater in New York City, Paris or Moscow. Barry and Mei come up from the Level One Parking Garage and get out of the elevator at Level Five Main Floor Theater/ University. To say that this grand place is overkill for a tour group of seventy-two is a gross understatement. They walk down an aisle on the main floor and join others who have already seated themselves in the first few rows behind the orchestra pit.

At 10am a man walks out onto the stage. He has an average build and height, but even though he is in casual attire, he has the look of a business executive. Behind him there is a large screen that has been lowered from above. He takes a control pad off of a podium and walks down to the group.

Standing in front of the first row he addresses the tour group. "Hello, my name is Jacques Laplace." He has a distinct Parisian French accent. "I'm here to begin your tour day or as I prefer to call it, *open house*." Jaswinder has already recognized him. "You have all met my wife, Genevieve, and I'm glad she has given you all a clean bill of health."

"Let me start by telling you about this theater that you are sitting in. It was designed by a friend of mine, Pierre Montrieux, to equal some of the grandest theaters on Earth. You probably have figured out that it is so large, because it is meant to hold our entire population if necessary. In a few generations this may be as many as 3000 people. This theater will serve a dual purpose. It will, of course, be our center for entertainment, but will also function as a safe refuge. Whenever we do an acceleration transition such as when we change from our current state of constant velocity to a stage of constant acceleration we will need all Gaians to go to one of three places. This theater is one, the gymnasium at the grammar school between Little Rio and Chianti Villas is another and the third is the conference auditorium at the Health and Sciences Center between Wicklesby and Sonora. In case of a more serious emergency, we may ask everybody to come to this location. We have fortified the theater several ways including additional radiation shielding and an independent life support system. We also have located the nanofactory and raw material storage in the levels below us. On a lighter side, we are very privileged to have John Diallo and his beautiful and talented wife Dakore Maredi as co-directors of the arts at this theater. They may be recruiting some of you to perform in this wonderful place."

"So, you are probably wondering who I am and why I am the opening presenter today. I am an architect from Paris and I was part of the Disney team that designed the six habitats of Gaia II. We wanted to show you our gratitude for the sacrifices you are all making by creating as nice of a place to live as we could imagine. In addition to the designs for these six areas, we have designed software for an additional twenty other habitats. Someday, you may decide to live with your neighbors for a little while as we completely rework an entire region of a Living Area. Also, we have some very imaginative minds on board who may want to try their hand at their own design. If so, our computer aided design tools are available to anyone interested."

"I am going to show you a short movie now about the designing and building of Gaia II. When the movie is over we can have a short question and answer period followed by an electric cart tour of Europia." With this Jacques Laplace uses his control pad to lower the lighting and start the 3D movie.

The movie starts by showing the design studios in Paris where the initial drawings and concepts were created. Members of the Disney team are interviewed and it is obvious that they are all taking this project very seriously. Then, there is a mini-documentary explaining claytronic atoms, commonly called *catoms,* to those who are not familiar with the technology. The movie explains that *catoms* are essentially very tiny building blocks about the size of a plant cell. The original concept imagined them at the molecular size range, but the sheer number that would need to be created is too immense for today's technology. The genius behind *catoms* is that they all have a unique placement of positive and negative electrodes so that when they move freely in three dimensions, they self assemble into a desired object. The programming and assembly are done with special algorithms using molecular computers and nanomachines all working in parallel to minimize the time frame. Once a complete set of *catoms* has been produced the work is done. It is a real pleasure to sit back and watch them assemble themselves into a building or a palm tree.

After the *catom* part of the movie, the next section documents the entire building process of Gaia II. It starts with the assembly of the shell and follows the process step by step through the installing of the fusion reactor and new technology propulsion engine. It explains how materials, which are mined on the moon, asteroids and even a comet are transported to the ship. The film shows the day that the ship was first made to rotate. Many short segments about the habitats and industrial areas being created are accompanied by interviews with workers on the projects. Finally, interviews discuss the selection of the crew to be asked to take this historic voyage.

When the two hour movie concludes, Jacques Laplace brings the lights up and asks if there are any questions from the audience. James Rowland has a good one. "You mentioned that we all have to come to the theater, the gymnasium or the convention center when the ship starts to accelerate. Why is that and what is happening while we are in here?"

Thank you. I can't believe that this wasn't covered in the film. Most of you are aware that we will be accelerating constantly at about one-tenth gravitational acceleration for about 7.2 years. This creates an additional vector of artificial gravity that adds to that from the spin of the ship. So that you still feel gravity as a downward force we have to change the slant of the surface. This slope changes gradually as we slowly increase acceleration over the course of about twelve hours. The soil we live on is about ten meters deep. Beneath that is a very rigid graphene barrier and below that is a very unique synthetic solid that flows smoothly like a liquid. By the time we have reached .1g acceleration the back end of each living area will be 50 meters higher and the front end will be 50 meters lower. The transition buildings which are the school, the hospital and the university are ingeniously designed to shift gradually also. You will be entering the university from the Alpenhausen side at Level J and the theater from the Hanalei side at Level 10. Even though the Disney designers have made every attempt to minimize any flooding or damage due to the inclination change, we feel that it would be wise to have you all wait in here while it is happening."

Another person in the crowd raises a hand and asks, "If we are gathering everybody in three different locations aren't they going to be isolated in the case of an emergency?"

"There are two maglev shuttles that run between the transition buildings. The tunnels they go through have added protection for an emergency situation similar to the theater. It's okay to use these shuttles for everyday use if you choose to."

Leela raises her hand. "Will we have snow or rain or seasons here?"

"We are leaving this up to the residents. Your only limit really is your imagination. We have software files on this ship with a large portion of the collective knowledge of mankind as well as some of the brightest young minds from Earth here. There will be community meetings. Create your own world."

"Now, if you will follow me there is a young lady, who I am sure you all will like, waiting for us in the parking garage to take you on a tour of Europia." Jacques leads the group to the back of the lower level of the theater and through double doors into the lobby. They follow the hall through the university and arrive at the elevator that takes them down to Level One parking garage.

Jacques introduces them to their new guide. "Everybody, this is Greta Mueller. She will be your tour guide to Europia. I won't spoil the surprise and tell you what she really does for a living. Have a wonderful time. I look forward to getting to know all of you on our journey." With that Jacques returns to the elevator and heads back up.

Sitting on a cart that she has decorated with a couple of strings of lights and some greenery is a young *blonde* woman.

She's on the short side, a little heavy set and not overly pretty, but she has the most infectious smile and laugh that one can imagine. She is dressed up to the hilt in Bavarian lederhosen and greets them with a heavy German accent. Some in the group are debating whether she is putting on the accent or always talks this way.

Greta waits until everybody has chosen their electric carts then speaks to the group through a speaker in her cart. "Vilkommen meine damen und herren. I want to tell you right now that my tours are audience participation. I am giving you each a hat to wear and a display pad to put on top of your dash." As she passes them out she says, "Put the pad in the middle of the dash so you both can see it. There will be words going across the screen so that you can sing along with the music that is coming from my cart. I'm not too worried about safety with these carts creeping along at about ten kilometers an hour in no traffic. Are you vith me?! More enthusiasm please. Okay let's go." She leads the parade out of the parking garage and starts up the music for *Roll Out the Barrel.*

The first stop is *La Chocolaterie Suisse*. Greta turns off the music and tells a little story about the inspiration of some of the shops in Alpenhausen. She explains, "Most of the shopkeepers came a week early to prepare their shops for all of you. Therefore, we have chocolate!! It's free, but we must ration a little so that everybody gets some and we don't all become fat little Gaians. You may have two chocolates a day on the honor system. So, turn off your carts, push the override button and let's go have some chocolate."

Barry has a dark raspberry truffle and Mei has a piece of amaretto fudge. "Two per day folks, let's get on with the tour."

Greta keeps them entertained with her stories as they ride along and occasionally she puts on another karaoke song. She drives out Inverness Road following the route that Jaswinder and Leela had taken when they arrived. It is full daylight now. The *sun* is bright and the *sky* is blue. They can see the entire cylindrical world above and around them in its full glory. Mei states, "I read an old book once of great historical importance. It was called "The High Frontier" by a professor at Princeton University by the name of Gerard O'Neill. If only he could have lived to see this."

The path winds through the forest. Greta comments, "You have noticed that we don't like straight roads and paths here on Gaia II. It's nice when you're sight-seeing, but a pain in the arse when you're in a hurry."

Emerging from the forest the lovely English countryside scene unveils before them. Green rolling hills are lined with hedges and a trickling creek completes the scene. In the distance is the tiny town of Wicklesby with a tall Roman Gothic building at its center. They cross a little stone bridge over the creek and see an engraving on the bridge that reads *Lovelock Creek*.

Greta stops the group on the path in a grassy pasture just past the creek. "Attention everybody, if I can get you all to look up at our sky cylinder now. I'm sure that you have all noticed that we have three suns in each Living Area. The suns are each centered over one of the three Living Regions that the areas are divided into. The sun and the moon are actually the same light fixture putting out light at a different brightness. The lights are on a track that travels across the *sky* in twelve hours from 6am to 6pm. The light that rises and the one that sets on the panorama walls is a different fixture. The sky on the walls is programmed for random sunrises and sunsets. No two will be alike. This is all powered by the fusion reactor at the tail end of our ship as is all of our other power. At this time the fusion reactor is being fueled by large back up tanks of Deuterium and Helium3. When we are on the move and out of the solar system, our scoop will be supplying interstellar hydrogen through a long conduit in the center of the sky cylinder. We have an expert among us who is one of the few who understand the workings of our main propulsion system. Her name is Mei Sun." Mei waves. "However, if you want to talk to somebody about our fusion reactor you need look no further than this cart. What Jacques Laplace didn't tell you is that I am the lead nuclear engineer in charge of all of your power. So don't mess with me or I'll turn the lights out."

Greta has the stunned group speechless. "Now that I have your attention I must apologize. When we should have been eating lunch I fed you chocolate. I intend to make it up to you by taking you all to a nice afternoon tea at a little town we call *Wicklesby.*" With that she drives off down the path followed by 36 carts each carrying two people with a new found respect.

The group drives within a stone's throw of Jaswinder and Leela's new home and stops at a little place called "Gran Polley's Tea Room". All are pretty used to the electric carts now and find a place to park. They, once again, push the override button to keep the carts from returning to one of the cart stations.

A sweet young lady by the name of Betty Jones invites them all in. She has been expecting and preparing for the tour. She has eight tables, each seating ten people, fully laid out with numerous wonderful little finger foods on decorative *English Garden* style plates. There is a place setting at each seat complete with matching tea cup. Table covers of lovely English linen drape from each table.

Greta introduces the group to Betty after all have been seated and she addresses the group in her very British accent. "Thank you all for coming to tea. Teatime has been a tradition of my family for generations so it is something I wanted to bring along on our trip. Let me tell you about the food in front of you. First, I must say that since there will be no real meat, dairy or eggs on this ship we have gone to great lengths to duplicate familiar foods with food fabricators. Whenever possible we use products grown on-board ship without any alteration. On one plate you will see little crustless sandwiches cut into triangles. These are cucumber sandwiches, a must for an English tea. The plate next to these is the best we could do at replicating sausage rolls like my great-great-great grandmother used to make. Similarly, there is a plate of pork pies and another of mincemeat tarts. Of course, what makes or breaks a good English tea are the biscuits or cookies if you will. The assortment in front of you is mostly varieties of shortbread biscuits, some with jam made with fruit also grown on the ship. Finally, there is plenty of freshly brewed tea with teapots at each table. My great grandmother would have loved to have had cozies like the ones on these teapots. They keep the tea hot for hours. There is more of everything so enjoy yourselves."

Mei Sun is not too fond of the cucumber sandwiches, but loves the pork pies. Leilani is not too impressed with the health benefits of most of the food items on the table, but enjoys herself anyway. True to her word, Betty keeps bringing out more food as plates empty and makes sure they don't run out of tea. Leela follows British tradition and has *milk* and sugar in her tea. The group finds out that there is one way to silence the boisterous Greta Mueller. Put tea and biscuits in front of her. At about 4:30 in the afternoon they continue the tour.

As the parade of carts rolls out of Wicklesby, Greta gives everybody a break and lets them enjoy the countryside scene in silence. Leela notices that there are daisies growing on the green rolling hills. The cart path crests a hill and before them is a moderately sized grape vineyard. Greta stops the group.

"This is the third Living Region of the Europia Living Area called Chianti Villas. There is no town here, just scattered villas that give the feel of living in rural Tuscany. The vineyard you see in front of you produces the only consumable item that is grown in the Living Areas of Gaia II. There will be a small winery that will be in full operation when we start getting crops of grapes. For now, we have brought up a few cases of wine from Chianti Classico Vineyards near Florence, Italy. Our winery operators, Don and Isabella Bertoni intend to strive to attain the robust flavors and bouquets of the Classico wines."

Barry speaks up. "Per chance, are we passing a tasting room on our tour?"

"A man after my own heart; I may be German, but give me a nice glass of Italian wine over a stein of beer any day." With that Greta starts up a little Italian mood music and drives down the path toward the vineyard.

The Bertoni villa is a lovely open-air building of Mediterranean style adorned by flowers and statues. It even has a small water fountain in the middle of a decorative garden. Don and Isabella are there to meet them in front of the tasting room. There's not a lot of room for parking so the carts line up in a single file on the path.

Jaswinder and Leela decide to forego the wine tasting and sit on a bench in the garden. Jaswinder is not really a wine drinker and Leela has had an awful lot of tea at Gran Polley's. They consider leaving the group and heading back to Wicklesby to have dinner at home, but decide to finish the tour.

Soon it is time to continue on and Greta puts the romantic Italian music back on. The group winds through the Chianti Villas enjoying the warm, inviting Tuscan charm and ambiance. Barry and Mei are now in the cart behind Greta. Barry asks, "Greta is there an Italian restaurant or café with authentic Italian food here somewhere?"

"Of course, Mr. Donaldson, soon we will be crossing a road called Via Siena. If you take that road to the right it winds up a hill past a couple of villas through a cypress lined alley to a small hotel at the top of the hill called Villa Dievole. Dario Russo operates a wonderful Italian café there. You can sit on the veranda, have a nice meal, look out over the Chianti valley and watch the sunset."

"Sounds like you're talking from experience."

"He's only been open for a week, but I did go there with my husband. I haven't tried the rest of the menu, but I can definitely vouch for the pappa al pomodoro."

Mei is actually a little hungry as she didn't eat a whole lot at the tea. She asks, "Are we eating dinner as a group or are we on our own?"

"You two have a one track mind. Actually, what I have planned is a little German garden party back in Alpenhausen. Do you like German food Mei?"

Mei looks at Barry as if to say, "You owe me". "Sounds wonderful Greta, should be a good opportunity to get to know our neighbors better."

On the way back to Alpenhausen, Leela is spellbound by the computer generated sunset above the mountain panorama. She knows that it isn't real, but rationalizes that they should make the best of and enjoy what they have. This was her philosophy on Earth after all. The temperature seems to be getting a little cooler or is this just her imagination?

Greta announces the plans for the evening. She lets the group know that they can stay as long as they want since there will be beer and music until 2am. At about 7:30, they drive up to a very ornate building with a sign informing them that their destination is called Gasthaus Rauch. Greta informs the group that food and beer are in the beer garden in the rear of the building and reminds them once again to put their carts in standby unless they want to walk home.

Barry and Mei share a small table in a corner of the garden with Jaswinder and Leela. When all have gotten their food and have settled in, a man in lederhosen walks up onto a small stage and addresses the guests. "Welcome friends. My name is Herbert Rauch and this is my wife Ilsa." Ilsa walks up onto the stage, makes a gesture to the crowd and sits in a chair with a piano accordion next to it. "We are your hosts here at Gasthaus Rauch and tonight we will also be the entertainment. If any of you have musical inclinations and would like to do a little moonlighting, we would love to let you display your talents on our stage in future engagements. Also, my wife will be giving accordion lessons. I hope you are enjoying the food and beer that we brew from scratch here on the premises." The guests give a polite applause. Herbert picks up a guitar and announces, "We would like to start tonight with a popular polka melody called *Valley Spring Polka.*"

As the night goes on and kegs of beer get low, most of the group loosens up and mingles with their new acquaintances. Leela once again surprises everybody as she pulls Jaswinder up and makes him do the traditional *Chicken Dance* later that evening.

Somehow they all manage to find their way home after laughing, dancing and singing well past midnight.

* * *

Morning comes too soon and there are a few less people present for day two of the tours. The time and meeting place is 10AM at the meeting room of the nanofactory below the theater in the university transition building. They all have instructions as to how to get there.

Barry and Mei (and everybody else coming from the Tropicania Living Area) come under the waterfall and through the sea cave to the parking garage below the theater. Taking an elevator downward as per tour instructions, they arrive at the level with the nanofactory meeting room and lunch area. The welcoming guide for day two is none other than Paul Drake, whom most of the group recognize.

Paul gives a visual presentation in the meeting room and then leads the tour through the factory. There are a couple of oversized elevators for transporting large items that aren't in use at this time. These are convenient for taking the entire group from level to level in the nanofactory. He shows them where the tiny nanomachines assemble small items and components for larger items then how these are assembled using common scale robotics into the items being requested by residents. A handful of human workers monitor the process for quality control and occasional mechanical problems.

After the tour with Paul Drake, everybody meets back at the Parking Garage where electric carts have been summoned for today's tour of Living Area 2 otherwise known as Tropicania. Beginning at Hanalei Village, the tour crosses the beautiful desert land of Sonora. This is where Kayla Novac and Ali Zamani have decided to make their home. When they arrive at Little Rio, the tour group is greeted by John Diallo and Dakore Maredi who put on a little show. The entertainment has a Brazilian Carnival theme, but is something thrown together quickly since John and Dakore have only been on the ship a couple of days. Leaving Little Rio the carts follow a road along the beach to the train station and ride the little open train back to Hanalei. Since their electric carts were left behind, the guide for day two of the tours walks everybody down to Crescent Bay where the day culminates with a luau.

As new arrivals keep boarding Gaia II, the full day Living Area tours continue. The final shuttle brings the last people to the ship and returns to Noda Geostation on January 15. The last full day tour travels through Tropicania on January 19. Shorter tours and presentations are scheduled from January 21-25 as all of the Gaians are getting ready for the January 28th departure.

Tours include the other transition buildings that are located between Europia and Tropicania. Between Little Rio and Chianti Villas the building is a primary school and a gymnasium with the Computer and Data Storage Center headed by Renata Toscini in the lower levels. Between Wicklesby and Sonora is the Zhang Health and Sciences Building where Genevieve Laplace heads the medical department and Leilani Matogawa is in charge of the physical fitness department. Also, Leela Singh has her psychiatric counseling office here. In the levels beneath the Health Center are the biological science labs where Jaswinder Singh heads up the Astrobiology Research Center. A large conference auditorium and banquet hall is located in this building. Along with the theater and gymnasium, this room is also designed to be a refuge.

The other major tour is conducted by Kayla Novac and Ali Zamani. Together they operate what is arguably the most important area of Gaia II. One third of the starship is devoted to food production and life support. This is especially challenging since for most of the voyage there is no solar radiation. Life support systems are far more complicated than just maintaining oxygen and carbon dioxide levels. There has to be a constant monitoring and balance maintained of the microbiology of the environment and numerous other essential systems to control. In giving their presentation and tours Ali has fun with the fact that they both came to the ship from Mars.

Mei Sun decides to skip her tour of the Life Support Area of the ship as she has to prepare for her own presentation on January 25. Together with Greta Mueller they are giving a talk and visual program entitled *The Energy and Propulsion Systems of Gaia II*. She meets with Greta a couple of times at the university to coordinate. They manage to work together in a professional way, but the two amazing women have a distinct conflict of personality. They mutually agree to essentially give two separate presentations within the one program.

Precisely at seven, Greta and Mei walk out onto the stage of the large, intimidating theater. There is a larger turn out than Mei has expected since the new propulsion system seems to have captured the imagination of the scientifically minded crew. The two presenters are a little cold to each other suggesting that the collaboration hadn't gone so well.

Lights dim and a spotlight shines on Greta as she walks to the front of the stage. She picks up a control device off a podium and adjusts the volume. "Hello, I'm sure you all know me by now. My name is Greta Mueller and I am the lead nuclear engineer in charge of our fusion reactor which gives our ship energy. My co-presenter here is Mei Sun who will try to explain our new propulsion system that makes this first interstellar voyage possible. I'm sure that Kayla Novac and Ali Zamani may argue about who has the most important job, but without energy there is no food or life support and we all freeze and starve to death. If Mei Sun's propulsion system fails then we all wind up drifting through space waiting for the lights to go out."

"I am going to be the first to talk tonight to show you how we plan to keep you all alive on our 42 year trip to Gliese 250 and beyond." With that Greta pushes a button on her remote and a three dimensional interactive image fills the stage behind her. Unlike the film that Jacques Laplace played here during the tours, Greta is a living part of this presentation.

Using images of the actual reactor and computer generated animations and simulations Greta explains, "Many people back on our home planet still think of fusion as just one process of converting sea water into electrical energy. Actually, there are many different possible fusion reactions all based on the fact that the final product, which is mostly stable helium4 with two protons and two neutrons, exists at a much lower energy state than the various isotopes of hydrogen. Therefore, due to the conservation of energy, when you combine forms of hydrogen to make helium you also get a large amount of excess energy in the process. As you all know, this is the process that occurs in the sun's interior which gives us life on Earth. The trick is creating conditions similar to the middle of the sun to get the reaction to happen." Greta manipulates the visual images as she talks.

"On Earth the primary process used for fusion is one combining deuterium, which is an atom of one proton and one neutron, with tritium, which is one proton with two neutrons. The results are a helium4 atom and an extra neutron. This process was chosen since the reaction can be achieved at much lower temperatures than other reactions and the fuel is abundant in sea water." Simulations show a deuterium atom combining with a tritium atom producing helium, a neutron and energy.

"The problem with using this process on our ship is that extra neutron."

Greta changes the image to the ships fusion reactor. "On Gaia II we will use two different fusion reactions. First, we will use deuterium and helium3, which is two protons and one neutron, to produce helium4 and a proton, which can be manipulated to get additional clean energy. We have been acquiring both of these fuels on moons, asteroids and comets and we hope to do so again in star systems we will visit." Greta shows with the interactive images behind her how helium3 is being mined from the moon and deuterium is being acquired from subsurface ice in a near-earth asteroid.

"That brings me to the second reaction that will be used on our ship. This reaction uses carbon, which we have stored in our reactor as a catalyst, to process interstellar hydrogen for fusion. What is important about this is that it can give us power without using up our fuel supply." She creates an image of the starship moving through interstellar space. An animation shows interstellar hydrogen atoms permeating the space in front of the ship."

"Contrary to what was once believed, we find that interstellar space is not empty. Atomic hydrogen permeates space outside our solar system with a density of about one atom per four cubic centimeters. This is still a lesser density than the best vacuum we can create in a laboratory. Your initial thinking may be wondering how we can use such a low density of fuel to power our ship. The answer is that during a large part of our journey we will be traveling at a significant percentage of the speed of light. At velocities over about 13% of the speed of light we will be able to scoop up enough atoms in addition to using their kinetic energy to produce the energy that we need."

Greta changes the scene behind her to a bubbling hot representation of the center of a star. "This fusion process is actually the primary process that occurs in hot stars. Our sun actually uses a reaction called proton-proton fusion predominantly, but stars about 10 to 20% larger than the sun use carbon as a catalyst for a reaction that is much better at producing energy. The process is called the CNO cycle." She changes the background to an animation showing how the CNO cycle works. "As you can see behind me, the reaction takes four incoming protons and converts them into a helium4 atom, two positrons, two neutrinos, three photons and 26.8MeV of energy. The positrons are created when two of the four incoming protons are divided into a neutron and a positron. In a very short time they will encounter an electron and the annihilation will produce more energy." The animation shows the carbon atom going through the following cycle:

Carbon12 – Nitrogen13 – Carbon13 – Nitrogen14 – Oxygen15 – Nitrogen15 – Carbon12

The second half of Greta's presentation shows how the energy produced from the fusion reactor powers the ship and then she once again introduces Mei Sun. After the applause dies down Mei Sun takes over the show.

Mei takes the hand-held video control pad from Greta. "We live at a wonderful time in the history of the human race. Not only have we survived our transition to a planetary civilization, we are making our first step toward becoming a galactic civilization. Humans have learned, as Greta has eloquently demonstrated, how to harness the energy producing processes of stars." Mei produces a computer generated image of a rotating Milky Way galaxy behind her.

"As is the nature of our species, understanding and using fusion was not enough. We wanted more. We wanted an energy source that could allow us to travel to another star in a human lifetime. When it became apparent that it was wishful thinking that we would ever be able to travel through wormholes or push a button and flip to a universe where superluminal *warp* speed is possible, there appeared to be only one answer." Animations of science fiction's representation of wormholes and warp drives fill the stage behind Mei.

"We needed an energy source that we could take advantage of for the entire interstellar journey so that, with constant acceleration, we could build up slowly to the high velocity needed to cross the void. A spaceship design called a Bussard ramjet was imagined by a creative scientist of the same name. This *ramjet* would scoop up its fuel as it went along. The fuel would be the interstellar hydrogen that Greta has mentioned.

The problem with this idea was also mentioned in Greta's presentation. There is nowhere near enough interstellar hydrogen to accelerate a small starship, let alone one this size, without an unbelievably large scoop. Other considerations make even an immense scoop (planetary size) an unlikely solution."

Mei projects an illustration behind her that looks something like a Mexican hat. "The answer has come from our research of the nothing less than the Big Bang. This drawing behind me, that looks like a Mexican hat, represents an energy distribution of space itself. As many of you know, this comes from a theory that has stood the test of time and observation called inflation. I won't explain the details of the theory, but what is important to us is that this lowest energy state," she uses a laser pointer to delineate the lower part of the brim, "is not zero! It has been known for over a century that there is a large amount of energy in *empty* space. One of the ways it makes itself known is by way of what we call *quantum fluctuations*. Particle-antiparticle pairs are constantly being produced, but last for such a short period of time that they can never be directly detected. In 2088, the now famous Nobel Prize winning Russian physicist Petr Romanov discovered a way to harness this *vacuum energy* of space. By using a unique combination of layers of graphene and a new substance he discovered which he has named *quantene*, along with a polarizing magnetic field produced by our fusion reactor, our version of Bussard's ramjet is able to keep the particle-antiparticle pairs apart long enough to be captured and used to propel our starship through space."

"This, of course, is more complicated in reality than I have described. I hope that the following video presentation of the development and testing of what we have called a Quantum Fluctuation Temporizing Ramjet (or QFT ramjet) will help with your understanding." Mei starts the three dimensional documentary and lets it speak for itself.

As the video concludes, Mei asks if the audience has any questions for Greta or herself. One good question is for Greta. The question is, "It obviously takes a great deal of power to get a fusion reaction started. Where does it come from?"

Greta looks directly at the questioner. "Plenty of power is stored in huge nano-batteries that have been charged by solar energy while we have been in orbit. Similarly, we will recharge these batteries during the planned one year stays at our destination stars and with any excess energy from day to day production. Once the reaction gets going, the fusion system will supply most of its own operating energy."

Just about everybody has a question they want to ask. One for Mei is, "Doesn't this QFT ramjet defy our sacred second law of thermodynamics not to mention the first. "

She answers simply. "As far as the first law is concerned, the energy is acquired from a potential energy in space itself."

"The violation of the second law is more complicated and less understood. For the longest time there has been a conflict about how much energy is in empty space. Quantum field theory says there is a very large amount and dark energy observation says there is some, but it is a very small amount. It turns out they are both right. There is some kind of negative energy in space that offsets the positive energy. We have experiments now that show this independently of our new propulsion technology. The universe is finely tuned, but just as matter won out over antimatter in the early universe, positive energy slightly dominated and is what we call dark energy."

"When we extract energy for our propulsion we are decreasing the entropy of our small part of the universe. It works, so the question is, how. Some will say that our laws do not hold for the fabric of space, just as space itself can expand faster than the speed of light. Others think that we may be increasing the entropy of another universe. The truth is we don't know the answer."

After numerous other questions and answers, the audience seems satisfied and Greta and Mei leave the stage to a standing ovation.

* * *

The next morning Mei Sun meets Leilani Matogawa, as planned, outside of the Tahiti Nui Café in Hanalei Village for their morning jog. They are both in excellent physical condition and will have no problem traversing the ten kilometer path that circumnavigates Tropicania. The sunrise simulation on the east wall of the living area casts a glow on their new cylindrical world that gives it an even more surrealistic appearance. Mei and Leilani have decided to go south toward Little Rio, which would be clockwise when looking toward the west wall in the direction they are jogging. Because of the water between Hanalei Village and Little Rio, they have to follow a path to the train station and then follow the path that parallels the tracks along the west wall.

Leilani is admiring the waterfall on the west wall. "Mei, I just can't get used to seeing a waterfall that curves to the left. It reminds me that no matter how hard we try to create an earth-like environment that we are really just living inside a giant rotating tin can."

"True, the Coriolis effect tells us that our habitat is rotating in the counterclockwise direction since the waterfall curves to the south. It's also the reason for the light breeze you are feeling. Due to the spinning, the air reaches an equilibrium state, which is a circular pattern between the sky cylinder and our surface." Mei picks up the pace a little. "You know what else? Since we are jogging in the opposite direction of the rotation we will actually weigh a little less while we are jogging."

Leilani laughs a little at the thought. "I wish I could have had an incentive like that for my weight loss clinics in Hawaii."

As they are running along, Leilani changes the topic. "I was at your presentation last night. It was very informative and entertaining. Do you ever consider the notion that it might not work?"

Mei responds casually as they are not even breathing hard. "Every minute of the day. Romanov's quantene has performed as promised when used for nanocraft or even the small prototype interplanetary ship which has made a couple of trips to Mars, but nothing of this scale has ever been tested."

"I bet Jacques Laplace is just as concerned that our shift to constant acceleration may wreak havoc on our living environments."

"Two more days, can you believe it?"

"It's like a dream. I keep waking up in the morning thinking I'm back in our home in Honolulu."

"Why did you decide to come on the journey?"

"Well, for one thing, Ishii feels that this trip is his reason for being, but I'm excited, too. Why did three shiploads full of people sail off from Europe in 1492 to what many thought were the ends of the earth?"

"Yeah, except they had the option of turning around and going back."

Leilani and Mei continue their jog and their conversation. Mei finds out that, if they are ever ambitious enough to swim the first leg, it is possible to swim from Hanalei to Rio. The dividing wall, which was created for illusory purposes, will open in several places if an object is detected to be approaching. Similarly, the wave making machine is deep enough not to be a danger and will also shut down for a short time."

Leilani's favorite part of the run is through Sonora. There is a certain feeling of freedom jogging through a desert environment. Upon return to Hanalei Village, the two agree to meet again after the journey is underway and go their separate ways.

When Mei gets back to the condo, Barry is awake and has breakfast ready. He welcomes Mei home. "It's going to be a very busy couple of days."

January 28, 2112
Launch

It's six in the morning on Friday in a little town called Wicklesby on a starship orbiting 36,000 kilometers above the Earth. Down on the Earth many people are going about their daily routine, but a good percentage of the population is intently watching internet coverage of this historic day on various types of monitors and comm-devices.

Jaswinder and Leela are already awake and having coffee in their little breakfast nook. They both realize the magnitude of this day and are much quieter than usual. There is no packing to do as they will be returning to their home late this evening. The deadline for the population of Gaia II to be in the theater, gymnasium or conference center is 10am.

The Singhs have chosen to ride out the launch of Gaia II in the gymnasium at the school. They made their choice based on the entertainment and food rather than the proximity to their home. On the gymnasium floor, where one day Jaswinder's and Leela's children may participate in sporting competitions, a three-dimensional, holographic presentation has been planned. A twelve hour concert has been coordinated with many of the most popular performers on Earth playing. The real artists are performing in different venues all over the planet. The shows have been timed to be simulcast live for this holographic concert on the starship.

To get to the gymnasium, Leela suggests that they walk to the Health and Sciences Building since they have plenty of time. The couple follows a path out of town that leads to Lovelock Creek. While walking alongside the creek Jaswinder breaks the silence. "I read that James Lovelock used to love to take walks through the English countryside. Kind of poetic that we are walking along a creek named after him as we prepare for the launching of a starship bearing a name he made famous in his writings." Both Leela and Jaswinder are very familiar with Lovelock's Gaia series of books that created a whole new way of perceiving the planet Earth.

Leela is quiet so Jaswinder continues. "You know, it could be said that he was one of the first astrobiologists. He once told the Jet Propulsion Labs that they weren't going to find life on Mars. This was before the landing of the Viking probes in the 1970s. He based his argument solely on the known atmospheric composition of the planet."

"I hope you keep an open mind when we get to Gliese 250. You of all people know that life could be much different than what we are familiar with."

"Yes, but any kind of life form that encompasses an entire planet or moon is going to change that world in a way that makes itself known."

Jaswinder has a question for Leela. "Leela, you have a very important job, too. Do you think that the people aboard this ship and their children and grandchildren can psychologically handle being taken away from their home planet to live on this floating, isolated *island* in space?"

"Jas, I'm afraid we are in new territory here. I have studied records of groups of primitive peoples who spent their entire lives in isolation on South Pacific Islands, but they never realized that there was a whole world out there that they were missing."

"Do you ever consider that it may be better not to teach our children about the Earth?"

"No, it's better to be open and honest with children and tell them everything. Besides, they would find out anyway." Leela has a look on her face as if she is trying to decide whether to say something. "Jaswinder, I have something I've wanted to tell you all morning."

"Leela, my love, I know already. I could see the twinkle in your eyes." He gives her a big hug. "I hope that we have a little girl who grows up to be a beautiful, wonderful woman just like her mother."

They walk hand in hand along another path that takes them to the Zhang Health and Science Building where they catch the maglev shuttle to the Romanov Primary School gymnasium.

Meanwhile, many Gaians have decided to wait out the launch transition in the Andrew Lloyd Webber Theater. Similar to the gymnasium, performances around the world are being simulcast to Gaia II. In the theater, however, the best currently running musicals, plays, operas and ballets are having special showings for the occasion. There is a mix of classical works such as *Swan Lake* by the Moscow Ballet in the newly renovated Bolshoi Theater and *Les Miserables* from New York City. Also, more recent hits include *Viva La Vida*, a new musical based on the music of the early 21st century group Coldplay and the modern Chinese opera performance of *Shangri La* which has recently become the highest grossing stage show of all time. *Viva La Vida* is being simulcast from London and *Shangri La* from Beijing.

The third venue, which is the Conference Auditorium and Banquet Hall in the Zhang Health and Science Building, is also popular. This area has been decked out for a huge Super Bowl Party. The game has been scheduled a few days earlier than usual to coincide with the Gaia II launching. Those lucky enough to be at the game are also getting to watch the minute to minute festivities erupting in every country on the planet on huge video screens. The football fans on Gaia II will be watching the game in Holomax.

Mei, Greta, Barry and Greta's husband Ernst have to spend at least the first few hours in the Energy Control Center. This is in the rear of the ship near the fusion reactor and shuttle port. They are monitoring the tense moments of launch and the engaging of the QFT propulsion system. Renata and Paul are in the Computer Control Center prepared to take care of any unexpected problems that may arise. Jacques Laplace and his crew are monitoring the morphing process of the living areas. Everybody else on Gaia II is having the time of their lives.

The global internet coverage starts at 8am Pacific Standard Time, which is also the time on Gaia II. Never has there been such a hyped event. Not even the moon landing back in 1969 had this kind of a galvanizing effect on the human race. Famous news anchors, celebrities, scientists and others from all walks of life try to catch some of the limelight. For one day anyway, our species is able to take its collective mind off of socio-economic problems and gaze in wonder at the stars.

Barry is watching the mania on a comm-device while Mei does some last minute checks. He comments to her. "There have been a lot of people, including myself, who have questioned the wisdom of putting such immense resources toward this project. I think what is happening today alone already proves that it's been worth it."

Fifteen minutes until 10am. The Times Square ball is starting to rise, the opposite direction of the tradition on New Year's Eve. Special effects at the Eiffel Tower give the impression that it is about to take off like a rocket. Clocks of all shapes and sizes everywhere are counting down.

The beginning is Greta Mueller's show as she oversees the shift of the energy produced in the fusion reactor completely to thrust. The ship must get into an accelerating reference frame to be able to *turn on* the QFT propulsion system.

An announcement is made on Gaia II. "Attention all Gaians, ignition is in ten minutes. We need everybody to find a seat now. This isn't because of our acceleration. It is because all power is to be temporarily diverted to our initial thrust to start us on our way. If all goes well, about three minutes later QFT propulsion will kick in and we will get our power back."

Comm-devices are lit up everywhere in the transition buildings as people say their goodbyes to family and friends. High and low emotions, exultation and crying, fills the arenas.

Five minutes, Mei, Greta, Jacques and many others on the ship and on Earth are on the edge of their seats.

Ten, nine, eight …. three, two, one. Ignition!! The power on Gaia II goes out. Greta's reactor puts all of its energy into the thrusters, but to an observer outside the ship it would look like a spewing bottle of champagne trying to push an ocean liner. Applause erupts all over the globe.

The feeling of the thrust is very anti-climactic for the Gaians as they can barely tell that the starship is beginning to move.

Now it's the moment of truth for Mei and the thousands of people who have spent the last several years planning, developing and constructing mankind's first interstellar propulsion system. Mei takes the lead. "We are approaching the minimum acceleration necessary to engage QFT. Powering up the scoop's magnetic field. We should see the first energy reading in about two minutes."

Two minutes pass, then three minutes, four minutes, five minutes and still no sign of any energy from the new propulsion system. Mei exclaims to Greta, "We're not getting the thrust you promised we'd get from your engines.

"My engines are doing what they are supposed to do, miss high and mighty. We're past what you thought was the minimum acceleration. This one's on you not me!!

One of Mei's bright young engineers shouts, "I'm getting a reading. Power increasing." The announcement is made to the Gaians and to Earth, "The QFT ramjet is working, the mission is a go!! Two more minutes until full transfer to QFT propulsion."

After being off for a very long ten minutes, the lights on the ship go on and once again there are shouts and applause everywhere. Then, as has been planned by a few select members of the planning committee, every venue on Gaia II and on Earth broadcasts the following famous statement in a slightly altered form. A computer generated voice of one of the original Star Trek actors, Leonard Nimoy, announces:

"Space ... the final frontier. These are the voyages of the starship Gaia II. Its 600 year mission: to explore strange new worlds, to seek out new life and new civilizations, to boldly go where no one has gone before."

Another voice proclaims, "Let the show begin!!"

The amazing intro to the musical "Viva La Vida" starts up in the theater. The hottest musical group on Earth, *Action Figures*, kicks off the concert from Istanbul, Turkey. At the same time, the San Francisco 49ers kick off to the Denver Broncos and Super Bowl 146 is underway. The twelve hour transition to constant acceleration has begun.

You can hardly tell that the living areas have gone through the morphing process now. The entire cleanup has been done and small damaged personal items have been recycled and replaced. There was some flooding and landscape damage, but most of it had been anticipated by Jacques Laplace and his team. The west walls of each living area are 50 meters shorter now and the east walls are 50 meters taller. Entering the transition buildings from the Tropicania side, the only sign of the twenty level, one hundred meter high structure is a parking garage and elevator building that sits on the roof. The exit from the buildings on the Europia side is at Level J. Because of the 0.1g acceleration of the ship, the Gaians still perceive the ground to be flat and the buildings upright, but the walls and transition buildings are atilt. Jacques and the Disney designers have used architectural design to minimize this effect.

It has been two weeks now since launch. Gaia II is now nearing the orbit of Saturn. The ship doesn't pass anywhere near the planets themselves since it is not necessary to use gravity assist velocity boost and they would rather not have the ship's trajectory altered.

Fabricators have been creating large amounts of artificial flowers of all varieties. The bakery in Wicklesby is doing the final touch up of a huge cake designed to feed 750 people and transport it to Bertoni Vineyards. Chairs have been set up in rows on a large lawn area with a beautiful, intricate arbor at one end and flowers everywhere. People are slowly starting to show up and find chairs to sit in. John Diallo is sitting at a piano on one side of the lawn with Dakore at his side.

One hour later, with every guest seated, a groom and his best man are standing on the right hand side of the arbor in elegant white tuxedos. On the left is a maid of honor in a beautiful lacy dress. John Diallo starts playing the music that has signified the beginning of a new life for billions of people over the last two centuries.

A lovely lady in a beautiful, classic wedding dress starts walking down the aisle between the chairs in step to the Wedding March. Renata Toscini is about to become Mrs. Paul Drake.

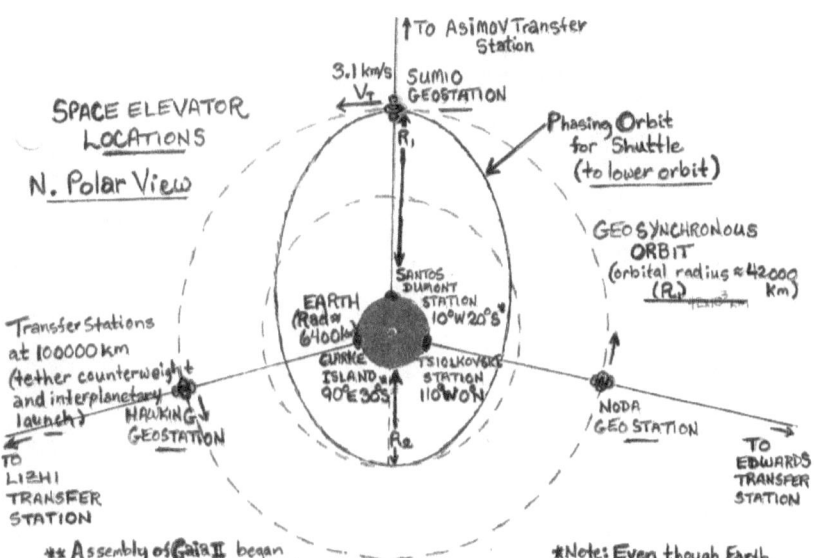

SPACE ELEVATOR LOCATIONS
N. Polar View

↑ To ASIMOV Transfer Station

3.1 km/s V_T SUMIO GEOSTATION

R_1

Phasing Orbit for Shuttle (to lower orbit)

GEOSYNCHRONOUS ORBIT
(orbital radius ≈ 42000 (R_2) km)

SANTOS DUMONT STATION 10°W 20°S*

EARTH (Rad ≈ 6400km)

CLARKE ISLAND 90°E 30°S*

TSIOLKOVSKE STATION 110°W 0°N

Transfer Stations at 100000 km (tether counterweight and interplanetary launch)
HAWKING GEOSTATION

TO LIZHI TRANSFER STATION

R_2

NODA GEO STATION

TO EDWARDS TRANSFER STATION

** Assembly of Gaia Ⅱ began in late 2100 at a location of 10km "above" Noda Geo station. Slower orbit at this location caused an intentional lag behind Noda of ~32 km per day (52800 km in 5 yrs)

Gaia Ⅱ (2111)**

*Note: Even though Earth stations are not all on the equator the elevators all extend toward an equatorial orbit location

GEOSTATION/GAIA Ⅱ SHUTTLES

Shuttle Departs/Arrives	Phasing Orbit ★	Transfer Time	$R_2 (10^3 km)$	$\Delta v_T \frac{km}{s}$
Hawking/Gaia Ⅱ or Gaia Ⅱ/Noda	Lower	18ʰ40ᵐ	29.1	−0.29
Noda/Sumio or Sumio/Hawking	Lower	17ʰ20ᵐ	25.6	−0.40
Hawking/Noda	Lower	13ʰ20ᵐ	14.8	−0.86
Sumio/Gaia Ⅱ or Gaia Ⅱ/Sumio	Lower	12ʰ00ᵐ	12.9	−0.97
Noda/Hawking	Higher	34ʰ40ᵐ	65.2	+0.32
Sumio/Noda or Hawking/Sumio	Higher	30ʰ40ᵐ	56.9	+0.22
Noda/Gaia Ⅱ or Gaia Ⅱ/Hawking	Higher	29ʰ20ᵐ	54.1	+0.19

★ Slow to lower (faster) orbit to catch up (½ orbit or less). Speed up to higher (slower) orbit to let destination, over ½ orbit away, catch up with you.

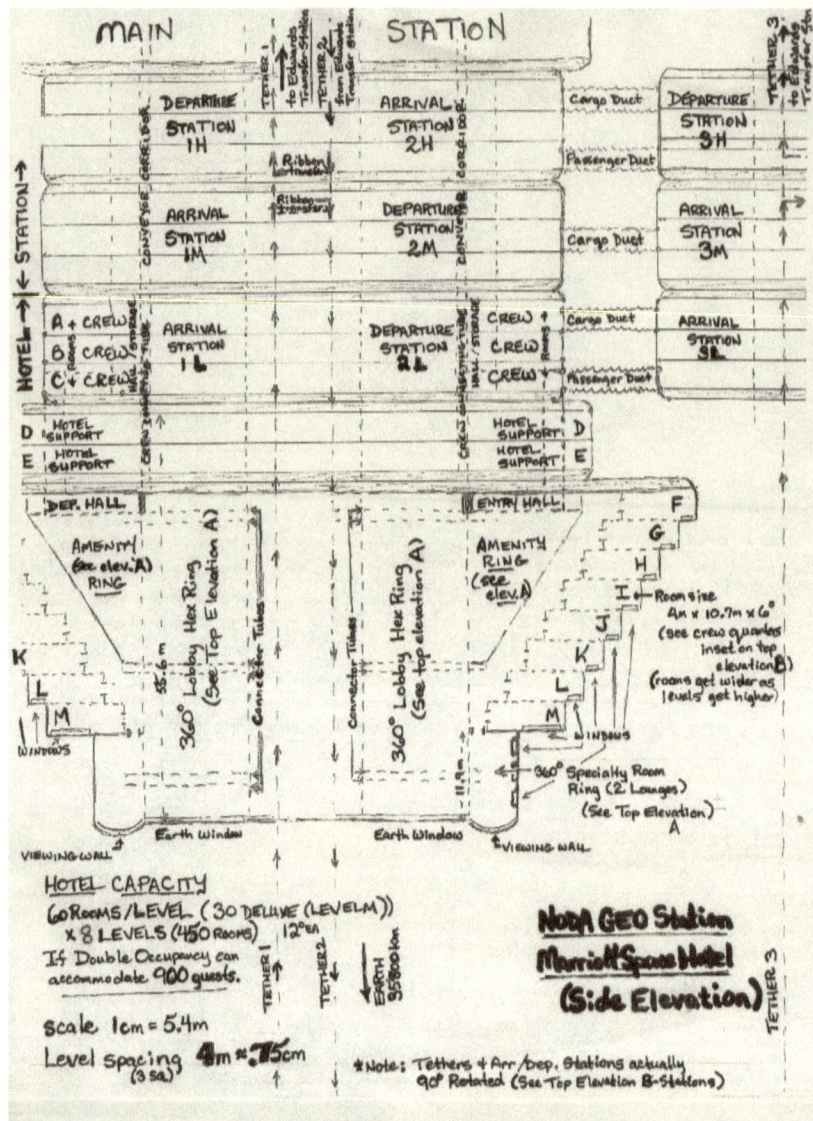

Lobbys, Restaurants, Atria : Extend 55.6 m from top of Level F to
(2)   (2)   (2)   Earth Window. Floor width 8m. Ceiling are 22m
                                Ceiling Height 21m.
Recreational Rooms: R1-R12: Extend from Level F to Level K (6 Levels)
        (12)   At level F height is 16m at Level K height is 3m
Banquet Rooms (4) + Lounges (2): All below Level M. "Floor" above Lobby
                                 "ceiling" to Lounge "ceiling" 6.7m. Length
                                 from bottom of Level M to Window 12m.

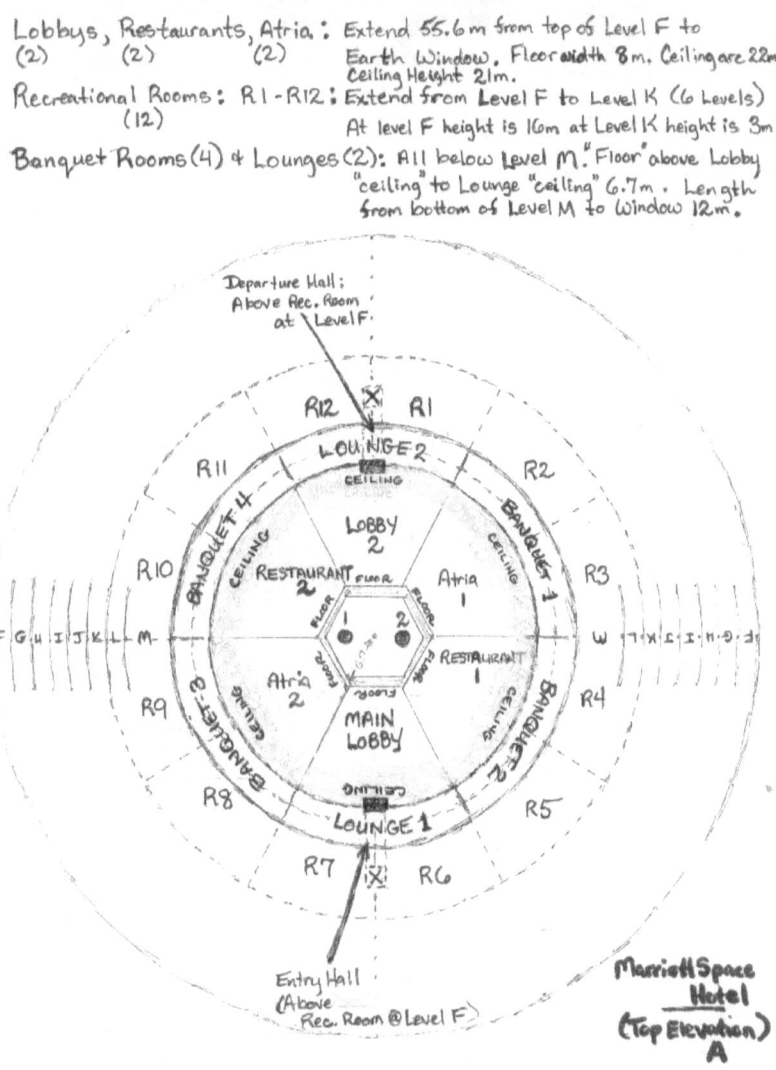

Departure Hall;
Above Rec. Room
at Level F.

R12 X R1

R11   LOUNGE 2   R2
                 CEILING

R10   LOBBY   R3
        BANQUET 4   2   BANQUET 1
          CEILING RESTAURANT FLOOR Atria
                      FLOOR   1   1
F G H I J K L M   M L K J I H G F
                    Atria   1   2   RESTAURANT
R9   BANQUET 3   2 FLOOR FLOOR 1   BANQUET 2   R4
              CEILING   MAIN   CEILING
                        LOBBY
R8   CEILING   R5
                  LOUNGE 1

R7   X   R6

Entry Hall
(Above
  Rec. Room @ Level F)

Marriott Space
Hotel
(Top Elevation)
A

SPACE ELEVATOR / STORAGE / CREW QUARTERS

* Arrival/Departure Stations 3 Levels "High" A-C
* 3 Levels of Crew/Staff Quarters and Hotel Storage/Maintenance
* Arrival/Departure Cargo/Baggage 2 Levels "High" A-B
* Passenger Arrival/Departure Staging/Waiting Area Level C

LEVELS A B + C: (TOP VIEW)

TETHERS 1 + 3 : ARRIVAL FROM TSIOLKOVSKY (40 hr. trip)
TETHERS 2 + 4 : DEPARTURE TO TSIOLKOVSKY (28 hr. trip)

CREW QUARTERS:
60 / Level (ABC)
(180 Rooms)
6' / room

Room design: 273A
              -357A
Angle/Level   273B
              -357B
i.e.   273C
              -357C
3A
9A
15A
21A
"   radius
357A   98.2m

(Same for levels B+C)

Scale: 1cm = 5.4m

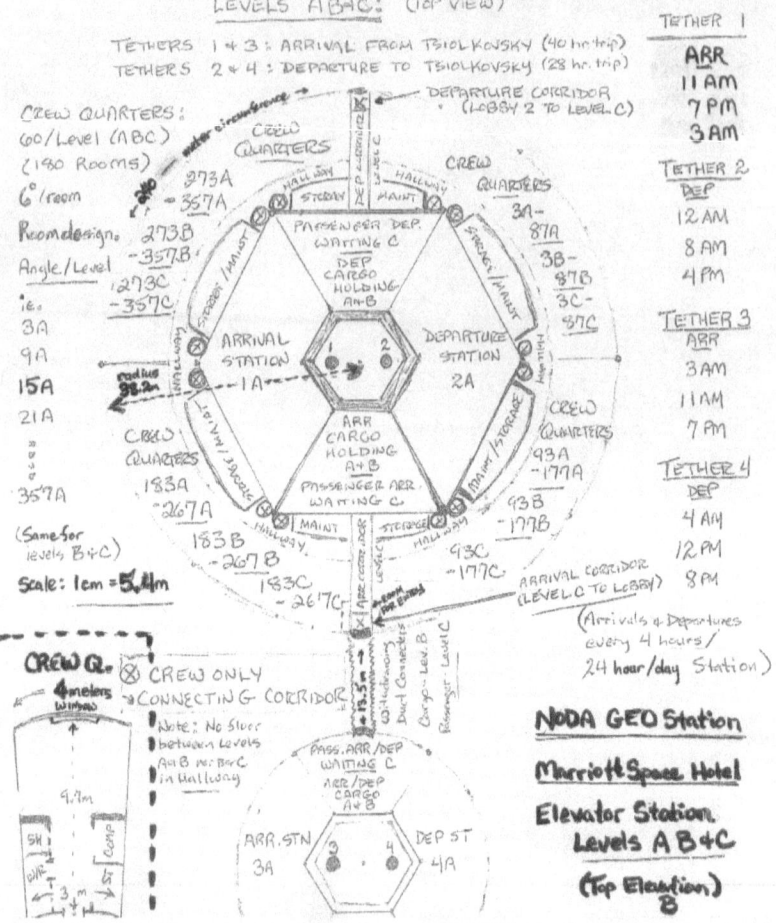

DEPARTURE CORRIDOR
(LOBBY 2 TO LEVEL C)

CREW QUARTERS

PASSENGER DEP.
WAITING C
DEP CARGO
HOLDING
A + B

ARRIVAL STATION
1A

DEPARTURE STATION
2A

ARR CARGO HOLDING
A + B
PASSENGER ARR.
WAITING C

CREW QUARTERS
273A - 357A
STORM / MAINT

CREW QUARTERS
3A - 87A
3B - 87B
3C - 87C

CREW QUARTERS
93A - 177A
93B - 177B
93C - 177C

CREW QUARTERS
183A - 267A
183B - 267B
183C - 267C

ARRIVAL CORRIDOR
(LEVEL C TO LOBBY)

TETHER 1	
ARR	
11 AM	
7 PM	
3 AM	

TETHER 2	
DEP	
12 AM	
8 AM	
4 PM	

TETHER 3	
ARR	
3 AM	
11 AM	
7 PM	

TETHER 4	
DEP	
4 AM	
12 PM	
8 PM	

(Arrivals + Departures every 4 hours / 24 hour/day Station)

CREW Q.
4 meters wide
⊗ CREW ONLY
* CONNECTING CORRIDOR
Note: No Stair between Levels A+B no: B+C in Hallway

9.7m
5H   ST COMP
3m

PASS. ARR/DEP
WAITING C
ARR/DEP
CARGO A+B

ARR. STN
3A

DEP ST
4A

NODA GEO Station

Marriott Space Hotel

Elevator Station
Levels A B + C

(Top Elevation)

8

GAIA II : QFT (Quantum Fluctuation Temporizing) Ramjet

* Each section has a surface/living area of ≈ 6.28 km²
  (ONeill Cylinders)
* Initial Crew ~750 / Maximum Capacity-3000
  (Max pop density=1 person/4200m²)
* Designed for 1m/sec² (0.1g) acceleration for 3LY dist (17.6yr)

Scoop Larger than Drawn (Diameter (max) = 10km)

Interstellar Hydrogen

Strong magnetic field generated by fusion engines

reverse thrust when decelerating

Quantum Fluctuations in Space

+ − + − Virtual
+ − + − Particle
+ − + − Pairs

* "Living" sections also referred to as living "areas". Each are divided into three living "regions".

$U_{max} \approx 0.64c$

3km

1600m | 1000m | 1000m

Living Section I | Living Section II | Life Support / Agricultural Section

100m

950m | 1000m | 1050m

Sky Cylinder

QFT Ramjet

30-meter deep surface

Slope of landfill when accelerating @ +1m/sec² (0.1g)

FUSION ENGINES (Initial start/pause)

Shuttle Docking Ring

Pods Assembly Launch

Landfill (~3.5 km²/living cylinder)

Slope of landfill (~3.5 km²/Living cylinder)

POWER OF THE SUN → * Fusion engines have deuterium fuel tanks for initial acceleration but also use interstellar hydrogen for ship power and small velocity adjustments

POWER OF THE BIG BANG → * Quantum Fluctuation Temporizor is able to prolong duration of natural fluctuations in interstellar space long enough to capture large amounts of energy for propulsion

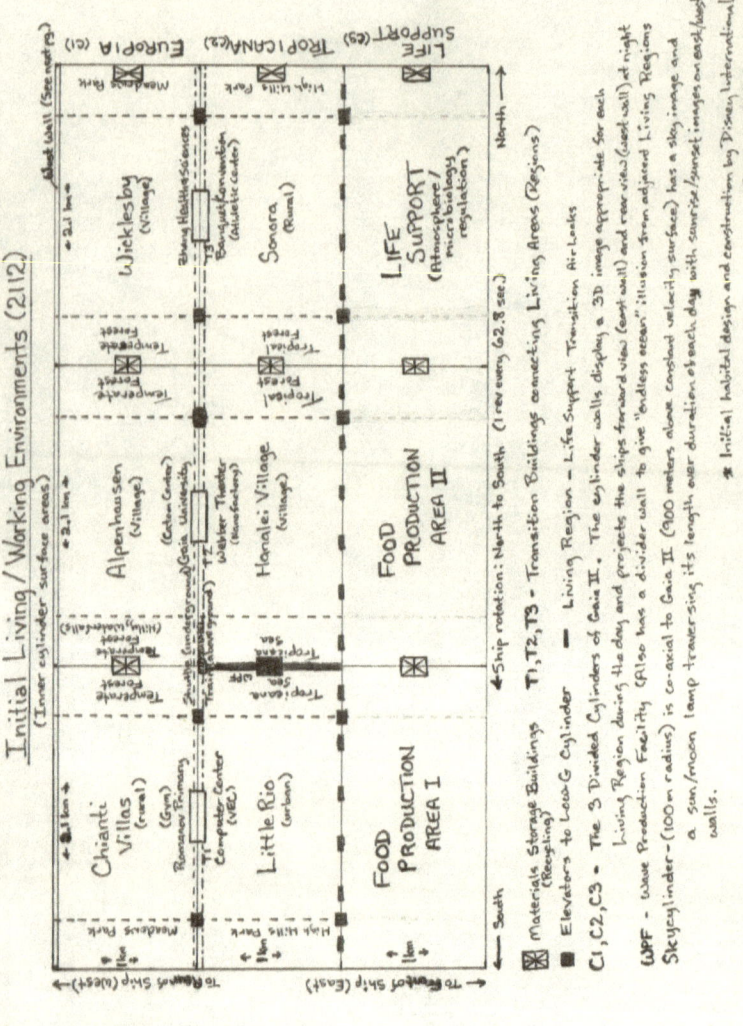

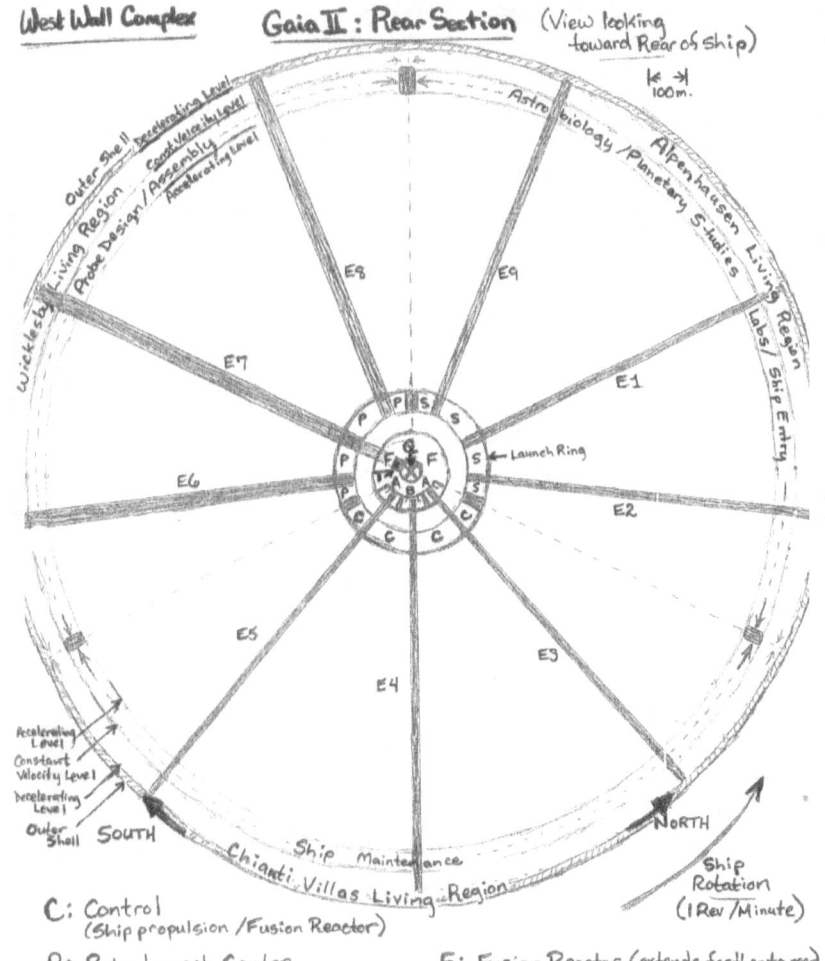

Gaia II : Rear Section (View looking toward Rear of ship)

West Wall Complex

|← →|
100 m.

Outer Shell
Decelerating Level
Constant Velocity Level
Accelerating Level
Wickleslot Living Region
Probe Design / Assembly

Astrobiology / Planetary Studies
Alpenhausen Living Region
Labs / Ship Entry

E8
E9
E7
E1
E6
E2
E5
E3
E4

P P S S
P S S
G F
F A F
T A B A
C B C
C C C

← Launch Ring

Accelerating Level
Constant Velocity Level
Decelerating Level
Outer Shell

SOUTH

Chianti Villas Living Region

Ship Maintenance

NORTH

Ship Rotation
(1 Rev / Minute)

C: Control
(Ship propulsion / Fusion Reactor)

P: Probe Launch Center
S: Shuttle Port
A: Sky Cylinder Access
B: Fusion Reactor Access

F: Fusion Reactor (extends farther to rear)
Q: QFT Propulsion Conduit ("   ")
E: Elevators
T: Low-G Training Center

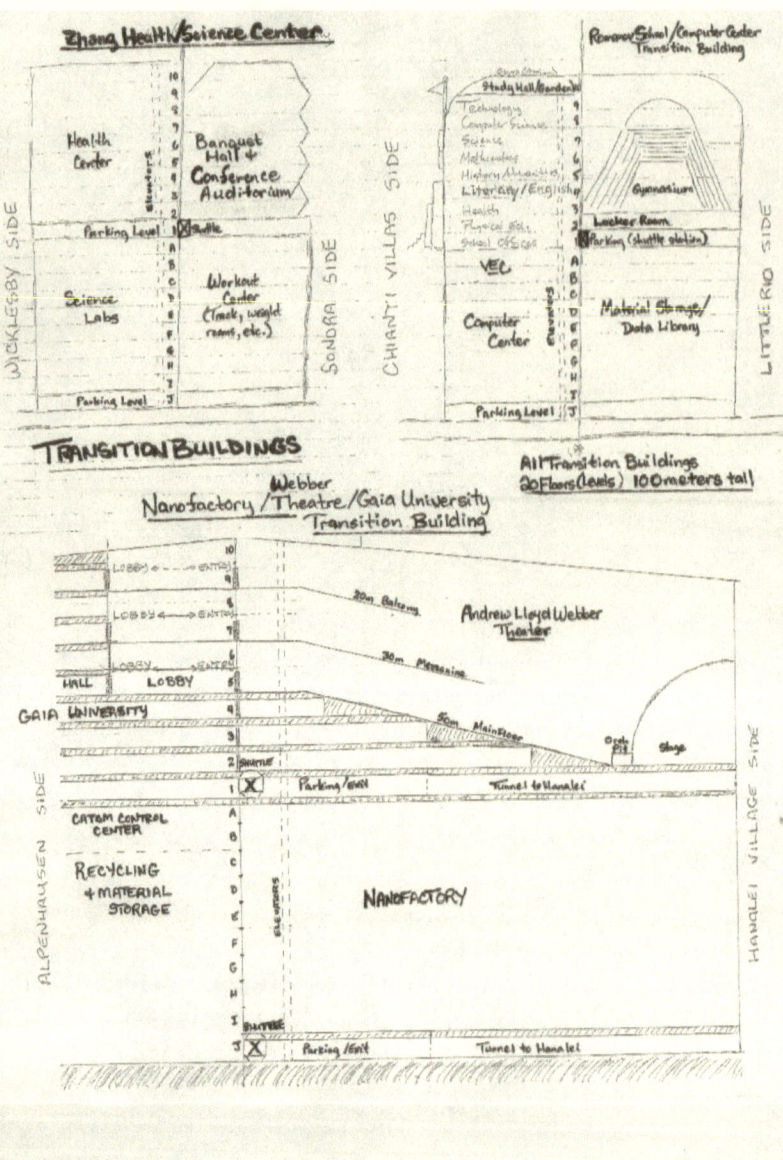

BEGINNING OF VOYAGE OF GAIA II:

Date: (Days after departure)

- Constant acceleration: $a \approx 1$ m/sec² $\approx 0.1g$, $v_0 \approx 53 \times 10^4$ m/sec
- (note: 1 AU $\approx 1.5 \times 10^{11}$ m, 1 LY $\approx 9.4 \times 10^{15}$ m, $c = 3 \times 10^8$ m/sec)
- Noticeable crossings:
- Termination shock @ 140×10^{11} m
- Bow Shock @ 350×10^{11} m — Only ~1 headwind in same distant sun
- ‡ Attain 0.1c @ 486 days
- ‡ Attain 0.64c (c_{max}) @ ~6 years
- ‡ Determined classically with non-relativistic equations
- Leave Local Interstellar Cloud (@ ~10 light years / ~2.0 yrs s)

Cross orbit of Saturn

Cross orbit of Jupiter

Cross orbit of Mars

** velocities at these times and distances (in 10⁶ m/sec)

TIME (DAYS)

Distance traveled (×10¹¹ meters)

2/12 25
2/11 24
2/10 23
2/9 22
2/8 21
2/7 20
2/16 19
2/15 18
2/14 17
2/5 16
2/1 15
2/1 14
3/0 13
2/? 12
11
10
9
8
2/4 7
2/3 6
2/2 5
2/1 4
1/31 3   ** 2.92
1/30 2   ** 2.26
1/29 1   ** 1.15 **
1/28 0

14.16
13.25
2/1 12.93
11.52
10.70
9.83
2/10 8.07
7.24
6.59
5.51
4.65
2/2 3.79 (2/1)

NOTE $v_0 \approx 0.1g$ **

RAHII

Beep… Beep… Beep… A flip-number digital alarm clock is going off on a nightstand. A young boy with dark hair and a light brown skin complexion reaches over and pushes down a button to turn it off. He reaches a little further and touches the bottom of a goose-neck lamp and it comes on lighting up the room.

The bedroom is full of gadgets and the walls are covered with posters. One poster shows a group of young men with a lot of hair and the name *Def Leppard* across the bottom. Another has a young man in a costume looking at his watch next to a classic low-riding sports vehicle with flaming tire tracks trailing off into the distance. On the nightstand, next to the lamp, is a cube that has sides divided into nine sections with each side a different color. In a corner of the room is a large pillowy object covered in a soft material that resembles the fur of a tiger like those seen in data library videos. Against the wall by the boy's clothes closet is a very shiny red electric guitar replica. It has white lines with black highlights randomly crossing the body and a light pine neck and head.

The boy darts across the hall to the bathroom, thankful that his sister has already finished her morning ritual. He opens the lid to the toilet. With a sigh of relief he empties his bladder. The stream hits an invisible screen and seems to magically disappear. He puts a hand under a dispenser on the wall and a dab of gel squirts into it. He rubs his hands together while looking into a mirror. An image of the boy's mother displays in the corner of the mirror and speaks to him. "Good morning,

Rahii. Today is the day of your weekly vitamins and health test. Don't forget to wash your face and brush your hair. I love you."

Rahii takes his vitamins out of a small storage unit in the wall and fills a small disposable cup from a drinking water spigot. After taking the vitamins, he takes another dab of gel from the dispenser and rubs it on his face. He grabs his brush out of the cabinet and runs it through his hair. The brush takes out static and revitalizes hair while brushing. The boy pours a little mouthwash into his cup and rinses, keeping the liquid in his mouth about 30 seconds and spits it into a special disposal. Leaning over to look into a small lens in the mirror with one eye, he tries not to blink. A faint light flashes into Rahii's eye, then he stands back awaiting the results. Again his mother's face appears in the mirror and talks to him. "Almost everything is normal, Rahii. I am going to increase your vitamin D dose. I can tell that Mary at the chocolate shop is letting you have an extra chocolate. Only one from now on, Rahii."

After getting dressed, even his clothes are a style popular in the late twentieth century on Earth, he sits down at a computer in his bedroom. It looks like an old computer out of a museum on Earth. The computer is a big, clunky looking thing that has the words *Apple II* across the bottom. This is all a façade, however. Rahii himself has tweaked the interior for maximum efficiency. With voice command, he can access and update any of his several constantly running programs. He can even get to virtual places, in the ship's cyberspace, that aren't meant for the entire population. His fascination is with the quantum computer that Renata Drake and a team of her assistants is developing.

Rahii, at age 14, is a computer prodigy. He is a student at Romanov Primary School. Rahii is actually having trouble in a couple of his subject areas, mainly due to lack of interest, but he excels in math, science and particularly computer science. Two of the programs, which he is running on the computer in his bedroom, are actually self-writing programs to be used with the quantum computer when it becomes operational. Given direction and algorithms by the user, his programs use several utility programs from the cyber-function library to write themselves in a similar way that self-replicating nanobots would create duplicates of themselves.

Sitting in his chair, Rahii taps his foot obsessively. It's a way he expels nervous energy while he is thinking. He asks for a program status update for one of his quantum computer projects. What he sees horrifies him. Three of the four branches of the program have gotten trapped in an infinite regression and have made no progress at all. It takes Rahii an hour to figure out the fix for all three branches. This pushes him to the brink of being late for school.

Rahii's mother, Leela, has been nagging him for the last half hour that he needs to eat something and get off to school. This was very frustrating for him since he was trying to focus on his dilemma. Finally emerging from his room, there is no time to eat. He grabs a piece of fruit and a slice of cinnamon bread and runs out the door.

Leela is sitting at the table in the breakfast nook with Jaswinder. "That boy, I worry about him. His history teacher tells me he is behind the rest of the class and he spends so much time in his bedroom."

Jaswinder dismisses her concern. "Don't worry. He knows computers better than everyone else his age, by far, and is at level 12 in both math and science."

"Still, did you see how he was dressed?! When he first started requesting those styles from the fabricator, I thought they were costumes for some school project. He's so different from the other children. It must be hard for him socially at school."

Jaswinder is dismissive again which infuriates Leela.

Rahii catches a maglev shuttle from the Health and Sciences Center transition building to Romanov School. He then takes an elevator to General Arts Level 5 to go to his 21st Century History class. In the hall, on the way to class, Rahii sees Stephanie talking with some of her friends.

Stephanie Maria Drake is a very pretty young lady with flowing dark blonde hair whom is one year older that Rahii. She never notices him, even in his 1980's style clothing, but he is definitely infatuated with her. What's not to like? She is beautiful, popular and the daughter of a woman he idolizes. Rahii accidentally bumps into somebody while distracted by Stephanie. With a menacing look from the other student, he speeds off to class.

Rahii chooses a seat in class near the window and touches the desk top to activate his learning program and prove his attendance. His personal data appears on the desk in front of him and shows that his arranged schedule puts him in History at this time. The display shows that he is at level six and currently studying 21st Century History. As is the daily routine, the instructor, Mrs. Helena Abbasi, starts with a short lecture. The students in her class are at different levels, so her lecture is usually a story about an important historical event randomly chosen from the different time periods being studied.

Today's story follows a family living through a troubled time that Rahii is supposed to be studying. She tells the class about terrible conditions in Northern Africa caused by global warming. Mrs. Abbasi explains how the family tried to emigrate to Southern Europe. They were very coldly and sometimes violently received since the Europeans were having their own problems. Immigrants have, historically, been a convenient scapegoat. By comparison, the trouble on the U.S./ Mexican border was very minor. When Italy, Spain, Greece, France and other countries started closing their borders the family was cut off from friends and relatives. Some family members still in Africa were involved in repercussions. At the time Europe was getting a great deal of its power from solar grids in the Sahara Desert. Many lives were lost as Africans protested by sabotaging the power stations. The family was essentially forced to live in a ghetto development in France that became somewhat of an internment camp. Unfortunately, as in many real life cases, there was no happy ending for these poor people.

The second half of the class is for self-paced, individualized learning. Mrs. Abbasi is available to answer questions. All of the students put on their comm-goggles so that what they see and hear doesn't disturb the others. Rahii presses the *begin* button on his desk display and then chooses the icon for 21st Century History. Another set of icons appear and he picks *2040s*. One more group of choices appears and he touches *geopolitical*. He really has very little interest in the topic, but knows he has to get through this to attain the level 10 that is required before he can attend the university.

The learning program that Rahii sees and hears with his comm-goggles actually gets his attention this time. The subject is the decision to build *Tech City* in West Antarctica where his mom and dad came from. After a short time, however, he is back to recoding one of his quantum computer programs in his mind.

When 10am finally comes, Rahii wanders to the break area for a snack along with the rest of the students. He gets an energy bar and a drink from the food fabricating vending area and sits by himself at a table. He looks around and sees a few like him, but most are in groups laughing and talking about topics he considers trivial and meaningless. He wonders if school was like this back on Earth. Stephanie, of course, is at a table of popular kids, all a year or two older than he is.

Rahii actually welcomes the very kind, fatherly voice that comes out of the school audio system announcing that it is time for all of the students to go to session two. He enjoys this class far more than first session since it alternates between science and mathematics.

At noon, he grabs his lunch to go because his next subject is computer science. Rahii is at a level 15, which is astounding for a fourteen year old. Due to his high level he gets to spend his class time in the computer center where Renata Drake is developing and testing the quantum computer. While one part of Renata's team works on the technical problems of integrating the new computer system with the existing, another group is developing the software to use with the quantum computer when it comes on line. Rahii is working with the second group.

Renata gives a little pep talk to the entire group. "If I could get everybody's attention for a minute, I really appreciate the long hours that you are all putting in, even the newest member of our team." She smiles at Rahii. "I have to give you some bad news or, if you prefer, more of a challenge. Our sensors are now telling us that our starship will be leaving the Local Interstellar Cloud sooner than we thought. The best estimates are telling us about two years, six months. As you all know, when we leave the cloud and enter the Local Bubble hydrogen density, and thus fuel for our fusion reactor, drops off dramatically. By this time, we need all computational operations to be done by quantum computer. That said, I want to compliment a couple of successes that have been made recently. On Saturday, John came up with an idea that may solve our interface problem." Everybody applauds. "Also, a huge contribution has been made by Ivan and Yasmin. Together they have discovered a method that will make production of the minute quantene-graphene sheets for the central processing units much easier." Another round of applause and pats on the back then they all get back to work. It seems like no time at all has passed when Rahii has to go to his final session, physical fitness.

* * *

That night at dinner, Rahii asks his father out of the blue. "Dad, what was Tech City like?"

Jaswinder is caught off guard. "Why do you ask, son?"

"My 21st Century History video today was about the decision to build it and the early days of its creation."

"I'm glad to see that you are showing some interest in history, Rahii. Well, I'm sure that your video told you that in 2048 a counsel in Geneva, Switzerland made the decision to fund the creation of a new city to be located in West Antarctica. Antarctica is the coldest, most uninhabitable place on Earth. At this point in time, global unrest, terrorism and conflicts were so bad that it was getting harder and harder to work on the technological advances that were needed to save man from himself. The wealthiest countries on the planet all committed to the construction of this new, technology based city that was to be extremely isolated to insure uninterrupted progress. Also, secretly, the world's first self-sustaining, positive output fusion reactor had already been built and tested in this West Antarctic location. It was to be ready for *turn on* in 2052."

"What your video probably didn't tell you is that this city, which later took ownership of the name *Tech City* that everybody was calling it, was also somewhat of a social experiment as well as a safe refuge. It was decided from the beginning that there would be no currency exchange in this new city, unlike the rest of the world. Also, this new city was to be populated by some of the brightest minds on the planet. Very little immigration and emigration was allowed and definitely no tourism. The entire city was to be connected by its own closed computer system, not to be accessible from the outside world. Since the city was being built from scratch, it was designed with a maglev transportation system connecting every building so no residents would have their own vehicles. All structures, of course, were totally enclosed and protected from the extreme Antarctic weather. All of this was made possible by the success of the fusion reactor which provided the unbelievable amount of power that Tech City needed to function."

"Sounds a lot like our home."

"In many ways it was. If anything, life in Tech City was actually more virtually assisted than Gaia II. We have learned that, just because we can let machines and computers do everything for us, doesn't mean that we should."

"Yeah dad, I get all that, but what was it like living there?"

"For the first few years I loved it. I was able to write my own agenda to study what I loved the most. I had access to the best computers available at the time and was a voice request away from the latest discoveries of cutting edge research. The team I was working with was amazing. Also, we were surrounded by beautiful architecture and garden areas. To go anywhere in the city all your mom and I had to do was hop in a maglev car, which were always readily available, and tell it where to go. There was plenty of real and virtual entertainment along with numerous wonderful places to go out to eat. On top of all this, we developed some very close friendships and there was a wonderful feeling of community and security."

"What about after the first few years?"

"I guess I got something called *island fever*. I missed the rest of the world. The once a year vacations to see family and friends only added to the longing."

"Why didn't you move away?"

Leela is listening and gets in on the conversation. "We talked about it many times, Rahii, but your father's work was there and there were some terrible things happening back in India where we came from."

Jaswinder adds. "Yes, and then they offered us the chance to be on Gaia II. What astrobiologist in his right mind would say no!?"

Leela looks lovingly at her husband. "And my life and place is with you wherever you are."

"I love you, too."

Rahii gets up. "Okay, enough. I'm going to my room."

Stephanie Drake is taking the elevator to level 5, where the history and humanities classes are. She always gets to school fifteen minutes early because she likes to talk with her friends in the hall before class. As she exits the elevator and walks down the hall, she sees her best friend Tessa and Tessa's boyfriend Ryan. Tessa has dark brown hair and is thinner than Stephanie. They ironically envy each other's hair and body shape. Ryan is not athletic or unusually smart, but is taller than the girls, has wavy brown hair and is well liked by the other guys. He and Tessa are in the usual spot near a vending area. Stephanie joins up with them and asks, "Where are Matt and Shakira? I bet they are up in the roof garden making out and looking out at Little Rio again."

Tessa counters. "When are you going to get a boyfriend, Steph? A lot of guys like you."

"Since you're mentioning it, what do you know about Derek Scott?"

"I see. You like older blonde-haired men." Tessa likes to tease Stephanie. "He is really good looking and very mysterious. He seems to have a small group of people that are kinda like his followers. Nobody knows where they go or what they talk about."

Ryan adds what he knows. "I've heard from a friend that his group has formed a little club and call themselves the *Real Earth Society*. My friend was with them for a little while, but he told me that he quit because they were way too negative about stuff."

Tessa lights up. "There you go. All you have to do is show interest in his little club and you're in."

"I don't know. My friend didn't like Derek very much." Ryan is truly concerned.

"There's only one way to find out."

Matt and Shakira come out of an elevator and join them for a couple of minutes before it's time for first session. If Romanov followed the old tradition of having a king and queen of the Spring Prom, no doubt these two would be chosen. Shakira is the daughter of John Diallo and Dakore Maredi and looks a lot like her mother. Matt is a star player in the school's three on three basketball league.

* * *

That day, during the noon hour, Stephanie sees one of the people from the group that hangs out with Derek. She decides to approach her. "Hi, I hear that you might be someone I can talk to if I want to find out more about the Real Earth Society."

The pretty, but tough looking, dark haired Hispanic girl looks like she's been blindsided. "I don't know what you are talking about." Stephanie tries to push it a little bit more, but the girl tells her to get lost.

After classes, the Hispanic girl, named Rita, meets up with Derek and the rest of their group on the grounds outside the school. They are in a private spot in a garden where the group usually meets. Rita tells Derek about Stephanie. "Derek, I thought you might want to know that Stephanie Drake asked me about the *Real Earth Society* today."

"Who's Stephanie Drake? You didn't tell her anything did you?"

"No, of course not, her mom is Renata Drake who is in charge of the ship computers and her dad is Paul Drake who runs the nanofactory. She's a year younger than us, but she is pretty popular in school."

"What? Is she trying to write an article for the school newspaper or something?"

"I really have no idea." Rita answers honestly.

"I need somebody to find out how she knows about us and why she is asking."

"I have a class with a friend of hers, Tessa Richards. I could try to find out from her." The offer comes from a group member by the name of Rhonda.

"Okay, but be smart. We don't want people knowing about our club just yet. Can all of you meet at the usual place Saturday morning at 10?"

Everybody nods.

* * *

At about the same time that Derek's group is breaking up, Stephanie is getting home from school. The villa where she lives is not all that far from the school. When she walks through the door she sees her little brother sitting in the living room by himself watching old Earth animal videos. Her dad comes out of the bathroom looking like he has just spruced up a little.

Paul Drake addresses his daughter, "Steph, I'm glad you're home. Your mom sent a message that she will be late again at the computer center and I have to meet with some people from work. I need you to watch Roger. There's plenty of food in the kitchen and you know how to use the *mealmaker*. "

"Whatever, dad."

"Okay, give me a hug and I'll be home by nine."

Stephanie was used to this ritual. A lot of nights their dad would stay home with them and a couple of nights a week their mom would come home for dinner, but many nights were like this one.

Paul leaves and Stephanie goes and sits by Roger. Roger is six years old and looks like a tiny version of his dad. There are nine years separating the two siblings, which is close to the Gaian protocol of within ten years. Stephanie interrupts the video. "Didn't you watch this one last week? With all of the choices of animal videos to watch, why watch the same one over again?"

"I like it."

Stephanie doesn't want to argue with that logic, so she goes to the kitchen to get dinner ready. After eating, she sits in the living room with one eye on Roger and gets out her comm-goggles. She finds a friend that isn't eating dinner or busy some other way and chats for a while. She then logs into the school computer and does a little homework. After a while, Stephanie gets Roger off to bed. When her mom and dad still aren't home at nine o'clock, she decides to get an early night herself.

* * *

The next day, Rhonda from Derek's group, is in second session class with Tessa. It's a Chemistry lab. Rhonda strikes up a conversation with an acquaintance of hers near Tessa's lab seat. During the conversation Rhonda works in, "You know Rita Sanchez. Yesterday, Stephanie Drake walked right up to her in the cafeteria and just started talking to her. Those two are about as different as two people can get. It was really weird."

Tessa takes the bait and butts in on the conversation. "It's not what you think. Stephanie was only talking to Rita to try to find out how to get into Derek Scott's little club. She's got the hots for him."

"Well isn't that interesting and who invited you in on our conversation?"

Tessa says under her breath, "Bitch."

Rhonda pretends not to hear and goes back to her lab seat having achieved her mission.

* * *

After school Rhonda, Rita, Derek and five others meet in the usual place in the school garden. Rhonda tells Derek her discovery and he ponders for a moment. "You know, we might be able to use this to our advantage. It could come in handy having the daughter of Paul and Renata Drake in our group. Leave it to me. There may be another member of the *Real Earth Society* when we meet on Saturday morning."

* * *

The next day in the hall, during a break between sessions, Derek catches Stephanie by surprise. "I hear you are interested in the *Real Earth Society*." Stephanie is speechless as she is looking the other way to get a snack from a vending machine. Derek speaks before she has a chance to say anything. "Why don't you come to our meeting Saturday morning at 10am? We meet in a game room at the Virtual Entertainment Center. Don't tell anybody though. We like to keep our club very private." Stephanie is speechless and nods as Derek walks away.

For the first time in weeks, all four members of the Drake family are sitting together at the dining table having breakfast. Renata is going in to work again today, but not until noon. There are two plates of pancakes in the middle of the table along with butter, a small pitcher of maple syrup, a bowl of blueberry topping, a bowl of whipped cream and a carafe of juice. Of course, the only part of the breakfast that hasn't been fabricated is the blueberries in the topping which are grown in the hydroponic gardens on the ship.

Roger gets his dad's attention. "Daddy, how come we don't have any animals where we live."

Paul has a tough time answering. "The Earth where we came from is a very, very big place. We are part of a group of special people that were chosen by the people of Earth to make a very important trip. What we live on is a giant spaceship that looks like the Earth on the inside, but is too small for the animals that you see in your videos."

"But daddy, why can't we have small animals?"

"When you get older you will understand, son. Animals need to eat like us and have babies. We just don't have enough resources to take care of both animals and people."

This was obviously not a good enough answer, but Roger goes back to eating his pancakes.

Renata looks to Stephanie. "What are you planning to do today?"

"Tessa and I are going over to the VEC today."

"I wish you'd do something more physical and get some exercise."

"Okay mom, why don't you and I go skiing today?"

Paul jumps on her. "Don't talk to your mother that way. If you need some time to think about having respect for your parents, we could ground you for a couple of weeks."

Stephanie tries not to let her mom and dad see her rolling her eyes. "I'm sorry mom."

There's not a lot said for the rest of the breakfast and as soon as Stephanie is done eating she races to the bathroom to freshen up. A short time later there is a knock on the door. Tessa has come to pick up Stephanie.

The Virtual Entertainment Center (VEC) is a level above the computer center which occupies the lower levels below the school. Tessa and Stephanie walk into the main entrance of the school, which is always open, and take the stairs down to the VEC.

Tessa comments to Stephanie before they part company. "Are you sure you want to do this? It bothers me that this club is so secretive."

"Lighten up Tess. It's only a club. You're the one who suggested I go for it."

"Okay, but if it gets weird quit. Don't commit to anything."

"Yes, mom."

"Oh, kill it. I'll see you here at noon."

With that Stephanie goes into the VEC. She sees a couple of people, whom she recognizes from Derek's group, in a private game room. She enters the room.

At a little after 10am, Derek walks into the room and immediately has everybody's attention. He possesses an aura of confidence that draws people in. It has been seen before many times over the ages in leaders both good and bad. He speaks to the group.

""It's good to see everybody could make it this morning. I want you all to welcome the newest member of our group, Stephanie Drake." They all look at her and make a welcoming gesture, a couple of which are not very sincere.

"I have found a game in the archives that I want you all to see." He pushes a remote control button and a rotating holographic replica of the Earth appears above the round table which is centered in the room.

"This game is called *Google Earth 2050*. It is a detailed copy of our home planet as it was in the year 2050. Now let me show you what it can do." Derek gives the command, "Google Earth, voice recognition: Derek Scott. Stop rotation." The 3D Earth image comes to a stop. Then he commands, "Clear atmosphere." All of the clouds disappear so that the land masses and bodies of water are clearly visible.

"Zoom in on Alberta, Canada." The globe rotates until Canada is pointing upward and then lowers *into* the table until all that is left is a portion of the Earth's sphere protruding from the table. The region that is Alberta is centralized.

"Zoom in on Banff." Now there is a flat image on the round table of the Banff area as seen from space.

"Altitude 4000 meters above sea level." With this command the image becomes a three dimensional hologram once again as mountains rise out of the table. The view is a relief image centered on the village of Banff, Alberta, such that the highest mountain rises about 80 centimeters above the table top.

"That little village down there is the home of more people than will ever live on this entire spaceship. I am showing you an example of what you will never see in reality." The group is mesmerized by the beauty of the mountains, valleys and lakes.

"Image, pan northwest at one kilometer per second." The scene moves up the valley past Lake Louise toward Jasper. Derek lets it run for a couple of minutes to let everybody get an idea of the grandeur of the Canadian Rockies then says, "Google Earth, reset. End voice recognition." He continues speaking to the group. "If any of you want to see more of the Earth, I have this room reserved until two o'clock. I can show you how to put your voice into the voice recognition program." He leaves the rotating planet image on for dramatic effect.

Some of what Derek says next is for Stephanie's benefit as the rest of the group have heard it several times before. "Our parents decided to leave this beautiful planet and fly off to another star just to satisfy their own egos. They just wanted to be famous; to be the first to leave our solar system. They didn't even consider us. We have no choice. We will never see the Earth. At least they have their memories. You can play these virtual games and pretend that you are on Earth, but it will never be the same actually being on the Earth. This is why we call ourselves the *Real Earth Society.* We must not tell others about our group or our parents will stop us from meeting."

"I'd like to ask each member now to tell us what you have found out this week about the planet we have been dragged away from. At least talking about Earth we can feel a little bit closer to it."

One member, by the name of Glenn, always talks about the same thing. "I found another old Warren Miller film in the data library. The one I found is video taken in a place called Jackson Hole, Wyoming. There's no hole there, but there are some really great vertical drops. The music that was being played along with the video was pretty exciting, too. It created the mood while the best skiers and snowboarders of that era did some unbelievable things."

Rhonda is pretty predictable, too. She loves the undersea virtual reality room. "I found a great program that was created using real footage taken by underwater divers at a place called Bikini Atoll. This place is a perfect example of how good the Earth is at healing its wounds. During World War II an atomic bomb test was done there, but 50 years later it had fully recovered. At the time of this filming it was full of life."

Derek smiles at Rhonda in a way that makes her blush. "Thank you Rhonda. That is a perfect example of what an amazing place our home planet is. It is fairly well accepted now that the biosphere of the Earth is one large self-regulating and self-healing entity. We are a part of this organism and there is where we belong."

As other members tell the group about what they have discovered since the previous meeting, something becomes very obvious to Stephanie. Right here is where Derek recruited his group. Most of these people have spent countless hours in the VEC. When the meeting is over they all go to play in their favorite virtual booths and rooms.

Derek approaches Stephanie. "Would you like to go to the chocolate shop with me? I'd like to talk to you about joining our club."

Stephanie is caught off guard. She's not sure what to make of Derek yet, but he can be very persuasive. And he's damn good looking! Stephanie says okay and they leave together. A couple of sets of eyes watching them walk out together have a very disapproving leer.

Derek really turns on the charm at the chocolate shop. He assists Stephanie from the electric cart and holds the door to *La Chocolaterie Suisse* open for her to enter. They pick out their favorite fudge. It's vanilla walnut for Stephanie and white cranberry for Derek. He finds a little table in the corner.

Holding the chair for Stephanie, Derek begins the conversation. "I've been noticing you at school. You seem to be very popular."

"But, I didn't think you knew I existed."

"How could I not notice you? I'm just very good at hiding it. If it was obvious, I wouldn't be so mysterious, would I?" Derek has perfected the art of saying what people want to hear. "You are by far the prettiest girl in school. I figured you probably wouldn't give me the time of day anyway. Besides, you must have a boyfriend." He knows that she doesn't.

Stephanie is pretty sure that she is not the prettiest girl in school, but she falls for his lines. "No, I don't have a boyfriend. I'm sure you have a girl friend. What about Rita? She seems pretty devoted to you."

"Are you kidding? The people in the club are all gamers. They're all just friends. I'm looking for somebody much deeper than that for a relationship. Somebody kinda like you…"

After more small talk, they finish their fudge and milk and Derek drives the electric cart back to the VEC. Stephanie sees her mom heading back into the computer center, after taking a break in the garden. She cowers a little in the cart as a natural reaction even though she's pretty sure that her mom didn't see her.

"What was that all about?"

"That was my mom walking into the building. She thinks I'm spending the afternoon with my friend, Tessa."

"What's your mom doing here on a Saturday?" Derek knows what Renata Drake does.

"She's in charge of the computer center. They have some big, important project they are working on that has to be finished in a year or two. I hardly see her anymore."

"What about your dad?"

"He's home with us most of the time in the evenings, but he never seems to be there mentally."

"You must really hate them." Derek is somewhat sincere for once as he really does feel hatred toward his own parents.

"No, not at all. Sometimes I wish they had never taken this journey though."

"So, does that mean you're joining us?"

"Sure, why not. I'd like to learn more about the Earth anyway."

"That's wonderful, Stephanie. I really would like to get to know you better."

"Me, too."

"Can I take you anywhere? I'm going to meet a friend in Little Rio." Derek lies again.

"No thanks. I'll have you let me off here. I'm meeting up with Tessa."

Derek leans over close to her. "I want you to promise me that you will keep our club a secret or my parents will never let me see you again." He leans over further and gives her an unexpected kiss and then helps her off the cart.

"Alright, I promise."

As Stephanie walks away to the school, Derek drives into the parking garage and then the tunnel that goes through to the Tropicania Living Area. He just decides to go home, where he is by himself most of the time.

When Stephanie meets Tessa in the VEC, Tessa is enthusiastically excited for her friend and has a slew of questions to ask. None of the questions are about the club though. "How did it go? What's he like, Steph."

"I feel so special when I'm with him. He treats me like I'm very important."

"Does he have a girl friend?"

"No, apparently not. He says that he's been noticing me at school."

"Well, he sure hides it well. Are you going to see him again?"

"I'm going to join his little club."

"I noticed that most of the club is gamers. That's not really like you, Steph."

"It's actually kind of interesting and fun, but I promised to keep it a secret so don't tell anybody."

"Why not? What's the big deal?"

"It seems that the group is mad at their parents for taking them away from Earth. Derek says that if his parents find out, then we won't be able to ever see each other again."

"That's weak, Steph."

"I know, but I promised."

"Okay, your secret is safe with me."

"Oh, and did I tell you? When he dropped me off he kissed me!!"

"No way!"

The next morning at 9am there is a *special* meeting of the *Real Earth Society*. The four core members of the club: Derek, Rita, Rhonda and Rhonda's boyfriend Steffan meet at a park in Little Rio.

Rita is the first to speak. "What happened with Miss Popular?'

Derek glances at Rita with fire in his eyes. "I want you all to be nice to her. We all want to get this ship turned around to take us back to Earth, but have no idea how. Stephanie may be the answer."

* * *

A Living Area and 120 degrees away, in Wicklesby, the Singh family are celebrating the 16th birthday of Rahii's sister, Chakori. The people of Wicklesby have decided to make sixteenth birthdays a community event. Friends of the family, including Barry and Mei, have helped assemble and decorate a small stage in Wicksteed Park on the edge of the village. Others have set up chairs and tables and have organized food and drink for the occasion. The bakery in Wicklesby has made a big cake with *Happy Birthday Chakori* written elegantly across the top and colorful frosting flowers decorating the edges.

People are supposed to start showing up around 11am when the Wicklesby Church gets out. Festivities are to begin at noon. Several people including Herbert and Ilsa Rauch have volunteered to provide entertainment. The Singhs have decided to attend church today and leave the preparation to others. The main service at the chapel is an attempt to find a commonality among the many beliefs represented on Gaia II. After church, the Singh family walks down the stone stairs of the old Roman Gothic inspired building in the center of town. They stroll along with many others to Wicksteed Park.

During most of the celebration, Jaswinder and Leela play host and socialize with many of the townsfolk. Chakori is the center of attention and hangs out with her friends. This leaves Rahii alone again. He sits in the grass, eats and reads an e-book. He started the book the day before. It is about a group of students in detention at high school in the 1980s. He can identify with the characters in the book, because he too feels like an outcast. He wishes that he was back on Earth in the 1980s, so he could meet kids like himself and have friends.

Chakori walks by with some of her friends and teases Rahii. "Come on Rahii. Join the party. I bet you'd be joining in if Stephanie were here."

This is horrifying to Rahii, because the last thing he wants Chakori's friends or anybody for that matter, to know is that he has a crush on Stephanie Drake. Rahii doesn't respond to Chakori and she keeps walking with her friends to where people are dancing now.

Rahii decides to go home to his computer and misses Chakori's big moment. Chakori wants to be an actress and a singer. She idolizes Dakore Maredi. For Chakori's birthday, Jaswinder has gotten Dakore to perform at the party. Halfway through the performance Dakore invites Chakori up to the stage to sing a duet with her. It's Chakori's favorite song, so she knows all of the words by heart.

* * *

As time goes on, Derek and Stephanie get closer. He has gotten her more and more brainwashed into hating her parents and wanting to return to Earth. Tessa is worried about her as she seems so much more serious now than she used to be.

When the time is right, Derek decides to make a suggestion to Stephanie. "Steph, my love, your mom controls all of the computers on the ship. Do you think there is any way we can take over the computers and make this ship go back home?"

"There's no way, Derek. I could never talk my mom into doing anything like that and I know nothing about computers."

"Still, think about it. If we could turn this ship around, I could see us as a married couple sitting in a park on real ground, looking at a real sky, watching our grandchildren play."

Stephanie is shocked by the statement, but she is caught in Derek's spell. "I'll see what I can do."

After school, Stephanie visits the computer center to see her mom. Renata is surprised to see her daughter. "Good to see you, Steph. I must say though, you don't usually come here. Is something wrong?"

"Everything's fine. I just want to learn more about what you do."

"But you've never been interested in computers."

"Derek doesn't get along with his parents at all, so I thought I'd get to know mine better."

"Well, I guess there is something good coming out of this relationship of yours after all."

"You just have to get to know Derek, mom. He's wonderful to me."

"Okay, since you're here what do you want to know?"

"I want to learn about this new computer that you are developing. I figure that, if I can get to understand it better, I will know why you have to spend so much time at work."

"I'm sorry that I'm away from home so much, sweetheart. If it wasn't so important for all of us, I wouldn't be doing this."

"How do I learn about this quanta-computer?"

"For starters, Steph, it's quantum computer. Are you sure you are really interested in this?"

"More than anything, mom. Can you teach me?"

"I'll tell you what. I'm afraid I am way too busy, but I have an idea."

Renata takes Stephanie into an adjacent room in the computer center. Rahii is sitting at a computer working away. "Rahii, have you met my daughter, Stephanie?"

Rahii is dumbstruck. He manages to form a few words. "No, but I have seen her at school."

"I'd like to ask a big favor of you. Stephanie is interested in learning about the quantum computer. Do you think you might be able to teach her a few things?"

The phrase "teach her a few things" puts an even higher level of anxiety into Rahii's already cloudy mind. He mumbles, "Okay."

"Thanks, Rahii. I owe you one." Renata looks at her daughter. "Now, listen to what Rahii has to say, Steph. He may be a year younger than you, but he knows as much about quantum computers as most of the people I work with."

If he was talking to Stephanie about anything else but computers, Rahii would be a bumbling idiot. As soon as he starts teaching her about the quantum computer, however, he is in his domain. He completely impresses her with his detailed knowledge, both about how the computer works and how to program it. She also finds out just how powerful the quantum computer will be. Other than that, every word Rahii says goes in one ear and out the other. When she has had enough, she stops him and says, "Rahii, how would you like to join my club?"

At precisely 9am on Monday, December 6th, every computer display on the entire spaceship shuts down. Every student's desk top, every monitor in the computer center, every home video display, and every comm-device simultaneously goes blank.

Cynthia Rowland is in her kitchen entering her food request list on the countertop display when it disappears.

Rahii Singh is in his 21st Century History class in the middle of his learning program. The program is explaining how, in the 2060's, many of the world's governments were forced by pressure from their civilian populations to install socialism to share food, water and health resources. His desktop shuts off.

Leela Singh is reading an e-letter from her mom in Bangalore. It was sent almost nine years ago. The ship gets and sends messages once a week on Mondays. The data is strictly text due to transmission and reception limitations. Information, as always, is carried by twisted optical lasers. It is received at Gaia II at a wavelength a little over twice that emitted due to the Doppler shift. This nine year old e-mail suddenly disappears.

Tessa Richards is getting text from her boyfriend, while in her first session class, when the display goes dark mid sentence.

On all of these and every other video display on the ship, a face appears. It looks like an alien from a science fiction series that aired on Earth in the late 21st century. Then, there is audio with text streaming across the bottom of the image.

"Please, do not be frightened. You are not in any immediate danger. I represent a civilization that has had technical capabilities for much longer than yours. We have taken over your computer systems and have learned all about your life form. This is how we can communicate to you in your language. The face you are seeing was chosen from your entertainment data bank. It is a creation called a *Kalon* from a series called *Galactic Civilizations*. It was the closest we could find to what we are."

"We coexist with several other intelligent life forms, in this region of our galaxy, and do not wish to harm you in any way. Unfortunately, you are proceeding into what you would call a quarantined zone. We cannot allow you to go any further."

"We have evaluated your fuel storage and estimate that you have enough to change direction once you have decelerated your ship. It is highly recommended that you return to your home star to refuel and then you can continue on in any other direction."

"We want to make it clear to you that this is not an option. You have one day to make the decision and start the deceleration. If you do not, we will start to shut down your life support systems."

"Do not attempt to break the connection between the new computer, which we control, and your main computer system or our program of life support shutdown will continue automatically. Even if you do manage to regain full control of your computer systems we have other ways of stopping you. We just chose this option in order to learn about you and communicate to you."

"To show you the extent of our control, we are now shutting off an artificial sun in one of your habitats. We are not allowing any communication using your computer system, but you will have all other basic functions and power for now. You will all meet at 9am tomorrow morning in your theater at which time we will give you final instructions. Please prepare to decelerate."

The best computer people on the ship try to no avail to get communications back on line and the message repeats five minutes later.

Barry Donaldson is teaching a tai chi class at the primary school when the alien message is broadcast. There has been no need for his security expertise or physical talents since he has been on the ship, so Barry has been trying his hand at teaching. The benefits of confidence and self control learned in martial arts training go far beyond physical self defense.

Watching the broadcast, Barry knows from experience that something like this can cause panic among even the most rational group of people. He instructs all of his students to go home and stay there for now. When Barry sees the school principal, Frank Dobrowski, in the hall, he finds out that all of the other instructors are doing the same. Something else Barry learned from his Homeland Security days is that when a large group is confronted with an external threat, there is a need for a strong leader. He says to himself, "Well Barry, I guess it's about time you earn your ticket for this trip."

Barry decides to get an electric cart and go to visit the villages. He rides through Little Rio, Hanalei Village and Sonora stopping at key locations to get the word out that they are having a meeting of the adults at 7pm in the theater tonight. Just the fact that there is some action being taken is helpful to the shocked populous. He drives through the connector tunnel at the Zhang Health and Sciences Center transition building and does the same in Wicklesby, Chianti Villas and Alpenhausen. It feels strange driving though Alpenhausen, because it is just past noon and it is dark except for ambient light coming from the neighboring living areas. Street lights, shop fronts and homes are lit up there like they would be seven hours from now. When he is pretty sure that everybody is going to find out about the meeting, Barry decides to pay Renata Drake a visit.

The computer center is in mayhem. All of Renata's best people are trying to figure out how this has happened. Their computers are part of a closed system and no technology known to man could take control of this system from outside the ship. Of course, they all know that if an alien species has been technological for even a few thousand years longer than us, that their capabilities would seem like magic.

Barry asks Renata for her assessment of the situation. Renata is baffled. "It's almost as if our friends have programmed the prototype quantum computer to control the entire computer system. As far as we can tell, there is no reason not to believe what they have said about breaking the connection between the QC and the molecular computer system. Also, for what it's worth, trying to break the encryption to access and deprogram the quantum computer would take another one just like it or better."

"Do you have any notion of how they could program the quantum computer from outside the ship?"

"Impossible. Of course, what we are doing now was considered impossible a century or two ago."

"Nevertheless, we haven't broken any of the laws of physics to do what we are doing. Can you imagine a way beyond our technology that this could be done?"

"It seems to me that there would have to be some sort of information transfer through the hull of the ship that would somehow search our ship to find and program the quantum computer. The information itself would have to have intelligence!"

"Something just doesn't seem right. For a moment, let's consider that maybe there are no aliens. Could any of your people have done this?"

"All of my team and I have been working together night and day for years now. I know them better than my own family. There's not one of them who would have done this."

"Yes, but for argument sake, could they?"

"I suppose that I have a few people who have been working with the QC enough to have pulled this off."

"Thanks, Renata. I have to ask you to watch your people closely for the next 24 hours and let me know if any of them behave unusually."

Barry leaves the Computer Center and decides to go and pay a visit to Leela Singh. He takes the shuttle to Zhang Health and Sciences Center.

This is actually the first time he has visited the Health Center in at least a year and he has never been to Leela's office. There are very few people in the building due to what had transpired that morning. When he finds Leela's office and she is actually in it, he is a little surprised.

Barry walks in and admires the room. It is designed for relaxation. Soft colors, tropical plants, rock fountains, art and accent lighting create a very soothing effect. He approaches Leela and speaks her name startling her a little.

"Leela, can I speak with you for a moment."

"Sure, Barry. Won't you have a seat? Can I make you some tea?"

"No, thank you. I see you decided to come to work today, even after that message this morning."

"I figured that if I was going to be of any help, then here was as good as anywhere."

"Well, I'm glad you did. I need to ask you if you are seeing any patients that may be experiencing depression from being away from the Earth."

"You mean that you think one of us may be behind this?"

"I'm just trying to eliminate the possibility before we give up and go back, making fifty years of our lives nothing but a waste of time."

"There have been some cases of depression, along with other symptoms, that could be attributed to an *island fever syndrome*. Honestly though, professionally speaking, I don't think that any of them would have done this. I should maintain confidentiality unless you have a good reason to suspect one of them."

"Why do you say that you don't think that any of them would have done this?"

"You said it yourself, Barry. If we turn around and go back, the decelerating time and then the reversal of the journey won't get us back to Earth until almost 2160. Most of the adults on this ship will be in their seventies. Plus, they all volunteered for this mission and thus have a strong motivation for seeing it completed. The depression, that some are feeling, is just something that they want to work through. I really can't see any of them wanting to sabotage our mission."

"Thank you, Leela. No matter how this turns out, Mei and I would like to have you and Jaswinder over to the condo for dinner soon. The kids could keep each other company."

With that, Barry feels like he has hit a dead end. All there is to do now is to plan what he is going to tell everybody at the theater tonight.

* * *

As the students leave the school, they are quieter than usual and seem to be in a type of trance. This has been seen before when schools have been let out due to the assassination of a leader or some other national crisis. The reaction seems to be a mixture of shock and fear.

There are a few students who don't show the fear like the others do. Eight of them meet in their usual location in the school gardens. Once out of sight and sure they are not being watched, the group is able to quietly express its elation.

Rahii is the hero of the day. The other seven members of the group congratulate him and pat him on the back. Derek is impressed. "Unbelievable. You are a genius, Rahii. The generation one people will never suspect a thing."

Stephanie, whom has been leading Rahii on and keeping her relationship with Derek a secret, gives Rahii a kiss for the first time. "I'm so proud of you. You did it!"

Derek speaks to everybody. "Okay, now I want all of you to go home and be just like every other person in this school. This will be the last meeting of the *Real Earth Society.* If all goes well we will watch our grandchildren grow up back on Earth."

They all break up and go home as Derek has asked, but Derek stays behind in the garden. When she is sure they've all gone, Rita comes out from behind a hedge in the garden. She walks over to Derek and they smile at each other. Then Rita and Derek have the most passionate kiss that either has ever experienced. The feeling of triumph and the anticipation, which has built up from having to keep their secret, multiplies the strong attraction they have for each other. Both Rita and Derek have that moment that everybody dreams of, but many go through an entire lifetime without experiencing.

Derek holds Rita and speaks to her. "We still have to play this cool. Over the next few months I'll break it off with Stephanie and then we can be together."

"Does it have to be that long? I hate every minute you spend with that bitch."

"I'm afraid so, my love. We must make sure that she doesn't tell anybody what we have done."

"And what about Rahii? She will have to keep pretending with him. If he finds out he's been tricked he could ruin everything."

"I need to talk to you about that, Rita. Rahii is the only one on this ship that can stop this program and return control of the computers to the parents. If he has second thoughts, we are screwed. We need to arrange for Rahii to have an accident."

"Derek! What are you suggesting?!"

"We have to make sure he can't tell anybody anything ever again. It's the only way. Until this ship is fully decelerated seven years from now and the excess fusion fuel is used to reverse course, they could still end this and re-accelerate."

"There's got to be another way."

"I've thought this all the way through. It's the only choice."

"How do you think we can do this? Surely somebody will find out that we are responsible and it will have been all for nothing."

"I have a plan. Tonight, after they have eaten dinner, I will go to Rahii's bedroom window. He always hangs out in there with his beloved computer and will for sure tonight with everything that's going down. I will tell him to make up a good excuse to leave the auditorium tomorrow morning. He can say he has to go to the bathroom or something. I'll tell him that there's an emergency meeting in the university cafeteria at quarter till nine. I'll say there is a problem that we haven't thought of that needs to be addressed."

Derek looks intently at Rita. "I'm going to need your help. We'll meet with Rahii in the cafeteria. Nobody will be there since the university isn't in full operation yet and everybody is supposed to be in the theater. You are going to have to get his attention and I will club him over the head. That is all you need to know. You can go back to the theater then and I will take care of everything else."

"I'm scared Derek."

"Rita, you are in this as deep as I am. We have to do this. Thirty years from now when we are back on the Earth with our children, this will all seem like a distant memory."

"Okay, Derek."

They kiss again, without any of the passion this time, and leave for their homes.

The dinner table is very quiet at the Singh's house that night. Jaswinder, Leela, Chakori and Rahii are all eating a rice curry dish with fresh vegetables courtesy of the gardens of Kayla Novak. Leela is the first to say something. "No matter what happens, we will all be together. Family is the most important thing. Everything else in life is just an adventure."

Jaswinder can't help himself. "But fifty years of our lives all for nothing! I studied astrobiology in Bangalore, and then in West Antarctica, never imagining that I may get to see extraterrestrial life forms first hand. When this opportunity arose I felt that I was born to do this. Now by the time we decelerate and return to Earth I will be an eighty year old man. Even if we replenish our fusion fuel and go to a different star, I doubt that I will live to see my dream become a reality."

The stress shows on Rahii's face and he tells his parents that he isn't very hungry and would like to go to his room. His mom says she understands and tells him to go ahead if that's what he wants to do. As he goes to his room, he thinks to himself, "Mom, if only you really understood." When he gets to his room he lays on his bed. Rahii won't be turning on the computer tonight. He has a lot of thinking to do.

At 7pm at least one member of every household is in the Webber Theater with the exception of a few that are still working in the Computer Center and the Catom Control Center preparing for morph to deceleration. The children of Gaia II are between the ages of 5 and 16 and thus under normal circumstances many could be left home alone, but tonight they need a parent to be with them.

Barry has asked his wife Mei, Greta Mueller, Renata Drake, and Jacques Laplace to join him on stage to talk to the group. He has to speak loudly to get the attention of the understandably noisy crowd. "Could I ask everybody to take a seat, please?" They all settle in to seats in the front rows. "We will tell you everything that we know and then there will be a discussion followed by a vote as to what we are going to do."

One man in the crowd shouts out. "What is there to talk about? If we don't turn around they will kill us all."

Barry fields the outburst. "I'm sure that George speaks for a lot of you. I must tell you all that I'm not fully convinced that these aliens really exist."

Another member of the audience speaks up. "Do you have any evidence to support that, Barry?"

"I'm afraid not. There hasn't been enough time. I have been told by Renata, whom I have asked to join me on the stage, that it is possible that someone on the ship may have been able to program the quantum computer to do this."

George speaks out again. "Who? It would have to be one of the computer center team if that is true."

Barry answers. "My apologies to anybody in this audience on Renata's team, but I have asked her to watch her people all day to see if anybody acts in the least bit suspicious."

"And??"

"I'll let Renata answer that one."

"Like I told Barry, I have spent more time with these people over the last few years than I have with my own family. They were all just as shocked about this as I was. I'll vouch for every single one of them."

Kayla Novac speaks up. "Renata, I know you've had your team trying to figure out what these aliens or whomever have done to our computer. Have they found out anything?"

"It seems that they have put an encrypted program into our prototype quantum computer. This computer is linked to our main system by an interface just completed recently. Theoretically, the quantum computer could control any cyberfunction of the molecular system. It is also possible that removing the interface or breaking the connection could send a final command to shut down systems controlled by computer."

"Which is everything!!", a frightened audience member exclaims.

"What about breaking the encryption to deprogram the QC?"

"Not going to happen. It would take another quantum computer or several decades using our current system."

George butts in loudly. "You people don't get it. If we thwart their computer attack, these aliens will just blow us into a zillion pieces. They are obviously far more advanced than we are."

A woman, who has been taking this all in makes a contribution. "Even if we start deceleration, we still have seven years before we have to use our fusion fuel. We can reaccelerate if we find out that the aliens don't exist."

Greta Mueller joins the discussion. "I need to remind everybody that our Deuterium and Helium3 reserves are limited. As the alien message said, we have just enough to do a reversal and get back to Earth. Whenever we are traveling at less than about 13 percent of the speed of light we can no longer rely on the interstellar hydrogen for our fusion. It's a onetime shot, folks. If something goes wrong, it's over."

An audience member asks Mei and Jacques, "Can we be ready to start deceleration in a day?"

Jacques answers, "All of the procedures are in place. We would be doing this anyway in about 19 years."

The rest of the question and answer period with the panel essentially just allows the Gaians to air concerns. When there are no more questions, Barry asks for a vote.

Only three people vote against complying with the alien demands. One is Barry. The others are Greta Mueller and Kayla Novac.

"We'll see you and your families all here at 9am tomorrow morning. Jacques and Mei will be preparing for deceleration."

Barry spends the rest of the evening talking with the members of Renata's team and anybody with computer experience, such as Jaswinder. He knows he is missing something, but is running out of time. Fully frustrated, he finally decides to try to get a few hours sleep to be ready for a very eventful day to come.

That night there is a knock on Rahii's window.

Tuesday December 7, 2128
Gaia II Theater

It's about twenty minutes till 9am on Gaia II. Almost every adult and child is in the theater. Renata and a couple of her best people are still in the computer center after being there all night. Similarly, Mei, Greta and their teams are in Ship Control on the other side of Europia near the fusion reactor. Also, Jacques Laplace is making final preparations to begin landscape morphing in the Catom Center below the university.

Rahii is with his mom and dad and sister looking like he has the weight of a planet on his shoulders. He notices it is 8:40 and tells his mom that he has to go to the restroom. Leela tells him to hurry since everybody needs to be seated in the theater at nine.

At 9am, to the second, the same alien face from the previous day appears on the monitors in the theater.

"People of Sol. We are instructing you now to begin your deceleration in one hour. As we have told you, failure to do so will initiate the shutdown of your life support systems beginning with power to your living areas. If at any time, during your deceleration, you disengage your propulsion system, for any reason, the shutdown will commence. We remind you again that this is not the only way we have to stop you. We advise that you make sure that all of your people are in a safe location to be ready for a 10am start of the decelerating process. Once you are at full deceleration, we will turn back on the light above the living area you call Alpenhausen and restore your communications."

Rahii is still not back from the bathroom and an angry Jaswinder goes to find him.

* * *

Fifteen minutes earlier, Rahii walks down the hall from the theater lobby into the university. He takes a flight of stairs up two levels and enters a door to the university cafeteria.

Derek and Rita are sitting at a table with an empty chair in between them. Rahii is confused, but walks over to the table and asks, "Where is everybody else?"

Derek looks at Rita as if to say he'll do all the talking. "We don't need to talk to them. Come over and have a seat and we'll let you know what this is all about. It should only take a few minutes."

As they had planned, when Rahii is seated, Rita turns on the table computer display in front of her and logs into the ship's main screen for access to information about the life support systems. She looks at Rahii seeing a very frightened, innocent fourteen year old boy. As Derek has told her she asks for Rahii to show her the order in which the life support systems will shut down if their demands aren't met.

Meanwhile, Derek pulls out a heavy metal mallet, which he has somehow acquired, from under the table. Rahii is just about to confess to Rita that his program doesn't go any further than turning off the power on the ship when Derek raises the mallet behind him. As Derek comes down with the fatal blow, something snaps in Rita. She jumps up and shouts, "Rahii!!" and tries to deflect the mallet. It glances off the intended target. Rahii falls to the ground unconscious and Derek starts to go after Rita.

Rita is much stronger and more capable than Rahii though. Derek goes after her with the mallet and she body slams him into the next table over. He hits her and she tries to knee him in the groin, but Derek is able to maneuver away. The struggle goes back and forth with neither gaining a permanent advantage, while Rahii remains unconscious on the floor. After what seems like an eternity of fighting and name calling, the fight works its way into the kitchen. Derek grabs a sharp kitchen knife and comes at Rita. She decides that it's time to escape and try to get help. Rita breaks for the dining area with Derek close behind.

When he is almost on top of her, Rita throws a chair in his way and makes it out the door. Derek turns his attention to Rahii.

Rita runs toward the stairs screaming for help. Barry and Jaswinder meet her half way up the stairs and Rita says, "Cafeteria!"

* * *

A few minutes earlier, when Jaswinder had come back into the theater with the realization that Rahii was missing, the first thing he did was tell Barry. It was as if somebody had flicked a switch in Barry's mind. It was something Leela had said yesterday, "None of the *adult* members of the crew had motivation to pull this stunt."

Barry yells at Renata. "Renata, how well does Rahii know the quantum computer!"

Renata answers the question with the reply, "Oh, shit!!"

Barry yells again at the top of his lungs, "Has anybody seen Rahii, a fourteen year old Indian boy, leaving the theater?"

One person answers. "I think I saw him walking toward the hallway to the university."

Barry and Jaswinder are out of the theater as fast as their legs can carry them. Running down the hallway they hear Rita's screams. They both pass her on the stairs where she says, "Cafeteria!"

Hoping it's not too late they burst through the door to the cafeteria with Barry in the lead. There's nobody in the dining area and they hear the noise of a familiar machine coming from the kitchen. Crossing the dining room so fast it seems he doesn't touch the ground, Barry bursts into the kitchen. In the kitchen, Derek is standing over an unconscious Rahii with a raised cleaver. Seeing Barry, he charges at him with the cleaver instead. With an instinctual evasive action that has come from years of training and experience, Barry dodges the cleaver, disarms Derek and throws him to the ground all in one fluid motion. Jaswinder is in awe and rushes to Rahii.

Paul Drake is the next one to come into the cafeteria, always wanting to be where the action is. As he cautiously enters the kitchen, Paul sees Barry on top of Derek and Jaswinder with Rahii and exclaims, "What the hell is going on here?!"

Jaswinder is out of breath and tending to Rahii but says, "He tried to kill my boy!!"

Barry is restraining Derek, but the boy's adrenaline rush is making him hard to handle. "Paul, try to find something we can use to restrain him."

Paul searches the kitchen and comes up with some pull straps used to seal bags of vegetables that are transported from the gardens. "Will these do?"

"Perfect." Barry uses the straps to keep Derek's arms behind his back. "There. He may complain about these hurting him, but frankly I don't care and there's no way he's getting cut free."

Barry makes another request of Paul. "Do you think you can take care of this while we take care of Rahii and try to get our ship back to normal?"

"My pleasure."

Jaswinder is holding Rahii in his arms when Barry comes over. "He's alive, but he's out cold. We need Genevieve."

"Stay here, I'll get her." Barry runs back to the theater. He is genuinely concerned for the boy, but he also realizes that the secret of stopping the quantum computer program lies unconscious with Rahii.

When Genevieve comes back with Barry, she has her hand-held diagnostic device that she carries everywhere with her. A scan of Rahii's head and the look on her face scares Jaswinder. "He's going to live, but it's not good. There is a crack in his skull and there's pressure to the brain. I can't tell if there is going to be permanent damage or not. He may be in a coma for a while. I've got to get him back to the Health Center.

Genevieve, Jaswinder and Barry carefully take Rahii out of the cafeteria. Paul is in the hall strongly holding Derek. Paul asks as they are going by. "Barry. Was that noise in the kitchen what I think it was?"

"Yeah, that was the food disposal recycling unit." Paul cinches the straps even tighter and Derek cries in pain as Paul takes him away.

As the three adults carry Rahii to the theater elevator, they are met by concerned people in the lobby. Leela is the first to meet them. "My boy! My boy! What has happened?!"

Jaswinder tries to console Leela. "He is unconscious, but alive. We are taking him to the Health Center."

Chakori sees her brother's bleeding head. "Oh my God!"

Stephanie is in a corner of the lobby crying her eyes out.

Barry sees Ali Zamani. "Ali. There are no aliens, but we still may have to do this if we can't stop the computer program. Could you tell everybody and keep them in the theater to prepare for deceleration?"

Ali goes back into the theater and gets the crowd's attention, something he is very good at.

Jaswinder tells Leela to stay with Chakori as they get into the elevator. At the parking level a shuttle is ready and they board to take the two kilometer trip to the Zhang Health and Sciences Center. Genevieve does everything she can to take care of Rahii as the shuttle seems to go maddeningly slow.

After Ali addresses the crowd, there is still a lot of confusion. *If there are no aliens, why are we still preparing to start deceleration? Why was an unconscious boy being rushed to the elevator?* Ali keeps control of the group, but there is a terrible feeling of helplessness.

Renata finds her daughter crying in a corner. "It's all my fault mom! I didn't know he was going to hurt Rahii!! It's all my fault!"

Renata is shocked and shakes her daughter a little to try to snap her out of it. "What are you talking about?"

"I made Rahii create the aliens so Derek and I could go back to Earth and have grandchildren." She is so upset that she doesn't seem to be making any sense.

Renata realizes that the hope of stopping the computer lies with Rahii, his father, Genevieve and Barry. There is nothing she can do, so she embraces her daughter. "I forgive you. I promise to be there for you from now on, no matter what." She takes Stephanie back into the theater to wait with everybody else.

Barry and Jaswinder watch patiently as Genevieve tends to Rahii in a medical room. She is monitoring all of his vital signs externally and injects some specially programmed nanobots into his bloodstream to work on brain repair. After about twenty minutes, she tells them, "He's stable, but only time will tell."

After a while, it becomes apparent that Rahii isn't going to come around in time to help them. Barry asks Jaswinder,

"Jaswinder, I need your help. Is there anything that Rahii might put a very special value on or something or someone that he is always talking about?"

"I don't know. He loves computers and he is obsessed by the 1980s decade. His bedroom is full of mementos from that time period. Why?"

"Ever since computers were invented, programmers have been putting *backdoors* into their programs so they could access them quickly. I would bet that Rahii would have done the same."

"But, it could be a lot of things."

"Would you go with me to look at his bedroom? Rahii should be okay now with Genevieve here to watch him."

"What if he wakes up?"

"This shouldn't take long and Genevieve doesn't think he will for quite some time. It's only twenty minutes until morphing starts. If we grab a cart, we should be back in time."

Jaswinder reluctantly agrees because he knows what is at stake. They go quickly down to the parking garage and grab an electric cart. Driving off to Wicklesby as fast as the cart will go, Barry wonders if they really will make it back in time and if so, then what?

In a short time, they are at the Singh's home and go straight to Rahii's bedroom. Barry asks Jaswinder to think hard. "You know your son better than anyone. What does he treasure most?"

Jaswinder looks around the room for a second. "He really takes great care of that guitar replica standing up by his closet. He is constantly polishing it."

Barry thinks, "Guitar? No, that wouldn't be it. Think Barry. Why does he like the guitar so much?" Then he sees it and asks Jaswinder. "Who is the musician in that poster?"

"I have no idea. Why?"

"Look at the guitar in his hands."

"It's the same!"

"This is a long shot, but I think it's the best we've got. I need to borrow that poster."

"Sure." Time is running out so they speed back to the Health Center. As they arrive, Jaswinder looks at the time. "Not even close. We have three minutes to spare."

The two friends hurry back up to the room Rahii is in to see how he is doing. Genevieve is in a chair keeping an eye on Rahii's vital systems monitor just as when they had left. Then, they feel a little rumbling. "It's started."

Barry looks at Jaswinder and words need not be said. Jaswinder tells Barry, "Go."

On the way out Barry says under his breath, "Why the communications, Rahii? For God's sake, why the communications?" Before leaving the building, he logs into a desk computer monitor and commands, "Google pictures, famous guitarists of the 1980s." An array of photo images comes up and Barry quickly finds the one in the poster with a name underneath. "Oh yeah, I've heard of him."

As he gets on the shuttle, Barry feels the deceleration, but it is still pretty feeble, as it was seventeen years ago. Today, however, there will be no celebrations or concerts or football games. A long five minutes later the shuttle pulls into the parking garage below the theater and Barry heads for the elevator.

As he comes through the entrance, he scans the room for Renata Drake and finds her in a seat beside her daughter and son, Roger. "Renata, I have a couple of *backdoors* I'd like to try."

Renata makes a little joke as she remembers an old classic movie. "Let me guess. Is one of them Joshua?" She quickly gets serious and asks Barry. "Do you really think Rahii used a backdoor and you know what it is."

"Maybe, it's worth a try."

Renata sees one of her team members and calls him over. "Barry, this is Gordon Chang. He's my best QC man. I need to stay here with my daughter and son, but he can try your idea."

"Gordon, do you think your family would mind if you went to the computer center with Barry?"

"Why? What's up?"

"Barry thinks he might know Rahii's backdoor."

Gordon immediately understands the importance. "I'll let them know. Meet you at the elevator."

On the way, in the shuttle, Gordon asks Barry how he discovered the backdoor. Barry tells him about how he went with Jaswinder to Rahii's bedroom. Gordon shakes his head, "Man, that's pretty weak."

"It's the best I could come up with."

"I'll try anything, but you know that most likely it's not going to work."

It's about 10:15 when Gordon is sitting at the programming station for the quantum computer. He is ready to try a backdoor. Barry is looking over his shoulder. "Okay. Try Van Halen." Gordon inputs the appropriate commands. It doesn't work. "Maybe Eddie or Eddie Van Halen." Again Gordon tries and nothing happens.

"Barry, it was a nice try, but I think we're going to have to wait for Rahii to wake up."

"I was so sure. Try a couple more things. How about *vanhalen* with no capitals and no space?"

Gordon gives it another try, not expecting much, and a big grin appears on his face, "We're in!"

"How long before you can disable control over power, communications and other life support systems?"

"Stopping the program from doing something should be easy. Undoing what has already been done will take longer, maybe an hour or so."

"So, still no communications. I can't tell Greta, Mei and Jacques to stop deceleration and morphing."

"What are you going to do?"

"Keep working, Gordon. I'm going to tell Mei and Greta in person. Once we stop deceleration, morphing will automatically stop."

"It's too dangerous, Barry."

"I've just got to go one kilometer from here to the Ship Control Center. I should be able to get out a second level window from the school then find a way to get to the entrance at the other side."

"You're crazy, but do what you've got to do."

By the time Barry gets to a second level window looking out into the Europia Living Area, the time is almost 11am. The area has been morphing for about an hour of the twelve hour process. After twelve hours, the ground level will be 50 meters higher at the school and 50 meters lower at the other side of Europia, where Ship Control is located. At this time it is a little over four meters higher at the school than during constant velocity. Barry climbs out a second level window, closes it behind him, and drops into a sea of landscape catoms.

He sees a very strange sight in front of him. In many ways the Chianti Villa area looks the same as always, but there is fluidity in every major structure. Occasionally, there is a noise caused by catoms making a large shift after tensions have built up. This is similar to the process that happens causing earthquakes, but on a much smaller scale.

As Barry makes his way across the top of the catoms, a foot slips into the ground and then is just as quickly pushed back up as the catom *building blocks* try to get back together where they belong. It is one of the strangest sensations that he has ever felt. The best way to describe it is like quicksand then anti-quicksand. Luckily, since he is in the Chianti Villas region, he doesn't have to go near any buildings to get where he is going. However, the landscape is very hilly by design and he has a particularly hard time getting through a vineyard. The grape vines are not made of catoms so they tend to shift in his direction.

Barry stops at a supply building next to one of the villas. He knows he is going to have to get up a wall at the far side so decides to look for a ladder. He figures that if it takes him a half hour to cross the terrain then he will need to scale six or seven meters to get to the entrance to the building housing Ship Control. The best he can find is a four meter a-frame ladder. While he is grabbing for the ladder a rake falls off its hanging storage and narrowly misses hitting Barry on the side of the head. The storage building does a little jerky shift and he decides he better get out of there fast. He doesn't think that the ladder is going to be enough, but can't find anything better and hopes he can figure something out when he gets there.

The trip is even slower going carrying the ladder. About three quarters of the way across, Barry has another obstacle. One of the irrigation canals through a vineyard has flooded. At one point he actually lays the ladder flat to get across a ditch.

Finally, Barry makes it to the far wall. Making his way along the wall he sees an entrance above him. As he feared, the four meter ladder is not enough to get him to the door and there is nothing to grab onto to scale the rest of the way. He decides to try to make it to another villa about a tenth of a kilometer north along the wall, to find something longer. As he walks away dejected at the thought of another trek through catoms, he hears a familiar voice calling out to him. "Hey, where are you going?"

Barry turns around and sees his wife Mei standing at the door she has just opened.

"How did you know?"

"We actually have a viewing window looking out over the Chianti Villas from Ship Control. I couldn't resist my natural curiosity to watch the catom shift. I couldn't believe my eyes when I saw some crazy guy trying to carry a ladder through a vineyard during a morph. Let me try to find something I can use for rope. I'll be right back."

"Wait, Mei! Stop the deceleration! There are no aliens and we're disabling the program."

"Damn, Barry! What happened?"

"I'll tell you about it later. Can you stop this?" As he calls out to her, a foot slips into the catoms again.

"Can you ride out the return to constant velocity? We have to do it slowly because of the catom shifting process."

"Yes, go. I'll be fine."

Mei heads back up the elevator to Ship Control about 800 meters away and gives the command. "Reverse deceleration process. Return at same rate to constant velocity."

Barry is impatient, so when ground level is high enough, about a half hour later, he uses the ladder to get up to the door Mei has opened and takes the elevator to Ship Control. When he gets there she gives him a hug and they kiss. "You have some explaining to do, bud."

At about fifteen minutes before reaching constant velocity, Gordon Chang gets the communications back and makes a call over to Barry's comm-device. "Hey Mr. Donaldson, did you have a nice swim."

"Very funny, would you call Ali for me? Tell him to let everybody in the theater know that constant v is in about fifteen minutes and then, when Jacques gives the okay, we can go home."

"What about Jacques? Shouldn't I call him?"

"I'll call him. He knows that we've reversed the deceleration process, because the catom shift is closely tied with the deceleration. He could tell you himself that we're fifteen minutes out. I'm sure he's going to want an explanation though."

Gordon Chang decides to go back to the theater after calling to be with his family. He walks in to a standing ovation. Renata and Paul are the first to meet him. Gordon is surprised to see Paul. "I thought you were watching the person that caused all of this trouble."

"I took him down to my nanofactory and made a temporary jail cell for him. His parents were notified and they didn't really seem surprised. He hasn't talked to them in years. It's pretty sad."

Renata echoes the sentiment. "It appears that the age of innocence for Gaia II is over. Let's go home. Jacques has already said its okay." Paul, Renata, Stephanie and Roger leave the theater together and catch the shuttle to the school for a short walk home. It's the closest that the four of them have been in years.

Announcements are made that there is no school for the rest of the day and that the next morning there will be a special assembly for all students in the gym.

Wednesday morning, at 8:30am, Barry, Paul, Leela, Leilani and the school principal, Frank Dobrowski are on a stage on the gym floor as the students settle.

The principal gets the student's attention and starts the assembly. "What has happened over the last two days has been a tragedy for all of us. A young boy was almost killed and another boy is awaiting our first criminal trial since we have left Earth. There will be a serious debate about his fate. Others involved will also be evaluated and the best course of action taken. That being said, we understand why this has happened. All of us are on the most important mission in the history of mankind and we don't plan on turning back, but we will make every attempt to get you all involved. Also, we will take seriously any suggestions that will make your lives more interesting and enjoyable. The four adults behind me have volunteered to be a committee for this purpose. They will all have offices in this school and will be here for you."

"Mr. Donaldson, would you like to address the students?"

"Thank you, Mr. Dobrowski. Starting today, we are expanding our total openness policy at the school. Every Tuesday and Thursday from 8 to 10 in the morning will be Earth Awareness Session. I will be coordinating instructors, from a range of disciplines, to come and answer questions, give presentations, show movies or whatever they come up with to help you all learn about our home planet."

"During this time also, Leilani Matogawa will be working with you to invent ways to be more active. I'm not referring to virtual reality games, but things we can do to make the best use of the home we have here on Gaia II. One suggestion is to create a low-g sports facility in a sky cylinder." Leilani stands up and waves to the students.

"Mr. Paul Drake, behind me, can build anything you can imagine. When the quantum computers go on-line, his capabilities will be vastly increased. You are the future of Gaia II. We want to make this place yours."

"The other member of this committee is the lovely Mrs. Leela Singh. She will be our new school counselor. Mrs. Singh is opening a second office here and will be there before school from 7 to 8am and after school from 5 to 6pm, as well as Saturday mornings from 8am to 10am. Any student can walk in and talk to her during these hours without an appointment. You can get her professional advice about any concerns you have no matter what they are. The meetings will be private and confidential."

"Now, we would like to try to answer your questions. It can be about the events that have just transpired or anything you like, that you want to share with everybody."

There are a few questions from the students. One asks about Rahii. Another asks about whether laws and penalties on Gaia II are the same as back on Earth. For the most part, however, when people are put on the spot, especially young people, they have a hard time formulating questions. Many concerns and questions will need to be addressed in the days to come in smaller groups.

Sunday Morning December 12, 2128
Singh Household, Wicklesby

Rahii awakens in his own bed. He thinks to himself, "I just had the weirdest dream ever." He slowly gets out of his bed. As he stands up, he has a sharp pain like a very short-lived headache and he sits back down on his bed. After a couple of minutes, he gets back up and slowly walks out of his bedroom in his pajamas. Rahii sees his mom in the kitchen and his dad and sister in the living room. Then they see him. The three drop what they are doing and rush over to him. Chakori exclaims, "Rahii!!" Leela is the first to get to him and gives him a big hug.

Rahii says, "What's this all about? I was just coming in to see what we are having for breakfast." Then he thinks to himself, "That was a dream, wasn't it?"

Roger Drake wakes up at 6am and rushes into the living room. When he gets there, he lets out a shriek. Under the Christmas tree, in a pet bed, Roger sees a very realistic looking golden brown puppy. Paul Drake walks in behind Roger. "His name is Winston. Why don't you call his name?" Paul has programmed the puppy to react to only Roger's voice.

"Winston, come here Winston." As Roger calls him, Winston gets up from the pet bed and walks over to Roger with his tail wagging and a happy look on his face. When he gets to Roger he looks at him and lets out a yap.

"Tell him to sit."

"Winston, sit."

The robotic puppy sits back on his tail and pants. Paul has done his best to make Winston look and act like a real puppy.

"Come with me Roger and I'll teach you all about Winston." Paul thinks, "I believe I will be making a lot of these."

GLIESE 250

Saturday August 11, 2153
Waioli Beach, Hanalei Village, Tropicania

A mynah bird flutters through the sky above a white foam of waves that are crashing onto the crescent shaped beach. The black bird with the bright orange beak flies up to a higher altitude and makes a wide arc toward the shore. Flapping against the light breeze, it slows itself in the air and makes a perfect landing in a nest high in a palm tree.

Under the palm tree, two people have been watching the bird in flight. It's a lazy Saturday morning on a warm day in August. The residents of Gaia II had voted ten years prior to have a greater temperature variance on the ship. The extremes in Europia are greater now and Tropicania has a considerably higher average temperature. Today on the beach at Hanalei Village the temperature is 29° C. The female under the palm is nearly seventy years old, but is still in excellent physical condition and looks about fifty. The male she is talking to, however, looks every bit of his seventy-one years.

Leilani Matogawa rolls over to face her husband after watching the bird. "Ishii, you and Roger did a nice job of imitating the random movements of a bird in flight."

"That was a perfect task for the quantum computer. Much of the actions you see in a living organism originate with random action and non-random reaction at the quantum level. Nature actually invented the quantum computer a couple of billion years before we did."

"Still, I really like some of the subtle little touches you came up with like having recharging stations in the nests."

"If you really want realism, there's something else we could do, but you probably wouldn't want to be under this tree."

"Ha! Ha! Very funny. Speaking of which, why are we under a tree anyway? Hardly any of our heat comes from the artificial sun."

"Allow an old man his memories please."

"Hey, look at Suki out there! She's up! I think she's getting the hang of it."

"You're a good teacher, Leilani."

"Any child or grandchild of mine is going to know how to surf."

"Do they have any idea what you used to be able to do on the North Shore back home?"

"They watch the videos, but may never understand the spirituality of the sport."

"You know, I've been thinking, Leilani. It seems that almost every idea or project we come up with here somehow tries to re-create something that exists or used to exist on Earth. I think that it's time we start to create our own world."

"The Low Gravity Park is pretty unique to us. We have even invented a couple of new sports to make good use of the facility."

"That's true. I bet the kids will be glad when we stop decelerating and they can lose that extra point one g."

"There's a lot more space, too, when the floor doesn't have to be at a 45° angle."

"Do you ever go up there?"

"No, I leave it to the young people. I like gravity!"

* * *

Elsewhere on the ship, astronomer Leonid Shevchenko is evaluating his latest data to prepare a report for the Arrival Committee on Monday morning. The white haired, 70 year old man looks about the same now as he did in his forties since his hair was white even then. Deep contours of his facial structure, that give him character, accentuate the concern he is feeling. Leo is thinking to himself as he looks over the new information he has to share. "What I'd give to be able to get the resolution of NGIRI*. I suppose we'll just have to be patient and wait till we get a little closer. At least I've got some good info about the satellites of 250B." He starts dictating and editing a short presentation he will be making at the meeting

*Next Generation Infrared Interferometer: Launched 2032

Monday 9am
Meeting Room 2, Zhang Health and Sciences Center
1000 AU from destination

Fourteen key members of the Gaia II crew are sitting at a large, round table in a dome shaped meeting room. A fifteenth chair is still empty. These people are all good friends and most are talking about children and grandchildren, with a few discussing their projects.

Jaswinder Singh is talking with his assistant and prodigy, Vera Greene, who is sitting to his left. She is a stocky, red-haired woman with a freckled face that she tries to hide with makeup. Vera is wearing a lab jacket since she had just been working on a terrarium project a few levels below the meeting room. At Jaswinder's request, the committee has allowed a second astrobiologist to sit in. At 38 years old, Vera is one of four second generation members of the group. The other three are Robert Tjoelker, the flight director; Henry Rowland, planetary science lead; and the youngest member Nova Szkody, who is an astronomer specializing in stellar studies.

Other members going clockwise around the table are Leonid Shevchenko, lead astronomer; Renata Drake and Gordon Chang, computer support; Jacques Laplace, Catom Center lead; Keiji Kusakabe, mining and refueling probe coordinator; Cheryl Bailey, Earth communications specialist, Inga Larsson, probe design and assembly lead; Mei Sun, quantum physicist/ QFT propulsion lead; and Greta Mueller, Energy Plant lead.

The fifteenth member of the committee finally comes walking through the door with the usual big smile on his face. Life support guru, Ali Zamani, takes his seat at the table.

Jaswinder is chairman of the Arrival Committee and so opens the meeting. Today, he is wearing an immaculate white collared shirt, that contrasts his dark hair and complexion, and wrinkle-free denim pants. He stands and addresses the group. "Welcome everybody. I'm glad to see that you could make it Ali." He grins at Ali. "These things can be pretty boring without you, my friend." He then looks at Leonid. "We will get Leo's report first, since most of our jobs depend on what he has to tell us."

Leonid takes a data chip out of his organizer and plugs it into the table. The committee members adjust the angle of their monitors and look at the data in front of them.

Leo begins. "Since our last meeting, we have been able to get IR confirmation of the three outermost known planets of 250A and what appears to be the only two planets of 250B. What's more, I think we have a moon orbiting the outer planet of 250B. If this is real, it will be our first finding that hasn't already been discovered by NGIRI."

"The data in front of you is pretty self explanatory. It gives you the masses, distances from the star and orbital elements such as eccentricity, orbital plane inclination and period. We do not have diameter, density or rotation information yet, although we do expect the planets of 250B to be tidally locked. You will see that the orbital planes of the planets of both stars are very close to the orbital plane of the stars themselves. This suggests that they were all formed in the same protoplanetary disc."

"Due to the angle of this orbital plane, we still haven't had a transit and we won't until we, ourselves, are in the plane after swinging around 250B. The computer has taken the data and made a visual image of the planets of 250A and 250B orbiting their stars, which is what you are seeing now."

"I do have some interesting information now about planets 250Bb and 250Bc. Since we are only 500 AU from the star and because it is a star of only about $1/250^{th}$ the luminosity of the primary and $1/1700^{th}$ that of the sun, we have been able to make the first visual observations of the planets. This is interesting because what we are seeing is reflected light from the star. We can combine this with the infrared data to get a better model of the planetary characteristics."

"The most interesting planet is the one closest to the star at 0.1 AU. Infrared data has already shown that there is a substantial CO_2 atmosphere that does contain water vapor. The visual data makes us believe that water may be the dominant component of the planet. This ought to keep the theoreticians busy making migration or accretion models, since a planet this size, only one-twentieth the mass of the Earth, in the habitable zone, should have lost all of its water. We can only see the side facing the sun, assuming tidal locking, but if the whole planet is uniform then the far side has a frozen ice cap that stretches from one polar cap to the other in a kind of hourglass shape. The near side has a liquid water surface. If our temperature estimates are accurate then the near side ocean may circulate enough heat to make the transition zone habitable. I can't wait to see what the probes turn up."

"The outer planet is a cold, rocky planet that appears to be a larger, colder version of Mars. It is very dry with a thin CO_2 dominated atmosphere. Unlike Mars, the atmosphere is about 20% nitrogen and 1% methane, which are probably being retained by the planet due to colder temperatures. Its moon is large enough to be spherical and may be more interesting than the planet. Once again, we will only know the truth when probes give us first hand evidence. What we have learned from the history of space exploration is to expect surprises. A full report of what we have found out is available to download at the usual address."

"From our current location, the apparent magnitude of 250A is -12.5 and 250B is -7.6. Thus, our view on the east walls shows us 250B in the center with brightness of about 16 times that of Venus at its brightest from Earth. At a viewing angle of about 12° from 250B, when looked at from the center of a Living Region, the primary star is now about the same brightness as a full moon from Earth. For more information about the stars themselves, I would like to introduce Nova Szkody to those of you who don't already know her."

Most of the members of the committee do know Nova well, but this is her first meeting so she has to say it. "Yes, I know, my mom destined me to become a stellar astrophysicist when she named me." Nova Szkody exudes a great deal of confidence for a 32 year old. She would probably already be a university professor if she were back on Earth. Her small frame and long, dark, fine hair give her a girlish first impression that disappears as soon as she begins to talk. Nova shows spectral and photometric data of the stars. She discusses composition, temperatures, sunspot cycles and other stellar parameters such as magnetic fields and solar wind. Most of this information is known already, but their observations have confirmed and improved upon existing data.

When Nova is finished with her presentation, Leonid completes his talk. He gives information such as time frames for crossing termination shock, the flyby of 250B and its planets and the arrival at 250A, where they will establish orbit around 250Ac. He also gives the status of the infrared, ultraviolet and visual telescope systems around the outer rim of the ship's scoop. Several receivers have been destroyed or disabled by impacts, but the redundancy built into the design has assured that they are still getting good data. At any rate, the repair crew will have their hands full when the ship settles into planetary orbit.

When Leo is finished, Jaswinder thanks him and asks for the probe status reports.

Inga Larsson is in charge of the probe program and so is next to speak to the group. She stays seated as usual while addressing the committee. Inga is a tall, large framed, blonde Swedish woman who is very physically intimidating. This may be why she doesn't stand. "First, I will give a recap of the probes we have decided to deploy for this mission."

"We have built three probes that we will leave behind at Gliese 250B. Each will actually be a pair of probes, an orbiter and a lander. It took our best people to be able to figure out how to decelerate these into orbit. We will be using the star for braking and have to use special magnetic field shielding to protect the equipment. This is a very risky endeavor, but we figure that it is worth a try since the scientific discovery could be revolutionary. Two of the probes will be following a trajectory to establish an orbit around 250Bb and the third will be using a couple of gravity assists to attempt an orbit of 250Bc. After what we have found out from Mr. Shevchenko, we will try to rush through an extra probe for the inner planet. If both outer planet probes survive, one will attempt to explore the moon. Otherwise, it will act as a replacement for a disabled probe. Once attaining orbit, the landers will detach from the orbiters and try to land on the planet's or moon's surface. We will be half way to 250A before we find out if the probes have succeeded or not."

"Similarly, we will release six probes for the outer planets of 250A, two each for planets b, *d* and *e*. These will be much easier to put into a stable orbit than those sent to the planets of the companion. Even if there is a malfunction, we will have a year to build replacements so redundancy is not as important. The main reason for sending two probes to each planet is that we may decide to land in two different places on the planet or possibly on a moon if we find one particularly interesting. Although delayed, we will be able to send commands to these planetary probes from Gaia II."

"There will be four mining probes launched, two reconnaissance and two diggers. These are the least complete at this time for two reasons. First, we don't know what the targets are going to be like and thus what mining method will be used. Primarily, we don't know the extent of the gravity well that we will have to deal with. The ideal situation will be finding asteroids that have what we need. The worst situation would be needing to look, without conclusive evidence, on a large moon. If we want our probes back, in this scenario, the return trip will have to be made using fuel found on the surface. On a large body, our mined substances would need to be launched from the surface. This would require an additional probe to build the launching mechanism. We are preparing for both scenarios and all of those in between. The main fuel we will be looking for is helium3, of course, but we will also be looking for other elements, including carbon and radioactive fuel for future probes."

"When our ship reaches Gliese 250Ac, we hope that it will be interesting enough to devote our full attention to the planet during our one year of orbit. The initial two probes that are sent out will survey planet surface and take some samples. We will be controlling them from the ship as they fly over the terrain of the planet. The next step will be based on what is found. Two additional landing probes have also gone into production, but we are trying to stay as flexible as possible with these."

"Finally, the probe that is most complete is the main satellite that will be left in orbit around 250Ac to collect data from all of the other probes and relay it to Earth. We are as prepared as we can possibly be, but the final decisions about which instruments will be on the launched probes will depend on information we get from our telescopes on Gaia II. We may decide to build more probes if we find other planets or change plans."

"Giving you more details about probe launches, trajectories and time tables, I'd like to turn the floor over to Bob."

Flight director Robert Tjoelker is a 38 year old man with short brown hair and an average build. He is wearing a polo shirt and jeans. Usually, Bob is a laid-back, down to earth guy that you'd want to have a beer with, but he gets very serious when it comes to business. He uses the room's holographic system to display images above the round table. He also puts his data chip into the table so that each individual screen shows estimated launch times, flight durations, orbital data and other details such as delta v maneuvers. The larger, central image first shows the 250B system along with the flyby path of Gaia II and the trajectories of the three launched probes. Then, the same is done for the outer Gliese 250A system as they traverse their way to the inner planet. Bob explains the challenges facing each probe and the importance of accurate timing. Of course, all of the information is tentative and subject to revision.

Inga Larsson then addresses the group again. "Discussing our reconnaissance and mining probes will be Keiji Kusakabe." Keiji puts his data chip into the table. Schematics of the mining probes are displayed on the monitors.

Keiji makes sure that everybody has his attention by clearing his throat. He is a shorter, round-faced Japanese man with a very deep voice. The 68 year old engineer has a son, Michio, who works closely with him and may, one day, take over the mining operations. He begins. "Even with today's technology, we can only make best guesses as to where the resources we need are hiding. The reconnaissance probes, of which you see a simplified schematic on the right side of your monitor, will be orbiting moons or smaller objects that seem likely to have what we need based on density and other factors. We have learned a lot about how to make very good guesses from all of our experiences in the solar system we came from. Once landing sites have been chosen, the initial function of the probes we call the *diggers*, on the left side of your screen, will be to take core samples. When we find what we are looking for the drills will essentially inject nanomachines, which we affectionately call the *miners* to break up the regolith so that it can be drawn up into a processor. The processor contains another group of nanomachines, that we call *sifters*, which chemically separate out the helium3, where it is diverted to pods that are transported back to Gaia II. This is obviously not as simple as it sounds."

Keiji now takes advantage of the holographic projector in the room to narrate a short holo-movie. "Asteroid mining was perfected in the mid 21st century by the two companies that we subcontracted for Gaia II, while it was in Earth orbit. We will not have all of the machinery of Planetary Resources or Deep Space Industries, but we won't need to mine the large volumes of materials that they do." The movie shows a Planetary Resources mining operation at an asteroid. "The problem right now, as Inga told you, is that we don't even know if we will have any asteroids to mine. We have to plan for a worst case scenario of having to mine moons, where it will be harder to get the pods off the surface." The movie shows a helium3 mine on the moon with a mass driver launching pods into orbit. "This will make it necessary to send out other probes with the machines for building the pod launching system." He turns the holo-movie off.

"The good news is that this star, as Nova has informed you, has almost the same elemental abundances as the sun, so we expect to find everything we need here."

Inga Larsson thanks Keiji and does her final introduction, "Another committee member at her first meeting, whom I would like to introduce, is Cheryl Bailey. Cheryl has been, and will be, managing all of our communications sent to and received from Earth, which is now about 28.4 light years away. She is the one responsible for giving us messages that were sent from our parents when they were only about ten years older than us. Her role will be greatly increased now, as she is in charge of the orbital satellite that will be collecting the data from all of the probes and relaying the information back to Earth. We hope that this satellite will be functioning perfectly long after we are gone. It would be a shame to get good science from the probes and not be able to tell anybody."

Cheryl smiles confidently. "Thanks, Inga. No pressure." Cheryl Bailey really didn't need an introduction. She is a medium height, full-figured, very energetic, brunette woman who has been involved in many of the functions on Gaia II over the last forty years. She gives a presentation giving details about the communications satellite and how it will send data to Earth via the standard twisted optical laser method.

Inga finishes. "Once the operation commences, I will be the lead for the team that will collect data and send commands while we are orbiting planet *c*. We have a lot of good people, who are all equally important, so I hope to make the best of this exciting year to come."

Jaswinder stands again. "I'm sure that the remaining members of the committee, including myself, will be thrilled when we have something to present. I want to thank all of you for letting my assistant, Vera Greene, attend our meetings. I want to welcome the new head of our Planetary Sciences Department, Henry Rowland. And, of course, without Greta, Mei, Renata, Gordon, Jacques and Ali, we would all be lost. They will all be playing huge roles in the upcoming year. At this time, I'd like to ask if anybody else has something they would like to share with the committee?"

This, as everybody knows, is Ali's cue. "Excuse me, Jaswinder. I have an issue that is really bothering me."

"Yes, Ali." Jaswinder smiles and a few others roll their eyes.

"I think that this whole 250A, 250B, 250Ac, 250Bb stuff is a whole lot of horse pucky. Since we will be discovering most of the worlds at the stars we are going to visit, I think we have the right to be the ones to give them names."

"Ali, the powers that be on Earth have already left this to our discretion. They have purposefully not named the stars or planets that have already been discovered."

"Yes, but I think we should decide now how this naming should be done. Are we submitting proposals and voting on individual names or are we choosing from entire sets of names so that they will follow a theme? This could be our legacy folks."

Keiji clears his throat again. "Oh come on, Ali! Is this really something that this committee should decide?"

"Who else?"

Nova Szkody smirks at Ali. "Ali is right and I have a suggestion. We found out mid voyage how important it is to get the younger generation involved in our mission. Why don't we have a contest in the primary school? We should know all of the major planets and moons by mid February. How about having entries naming all of them to be submitted by February 15? Then, voting on a winner will give us all something else to do in our twelve hour stay in the theater on February 20."

Jaswinder makes sure there are no other comments. "Okay, all in favor raise their hand." All hands go up. "Good enough. Cheryl, I trust that you will be adding the record from this meeting to the data packet being sent back to Earth today. Thank you everybody. Meeting adjourned."

Tuesday September 25, 2153
Sonora, Gaia II
(One week from flyby of Gliese 250B)

Ali Zamani and Kayla Novak are taking their daily evening walk through the desert terrain of Sonora. The path winds through small ravines and over low hills past catom joshua trees and cactuses, surrounded by live desert shrubs and grasses. They usually walk at dusk to take in the random computer generated sunset image, but tonight they are strolling later in the evening. The reason is that there are now two stars that dominate the east wall of the habitat.

The designers of the living areas of Gaia II, Disney International, decided that images would be projected to cover the east wall and west wall of each habitat. Each of the three regions of both areas was given its own two displays. At 900 meters high and 1820 meters across at the base of each wall, these twelve video screens were the largest ever made.

In the evening, images are generated from actual wide-view cameras on the exterior of the spaceship. Cameras on the outer rim of the scoop constantly gather light from the view ahead of Gaia II and similar ones at the rear exhaust cylinder capture the view looking back. This visual information is processed by computer and projected onto the walls. These *screens* re-emit light at the desired wavelength, rather than reflect, for better clarity. The goal is that a person in the center of a Living Region should be able to look at the east wall or west wall at night and see the same view that they would see if the ship were to suddenly disappear.

All six Living Regions have elevated viewing places at their centers. In Sonora, it is a plateau at the top of a small mesa.

Ali and Kayla make their way up a trail to the viewpoint. The artificial moon traversing the sky cylinder is in a crescent phase now, but it still gives them enough light to navigate the very familiar path. They aren't alone as others coming from different directions have the same idea.

Directly in front of the Gaians on the mesa, centered on the east wall, is a red stellar image. It is almost a hundred times more luminous than Venus at its brightest as seen from Earth. One viewer with magnifying goggles says that she can see the star as a disc now and not just a point source. A knowledgeable man states that the angular diameter of the red star is just a little less than Mars at its smallest from Earth. Ali and Kayla don't really care about the visual details. They are thinking about the implications of human beings being able to see what they are seeing for the first time.

What's more, the red star in the center of the screen is nowhere near the brightest object on the wall. At a viewing angle of about 30° from the central star in the 7 o'clock direction, is another star about 80 times brighter. That would give it the luminosity of about five full moons. It is a bright point of white light, although some say they can see a slight yellow-orange tinge.

Kayla takes Ali's hand. "I can't believe we are about to visit two new solar systems. If somebody had told me when I was a girl in Israel that I would do this, I would have wondered what they had been smoking."

Ali is looking in the other direction. "The only way I can recognize the sun is by knowing that it's the one in the middle. Sirius and Procyon are much brighter. Did I tell you that I am making up my own Gliese 250 constellations? The sun is in the constellation I call *The Phoenix*. Can you see where Vega is the tip of the beak, Procyon and Alpha and Beta Ophiuchus make the right wing, Altair and Zeta, Gamma and Theta Aquila make the left wing, the Sun and Theta Serpens are the base of the body, Sirius is the base of the tail and Alpha Centauri and Nu and Eta Ophiuchus are the fiery trail?

"I'd rather look at the stars in front of us, Ali."

"But Kayla, you must understand where you have been to appreciate where you are going."

"Do you think you can just be quiet and sit with me for a while?"

* * *

The next morning, at Romanov Primary School, preparations are being made for the annual Fall Quarter Orientation Assembly. New students will be welcomed, faculty and advisers introduced, old and new programs announced, but most importantly, all of the students will be reminded about why they are on this mission to the stars.

The students are all starting to fill the seats on one side of the gymnasium and a stage is set up facing that direction. Some older, familiar faces are on the stage along with some newer speakers from Gaia II's second generation. By 8:30, most of the students are seated, but there is still a loud rumbling noise, which is the collection of conversations throughout the gym. The first day of fall quarter, and school for some, was on Monday, so a certain amount of excitement fills the room.

The principal of Romanov is still Frank Dobrowski. Some wonder if he is going to retire soon. He has had the same response for years. "What do you do when you retire on Gaia II? Travel? Go fishing? Play golf?" In seriousness, he has considered going back to teaching, but he still enjoys being the principal. He gets the crowd's attention speaking through his voice projector.

"Good morning everybody, please take your seats and we will begin this year's fall assembly."

When it quiets down a little the principal continues. "It's good to see you all here again. At this time, as is the tradition, we would like to have all of the students who are attending Romanov Primary School for the first time to please stand." Most of the new students stand. "I want you all to try to remember your first days in this school and try to make all of these new arrivals feel welcome." The crowd applauds and then the new students sit back down.

"We have a treat for you to start this year's assembly. Our one and only music and drama instructor, Mrs. Chakori Singh-Jones, will be performing a new composition by my friend, John Diallo. This is going to be part of a musical that will be premiering in December, being performed by the Performing Arts Club."

The lights are dimmed and beautiful holographic imagery fills the arena. A spotlight shines down on the location where John Diallo is playing an electronic piano. The inspirational intro to the song is perfectly in sync with the visual effects. One at a time other instruments are added, and spotlighted, as they are being played by some of the school's older students. As the vocals are about to commence, the spotlight fades and the audience can see that the entire stage, where the principal had been standing, has lit up and been transformed into a very vibrant, colorful scene. The holographic illusion is that of a bustling market place as it may have been in Mumbai or Kolkata, India back on Earth.

Chakori walks on stage in a colorful, traditional Indian sari. She is on the short side like her mother, Leela, but has a dark skin complexion like her father. Her extroverted personality and confidence give her a strong stage presence, in spite of her height.

Interacting with the holographics, she begins to sing the title song from their newly composed musical, *Bazaar!!*. Dancers from the Performing Arts Club, in full costume, fill the stage area and encircle Chakori. The song and visual presentation is very energetic and uplifting. It was chosen to start the assembly in order to *wake up* the students and get them into a positive frame of mind.

When the performance is over, the lights to the gymnasium come back on and the stage returns to normal, with Rahii Singh standing in its center. He is clapping along with the crowd. After a minute, he comments through his voice projector. "I still can't believe that the woman you just saw is the same person that used to torment me when I was your age." Most know that Rahii is Chakori's younger brother.

Rahii is a tall, strong man now and it is difficult to imagine Chakori picking on him. He still spends most of his time in jeans and a t-shirt working with quantum computers, but has borrowed one of his father's business outfit designs to fabricate what he is wearing today. After graduating from Romanov, he had volunteered to help his mother counsel students to try to atone for his own mistakes. He was asked by Principal Dobrowski to give this year's presentation at the Fall Assembly.

Rahii begins. "Now, for all of the new students, and as a reminder to the rest, I want to tell you about where we came from and why we are here." The stage lights are turned off and the gym lights are dimmed. The machinery, that had just created the visual effects for the musical presentation, now projects a two dimensional image that extends about double the width and height of the stage.

"I'm sure you all recognize this view before you. This is what we see every night when we look at the west wall of our Living Region. I'm also pretty sure that your parents and teachers have told you that the bright light right in the middle is where we are from."

Scenes from the Living Areas of Gaia II are presented next as the image becomes three dimensional. Residents are shown traveling through the cylindrical world in electric carts. "I am like all of you. I was born here. Sometimes it is hard to imagine what the place we came from must really be like. Gaia II is everything we know."

Now the holo-movie transforms to an image of Gaia II moving through space, with a blue, slightly cloudy Earth in the background. It was taken when the spaceship was in orbit before it left it's home planet. "This is what our home looks like from the outside. Our whole world is on the inside of this large object that was built by other people just like us. Your grandparents could tell you about these people."

An image appears again of a cart traveling between Wicklesby and Alpenhausen. "Our world is called Gaia II, because Gaia is another name for the place we came from. Gaia II is no different from this cart, which is driving from Wicklesby to Alpenhausen. It is just a very large *cart* that is taking all of us from one place to another."

The image in the gym returns to that of the west wall at night. "I will now take you on an imaginary trip back to our planet. The Earth is a very, very big place that is the home of enough people to fill a million Gaia IIs. This planet, we call Earth, is a big ball in space that circles (or orbits) an object that is much larger. That object is the ordinary star in the center of this nighttime view. The light and heat it gives off makes life on Earth, and us, possible. Most people call it the Sun."

Slowly the lights, which they all know are called stars, start to move a little farther apart. "This is what we would see if we traveled back to the sun. We have been on our journey for about 42 years now. The image you are looking at is changing quickly, because we have sped up time so that we cover this 42 year trip in 42 seconds."

Rahii narrates an imaginary voyage back to their home solar system. The holographic movie, which he has created, takes the audience on a *near miss* of an object in the Oort cloud and Rahii explains how some of these objects have been diverted into orbits that bring them close to the sun. Comets are shown in their full glory. Then he uses real images, taken by manned and unmanned spacecraft in the 21st century, to recreate flybys of dwarf planets in the Kuiper Belt and most of the solar system planets and moons. Rahii gives a short lesson about each object as they pass by, illustrating the surprising variety of objects orbiting the sun.

Finally, the students are taken by Mars and it's space elevator on their way to the final destination. The Earth-Moon double planet system gets larger and larger in the Romanov gymnasium. The imaginary ship slows even more as they fly past the far side of the Moon to see a crescent Earth rise above the lunar horizon. Taking one trip around the unique planet, Rahii's creation plummets into the atmosphere and flies above mountains, forests, lakes and oceans. As the holographic movie at last displays the presence of man by flying over farms, towns and eventually large cities, Rahii talks about mankind's stewardship of this island oasis in space. He explains how short-sightedness caused a devastating mass extinction of species and how human's showed their resilience by overcoming the problems they themselves had created. Rahii describes just how fragile and precious this world is. He explains that a primary reason why they have been sent on this mission in Gaia II is that the people of Earth have become aware that, in order to insure their survival, they must find other places to develop and call home.

"This is why we have been selected, and given the honor, to represent the billions of people of Earth, as we travel to the stars. The first star, which we are going to, has a planet that the smartest people on Earth think may be our best hope for a new home for people. Our spaceship will be traveling on, but if we discover what is hoped to be found, then future Gaia IIs will bring men, women and children to live and create a new world." The final part of the holographic movie shows a realistic animation of spaceships traveling to the new planet, people building cities and moving about in the cities with imaginary futuristic vehicles.

Nova Szkody walks onto the stage in an animated way as the lights to the stage come back on and the hologram fades. She approaches Rahii, "Wait a minute Mr. Singh. There is another reason why we are traveling to another star."

"Oh, did I forget something Mrs. Szkody?"

"Only the most important reason, at least in my opinion."

"You mean?"

"Why, science, of course!" Some of the students let out a sigh, because they have had Mrs. Szkody as a teacher. They love her energy and vitality, but she seems to live and breathe science. It can be a little exasperating when she goes on and on about her favorite topic, which is studying stars.

"But why do we need to go to another star, ourselves, when we have excellent telescopes and unmanned craft that can learn so much?"

This is where the presentation is turned over to Nova Szkody. The holographic image before the students now shows the largest optical telescope complex on Earth in the Atacama desert of Chile. The vision slowly pans toward and zooms in on the most dominant structure. Upon closer inspection the building has multiple domes in a ring surrounding a large central structure.

With computer editing and animation, one of the domes opens and the movie takes the audience inside. Several uniformed people are working on a huge telescope and its related machinery.

Nova begins. "When we left the Earth, this was one of the best instruments made for studying space. Six telescopes like the one you see are working together to create one very good image. A lot can be learned with telescopes like this. People can see things so far away that the light they see has been traveling through space since the beginning of the universe. We learned from all of the unmanned probes that were sent out to other planets and asteroids and comets, however, that to truly learn about a place, sometimes you just have to go there. Every time we have sent out a mission there have been wonderful surprises." Images of unmanned craft exploring planets and moons fly through the gymnasium.

"Starting in the year 2050, people sent the first unmanned machines out to explore other stars and their planets. These were very tiny spaceships called nanocraft. They were sent off in swarms by a very powerful laser satellite, which beamed energy to accelerate them to fantastic speeds." A holographic simulation shows this at a distance and then zooms in on a nanocraft to show its lightsails capturing the light from the laser.

"We learned important things from the nanocraft, but they were limited as to what they could do. The small percentage of probes, that were able to make it all of the way to the star, collected data as they sped past the destination system and relayed it back to Earth using their lightsails as antennae. There was no way to give the probes instructions from Earth after arrival, because it would have taken 20 years, on average, for a signal to travel the great distance. The nanocraft helped us choose where we are going, but to really find out what we wanted to know, we needed to send better instruments with people to make real time decisions at these specially selected stars."

A spotlight beams on another woman, who is walking onto the stage to join Nova and Rahii. Vera Greene's voice fills the gymnasium. "Nova, you're not telling the young people why I am here."

"Everybody, this is Vera Greene." The bright red haired woman is in her white labcoat as she walks over beside Nova. " You don't see her very often, because she likes to hide from everybody in her laboratory."

"Well, Nova, didn't you say that sometimes to do real science you have to put your hands on what you are studying and not just look at it from a distance."

"Vera, I would love to, but it is slightly difficult to put your hands on a star!"

"Exactly, Nova, which is why I study what I study and not stars." All of the students realize that this little confrontation is just a put on.

"And what exactly do you study, Vera?" This is Vera's cue to take over the presentation. The spotlight on Rahii and Nova turns off.

"I thought you'd never ask." The holo-movie now shows the lab where Vera Greene and Jaswinder Singh work with a few others. There are numerous enclosed terrariums and aquariums, each attached to temperature, gas and liquid regulating units to create different environments. Jaswinder is working at a computer on one side of the room.

"I study life!! Throughout the history of our species everything we think of as being alive, that we have encountered, has come from Earth. It never has really made any sense that Earth would be the only place in our whole galaxy of billions of stars with life. Then when you consider that there are billions of galaxies in the universe and possibly billions of universes, well, we'll stick to our part of our galaxy, the Milky Way, for now. Evidence from the nanocraft, which Mrs. Szkody was telling you about, gives us good reason to believe that at least two places, which we are going to visit on Gaia II, also have life. Until we discover and can study this life in our laboratories, we use the life we know and our computers to try to make good guesses as to what living things might be like on other planets or moons. This is important because, if we are going to find other life on this voyage of Gaia II, we need to know what to look for."

The holo-movie zooms in on a microscope and then computer animation takes over, as the students take an imaginary trip into the microscope and then into the world of microscopic life. "Every day you lose about 50 million skin cells, which are replaced by new ones. For about two billion years, life on the planet Earth never got any larger than one of those cells. So, it makes sense that most of the places away from Earth that support life are only going to have very tiny life forms like the ones we look at through the microscope. We will be looking hard for this life, but we really hope to find places where life has been around for such a long time, that larger things have evolved like on Earth."

Leaving the microscopic realm, the students are now back in the lab where Jaswinder is working at the quantum computer. "We know that life becomes more and more complex due to a process that most of you know about called evolution. Evolution of a life form is essentially determined by its environment or surroundings. That is, if nature comes up with some design by accident that makes it easier for a living thing to thrive in its environment, then it will live to produce more like itself. It will win the competition for survival over others without this gift. This quickly gets complicated, however, because the evolution of a life form changes the environment for all of the other living things." Holographic animation gives examples of primitive evolution while Vera is talking.

"We have been studying the evolution of life on Earth for almost 300 years now. For most of this time people found fossil records, like old bones or imprints in soft rocks, and were able to use ingenious methods to determine their age. We also learned a lot about what the early Earth was like by studying records kept by nature in layers of rock and ice. Scientists think they have a pretty good idea of what the Earth was like when the first life began and also when it evolved from one cell into more complex creatures. The term we use for early environments is a planet's *initial conditions*. What Jaswinder is doing at the computer is making guesses at what different initial conditions might be on other planets orbiting other stars. He is also guessing at what kinds of different varieties of one celled life are possible on different worlds. He puts his data into the quantum computer and lets the computer try to create possible evolutionary histories of entire planets."

"These are some of the interesting things that the computer has come up with." The holo-movie shows alien environments with alien plants and animals. "Even with our best computers, though, these are just guesses. Real evolution takes place over millions and even billions of years and is affected by unforeseen catastrophic events. Nature always surprises us and probably will again when we find and study life on other worlds, which we call exobiology, first hand."

The spotlight enlarges to reveal Vera, Nova and Rahii, now standing together on the stage. Rahii addresses the students. "We are here, because we need your help. Mrs. Szkody, Mrs. Greene and all of our parents and friends will only be able to keep this mission successful for a fraction of this 600 year journey of Gaia II. We will need all of you and your children to take over for us. What we all will learn together will be very exciting and should amaze the people back on Earth. All we can ask of you now is that you do your very best in school so that you can find out what you are best at and excel in it. We need to all work together as a team so we can make the people of Earth proud of us."

The principal, Frank Dobrowski, comes back on stage as the lights come on in the gymnasium. He joins the others. "Thank you Mr. Singh, Mrs. Szkody and Mrs. Greene for a very enjoyable and enlightening presentation." He claps and so does the student audience. "Our next three speakers would like to tell you about some of the opportunities there will be for you here on Gaia II. Jobs on our spaceship can be very interesting and exciting. Here to tell you about some of these are Greta Mueller, who runs our energy plant, Ishii Matogawa, who has devoted his life to making ours more fun on this long voyage, and Cheryl Bailey, who is in charge of maintaining our vital link with the people on Earth who sent us on this mission. May we please have a warm welcome for these three friends of mine, who have come here to talk to you."

Greta Mueller is the first to talk to the students. The lights dim, but a spotlight still shines on the presenters. Holographic images of engineers and other workers are shown working with the fusion reactor that powers the ship. Greta makes a case, in her own unique way, of how interesting it can be working as a nuclear or electrical engineer. She explains what education and experience will be needed to be able to work at these jobs. Greta knows that, even though this work is vitally important to their survival, recruiting young people for these positions can be difficult.

Next, on a lighter note, Ishii Matogawa makes his presentation with a short holo-movie illustrating his message.

What Ishii tells the students is that you don't have to be a nuclear engineer, computer scientist or astrophysicist on Gaia II. He uses the example of Chakori Singh-Jones, who performed for them earlier. Ishii talks about the many other careers on Gaia II that are beneficial to life in their world. There are hotel and restaurant operators, community event coordinators, artists, hydroponic food growers, physical fitness instructors like his wife and many other choices all important in their own way. Ishii is a favorite of the students since, even though he is over 70 years old now, he is still young at heart and has invented numerous things that they enjoy.

Finally, Cheryl Bailey has her turn to address the students. She explains that she is there representing all of the hard working people at the Probe Center. She tells the audience what they know about the stars and planets they are about to visit and adds that they will surely still find more planets and moons. Cheryl explains what probes are being completed at the Probe Center and what they hope to accomplish. She, of course, has to mention the probe that has been her focus for several years now, which will receive all of the data from the other probes and process it into an information package to be beamed back to Earth. While she is talking the holo-movie shows an animation of the planets circling Gliese 250B and 250A with probes being sent off from Gaia II on their missions. The images were created to be as real as possible with the latest information from Leonid Shevchenko and his astronomy team. Finally, Cheryl makes a plug for the Probe Factory, telling the students that several of them will be needed to design and construct the probes that will explore the next star on their journey.

The lights come back on and the only person on stage now is Nova Szkody. She has a final message for the students before they are dismissed for lunch and third and fourth sessions.

"I hope you have all enjoyed the assembly." The students applaud. "I have one more fun thing to tell you before you go. In about six days now we will have our closest approach to the star Gliese 250B and its two planets. Then, it will be a few months before we enter a constant velocity orbit around our destination planet. This is scheduled for February 20th."

"By that time we will know every major planet and moon around both stars. We have decided to have a contest for all of you. Any student from age 6 to 16 is eligible. We need names for the two stars, all of the major planets around each star and all of the major moons around each planet. Entries must be in by February 18th. A committee of myself, Ali Zamani and three others will pick the top five candidates and we will all vote for a winner during our twelve hour transition time in the theater on February 20th."

"In addition to having the honor of being the one to have named all of these objects and having that information sent back to Earth in a data package, there is another prize for the winner. He or she will get to be in the first group to take a spacewalk tour. We will be taking small groups in lifesuits outside our spaceship. They will be able to see the planet and its moons, if it has any, along with all of the stars and our home from the outside."

"Starting next week, the Tuesday Earth Awareness class will be devoted to keeping you updated about what we have learned about this new place we are arriving at. You may all go now. Have a nice lunch."

The students all leave the gym in an orderly manner, but now they are even more excited than when they arrived. The large room is filled with the drone of hundreds of conversations.

There are about 800 students now at Romanov Primary School, so the Earth Awareness Classes are divided into five groups, by age. The classes are held in the largest rooms on five different levels. The oldest and largest group, 14 and older, is on the Science Level or Level 7. The instructor for this session is Nova Szkody.

At a little after 8am, when the students have settled a little, Mrs. Szkody addresses the class. "Good morning. I'm very excited to be with you today. As most of you are aware, this will be the first Earth Awareness Class that is devoted to informing you about where we are going instead of where we came from. This may seem like any other day to all of you, but to the people of Earth and for the whole human species, in general, today is a very important, historic day. For the first time ever, people are visiting a star, besides the Earth's sun, and releasing probes to study its planets. Three probes are being launched today, two at 10:32 this morning and the third at 11:06. Our closest approach to the star Gliese 250B will be at 5:20 tonight. The probe launches are precisely timed to have two probes visit the closest planet and one to go to the other planet. We originally had two probes going to the outer planet, but the closest one is so interesting that we decided to change our plans. Also, due to how fast we are going by the star, the process of slowing these probes down to orbit the planets is very risky. We wanted to make sure that we had at least one operable probe at the inner planet. I am here to tell you what we know so far."

Nova uses a hand-held remote to dim the lights as the room's holo-projector creates an image of a red ball of fire over her head in the five meter high room. "This is the best image we have so far of the red dwarf star Gliese 250B. We are looking at it through special filters since it is much too bright to look at it directly. The image you see is of light emitted from the star in the ultraviolet part of the spectrum to best show features of the star. The colors are created by computer to approximate what you would see if you were able to look at the star unaided. We sped up the video in order to show you the star's rotation and the coming and going of events on the star's surface. In a minute you will see an ultraviolet flare from the star. We have known for a long time that red dwarfs commonly do this, but it is just a stroke of luck that our cameras were able to capture one happening."

The students watch as the star slowly rotates, with numerous bright and dark spots circulating on the surface. Then, what looks like an arm of flaming gas arches from the star at the 10 o'clock position. Seconds later what looks like an enormous explosion sends material spewing out into space. The flash is bright, but short lived.

"Younger red dwarf stars have so many of these flares that living on a planet or moon near them would be impossible. This star, however, has been around for quite a while and has settled down into a more predictable, friendly state. It was thought for a while that life could never get started around any of these stars due to their violent nature and something called *tidal locking* of the planets. Now we know, however, that most red dwarfs have been relatively stable for billions of years. *Tidal locking* is a term used to mean that the same side of the planet faces the star all of the time. We no longer think that this would completely rule out life and a moon of a tidally locked planet would still show different sides to the star and be another possibility for finding life." Nova goes on to teach the students more about the star before moving on to the planets.

She first discusses the outer planet to save the best for last. The holographic image above Mrs. Szkody zooms out and two small bright dots can be seen moving very slowly among the stars in the background. Then they zoom in on the dot that is farthest from the star. As the image gets larger, they can see another body, a moon, circling the planet. When the hologram above Mrs. Szkody is about the size of a basketball, the zooming stops. The planet is still a little fuzzy."

"This is the best we could do with our *enhanced resolution* system as of yesterday. We are traveling at the speed of 7AU per day and so will be passing by this system over the next couple of days. You should all know what an AU is from my class. The closest Gaia II will get to this planet is about 1AU, but, of course, we hope that the probe gets much closer. Even though our image is very hazy, there is still a lot that can be learned. It appears that this is what we would call a dead planet, but it will still be scientifically interesting. There is a thin atmosphere of mostly nitrogen and carbon dioxide. In short, this planet looks like a large, cold Mars. The difference is that this planet never gets any warmer than 100°C below zero. Mars is lacking in the nitrogen that this planet has, because it is warmer and slightly smaller so any nitrogen, in its early atmosphere, would have been lost to space. Mars was even warmer still and had liquid water when it was very young. This planet probably never did. Also, it doesn't appear to have anything going on geologically and the planet's moon isn't large enough to have tidal influences."

"This brings us to the moon of the planet." An image of the moon comes out from behind the planet. It is much darker to look at than its parent body. "Due to albedo, density measurements and absorption lines in the three to five micron range this moon looks similar to a very common asteroid type in earth's solar system. We will wait to see what the probe finds, but if this proves to be true, then as much as 20% of its mass could be frozen water and it may contain organic molecules like amino acids. The moon is about 43% of the diameter of the earth's moon, which makes it slightly smaller than the asteroid Ceres and just large enough to be spherical."

"The moon is also interesting because it couldn't have formed where it is right now. We think that it came from the outer regions of the nebula that formed into the planets and moons of the primary star. Somehow, it was dislodged and captured by the companion star and then the planet. How this happened is a mystery. We may be diverting the planetary probe to the moon."

"And now for the place we are most excited about!" The outer planet and the moon move to the left of the room and then out of view. The star crosses the room followed by a small object that seems insignificant by comparison. When zoomed in on, the object is even fuzzier than the first planet. The dark half of the planet appears to be larger than the side facing the star. A faint wisp of atmosphere trails away from the star side then seems to disappear into the far side.

"This object is nothing like we have ever seen before. You are looking at a very small planet. There are actually three moons in our home solar system that are larger. Due to density calculations it should have a silicate mantle and an iron-nickel core, but then the rest of the planet appears to be water. The water should be deep enough that it may go through a phase change before reaching the mantle. A liquid ocean covers the star side and a frozen one the other side and the poles. It appears that a state of equilibrium has developed where ocean currents from the hot side melt water deep under the ice of the far side. The current then must bring cold water to the near side minimizing evaporation. We think that a very strong wind, like nothing on earth, takes the water vapor to the far side where it condenses before a significant amount can dissociate and be lost to space."

A knowledgeable student raises his hand and asks, "Don't M dwarfs emit a lot of UV radiation when they are young? Considering this, the high rate of evaporation due to low atmospheric pressure and the estimated age of the star shouldn't this planet have lost all of its water a long time ago?"

"Yet, we are looking at a planet dominated by water. One thought may be that when the outer planet had the encounter that left it with its moon, a result may have been its highly elliptical orbit. This may have caused the inner planet to migrate closer to the star. I will leave it as a homework assignment to come up with any other ideas."

There are a few other questions and Nova Szkody talks in more detail about the probes that are being launched soon. Then she dismisses the students to break and second session.

* * *

For the last few hours the Probe Center has been in a frenzy. To an outsider it would seem to be chaotic craziness, but everything has been well planned and so far all operations are proceeding as scheduled. They are preparing to launch not one, but three probes which have been precisely timed to achieve orbit around their destination planets. Everybody in the center is aware that, at the speed that Gaia II is flying by the companion star the success of these missions is a crap shoot. All they are concerned about now, however, is doing their jobs perfectly to give the probes their best chance.

At 10:20am, the Flight Director, Robert Tjoelker, gives the command to start up the launch ring. This is the same maglev system that enabled the arrival of the shuttles that brought people to Gaia II over 42 years ago. The two probes are on opposite sides of the 400 meter diameter ring when it starts its revolution in the opposite direction of that of the ship. When the ring precisely offsets the spin of Gaia II, Robert announces, "Ready for launch."

Both craft are going to the same destination and so are being launched simultaneously. At precisely 10:32am, the orders are given that everybody in the Probe center has been waiting for. "Probe separation thrusters engage." Both probes fire thrusters and move a safe distance away from the ship. There is no propulsion exhaust from Gaia II to be concerned with because the ship is decelerating and it is being ejected in front of the QFT scoop. At the planned separation time, Director Tjoelker gives the next command, "Initial braking on my mark. Three, two, one detonate." What are in essence two controlled nuclear explosions speed the probes away from Gaia II. At exactly 10:46:30, the probes' light sails are unfolded to full extension and the rest is in the hands of the on board computer system.

The process is repeated for a third probe at 11:06 and all three are underway with everything going perfectly so far. The probes are using every trick in the book to decelerate, but the riskiest is when they have to use the outer atmosphere of the star itself for braking. The metamaterials of the shell of the craft are to be tested to the limits of their capabilities and beyond. The light sails will be ejected as they will no longer be useful. After this daring maneuver, a couple more precisely timed high delta-v thrusts should get the probes to where they need to be. It will take about a month and a half to attain stable planetary orbits, a little sooner for the outer planet probe, but the critical event will happen much sooner.

It is just after Gaia II's closest approach to Gliese 250B, when it is on the opposite side of the star, that the moment of truth occurs. The time is 6:15pm. Tension in Probe Control is at its peak. Inga Larsson and Robert Tjoelker are the main players in the control room, but all either of them can do is wait. The first two probes are now in the process of *stellar braking* and the third should be there any minute now. After the longest hour that any of them has ever endured, a signal from a surviving probe reaches Probe Control. It's the third probe. The first two have been lost.

A dejected Inga consoles Robert. "We knew this could happen. We were attempting something that has never been done before. At least one probe made it."

Robert stares at his monitor in disbelief even though he knows the reality. "But both inner planet probes!! I was hoping that at least one would make it."

"This is a good lesson that redundancy isn't very reliable unless the backup mission differs significantly from the primary. Of course, in this case, we didn't have much choice."

"Looks like we will be constructing another probe or two when Gaia II reaches final orbit."

"Yes, and maybe we can get Mei Sun and her prodigies in on the new probes."

"True, with QFT propulsion, a trip from 250A to 250B will take about seven months. We may even be able to get some data before Gaia II has to move on to its next star."

All fifteen members of the arrival committee are present as one of their most important meetings is about to get underway. Even Ali is there early. There is a certain tension in the room, especially after what happened to the probes at Gliese 250B. The ship is now about 50AU from destination and traveling at 2.25AU/day. Arrival day is still February 20.

As chairman of the committee, Jaswinder Singh, again begins the meeting, he stands at the oblong table. "Okay, is everybody ready to begin?" This is rhetorical, of course. "Let's hear from Henry first to see how the probe we left behind is doing."

At 36 years of age Henry Rowland is one of the youngest members of the committee. He is the lead planetary scientist, overseeing a team of four members at this time. Some think that Henry may have the highest IQ of anyone in this group, even Mei Sun. He is a thin African American of average height. Lines in his face give the impression that he is always deep in thought. His mother and father, Cynthia and James Rowland live in Hanalei Village and are good friends of Barry and Mei.

Henry stays seated and inserts his data chip into the table. "I have a short video presentation of the most recent images of the outer planet of 250B and its moon. Our probe has been orbiting now for about two months. During the second week of orbit, the lander was sent to the planet's moon. A successful landing, as you all know, was made on November 17th. Due to signal delay we received verification from the orbiter on November 19th."

"These first images you are looking at of the planet were taken every 10 degrees of the 360 degree orbit. The rotation of the planet itself is so slow that it is negligible during one orbit. There are a few interesting things we can learn. We suspected that this stellar system is at least as old as the sun's and this has been proven out by rock dating from the moon lander. The Gliese 250A/250B system is about 4.5 billion years old. What's interesting about the planetary surface is that, if you count the craters, the surface has not reached the maximum cratering threshold. Since we have no reason to suspect any past geologic activity, that means that every impact, since the planet solidified, is recorded on the planet's surface. Our home system has gas giants, mainly Jupiter, that in many ways protect the inner planets, but can also occasionally cause changes in the orbits of smaller objects and send them hurtling inward. Thus, to this day, impacts are still happening on Mars, the moon and even Earth. There are no gas giants here, so this planet is a perfect laboratory for testing the theories of the birth of solar systems."

Henry Rowland has the group zoom in on certain features on their displays by touching the area on the image. He attempts to explain the origin of craters, flows. rises and fissures along with their chronology. Then he moves on to the moon.

The first images shown, that were taken by the moon lander, still amaze them all, even though everybody on Gaia II has seen them for over a month now. The landscape is a dark gray color, which is intensified since the light from the star is red. "The crater density is higher than on the planet. This is one reason that we think that this object was formed in the accretion disk of the primary star. Somehow, it seems that it was dislodged long after the impact era, by some passing body, then captured by the companion star. I am working with Gordon on a computer model that could explain how this could happen. We think it could be similar to the way Neptune captured Triton in our home system." The committee sees images of the moon as the lander gets closer and closer and then lands.

"You have all seen what I have been showing you already, but now I would like to show you some images that the probe's rover has taken recently." The first image is of a rock on the surface. The rock is black and embedded with numerous small, shiny specks. When the camera zooms in they can see what looks like tiny glass spheres. "The shiny specks in this carbon rock are particles of magnetic iron and silicates. The little spheres are called chondrules. The rock is a meteorite in the sense that it arrived at this object long after it had condensed to form the spherical body we see today. This meteorite, folks, is not much different than many that have been recovered on Earth. Also, the moon, as predicted, has many of the features of Type C asteroids, including numerous organic substances and even amino acids. When taking into consideration the age information from the rocks, the elemental abundances of the stars, and now these chondrules, which are thought to have been formed by supernovae exploding in the central area of the sun's stellar nursery, I think it is safe to say that this system formed at the same time as part of the same event that gave birth to our sun and planets."

Leonid Shevchenko shakes his head. "Can't be. There are dynamical considerations. The galactic orbit of this planet doesn't trace back to being close to the sun 4.5 billion years ago."

"True, but I still think that we are looking at a solar sibling. It could be that an encounter with a large object, a massive dust cloud or even a concentration of dark matter may have altered the orbit."

Having gotten their attention, Henry gives more detail on the data and analysis from the science instruments on the

probe. He tells them the estimated percentage of water in the rock
and more details about the carbon compounds found. As in Earth
meteorites, there is a slight preference of left hand over right hand
amino acids, which is theorized as to why Earth life is based on
the left hand variety.

When Henry Rowland is finished with his impressive
presentation, Jaswinder prompts the next speaker. "Leo, what's
our latest object count?"

"There have been no new discoveries in the past few
weeks, so we think we have found all of the major bodies now
unless there are some not in the planetary orbital plane. To recap,
within the first two months after Gaia II entered the system's
plane we detected the two inner planets, one moon at the third
planet, four major moons at the fourth and largest planet, two
major moons orbiting the fifth and three the sixth. We have
confirmed that, as with 250B, there is a halo of smaller icy objects
orbiting well outside the orbit of the outer planet. We suspect that
these may be common for systems with no gas giants."

"Thank you, Leo. May we have a probe report?"

Inga Larrson starts the presentation. "The only probes we
will launch before reaching orbit of planet c are two each for
planets b, d and e. I will let Robert fill you in on the latest timing
and trajectory calculations. Keiji will give you an update on our
decisions with the mining probes."

Robert Tjoelker then puts in his data chip and gives the
group the probe launch data. He also informs them all as to when
each probe should attain planetary orbit and mentions that the
landers will be sent down when decisions are made about where
to land from orbital imaging.

Keiji has the floor next. "We had a hard decision to make.
There are plenty of small bodies to mine, but they all dwell in a
band from 5 to 30AU from the star. The decision has been made

that we will try to get what we need from the moon of planet c. The mass of the moon is estimated at about 30% of the mass of the Earth's moon so it will be a little easier to mine. Due to the proximity, we will first send two probes out that are strictly for reconnaissance, then depending on what is found we will send one or two landers. The lander or landers will be followed by one or two probes that will be designed specifically to build mass drivers to send pods of fuel into orbit about the moon. Then a final mission will gather pods and bring them to the ship. We have confidence that our team can have these probes ready as they are needed."

Inga speaks again. "Once in orbit, our plan is still to launch four probes to planet c. Also, of course, we will launch Cheryl Bailey's command probe. Orbital location of the command probe will depend on the landing sites of the planet c probes. New probes already planned are one for each of the inner planets and the QFT probe to go back to the inner planet of 250B. These and the additional mining probes will keep our production plants at capacity for our first six months in orbit."

Jaswinder thanks Inga and the rest of the committee gives their reports. Nova Szkody tells what they have learned about the primary star. Cheryl Bailey gives a briefing about what information has been sent to Earth and the finishing touches being done to the command probe. She mentions that they received a message from Earth hoping that they had made it, wishing them luck. Vera Greene gives a report on her research into what kind of life may theoretically have come to be in the ocean of 250Bc. Renata and Gordon give a report as to how quantum computers will be used over the next year and when the conventional system will be more suited for the task. Greta Mueller explains how the solar panels will be fanned out to collect energy for recharging the fusion reactor's nanocells. She also highlights the process as to how the fuel pods from the miners will be received, processed and stored in the ship's fuel tanks. Mei Sun presents her team's design for the QFT probe to be sent back to 250B. Jacques and Ali talk to each other and jokingly pose the question, "Why are we here?" Ali answers his own question, "I guess they need an audience."

Henry Rowland has one more thing to add before the meeting breaks up. He lets them all know that his mom, Cynthia, has planned a beach party for the arrival committee and their extended families. It will be at Hanalei Village's Public Beach and everything will be provided. Jaswinder says that he hopes to see them all at the beach and adjourns the meeting.

Leonid Shevchenko is doing a routine program run that enters latest positions and brightnesses in a search for additional planets or moons. The display tells Leo that there is about an 80% confidence that planet c has another moon. It has been predicted by the computer due to a slight motion of the planet perpendicular to the orbital plane and not due to a change in brightness that would indicate a transit. This means that this would be a very odd moon, which, unlike the others, is orbiting the planet well out of the plane of the rest of the objects in the system.

Leo's first thought is about mining and he decides to call Keiji Kusakabe right away to let him know the news. A second side thought is that he better let Nova Szkody know so that she can tell her students that they have one more moon to name.

Barry Donaldson and Mei Sun are awake before sunrise today. They have decided to take an early morning bike ride. Barry looks like the walking dead and moans a little. "Are you sure you want to do this? We have a long twelve hour wait in the theater today."

Even at age 70, Mei is wide awake and full of energy. "Exactly, there will be plenty of time to take a nap if we want to in the theater."

"Remind me, why are we doing this again?"

"I want to look at the planet."

"We will be orbiting around it for a year you know."

"What can I say? I'm curious."

Barry freshens up in the bathroom and then they both walk out the front door of their Wailea Park condo. Two bicycles are parked outside. They both hop on the bikes and ride toward the north of town away from the beach.

Barry and Mei pass the Tahiti Nui Café then take a right onto the road that leads north out of town. One block up this road is a softball field that had been created mid-voyage, partly due to the persistence of Leilani Matogawa. The field's bleachers face the east wall.

For the last couple of nights, the artificial moons on Gaia II have been *turned off*. The destination planet has been centered on the east wall, even when it hasn't been in the direction of travel of the ship. It is now at its largest since they are just about to establish orbit at 45000 kilometers. This distance was chosen so that, like at Earth, Gaia II will be orbiting the planet once a day.

Thus the view of the planet on the East Wall is almost as large as the view of Earth from Noda Geostation.

Barry and Mei park the bikes and sit in the bleachers. Barry is the first to comment, "Mei, I hate to say it, but there's not much to look at."

Mei agrees, but at least her curiosity has been satisfied. All they can see is a cloud covered planet with a few swirls showing signs of the slow rotation. She lets some dirt from the ground by the bleachers sift through her fingers. "It's too bad we don't have infrared imaging on the wall. Now that would be interesting."

Just the fact that they are this close to an earth-like planet orbiting another star is reason enough to sit there and take it in for a while. Eventually, they decide to head back, have breakfast and get ready for the twelve hour transition period in the Andrew Lloyd Webber Theater.

* * *

In a little house in Alpenhausen, eight year old Anna Mueller is already out of bed. It's only 6am, but she can't sleep. The cute, pudgy little blonde girl is busting at the seams with excitement. Anna is one of five finalists of the contest to name the stars, planets and moons. There is one other finalist about her age, but the rest are much older.

She goes and pounces on her mom and dad. "Wake up, wake up! We have to get ready to go to the theater."

Anna's mom, Debbie, rolls over and looks at the display on the side of the bed still showing a page she was reading when she fell asleep the night before. The time in the bottom right corner tells her it is only six o'clock. "Anna, we don't have to leave for another three hours."

"But mom, can't we get there early and get a good seat?"

Debbie knows why her daughter is so excited and gives in a little. "Okay, Anna. How about if we leave at eight-thirty? Can I get another hour of sleep now?"

"Mom, is grandma coming over to go with us?"

Anna's dad, Hans, rolls over now, awoken by the conversation. He stretches as he answers his daughter. "Now Anna, we told you, grandma has a very important job to do while we are in the theater."

"Oh yeah, how about grandpa?"

Hans and Debbie start to realize that they aren't going to get any more sleep and both sit up in bed. "We've arranged to meet your grandpa once we get there."

"But what if he doesn't get a seat with us?"

"Our seats are all reserved, sweetheart, your aunts and uncles and cousins will be sitting with us, too. Now, why don't you go and wake up your brother while your dad and I get washed up and dressed." Achieving her goal, Anna heads for her older brother, Ron's, room.

When Anna is gone, Hans laughs out loud. "That was a mean thing to do, sicking her on Ron."

"Hey, if we have to suffer, he has to suffer."

Debbie and Hans take turns in the master bathroom, get dressed, then go to the kitchen to make breakfast. It's a long hour and a half after breakfast before they leave for the theater. Ron does his own thing, but they try to keep Anna preoccupied by playing an animated movie on the wall display.

Anna makes sure that they leave at exactly 8:30. The Mueller family walks through Alpenhausen to Gaia University and the Webber Theater. When they get to the lobby the Muellers get a pleasant surprise. The entire lobby and entrance to the theater are decorated like a big city ballroom on New Year's Eve back on Earth. There is a big banner hanging above the entrance announcing, *WE MADE IT!* Confetti, streamers, an ice statue, flowers and other decorative ornamentation are artistically strewn throughout the big room. Everybody coming into the theater will come through this lobby either down the hall from Gaia University, like the Muellers, or up the elevators on either side of the lobby from the Parking Garage on Level J from the Tropicania side.

Hans, Debbie, Anna and Ron walk through one of the three double door entrances and are greeted by Herbert and Ilsa Rauch, who are dressed very formally. The four of them are given a program and a menu to share.

The inner theater is almost as impressive as the lobby. Down both sides of the main floor are food booths representing some of the eating establishments on Gaia II. There is a German sausage booth, with a small beer garden attached, run by the Rauch family, a booth for the Tahiti Nui Café, a chocolate stand worked by Mary Gautier of La Chocolaterie Suisse, a wine, cheese, bread and fruit stand offered by the Bertoni family, a British finger foods booth by the Joneses, a pasta booth operated by the chefs of Villa Dievole, a booth from Little Rio presented by Casa da Feijoada serving its title dish and a couple of re-creations of Brazilian stews, and several other small stands, including an espresso stand and a gelato stand. The food areas and the stage are also very beautifully decorated.

The Muellers take in the scene in front of them. Other than the hosts and the people who have assisted with the set up and decoration, very few families are here yet. They have all had breakfast, but Ron and Anna both walk directly to the La Chocolaterie Suisse booth and Hans and Debbie find the espresso stand.

Then Anna sees what she is looking for. There is a well marked table near the stage, on which rests the entries of the five finalists of the naming contest. Every chair in the theater has a computer access display panel, but voting will be done at the table for the fun of it. The winner is to be announced at the end of their 12 hours in the theater.

Hans and Debbie find the reserved seats. They look over the program together while enjoying the coffee drinks. It's still an hour before the transition performances begin so they make sure Ron and Anna are okay, then walk back up into the lobby and greet a few friends as they arrive. Franz shows up at about a quarter till ten and finds them in the crowd. By ten o'clock, all but a few stragglers are in the theater and most have found seats.

From behind the curtains, to the center of the stage, walks John Diallo. He opens the festivities with an announcement using his voice projector. "Welcome to the Arrival Celebration of Gaia II!! Before we start I need to let you know that our transition to constant velocity is still on schedule. It will begin at approximately 11am and last for twelve hours. We asked for everybody to be here by 10am, but our recognition program tells us that we are still waiting for twenty two people. They have all been contacted and assure us that they will be here by 10:15. Everybody please find a seat. At 10:15 we will turn down the lights and begin the premier performance of our musical *Bazaar!*"

Hans Mueller looks around and notices that instead of filling the main floor and getting the best view of the show as possible, Gaia II residents have spread themselves evenly over the main floor, the mezzanine and even the balcony. A few social groups of friends have formed. He wonders if Leela Singh would find this interesting.

Most are seated at 10:15 and, true to his word, John Diallo has the lights dimmed. Dazzling, colorful special effects lighting fills the stage area as the wonderful, dramatic music builds in volume and intensity. *Bazaar!* has begun.

Events in Ship Control and the Computer Center are fairly mundane. Reducing deceleration to enter an orbit is much easier than leaving the orbit. Fusion propulsion will not be needed for braking, but Greta Mueller and her team are there just in case. Jacques Laplace and his team are having a pretty smooth time preparing for the catom transition also. They are getting pretty good at this. At 11am the morphing begins.

The organizers of the Arrival Celebration decided that there would be an hour break in between performances to allow people time to mingle and eat. The performances last from one to two hours and are all family friendly, of course. There is a mix of performances by Gaians and holomovies or performances from the entertainment data bank. The live performances are a comedy play performed by the Wicklesby Players, an enchanting concert by a string ensemble comprised of older members of the third generation of Gaians, a group of second generation Gaians who formed a band called *Exploding Novas* (yes, the drummer for the group is Nova Szkody) and of course the musical *Bazaar!*.

Anna Mueller has been watching the contest table for a good portion of the 12 hours. She gets her mom's attention midway through the celebration. "Mom, when people look at mine, I can see them laughing. They think mine is silly. I'm serious, mom."

Debbie puts an arm around her daughter. "Let's just wait and see, sweetheart. I think your choices are wonderful."

Everybody seems to have a really good time at the celebration as, for most, the time seems to go by rather quickly. People from the Computer Center and the Catom Monitoring Center rotate out so that they too can enjoy some of the performances and food and drink. Unfortunately, those in Ship

Control and the Fusion Plant are on the other side of Europia from the theater and so have to stay there for the duration. During the last couple of hours many of the younger children are reclined and asleep in their seats. A movie that is more adult oriented is shown during this period. The one that has been chosen is a re-mastered version of the 20th century classic *Schindler's List*. Franz Mueller is somewhat of a historian and comments that it is good to remind ourselves of what people are capable of doing to other people so we can make sure that it never happens again.

Anna's body wants to sleep so badly, but her mind won't let her. Her mom and dad glance over at her occasionally as she starts to nod off and then forces herself awake. Hans can't help but be envious of youth, when simple things can get you so excited.

At 11:15pm, when the movie is over, John Diallo comes back on stage for a final announcement. "We have word from the Catom Center that the Living Area morphing is complete now and we can return to our homes whenever we want. I hope you have all had a good time at our celebration and I'd like to thank the organizers, decorators, food vendors and performers." There is a sincere applause from the audience.

"There is one more thing that we must reveal before you all go." The curtains open and a three dimensional simulation, not to scale of course, of the Gliese 250 system of stars, planets and moons takes up the entire stage area. Hans Mueller has to nudge his daughter who has nodded off. "This is it, Anna."

John Diallo walks to the side of the stage and is joined by Ali Zamani and Nova Szkody. Together they announce, "Residents of Gaia II, these are the names that you have chosen for the new worlds we have discovered." Next to each celestial body a name appears. A loud shriek comes from the direction of the Mueller family.

* * *

The next day when Cheryl Bailey is putting together her data package to transmit back to Earth she says to herself, "Oh, they are going to hate us!" She enters the following information: Names given to stars, planets and moons of the Gliese 250 system by vote of the residents of Gaia II:

Star: Gliese 250A: Zax

      Planet f: Mulberry

      Planet g: Yertle

      Planet c: Who   Moons: Horton, Grinch

      Planet b: Sneech Moons: One Fish, Two Fish, Red Fish, Blue Fish

      Planet d: Sam   Moons: Eggs, Ham

      Planet e: Cat   Moons: Thing One, Thing Two, Hat

Star: Gliese 250B: Lorax

      Planet c: Truffula

      Planet b: Onceler   Moon: Thneed

About 800 Gaians are signed up for spacewalk tours as of March 16th. Twenty people at a time will be taking the tour so it is booked up for forty weeks.

The week before each tour, everyone that signed up must go through a training session in a special, extreme low-g training room in the probe center near the propulsion conduit. All of the space-walkers are holo-scanned to make perfectly fitting lifesuits. These form-fitting outfits use sophisticated technology to maintain pressure, temperature, air supply and radiation protection yet still allow mobility. The duration of the training session is up to the trainer's discretion. She has to feel comfortable that everyone is totally ready for the following week's tour before dismissing the group.

At 9am on March 16th the elevator from the medical screening lab to the shuttle port begins its half hour climb with the trainer/guide and sixteen other passengers. This first tour group is short four people who have decided that zero-g is not for them. Two of the spacewalkers are a boisterous lady of 74 years and a sweet 8 year old girl. Greta and Anna are having the time of their lives. This is the same elevator with smart chairs that Greta rode down 43 years ago. It's hard for her to remember a time when she wasn't living on Gaia II.

Greta still spends a lot of her time in the Fusion Energy Plant at one-fifth g, in an advisory capacity, so is accustomed to low gravity. Anna, however, is just a natural. Greta enjoyed watching Anna during the low-g training. She thought to herself that her grand-daughter reminded her of a few children at the fair, when she was young, who would ride the spinning rides and roller coasters over and over and over, always wanting more.

Anna is tickled pink to be doing this with her grandma and hopes to be just like her someday. When the elevator reaches the shuttle port, Anna is the first out the door. Greta has to restrain her a little, since at 1/5 g you could jump up and hit your head on something.

The trainer/guide meets with the group when everybody is out of the elevator. She leads them all to the locker room, where their specially made lifesuits await. Thanks to the training session, most are able to don their suits with very little assistance.

The trainer has each person activate his or her suit for total life support. They even secure their head domes and start breathing the oxygen-rich air supply. Then, the guide uses a hand-held device to get readings from all of the sensors in each person's suit. Pressurizing is done by a steady mechanical counter pressure system with expanding foam buffers for concave areas of the body. Temperature is maintained by extreme insulation using a silica nanoskeleton coated by a flexible polymer and a cooling system of polymers coated with thermoelectric nanocrystals to absorb heat. Radiation protection is from hydrogen embedded throughout the suit and a special material in the outer layer. A high oxygen air supply is fed into a clear, domed helmet made of a special, see-thru, thin, super-strong ceramic. The trainer's hand-held device lets her know that all of these systems are working perfectly throughout each entire suit.*

The guide activates and checks her own suit, then tests communication by telling all of the group that it's okay to enter the shuttle bay now. She reminds them all that they will remain on full life support for most of the trip. Everybody was told in training that this would be the case so they could all get used to the high oxygen content of the air supply and to detect any suit failures, while they are still in the safe confines of the shuttle.

The guide escorts them all through the hermetically sealed door to the shuttle bay. Before them is a vessel like no one in the group, except the trainer, has remotely anticipated. It looks like a *flying saucer* out of an old science fiction movie from the entertainment data bank. The shuttle has four *legs* supporting the *body* of the ship and a staircase extending from the floor of the shuttle bay into the lower, central bulge of the bottom of the ship. There is a large, transparent half-bubble on the top, middle of the vessel.

Greta shakes her head. "Sally, who's idea was the design for this tour shuttle?"

Sally smiles. "The concept was suggested by Ishii Matogawa back in 2132. The probe people needed something to challenge them during that down period. I think they had a lot of fun designing and assembling this."

One by one they all go up the stairs into the *flying saucer*. Anna can't help but take two stairs at a time in the low gravity. The passengers are all welcomed by the pilot as they board. Staying with the theme, he is dressed up as an alien. Since everything is computerized, he is mostly there for entertainment, but is highly skilled at handling the shuttle in case of an emergency.

When everybody is strapped in, the pilot gives the signal to shuttle control. The shuttle bay is evacuated and depressurized so that the portal can be opened to the shuttle ring on the exterior of the ship. The four *legs* supporting the *flying saucer* fold down together and become the track that takes the ship to the shuttle ring. Once the track is connected securely to the ring, the portal closes.

As when launching the probes, the maglev shuttle ring moves slower and slower until it is no longer revolving about the axis of Gaia II. Some of the passengers feel an uncomfortable feeling because of this, but the automatically released medication helps a lot. The pilot uses touch icons on a control panel display to release the shuttle from the track and it hovers slightly above. Then, with the okay from shuttle control, the pilot gives the command to initiate a delta-v thrust that separates the shuttle from Gaia II. The on board computers take over from there.

After a second delta-v puts the *flying saucer* into an orbit ten kilometers closer to the planet than the *mother ship*, the pilot lets the passengers know that it is okay to undo their safety straps. They are all weightless, now. Sally points up and tells them, "Follow me." A hatch has opened leading to the clear bubble on the top of the shuttle.

Following Sally's lead, most finally manage to work their way into the bubble. Everyone in the group was taught extensively how to move in zero-g, but this is still all new to them and even the training room had a small amount of artificial gravity. Sally has to go back to get one person who is left floating in the middle of the room below.

The view is amazing in the bubble. The initial orientation of the shuttle has the bubble pointing toward their home ship. The tourists look up and see Gaia II from the outside for the first time. Since they are ten kilometers away and the ship's length is four kilometers including the scoop, the size is like looking at a four meter model from ten meters away. It's hard to believe that their whole world is in that small cylinder above. There is also a wonderful, clear view of stars in the background along with a crescent moon on the view horizon. They have seen this view on the walls in their Living Areas, but reality is quite different. Part of the view in the direction they are traveling is shielded to protect from the intense light of the star.

Sally talks to the group through the communications system in their helmets. "We will stay in this orientation for a little while to let you take in the amazing view above. Then, we are going to have a little fun!"

After fifteen minutes or so, Sally has everyone in the group grab on to one of several handles around the perimeter of the bubble room. There is a worried look on the faces of several of the passengers. Sally communicates to the pilot, who has been listening to all of their conversations. "I think we're ready, Jim." Slowly their ship starts to rotate. They all see the moon and then Gaia II leave their view and a bright object starts to appear in the direction they are turning. When the rotation stops, a large sphere, 35 times larger than a full moon seen from Earth, is straight *up* now. There is a feeling of having been turned upside-down, except there is no up or down.

Everybody is mesmerized by this amazing sight. The cloud covered planet is half dark and half light. Sally's voice snaps the tour group out of their trance. "The object you are now all looking at, thanks to a young lady here with us today, is called Planet Who. The moon you saw is called Horton and before this trip is over you may even see Grinch. We are now in an orbit ten kilometers closer to Planet Who than our home, Gaia II. That means we are traveling about 1.3 kilometers per hour faster. We will stay in this orbit for about three hours to clear the length of Gaia II. That should give us plenty of time for a space walk. If anybody has changed their mind about doing this, you can wait down in the room below. I'd rather find out now than when we are outside."

All sixteen stay in the bubble and Anna can't wait. Sally does one more check of everybody's lifesuit then does one additional test that catches them by surprise. Sally has a utility belt and takes a cutting tool out of a compartment in the belt. She has everybody stick out their hand one at a time. Then, she uses the cutting tool to slice a glove of each passenger. Each time, the abrasion quickly seals itself. The gloves and suit have a self-healing capability.

It's time for the spacewalk. Sally hooks a cable onto a loop on her waist. About every five meters of cable, there is another clip. She secures each traveler to the sixteen clips after hers. That leaves four clips for the missing passengers and an additional 20 meters of cable. Sally then fastens the other end of the cable to a designated spot in the bubble room and lets the pilot know that they are ready.

The hatch to the lower room closes and the bubble room depressurizes. When ready, the bubble fully opens up so that the entire group is now in open space. Sally is the only one with thrusting capability and gently thrusts away from the ship. The next person behind her is a little hesitant to let go. Greta thinks out loud. "This must have been what it was like letting go of a high bridge when bungee jumping or stepping out of an airplane when skydiving back on Earth." Sally coaxes the man and he releases his grip. One by one they follow her out into space.

Anna is behind her grandma in the middle of the group. She keeps moving farther away from the ship as, one by one, the rest of the space-walkers release to follow Sally out into the void. There is not much being said as most of the group is completely overwhelmed. Anna has been too busy with the mechanics of what they are doing to really look around and appreciate where she is. Finally, the last person releases and the remaining twenty meters of cable are played out. Sally keeps the line relatively taut using her thrusters. Greta checks on her granddaughter, at first with concern and then just to observe her joy.

When the line is at full extension, Sally starts to tell the group about what they are looking at. She explains the dark area they are seeing in their helmets. There are special filters embedded in the transparent material that darken in the direction of the star for eye protection. Sally gives the space-walkers information about the *flying saucer* they are tethered to, Gaia II, the planet, the moons Horton and Grinch, the stars they are seeing and other celestial objects, but at this point Anna is in her own world and doesn't hear a word.

Anna looks at the ship, the planet and the stars in the distance. She has spent her eight years knowing nothing but the inside of their big spaceship. It has been her whole world, her universe. The second generation adults on the spacewalk have spent 30 to 40 years in Gaia II and are truly overcome with emotion, but Anna feels it, too. Mentally, she knew it was out there from her schooling, but nothing could have prepared her for this.

A large band of stars, some areas obscured by dark patches, extends across her entire field of view. It is so beautiful. To Anna it looks like a halo of shimmering lights spread out on a black velvet cloth. She still has no true feeling for distances and sizes of the objects she is looking at, but she will remember this view for her entire life.

Anna then turns her attention to the planet below. It's so huge. She knows that it is a lot farther away than Gaia II so it must be way bigger. Anna has learned about Earth in her science classes and at Earth Awareness assemblies and has been told that this place is bigger than Earth. All she can see is a big fuzzy cloudy ball reflecting the orange-yellow light from the star. She knows about clouds and that they hide the hard surface of the planet. Maybe under the clouds there is some who-creature looking back up at her.

While she is taking in everything, Anna has many questions. Why, in this unbelievably big universe, is there such a small part of it where people can live? If all of those stars we are looking at are like the one we are near now or the one we came from, where Earth is, shouldn't a lot of them have planets where other people live? What star out there are we going to next? Why are the stars so far apart? How can scientists look at that band of stars and know it is a spiral shaped galaxy like the one on the poster in her science class? If there's supposed to be so many other galaxies, why can't I see them? (Andromeda is obscured by the star now.) Anna keeps her questions to herself for now, because Sally is talking to the grown-ups. She decides to just stare off into a dark part of space for a long time to see if she can see anything. In her mind, she is traveling through the stars. Anna feels very peaceful and happy. She almost forgets that her grandma is only meters away. When she does look in that direction, she sees that Granny Greta is smiling at her through her see-through helmet.

The time goes by fast and before long Sally is telling the group that it is time to go back in. The cable starts reeling them all in toward the bubble room. It stops when the first person is back. Sally then instructs that person to slowly reel in the cable until the next person is back in contact with the ship. The process continues, with each space-walker finding a handle to grab as before, until Sally is the last one. She gives a little thrust and joins them. The bubble closes and then pressurizes and they can all detach from the cable.

The hatch to the lower ship is opened and Sally informs the group that they are welcome to stay in the bubble or go back *below.* Anna goes through the hatch after a little while just to have more room to move around. The walls are well padded.

When it is time to make the delta-v speed-up to get out of the lower orbit, the passengers all have to strap in or hook on to one of the many available locations above and below. Now the shuttle is traveling in *front* of Gaia II. Only a small, select group of Gaians have ever seen the front side of the QFT scoop until now. Sally tells them a little about it. From the shuttle's point of view, the scoop is a huge dark vortex five times the diameter of Gaia II. They are able to see part of the inner scoop thanks to reflected light from the star. Anna comes back up into the bubble to look at the view. What she sees gives her a very eerie, scary feeling. It looks like there is a giant open mouth trying to draw them down into a bottomless dark pit. She leaves the bubble and goes back to the room below. The *flying saucer* continues on and then does another delta v to establish an orbit ten kilometers *above* Gaia II. Now they are going slower and will wait for the *mother ship* to pass them back up.

It is another three hours before the final velocity changes to rejoin the ship. Sally tells the group to all come up to the bubble after about an hour, if they aren't there already. She points out a light on their view horizon. It doesn't look much different than the stars in the view. "That is Planet Who's second moon, Grinch." She explains how Grinch is different than any other moon in this planetary system and mentions a couple of theories about how it came to be in orbit about Who. Sally tells them that they will be closing the hatch to the bubble in fifteen minutes.

When the tour group has had their last look out of the bubble and have all come back to the room below, the hatch closes. After a few more minutes, all are instructed to remove their head gear. The lower room now has a lower oxygen content to get them used to breathing normal air again.

The pilot comes over to the group, still in full costume, and asks if anyone is hungry for lunch. Those that are, which includes a certain 8 year old and 74 year old, get to see what it is like eating and drinking in zero gravity. The food is good and somewhat similar to the space hotel food that Greta has a vague memory of enjoying. They are advised to take only a few sips of liquid. It's okay to go to the bathroom in the suit if necessary, but it isn't a pleasant thing to live with during the rest of the tour.

Finally, the trip has to come to an end as the shuttle rejoins the maglev ring above the fusion reactor section of Gaia II. The ring slowly starts to move to catch up with the ship's rotation. Their flying saucer enters the shuttle bay and after a while, the passengers are allowed to disembark. Sally leads them out of the bay to the locker room where they all doff their suits, which will get recycled. Then, it is back down the elevator and home. It's been a day to remember, not just for Anna, but for all of the Gaians taking the trip. The second and third generation space-walkers now have a totally new perception of the place they live.
*From: www.popsci.com/technology/article/2012-10/deep-space-suit?single-page-view=true
Later the Same Day
An Isolated Building in Sonora, Tropicania

* * *

There is one person on Gaia II who hasn't been allowed to sign up for the spacewalks. He has a small home in Sonora that was made especially for him. The Gaians have tried to make the man comfortable, but he can never leave the immediate vicinity of the abode unless being escorted.

In the center of this home, there is a small, very plain room. It has white walls and a white ceiling, with a tile floor. There is a very simply designed rug on the floor in the room. Derek Scott is kneeling on this rug with his hands on his knees. Derek still has his blonde hair of youth, but he keeps it very short. He is very muscular and physically fit, since taking care of his

292 *Jack R. Woods*

body has been an obsession during his years of solitude. Derek is wearing a very basic khaki robe as he kneels and begins his ritual. He is attempting to reach a state of calmness before performing the *Salah* of *Isha*. This is the evening prayer, consisting of four *raka'at*, which are units of prescribed actions and words to be repeated. After *Isha*, Derek then does the first of the *Tarawih* prayers. Today is the first day of *Ramadan* in the Hijri Calendar year of 1579. Over the next 30 days, he will attempt a *khatm*, which is a complete recitation of the *Quran*.

It is about 8pm now and Derek has been fasting since 6 o'clock this morning. Before 6am, he had *suhoor*, a pre-fast meal. For Derek, this consisted of juice, dates, bread and a protein bar. After the *Tarawih* prayers, he will have *iftar*, the fast breaking meal. In addition to reciting the *Quran* and performing the five daily mandatory *salat*, Derek will again be attempting to forgive himself and those who have kept him prisoner for these many years. He is on his own personal pilgrimage to find peace in his soul. The simplicity of his prayer room and his kneeling position, called *ruku*, show his submission and humility before *Allah*.

Shortly after 8pm, Derek hears a knock on his door. He knows who it is as he doesn't get many visitors. Opening the door, he lets in Seker Zamani.

Seker has been coming to see Derek regularly now for about fifteen years. His first visit was also during the month of Ramadan, which fifteen years ago began near the end of August. While a student at the university, Seker Zamani decided that his purpose in life would be to keep the Islam religion alive on Gaia II. During the month of Ramadan, along with fasting, abstinence, prayers and recitation, it is also very important to increase charity to persons who are less fortunate. Seker decided one year that if he was going to attain the highest graces of *Allah*, he was going to need to help Derek Scott. After a very difficult couple of years for

Seker, Derek finally reached an understanding that Allah could give him a peace that he had never known and help him overcome his terrible feeling of loneliness.

Tonight, Seker has come by to enjoy a special meal with Derek. Seker, of course, has also been fasting all day. For the first *iftar* of this *Ramadan* they are having a small feast. Seker has brought a salad of berries and greens, grown in his mother's hydroponic gardens, all in a nice vinaigrette dressing. Derek has a large container of Brazilian stew from Little Rio that he will heat up along with some Hawaiian sweet bread from Hanalei Village. He had requested these items to be delivered in his weekly food and supply delivery. Seker has also brought a nice fruit cake from the bakery in Wicklesby. They drink water. Alcoholic beverages are not allowed for Muslims.

Seker and Derek have actually become friends, of sorts, over time. Even though he knows that Derek did a terrible thing when he was younger, Seker also realizes that forgiveness is very important in the eyes of *Allah*. Seker wonders if Derek will ever be accepted back into the Gaian society. The truth is, however, that Derek has gotten used to his life of solitude and prefers to keep it that way.

After an excellent meal, Seker bids farewell and arranges to come by in a few days so they can recite some verses of the *Quran* together. He then returns home to his wife and children, a short walk through the darkening Living Region of Sonora. Gaia II is still using the artificial sun for daylight and computer generated sunrises and sunsets on the east and west walls, even though they are near a real sun now. Once the sunset is over, the wall images of stars and the planet are obtained by moving wide field cameras that maintain a view 90° from the direction of the star. The sunset on the west wall was over about a half hour ago.

The reason Sonora is getting darker is because Seker is walking home during Who-set.

The staff of the Probe Center is working on all cylinders. This is another day of major importance for them and all of Gaia II. Today, two probes are being launched that will explore the surface of the planet, Who. On top of that, the two probes at Planet Sneech have been in orbit for about a week now and landing sites will be selected today. The probe to Planet Sam is having a close approach to the moon, Ham, and the final deceleration maneuvers are being made for the probe to Planet Cat to be able to establish an orbit. Two mining probe missions are also being monitored. One is orbiting Horton to find a site likely to supply helium 3 for the ship and the other is on its way to Grinch to search and mine for heavier elements. Finally, the planning phase of the new probe projects, which include the probes to the inner planets and the QFT probe to the Planet Truffula orbiting the star Lorax, has been completed and those projects will soon be going into production.

Gaia II makes an orbit of Planet Who in 24 hours, but the planet rotates once in 11 days 9 hours. So, since the orbit is in the direction of rotation, the ship takes a little over 26 hours to make a complete circuit of the planet. Scientists have already been studying the planet from Gaia II, while in orbit. They have found that there are large bodies of water on the surface, but it is opposite of the situation on Earth. Most of the surface area of Who is land. There are isolated seas on the planet with the largest being about the size of the continent of Australia. From thermal imaging the scientists can tell that there is a higher degree of plate tectonic activity and thus volcanism than Earth, which is to be expected from the larger planet. Another result of this is a greater differentiation of land elevation. If you take sea level of the largest body of water on the planet as the zero mark, radar data has shown that there are mountain ranges on Who that are over double the height of the Himalayas.

It is believed that the atmosphere of Who has come completely from the out-gassing of processes going on in the interior of the planet. The composition of the air is somewhat like early Earth, but higher in carbon dioxide as there is less water for it to dissolve into. The nitrogen content is high due to a long time build up from the out-gassing of ammonia. The estimated percentages are as follows: nitrogen 75%, carbon dioxide 17%, water vapor 3%, oxygen 2%, methane 1.5%, argon 1% and traces of other gasses especially nitrous oxide and carbon monoxide. The atmospheric pressure is almost double that on Earth at the surface, but the atmosphere doesn't extend quite as high. The cyclical processes, that maintain the balance of these levels on this 4.5 billion year old planet, are still a mystery.

Jaswinder Singh, Vera Greene and the rest of their team have been brainstorming for the last two months to make sure that the scientific instruments on the probes will discover any form of life that may exist on the planet. There has been a lot of second guessing, but in the end there has been little change in the original design of the experiments. With 2% oxygen and 1.5% methane in the atmosphere there is a good chance of finding some sort of life, but the abundances could also come from natural processes.

At 8:45am. Inga Larsson gives the command to her team to launch the first probe. The landing site for this probe has been chosen to be a delta, formed by the longest river on Who where it empties into one of the larger seas. The probe will not be landing right away. When it gets near the surface, a chemical reaction will inflate large air tanks so that the probe can *float* above the surface and explore the area before setting down for soil testing.

The second probe is scheduled for a 2:20pm launch. Since the primary mission of the probes is the search for life, the destination of the first probe and of this one have been chosen accordingly. One of the equatorial seas of the planet has a continental plate division right through its center. It is expected that there is thermal vent out-gassing at the sea bed along the fault line, as a higher amount of CO_2 and methane are being detected. Since one theory of the beginning of life on Earth is that it originated near thermal vents of this type, it seemed like a good place to look. The second probe is very different from the first. It will land and float on the surface of the sea and then send a submarine explorer to the sea floor.

* * *

At 2:30pm the next day, many Gaians are eating their lunch, but just about everybody is watching a video monitor of some sort. The surface of Planet Who is about to become visible for the first time. The probe committee has chosen the name Sagan for this probe, in honor of the late twentieth century astronomer who was such a strong, positive advocate for the search for extraterrestrial life. This voyage of discovery that Sagan is taking is of special interest to the younger Gaians. They have spent their whole existence living the day to day routine on board the ship and this is something external and new. For the first generation Gaians, of course, it is the culmination of a lifelong dream.

Henry Rowland, with his extensive knowledge of planetary science, is the narrator of the video that is being watched intently by the Gaians. So far, since entering the atmosphere, there hasn't been much to see, but that is about to change.

Many families have gotten together to watch the telecast on a wall display in one of their homes. Some of the teenage Gaians are with their friends and glance occasionally at their hand-held monitors to stay apprised of the situation. Ishii Matogawa has developed personal viewing helmets for members of his family so they can be completely immersed in the field of view of the probe cameras.

Something appears on all of the monitors. Henry Rowland makes the announcement. "There it is. We have our first view of the surface of Planet Who." The probe descends below the lower cloud layer and over a large river flowing through a dark steamy land mass. The light level is low due to the heavy cloud cover, but computer enhancement allows Gaians to see features that they wouldn't see with the unaided eye. Being already at a low altitude, it seems like no time at all before there is a jolt in the image telling the viewers that the air tanks on the probe have been inflated. Sagan settles down to establish a hover at about twenty meters above the surface.

Henry informs his audience, "Temperature readings by Sagan tell us that the surface temperature is about 80°C. Planet Who is far enough from the star that it get's less radiation than Earth does from the Sun, but the greenhouse effect is keeping the surface hot. This is a delta, just like the ones on Earth, which has been built up by sediments being washed down the river to the sea. In a few minutes, Probe Control will be activating horizontal propulsion and we will all take a little tour of the delta." The ground image starts to move as Henry attempts to explain what they are seeing. All of a sudden, the probe seems to be rising as the surface image becomes more distant and the viewers soon find out why. "The probe sensors have detected a large object and it is increasing altitude to fly over it." A gigantic rock crosses the image slowly. "Judging by the height of the probe now, you are looking at a boulder about fifty meters tall. It appears to be of volcanic origin, deposited here by an ancient eruption."

Hovering above the steamy landscape, Sagan approaches land that has a different color than what has been seen so far. Even in the low light a yellowish tinge can be seen. As the probe floats over, it becomes apparent that this substance extends like a rivulet for hundreds of meters. Henry gets confirmation from other team members then announces, "What you are seeing is a gold deposit. If the surface is any indication, this field would dwarf anything ever found in the US state of Alaska back home. If people ever live on this planet, the gold will be a wonderful resource. Most of you know that it has many important uses besides just pretty jewelry."

For about four hours, the probe explores the delta and finds no visible signs of life. There are many more boulders of various sizes, another (smaller) gold field, some reddish areas where there is exposed oxidized iron, and a few other features of interest to a planetary geologist. Before Sagan is about to prepare for landing, Henry informs his audience, "As much as we have hoped, we aren't really surprised at not finding plants or animals here. Multicellular life as we know it would have a difficult time surviving in this environment. For starters, the oxygen level is very low and the temperature is very hot. Also, the dense cloud cover would make it difficult for any larger life to use photosynthesis for energy."

"This does not rule out life at all, however. You must realize that life on Earth existed as single-celled organisms for two billion years before oxygen started amassing in the atmosphere. We have to expect that the majority of life in the universe is similar to our bacteria. Even photosynthesis cannot be totally ruled out yet. Cyanobacteria developed very early in Earth's history in conditions not too different than what we have here. This microorganism is still responsible for all photosynthesis on Earth to this day. The reason atmospheric oxygen levels stayed so low for so long in the presence of cyanobacteria is that the oxygen that was produced combined with so many other elements. At first oxygen on Earth combined with dissolved minerals, like iron, silicon and sulfur, in the oceans and then it oxidized the same elements on land until the land and seas were saturated to a point that it started accumulating in the atmosphere. If something like our cyanobacteria came to be here within the last two or three billion years, the low light level and thus the slow conversion of CO_2 to oxygen, might still not have gotten this planet to the saturation point. We will soon be testing the soils and waters of Planet Who!"

Henry's face appears on the monitor. "While Sagan is still preparing to land I will tell you a couple of other things that it will be looking for. There are several other ways, which we know of, that life can get energy other than by photosynthesis. One is called chemosynthesis. This is a process in which microorganisms convert carbon dioxide or methane into organic material without using sunlight. In photosynthesis, the sunlight strips a hydrogen atom off of a water molecule to be used as an *electron donor*. In chemosynthesis, the organism finds other *electron donors* in inorganic matter, such as hydrogen sulfide, sulfur or iron without needing sunlight. This process still happens on Earth near thermal vents on the ocean floor and is accomplished by organisms we call chemoautotrophs. Another, less efficient, method of energy production is an anaerobic (without oxygen) process called fermentation. Herbert and Ilsa Rauch are very familiar with this process. So, we are still hopeful as Sagan is about to land and our other probe will be doing tests near Who's version of deep sea thermal vents."

Sagan releases gas from its air tanks and descends. Its cameras show Gaians a panoramic view and Henry Rowland informs his audience that it will take time to get test results from the probe, but he will keep them updated.

The second probe has been dubbed Dixon, after a twenty-first century scientist who was a pioneer in the discipline of astrobiology. One of the key questions for astrobiologists was, and still is, the origin of life. The hardest step to explain is the emergence of self replicating cells from a *soup* of pre-life organic molecules. Jackie Dixon and her team at the J Craig Venter Institute created the first self-replicating, evolving and metabolizing synthetic life. She won a Nobel Prize for her work in 2132 and became a world-wide celebrity.

The probe, Dixon, is now descending thousands of kilometers away from Sagan. Henry Rowland gives the signal to Carol Day, who is monitoring the video transmission, to go to split screen. The right side of the screen displays the slowly panning view from Sagan and the left side allows viewers to now also see what Dixon is seeing. The probe is going through atmospheric entry so, in addition to obscuring clouds, occasionally hot plasma streams past the camera.

Henry tries to fill in the gap for those watching until things get more interesting. He comments, "We are expecting great things from Dixon since she and I share a common African-American heritage." He gives a short biography of Jackie Dixon. "We have a little treat for you. Unfortunately, the missions of the probes are scientific and not a sight-seeing trip. That being said, we expect the lower cloud layer to be higher for the second probe. Dixon will be passing over a small mountain range on its way to the landing site. I say small, but the heights of some of the mountains in this range are on par with higher peaks in the Rocky Mountains back home." Henry informs the viewers of what they know about the plate tectonics of Planet Who. He adds, "Since there is less water on Who than on Earth, the relative sea level is lower, so mountain ranges are much higher. However, even if you measure from the deepest point in the sea to the highest point on land, there is still a significantly greater difference on Planet Who due to the higher degree of plate activity."

A large rocky feature starts to materialize as Dixon comes out of the clouds. It is remarkably clear compared to the view from the first probe. The rugged mountain range below actually looks dry from the altitude of the cameras. As the probe passes over the final ridge the contrast is astounding. The far side of the range is buried in a sea of clouds. Henry comments, "What Dixon is seeing now is a rain shadow effect like the one that causes such a difference in precipitation between the East side and the West side of several of the Hawaiian Islands. If we could see through those clouds there would probably be some amazing waterfalls. The cloud build-up, and the weather in general, on Planet Who, happens more gradually due to its much slower rotation than Earth, but it also lasts a lot longer. A storm could last for weeks."

"Dixon will be landing in a calm sea today. It is now decelerating in a way that is, in principal, not much different than the earliest space vehicles that landed in the ocean using a parachute. Of course, today's methods are much more controllable and reliable." The probe has a successful splashdown in a central sea location. After stabilizing, Dixon's cameras can only see water with clouds on the horizon. "Dixon will be doing some water sampling before it releases the undersea probe. We will be leaving the cameras on, so you can log in any time you want to see live video, but I am leaving you for now. At five o'clock tomorrow night we will be passing over Sagan's landing site and I will come back on-line and update you on the first day findings of the probe's scientific instruments. Then at ten forty-five we will do the same for Dixon. The submarine is being launched at eleven pm tomorrow. This is Henry Rowland signing off."

* * *

The next day, the initial findings of both probes are disappointing as far as the search for life goes. There is no sign of even the simplest form of life as we know it. This poses a new question to solve, "Why isn't there life here, or is it just so different that we can't see it?" On the bright side, a wealth of knowledge has been gathered about the composition and chemical processes occurring in the soil that may help Henry Rowland and his coworkers piece together a history of the planet. Sagan will still be doing deep core samples in the days to come and will be releasing a rover to get samples and examine rocks in interesting locations away from the probe. Dixon has confirmed expectations of high salinity and pH of the sea water and the submarine is still analyzing seafloor samples near the thermal vents, that were located earlier today.

A small ornate dome rises out of the desert land of Sonora. Years ago, Seker Zamani had convinced the Gaians that Muslims on Gaia II needed their own place of worship. The churches on the ship in Wicklesby and Hanalei Village just weren't designed to accommodate some of the traditions of Islam.

There are about fifty adult, practicing Muslims and all of them are in the Sonora Mosque today. This is the first day of the month of Shawwal. The fasting month of Ramadan is over. Soon there will be a feast and celebration, but now there is a special communal *salat*, or prayer in progress. The mosque has a large open floor and each worshiper has his or her own simple rug on the floor in front of where they stand. They are all in basic white attire in reverence to Allah.

The *salat* of *Eid ul-Fitr* consists of two *rakats* or units. Each rakat has an additional three *Takbirs*, where each person raises hands to ears while saying "Allahu Akbar" or "God is great". In the second *rakat*, the *Takbirs* are before *ruku*, which is the tradition of getting down on the rug and resting hands on one's knees. Once attaining calmness, submission and humility before Allah, the prayer continues. After the *salat*, all leave the mosque in reverence to meet at the feasting area, which has been set up in a pretty area resembling a desert oasis on Earth.

Seker is with Derek. He has gotten special permission for Derek to join them as long as he is a *chaperone* of sorts. Seker sees that Derek feels out of place and starts a conversation. "So, did you have any revelations during the *Laylat al-Qadr*?" The Laylat al-Qadr was four days ago and is the holiest of Islam days. The name means *Night of Power* and is when it is believed that Muhammad received the first verses of the Quran from Allah. It is also believed that this is when Allah decides each person's destiny.

"I did not discover any specifics, but I did get the overwhelming feeling during prayer that Allah still has a very important plan for my life." The two join Seker's family and all of the others at the feasting grounds.

Along with other younger and nonpracticing family members of the worshipers, Kayla Novac has been helping with the set up and planning of the celebration. Ali Zamani has been in the mosque with Seker and Derek. He walks up to Kayla and gives her a kiss on the cheek and whispers in her ear, "This has to have been the longest Ramadan ever." They give each other a little sly smile in anticipation of the evening to come.

It has been two months now since the probe launching to Planet Who. All of the members of the Arrival Committee plus several others have been invited to this meeting today to get a wide range of points of view as to how their mission should continue.

A notable invite to the discussion is Paul Drake. Paul and his nanofactory have stayed very busy producing new products for the Gaians, but others in the room are not sure how his expertise will be valuable to the probe missions. His research department, with whom he spends most of his time, has been working on quantum computer applications and improved nanobots. Other than that, he mainly creates products ranging from furniture to lifesuits to anibots. His son, Roger, is in charge of the anibot project.

Jaswinder Singh is again presiding over the meeting. First generation Gaians, on the committee, had been briefed before leaving Earth, but younger members are just now realizing that Dr. Singh had been selected for the Gaia II mission to be more than just an astrobiologist. He has been given the responsibility, from the powers that be back on Earth, to be ultimately in charge of the entire mission. Sometimes they wonder who he will choose to carry on in his place as he gets older.

Room 701 of Gaia University is similar to the room where Nova Szkody presents Earth Awareness Class in Romanov Primary School. It is the largest classroom on the science level, complete with podium and 3D projection capability. Designed to accommodate two hundred students, the seating is tiered with fully capable smart chairs. Today, it is about one quarter full.

All of the invitees settle into their seats and Jaswinder begins the meeting. "Thank you all for coming. We will be discussing all of the probes and their findings today, but our key focus will be on the two Planet Who probes, which have been on the surface now for two months. If any of you are wondering why you have been invited to this meeting, it is because we think that your perspective and input may be valuable to important decisions we will soon need to be making. Our primary decision may be one of the most important ones that mankind has ever had to make, so if any of you have any thoughts or ideas, no matter how silly they may seem, we would like for you to share them with us."

"To start the meeting, we will have Keiji Kusakabe update us on the mining missions." Keiji steps up to the front of the room and uses a hand-held control device to activate the room's 3D imagery. Keiji stands off to one side of the image.

"What you are looking at is the *digger* probe on the moon, Horton. Landing went smoothly, but as you all know we didn't find the helium3 we were looking for at Site A. I'm afraid that this still isn't an exact science. Our next preferred site was too far away so the decision was made to relocate the *digger* to Site D, about one hundred kilometers from Site A. We were prepared for this contingency, but the move did use up a lot of the probe's power."

"Luckily, we did find helium3 in the regolith at Site D. Only traces were found, however, so our *miners* and *sifters* will have to process three times the regolith as on Earth's moon to obtain an equal amount. We do think we will be able to fulfill the needs of the ship with about four months of mining." The 3D live image of the *digger* is being taken by a rover sent out to visually monitor the operation. Processed regolith is seen slowly ejecting from the *digger* and filling an adjacent ravine. Great care is being taken to not create a cloud of debris in the low gravity environment.

"We will be sending out the probe next month to assemble a pod launcher, so that it will be ready when it is time to start putting pods of helium3 into orbit about the moon."

"The mining probe to the moon, Grinch, has been even trickier, but what we have learned from the trial and error of asteroid mining near Earth has been invaluable. Our digger is now on Grinch and attached to the surface. The extreme low-g mining here is totally different than that on the larger moon. In addition to finding heavy elements that will replenish what we have lost, including water and carbon compounds, we are getting some good science from Grinch. This body may not have even formed in the same protoplanetary disc as the rest of this system. For all we know, it could have come from ours!" Keiji gives more details and shows more video taken by the probes and finishes to a warm applause.

Jaswinder then asks Henry Rowland to give a presentation of the latest data from the outer planet probes.

"Good morning. I'm sure you all watched the telecasts of the successful landings of the probes that we have named Scott and Amundsen after the polar explorers." The group applauds. "We have taken a few pictures for our tourist brochures since then." He turns on the projector and everyone in the room gasps. "The image you are seeing is the view from the probe, we are calling Scott. It is taken through a filtered lens as it is looking directly at the planet's sun. The Planet Sneech is 1.2 AU from the star Zax, so the orange dwarf star has an angular diameter of about 70% of the sun's as seen from Earth. The star's luminosity is 15% that of our sun's, so Sneech only gets about 10% of the warmth as the Earth. As you can see, there is an atmosphere diffracting the light of this K-type star creating the beautiful lavender color in this image. The glistening surface and sparkling specks in the air are crystals from a very recent eruption of an *ice volcano*. You can see that, even though Sneech is very cold, it can be quite beautiful. Humans may eventually live on Planet Who, but Sneech is the one the artists will be visiting."

Henry changes the image. "This is a view of the rugged landing site that the probe Amundsen had to land at twenty hours ago. Sneech rotates once every 42 hours, so right now Amundsen is in darkness. This probe is on a fault line near a mountain range. Amundsen will probably eventually be destroyed by a sneechquake, but we decided that it would be worth it to get samples from this region."

Henry shows another image and again gets gasps from the audience. "There is little scientific value to this image, but it rivals any fantasy space art painting I've ever seen." What they are looking at is a twilight view of a rugged mountain scene with small white glaciers (probably frozen carbon dioxide) and two amazing moons, both full in the lavender sky.

"As well as pretty pictures, there is a lot of science we can do at Sneech. At 2.3 times the mass of the Earth this is the first so-called Superearth we have ever visited. It's radius is 1.3 times that of Earth so it has 70% more surface area to explore. There are plenty of heavy elements and frozen water in the crust of this planet, so I think we will probably be colonizing Sneech long before Who can sustain earthlife without biosphere protection. People will always need lifesuits on Sneech, but that is no different from Mars, where colonies are now being established." This last bit of information was from their most recent Earth communication that was sent out over twenty-eight years ago.

"I could talk all day about Sneech and its moons. Therefore, I think I will just answer any questions you may have for now so we can move on. Full reports are available on the probe site."

A lady in the back of the room raises her hand and is selected. "What surface gravity has been measured by the probes?"

"Readings from both probes are about 1.43g. This confirms our calculation made from our mass and radius measurements. The average density of the planet is about 6.2 grams per cubic centimeter making it about 12% denser than Earth. "

Another question comes from the other side of the room. "Is the closest moon experiencing any tidal heating?"

"No, Sneech isn't massive enough to have this effect. There won't be a liquid ocean underneath the surface of this moon, even though it has been named *One Fish* by our young contest winner." This gets a polite giggle from the room.

A couple more questions and Henry changes the topic to the probes exploring the fifth and sixth planets. The fifth planet, Sam, has an unusually thick atmosphere resembling Saturn's moon, Titan. The sixth planet, and third largest, Cat, isn't a carbon planet, but has a higher abundance of carbon and water than any other terrestrial planet in this system or the Earth's. Henry promises that there will be a broadcast to all Gaians, giving all of the details about what the outer planet probes have discovered, but for now the meeting time is devoted to the Who probes.

Jaswinder joins Henry at the podium. To everyone in the room, especially Henry, he apologizes. "I'm sorry, Henry. Thirty minutes is not nearly enough time to do this subject justice. One week from today, we will have another meeting totally devoted to the outer planet probes."

"Now, I would like to discuss what I brought you all here for. If you look at your personal monitors, I will go over the analysis of the data from the scientific instruments of our two probes on the surface of Planet Who." Jaswinder shows numerous tables, graphs, spectral images and other means of presenting data then gives his team's analysis of what they think the information implies. Jaswinder discusses soil composition, chemical processes, changes with depth, differences between the data from the delta and the thermal vents, sea and atmosphere composition, temperature gradients and other parameters that may give clues as to how this planet works and the probability of finding life.

After an hour of detailed analysis, Jaswinder announces his team's conclusion. "It appears that every process, abundance and all other data we have taken so far can be explained by inorganic reactions and cycles. In other words, no evidence of life has been found. I'm not satisfied with this, however, and I may never be. I think that this is why I was chosen to oversee this mission. Our prime objective, other than just adding to the collective knowledge of mankind, is to find a new home for the human race and earth-life. With Planet Who, this involves terraforming, which would be a one hundred to one thousand year process of making this planet livable for life as we know it. We know from Earth that once Gaia takes hold of a planet, it's there to stay. But at what cost? Can we really be one hundred percent sure that there is no indigenous life, completely different than ours, which we would be eradicating? On Earth, the Great Oxidation Event was the most catastrophic mass extinction in our history. Can we be morally right to even take the most remote chance that we will be doing the same thing here? I would like to open up this topic for discussion."

Gordon Chang asks the first question. "What about dormant life? We know that some forms of life can stay in a dormant state for as long as a thousand years, to be revived by special environmental conditions or some biological clock. How could we test for this?"

Vera Greene is now up front with Jaswinder and fields the question. "That is exactly one reason why it is so difficult to be sure. We would like to think that any life form would eventually evolve to the point to where some descendant would inhabit almost anywhere we choose to look. We would also like to think that we could tell it apart from common inorganic material. Once again though, what if we are wrong?"

One of the probe team members stands. "How do we even know we can terraform this planet? It has never been done before."

Jaswinder answers. "If you don't mind, we'll answer that question later. We have a special presentation after this discussion."

Mei Sun makes a statement. "I would like to bring up the question of morality. For the sake of argument, let's say that there is a dormant, silicon-based life form that lives ten meters underground and only surfaces during short periods when the magnetic poles flip. If we assume that this would be a very simple life form, would it really be immoral to replace it with our more advanced life? Isn't this just the way that nature works?"

Jaswinder responds to this question, also. "I don't think it's just a question of spiritual morality. One of the greatest mysteries of the universe is how life began, what different forms it can take and how common it is. This is why I became an astrobiologist. Finding life like you just described would be a huge step toward finding an answer. It would be scientifically immoral, if not spiritually immoral, to eradicate it."

Mei Sun counters. "Then we should never create any colonies in the galaxy and shouldn't be inhabiting Mars."

"Maybe we shouldn't."

Paul Drake takes a central position. "I would vote that we do every test and experiment, that we can conceive of, to look for signs of life and, if they all come up negative, we move on."

The debate continues for about an hour. The only decision made is to continue the debate. When Jaswinder feels that all of the important points have been made, he announces that a special committee will brainstorm to come up with more tests that the probes can do. Meanwhile, he lets them know that he would like to continue on to the next topic of discussion.

"We need to be prepared to attempt the terraforming of the planet in case we decide to proceed. Two people in this room are going to talk to you about how this might possibly be done. First, I would like for you to hear what Ali Zamani has to say." It makes perfect sense that Ali should be involved in this, but it still catches the group by surprise.

Ali takes the podium. "Hello friends. If you haven't guessed by now, I have a dual purpose on this voyage. First and foremost, my job has been to keep you all alive. This is not as easy as you would think. I have used every trick that I learned in Egypt and on Mars along with a few I came up with along the way. My other, less known, responsibility has been a generalization of the first. That challenge has been to attempt to figure out how to make an entire planet livable for human beings."

What really has most of the people in the room stunned is that they can't remember a time when Ali has been this serious. They find out that he has been spending a lot of the last twenty years in his lab perfecting genetically engineered algae. The algae he has *designed* is super temperature resistant, consumes an amazing amount of carbon dioxide and methane and spreads faster than any life form known to man.

Ali explains a three phase process that he feels would be their best shot at getting earth-life to take hold on Planet Who.

When Ali is done, Jaswinder asks his other surprise speaker to take the podium. He asks Paul Drake to fill everybody in on the status of his project.

Paul comes to the front of the room. "Thank you, Jaswinder. About two years ago, Dr. Singh came to me and asked how far we have come in our research to perfect self-replicating nanobots. We actually had some working models at the time. He asked if I would be able to develop one that could be airborne in 2 bars of atmospheric pressure, convert carbon dioxide to oxygen, duplicate itself on the order of once every ten minutes and handle high temperature, but would become inactive at temperatures below 30°C. I told him that it may be possible and he asked if I could make it a high priority."

"Since then, the specifications have been refined and numerous prototypes have been developed and tested. We decided to first focus on the self replication and then have a final replication into a nanomachine that would perform the atmospheric conversion. The machines need raw materials to duplicate so would not be able to be airborne until the final evolution. Mathematically, at one reproduction every ten minutes, the entire surface of the planet would be covered at a density of one nanobot every 100 square nanometers in about fourteen hours."

Jaswinder asks Ali to come back up to the podium. "Gentlemen, I have had you both working independently on your research products. I would now like to ask you if you could become the best of friends. Paul, I need for you to assist Ali in any way that you can. You have worked wonders developing your nanobots and I congratulate you. Unfortunately, there is a lot more to terraforming a planet than just changing carbon dioxide to oxygen. Ali, with help from Paul's nanobots, you can greatly reduce the time frame of this huge undertaking. I would like to ask both of you to work together to come up with a plan to terraform Planet Who in the shortest period of time possible and present your results eight weeks from today. Will you do this for me and the rest of mankind?"

Paul answers first. "So you are asking me to work side by side with this crazy man to develop a plan to do the impossible and then never get to see if it works, because a committee has decided not to proceed."

Jaswinder smiles. "Yeah, that's about right."

Ali looks at Jaswinder. "Really Jas, nanobots?!"

Paul and Ali shake hands and Ali makes a suggestion. "Meet you for breakfast at Tahiti Nui Café tomorrow?"

Paul smiles this time and quotes a famous movie line. "Ali, I think this could be the beginning of a beautiful friendship."

Jaswinder thanks everybody for coming and reminds the group that there will be a follow up meeting in eight weeks on Monday, July 15th where decisions will be made.

Jaswinder talks to Ali and Paul on the side after the meeting. "There's somebody else I want to have work with you. Planetary systems, even without biology, are incredibly complicated, interactive feedback mechanisms. You will need to run numerous models on the quantum computer. You need a computer expert and my son, Rahii, is the best QC man on this ship, even with the five years he was banned from the computer center."

Ali comforts Jaswinder. "We'd be honored to have your son work with us."

Suki Matogawa is especially excited about this year's Summer Festival. She has signed up for the ages 10-16 surfing competition. Suki has been practicing at every possible opportunity, even though her parents have made sure that school comes first. She is one of the youngest in the age group, so she doesn't expect to place, but she is really hyped anyway.

Michael Chang is awake early about two kilometers away from where Suki lives. He is eating a light meal, low on fats and sugars, because today is the day he has been training for all year long. Michael is in three different events of the *Low-g Games* that are a part of the Summer Festival. His best event is the high dive, but he is also performing in the trampoline and gymnastics competitions. While he eats, he is mentally going through his preplanned tumbles and spins.

Leilani Matogawa is eating a high-carb breakfast at her home in Hanalei Village. She is the favorite in the senior 10K race through Tropicania. Men and women are competing together. She has an added incentive to finish the race in a good time, since Suki's surfing competition starts one hour after her race begins.

Almost the entire population of Gaia II has gathered for the festival. There is something for everybody. As well as the numerous sporting competitions, there are food booths, arts and crafts booths, games and projects for young children, musical performances, a sandcastle building contest and other fun things to keep them all entertained.

There are large outdoor screens set up all over the festival area, which this year is in northern Hanalei Village. On the screens, the festival goers can watch on-going sporting events, musical performances and other entertainment.

The food booths this year are presented by volunteers from each of the six Gaian communities. They have decided to give the hospitality people, like the ones who catered the Arrival Celebration, a break so they can relax and enjoy the festival.

There are three musical groups performing during the day long celebration. A stage is set up on the western side of the festival area. From 10am to 1pm, the Alpenhosers are playing their fun music, which is traditional German polka with a twist. From 2pm to 5pm the Primal Percussion Ensemble from Little Rio plans to keep everybody dancing with their infectious rhythms. Then, after a two hour dinner break, the Exploding Novas have the 7pm to 10pm slot. The *Novas* are beginning when the sunset simulation is covering the western wall behind them and finishing their set with music complementing the choreographed laser light show that culminates the festival.

The *Low-g Games* have been going on all week, but today is when all of the final competitions are happening. The games are held in the Low-g Park that was created mid-voyage thanks in part to the vision of Leilani Matogawa. The western 100 meters of the sky cylinder above Tropicania was converted into the park. The sky cylinder has the same axis as Gaia II, of course, and has a radius of 100 meters as opposed to the 1000 meters of the Living Areas. Since gravity increases linearly with distance from the axis, the artificial gravity on the inner surface of the Low-g Park is about 0.1g. Some events actually take place or originate closer to the axis at even lower *gravity*.

Nine elevators ascend the western wall of Tropicania, accessing the park. They are equally spaced, with Elevator 1 beginning near the theater elevators in the parking garage that is accessed through the waterfall covered cave entrance from Hanalei Village.

At 9:30am, Michael Chang begins his ride up Elevator 5, which is the closest to his home in Little Rio. Michael is confident for a sixteen year old and has been very disciplined in his practicing. He is average height, but is very well toned from years of focused exercising. He knows he is ready for this,but is still naturally nervous. The ride takes half an hour and is very scenic, since the side facing the Living Area is transparent. Michael isn't thinking about the view, however. He is totally focused on his first finals competition on trampoline, which is scheduled to begin at 11am. Others in the games are in the elevator with Michael and in the other eight elevators which all departed at the same time. The competition coordinators and judges all took an earlier elevator.

Some of the events are similar to the old X Games competitions of the early 21st century, such as skateboard and BMX, which both have special facilities at the park. Other events, such as those Michael Chang is participating in, are more gymnastic in nature. A couple of events, like the high dive, take advantage of the still lower artificial gravity *higher* in the park. The one that begins in the lowest gravity is the hang gliding competition. It begins only twenty meters from the ten meter radius propulsion conduit. In other words, it takes place seventy meters closer to the Gaia II axis than the *surface* of the Low-g Park and therefore has only three percent of normal 1g gravity. There is a special access elevator to the Super Low-g Aerial Staging Facility.

Meanwhile, the senior 10K race is about to begin at the festival grounds *below*. The main 10K race was at 9am and has been completed now by all but a few recreational joggers. There is also a shorter race for children twelve and under at noon. The seniors are gathering at the starting line for the *go* signal set for

10am. Leilani is feeling good, which isn't a good sign for anybody attempting to defeat her in the race.

At 10am precisely, the race is begun and follows a route very similar to the first circuit of Tropicania ran by Leilani Matogawa and Mei Sun so many years ago. All of the runners race toward the waterfall and the path that parallels the train from Hanalei Village to Little Rio. The route winds through Little Rio and Sonora then back to the finish line at the festival grounds. The circumference of the Living Area is six kilometers, but the trail through Tropicania is planned so that the race is exactly ten kilometers.

Ishii Matogawa is one of the judges of the surfing competition and is fine tuning the wave machine that creates waves in Hanalei Bay. The machine and the contour of the surface below the water have been designed to produce the best waves possible in the surfing area, but they are still pretty feeble compared to those surfed at competitions on Earth. Therefore, the judging is more about style than athletic ability.

Suki is now on the beach with other contestants picking out her surfboard. She is quite short compared to the other surfers in her group. Being a little on the plump side she takes after her grandfather a little. Ishii is watching her from the judging booth and can't help but giggle. Still, he is very proud of her and she loves her grandpa. The surfboard Suki picks has drawings of surfers on big waves randomly oriented on the the surface. The competition boards being used are all essentially the same, except for artistic designs, to ensure fairness.

Also on the beach, there is a sandcastle building competition underway. Jacques Laplace is overseeing this contest. He has to separate the catoms from the ordinary beach sand to make the castle building possible. Gaia II has its share of wonderful sculptors and artists whom are seriously competing, but there are many participating just for fun. There is a special contest for young children as with many of the festival events.

Still one other event on the beach is the beach volleyball competition, which is also underway. There are so many things to participate in, it's surprising that there are any spectators, but there are numerous people cheering on their friends and family members. Most of these people will be doing their own thing later.

The premier event of the Summer Festival is the softball game between Europia and Tropicania. This takes place at the field where Barry and Mei sat in the bleachers, to look at Planet Who, just before arriving in orbit.

The field is set up with the direction from home plate to the center of centerfield being due north. There is a good reason for this. Gaia II rotates from South to North, so there is a coriolis effect that is apparent when looking at the waterfall which curves to the South. The playing area is a standard ball field with a first base foul line and a third base foul line. What is different on Gaia II is that balls hit in the air tend to curve in the foul direction. A ball hit twenty meters high, down the left field foul line will land about four meters foul not even taking into account breeze or aerodynamics of the ball. The ball also seems to travel farther when hit near the foul lines than to straight out centerfield. What's more, deviation due to the coriolis effect is height dependent, so the higher the ball is hit the more it curves. This effect also increases at greater angles away from the center of centerfield. A player brought here directly from Earth would have a heck of a time getting oriented to all of this, but these players have spent their entire lives in this environment.

Ali, Kayla and some of their family members are sitting with Jaswinder, Leela and family in the third baseline bleachers. The game is about to start. It is scheduled for 2pm, but running a little late. Neither family has any members in the game, but they enjoy watching. Jaswinder comments to Leela. "It's too bad cricket hasn't gained popularity here, but I guess this will do." The Singhs are from Europia and Ali's family lives in Tropicania, so Jaswinder and Ali have a little gentleman's bet riding on the game.

During the middle of the game, Ali has a short conversation with Jaswinder. "Jas, I have a proposal for you."

"Sorry, no backing out on your bet now."

"No, I'm afraid this has nothing to do with the ballgame." This piques Jaswinder's curiosity. "Paul, Rahii and I have been working day and night on the terraforming challenge and we have come to a conclusion of sorts."

Now Jaswinder completely turns his attention away from the game. "Go on."

"It's going to take about twenty years to get life to take hold on the planet and take over the terraforming process without our help. We have concluded that, because there are so many variables, this process is going to have to be monitored."

"What are you getting at?"

"A bio-dome on Planet Who!"

"But who would stay behind to staff it?"

"I've already had the conversation with Kayla. We have agreed to stay behind on the planet. By the time we reach the next star we will both be one hundred years old or dead. There are good people, who can maintain life support systems on the ship and we have the experience from our biosphere living on Mars."

"Are you sure you've thought this thing all the way through? Once we leave, we can't come back."

"We have. Both Kayla and I understand the gravity of the situation, so to speak, and we have decided."

"Well, I'll run it by the committee and see what they say."

"Okay Jas, but it's the only way."

Jaswinder watches the rest of the game with Ali, but after *the conversation*, his mind isn't on softball. Europia wins and Ali has to host Jaswinder and Leela to a nice dinner and evening at their home sometime in the near future.

After the game, the Singhs and Zamanis go their own way. The residents of Gaia II enjoy the food and music that evening, followed by an amazing laser light show to close down the annual event in style.

one week later…

The committee agrees reluctantly to Ali's bio-dome proposal, which is to be announced at the next formal meeting on July 15th. Ali and Kayla break the news to their family. There are tears of disbelief and Kayla reminds them that it's not for sure yet since the final decision hasn't been made to try to terraform the planet. Seker talks to Ali on the side. "If this all happens, there is somebody I would like to go with you to live in the bio-dome. I haven't asked him, but I think he will volunteer."

By themselves, or in small groups, people are exiting the elevators on the seventh floor of Gaia University. A few take the stairs. Attending the meeting today are all those who were invited to the meeting on May 20 plus several others. In addition, today the meeting will be telecast so that any interested Gaian can watch the proceedings. Everybody on the ship knows, by now, what decision is going to be made today.

As the seats of Room 701 fill, Jaswinder has a worried look on his face. The room is buzzing with conversation. Eventually, everybody is seated and the noise level in the room drops a decibel level. Jaswinder takes this as his cue.

"Good morning to you all. As you know, there is only one topic of discussion today. We are going to present all of the newest data from experiments being done by our probes on the surface of Planet Who. Our best data analysis people have been obsessively studying the results of these experiments and all of the previous findings of the probes. So, we'll get started right away. Vera……"

Vera Greene is sitting next to Jaswinder and stands up. "I am going to be the one presenting our findings, but everyone on our team, including Jaswinder, has put an incredible amount of time and energy into this to try to be as thorough as possible. Our probes, Dixon and Sagan, have been very busy. They have gotten core samples from deep in the ground. A rover from Sagan and the submarine seafloor explorer from Dixon have carefully taken samples over areas of about 2000 square meters looking for any surface anomalies. The probe labs have combined portions of these thousands of samples with every available chemical, both natural on the planet and brought to the planet by the probes, at a range of temperatures and pressures. Other variables, such as intensity of light and saturation of solution have also been varied. Let's look at what we found."

Vera uses her hand-held control to dim the lights in the room and present data using both the 3D room projector and the personal smart chair monitors. Her presentation lasts for so long that, half way through, everybody in the room is given a break to get something to snack on. Four hours later, each person in the room has a new appreciation of how much work the astrobiology team has done in such a short time and gives a standing ovation.

Jaswinder takes charge of the meeting again. "Now that you've seen one of the most intense two months of detailed data gathering and analysis ever done, I think you have noticed a common thread. We have done a lot of science and have learned a lot, but we still do not have any evidence whatsoever of life. That means terraforming is still on the table. Our subcommittee has decided to have a vote at this meeting to determine the fate of Planet Who. It's up to you. A two-thirds majority in favor of terraforming will be required for us to proceed on this course. I am putting a screen in front of you now. It's pretty simple, but this choice may be one of the most important ones you ever make. Please select *terraform* or *do not terraform*."

After about ten minutes, Jaswinder checks to see that all of the votes have been submitted and looks at the results. He is careful not to show any emotion when looking. "Ladies and gentlemen, the votes are in. By a margin of 76% to 24% you have decided to terraform Planet Who." There is a loud applause and lots of pats on the back. Jaswinder is a little more subdued. He was one of the 24%. He could have used his power of veto, but he chose not to. He hopes they are right.

After things have settled down somewhat, Jaswinder asks for everybody's attention again. "Okay, now that the decision has been made, there will be an afternoon session of this meeting today. We will break for lunch until 2pm. Then, for all of you who wish to return, we will get a report from Ali Zamani and Paul Drake as to how this terraforming is to take place."

Jaswinder has lunch with Vera in the university cafeteria. Very little conversation takes place between the two of them for the hour. Vera wonders what Jaswinder is more worried about, destroying an alien life form or leaving Ali and Kayla behind on the planet.

At 2pm, Room 701 is crowded. Every single person from the morning session is back to hear what Ali and Paul have come up with. When Ali walks into the room, most take their seats immediately in anticipation. Paul is already there at a table in the front of the room.

Ali begins the session. "First, I would like to echo what I am sure that Jaswinder is thinking. I hope we are doing the right thing." There is a contemplating pause then Ali continues. "If you recall from the meeting two months ago, Paul and I have been working together to develop what we feel is our best chance for making the planet below us habitable for human beings. I would like to acknowledge a third person who has been invaluable in our endeavors. Over the last two months, we have run twenty computer models using different parameters that would have each taken a full year before our new computer system. We couldn't have done this without a quantum computer expert. As we speak, he is rerunning the plan that we think will do what we want to do. His name is Rahii Singh." Ali gets a warm applause from the room.

Together, Ali and Paul explain their plan detail by detail. They break the process down into phases and describe the feedback loops that they are trying to create on the planet. After about two hours, everyone in the room understands what a difficult undertaking this is and Ali and Paul have only scratched the surface of the plan. They don't even mention the most important part, which is the introduction of terra microbiology to the planet.

Ali lets the group know that their talk will be about another hour and asks if anyone would like to take a break. Almost unanimously, they all decide to continue.

"Okay, we will go on. Paul, Rahii and myself have determined that the process we have just outlined should take on the order of twenty to twenty-five years to attain the point to where the self regulating planetary system takes over without our help. You have seen how complicated and unpredictable some of the steps in our terraforming can be. Even with QC modeling, we can't be sure that everything will go according to plan." Then Ali drops the bombshell.

"The bottom line is that we are going to have to have a physical presence on the planet during this critical period. To make this work, we have to establish a bio-dome on the planet. My wife, Kayla, and I will not be going on to Gliese 251 with the rest of you." There are gasps in the room and sounds of disapproval since only the central committee members were aware of this decision.

Someone in the audience speaks out. "You mean that with all of our high tech computer systems, we can't put in some sort of automated monitoring and regulating system?"

"Too many variables. Even today, computers are only as good as the information we program into them. There is no way we could possibly foresee every scenario."

Another very concerned voice is heard. "It's not worth it, Ali. Report your findings to Earth and let them send out a special mission to do the terraforming."

Ali counters. "It is worth it. We are talking about the beginning of the human race becoming a galactic civilization. Also, I hate to say it, but this mission may be a fluke. Who knows when the powers on Earth will commit the necessary resources again to develop a project of this magnitude? Kayla and I have both decided. You know we are the best choices for this."

The room is quiet and Ali moves on. "Okay, now for the next hour, Paul and I will describe our plans for the bio-dome we want to establish on the planet. We had design assistance from the Probe Center and the Catom Center. Also, a new quantum computer will be constructed and will be placed in the dome. Data gathered by an orbiting satellite, transmitted by sensors in land, sea and air will link to the computer in the dome for analysis and recommendation. We have decided on a nuclear fission reactor for energy as we feel that trying to establish a fusion energy plant is not going to be possible in such a short time with limited capabilities. Paul, if you could show them our plans."

Paul Drake takes over the presentation. He uses all of the audio and visual devises of the room to explain the details of their planned bio-dome and how it will self assemble using nano and catom technology. Several landers will take the materials needed to the chosen location. He then explains the life support system, the machines that will be used to access the planets resources and more details about the terraforming monitoring system.

After Paul's talk, he and Ali field an array of questions and then Jaswinder calls an end to the meeting. Several people in the room talk privately with Ali as people are leaving and there is a lot of handshaking.

It's a very emotional Thanksgiving Day dinner at the home of Ali and Kayla. All of the family is there. Their son, Seker, and his wife, Roya, are with their two sons, Nouri and Ahmad. Their daughter, Rachel, and her husband, Jeremy, have come over from their home in Chianti Villas with their son, Adam, and daughter, Delinda. Adam is the oldest of the grandchildren and has invited along his girlfriend, Diana. There is one other guest at their home for Thanksgiving dinner. Ali and Kayla have invited over Derek Scott.

Not long after the decision was made in July, Seker Zamani made a special visit to the home of Derek Scott. He explained to Derek the sacrifice that his mother and father will be making by staying behind on Planet Who while the ship moves on to the next star. Seker asked Derek if he would be willing to go with them, to help and protect them. He told him that he didn't want an answer right away.

On the next visit, when Seker was making his routine supply delivery, he got his answer. Derek told Seker that he had been praying during the week since his last visit. It became clear to him during these prayer sessions that this was the destiny that Allah had chosen for him on Laylat al-Qadr. Derek promised Seker that he would watch over Ali and Kayla for as long as they live and give his life for them if necessary. On a lighter note, he told Seker that he had always wanted to live on a real planet with real gravity. Seker could see Derek's sincerity and thanked him.

Now, they are all sitting around the Thanksgiving table preparing to eat dinner. Adam's girlfriend, Diana, observes the oddity of the moment with this strange gathering of people and feels that she has to make a comment. "I really hope that nobody takes offense, but I can't help but notice how unusual this situation is. We have a Muslim family with the patriarch from Iran and matriarch from a Jewish family in Israel, their daughter, who has chosen a secular life with a family in an Italian community in a different Living Area, an ostracized, rehabilitated criminal and me. On top of this, we are celebrating Thanksgiving which is an American holiday." One of the things that has attracted Adam to Diana is her honesty and willingness to speak what is on her mind. Sometimes it can be embarrassing, however.

Ali also enjoys Diana's honesty. "Yes, Diana, Allah loves wondrous diversity." He pauses for a second, trying to remember where he heard that phrase before. "Adam has told us that you are fascinated with Earth history. You are correct that Thanksgiving is strictly an American holiday, but essentially it was a festival celebrating the harvest and many different cultures had a similar celebration by a different name. We have chosen to adopt the name *Thanksgiving*, because we think it is very appropriate at this time to thank Allah for friends, family and the food on our tables that he has bestowed on us. Also, school is out this week for *Family Week*." His last comment gets a chuckle.

Ali, being the head of the family begins the dinner with a comment. "Now, before we eat, it is our family tradition that everybody takes five minutes of silence to pray or reflect on how fortunate we all are to be together here today."

Rachel tears up a little. She knows that in a short six days from now that her mother and father will be leaving them. She will be able to communicate with them from the ship occasionally, but she will never see them in person again.

Kayla comforts her daughter. "Come now Rachel. You promised us this would be a happy day. We can make the best of the here and now. Let's not say goodbye yet."

Rachel does a little half smile to her mother and asks if they would excuse her to go to the washroom for a minute. When she returns, they all honor the five minutes of silence and contemplation then begin eating their feast.

Derek is being very quiet, partly out of respect, but also because he has spent most of his adult life by himself with no one to talk to. As he enjoys some dates and sweet bread, he gets an occasional glance of distrust from Rachel and Jeremy. They were both students at Romanov Primary School when he did what he did.

It's impossible not to notice so eventually Derek says something. "Don't worry. I will take good care of your mother and father."

Jeremy can't help himself and blurts out. "Yeah, like you took good care of Rahii."

"That was a long time ago. I was a different person then. I've found Allah now and have had 26 years to think about what I did and why I did it. I will be paying the rest of my life for decisions of my youth, but I believe that Allah still has a purpose for me. Going to the planet to watch over Ali and Kayla is my destiny."

Rachel still has her doubts about Derek, but she knows that Seker has spent a lot of time with him. It appears that Seker trusts him and she really doesn't have much choice.

They all finish eating their Thanksgiving dinner without a whole lot of conversation. It hasn't been the happy family time that Kayla was hoping for, but Ali has a good time with his grandsons. He breaks out his *Braingate* helmet and smaller ones that don't use the chip implant, but are manipulated with hand held controls. Jeremy joins Ali and the boys later while Rachel helps her mom. Seker and Roya go for a walk with Derek. They return to the gathering, but Derek parts ways and walks home. Meanwhile, Adam and Diana watch an old movie with Delinda.

Even though Ali and Kayla aren't leaving for six days, Rachel gives them a hug like she will never see them again when she goes home with Jeremy.

December 2, 2154
Day of Bio-dome Lander Launch
West Wall Complex, Europia

The bio-dome on Planet Who has been ready for occupation for three weeks now. Final testing has been done and automated supply transports have been sent down to fill the living space with everything its new residents will need. If anything has been forgotten, Gaia II will still be in orbit for another two months. The planet-wide micro sensors are scheduled for deployment in early January and the orbital monitoring probe and Earth communications satellite are already in orbit and fully functional.

Launch of the lander to the planet is scheduled for three hours from now at 11am. Ali, Kayla and Derek have had a very nice, warm, emotional send off by friends and family and are now in the elevator making the ride to the Shuttle Center. They will board the lander at 10 and will await final checks before starting their trip. After initial separation, the craft will be totally operated by on board computers. There is a lot of trust being placed in technology today. This is a onetime chance, one-way trip. Unfortunately, if anything goes wrong, the landing party can't just be beamed back up to the ship.

Kayla breaks the silence in the elevator. "I think what bothers me most is that our new home is going to be a place where the average temperature outside is 80°C. For some reason, -40°C on Mars seems much more acceptable."

Ali corrects her. "You mustn't have heard. The bio-dome is in a high elevation mountain valley where the temperature is a balmy 70°C."

"Really, and I forgot to bring my jacket."

"The humidity's not so bad there either. We may have to build a resort and sell tickets to earthlings."

Derek seems perturbed. "Are you two going to go on like this all of the time? If so, I want my own dome."

Spirits are high among the three travelers. It seems to be easier to leave friends and loved ones when there is an adventure ahead. They reach the Shuttle Port and board the lander at 10am as scheduled.

The vehicle that is taking Ali, Kayla and Derek to the surface is a modified supply lander. A lot of special features and upgrading were added. If a supply lander is lost, then it's just a setback for the mission. Losing this lander is not an option. There are backup computer systems, extra environmental protection and, of course, life support including food and water. Even three lifesuits with oxygen tanks are supplied, even though it is hard to imagine a scenario where they would be used. All of the landers, that were sent to establish the bio-dome and to transport supplies, completed their missions without a hitch.

Kayla does seem a little worried that none of them are trained to manually operate the vehicle, but Ali informs her that entering an atmosphere this thick requires precision angle of entry adjustment and velocity control. Even the best trained pilot would have to rely on computers. Kayla thanks Ali for the comforting information.

At 11am, Robert Tjoelker gives the command for lander thrusters to separate the vehicle from the ship. Robert has been given the lead on this mission. The lander is to follow a trajectory as to reach the bio-dome in six hours. The most critical period of the atmosphere entry lasts only about ten minutes, but the entire deceleration through the atmosphere is dangerous. By the time the lander reaches the bio-dome, Gaia II will be about two hours past directly overhead.

The first five hours of the trip are very uneventful. They are all free to move about the cabin in zero-g except for the occasional delta-v thrust. Kayla reads a book and Ali listens to music and watches a movie. Derek studies data in the computer about the bio-dome life support systems and its array of machines.

The dome houses two hovercraft and two land rovers for exploration and other use outside the dome. There is a quantum computer with a back up molecular computer system. The molecular system has a vast amount of accessible data, including how to operate and maintain the quantum computer, and will be their main system for life support and bio-dome operations. The QC will be mostly used for the terraforming process. Also, the bio-dome has a material storage section with fabricators and recyclers. Hydroponic gardens are in place with everything Kayla needs to grow what they need, and a food storage unit is full to keep them going until the gardens start producing.

Likewise, other life support mechanisms are in place awaiting Ali's magic touch. They will be able to use compounds from the local environment to a much greater degree than they were able to on Mars and thus the use of the term bio-dome rather than biosphere. The life support section of the bio-dome will serve a dual purpose of producing the algae and, later, the higher forms of oxygen producing flora that will be used for terraforming. Derek wants to know as much as he can about their new home since he doesn't have a great trust of computers.

After a little over five hours in the lander, it begins to enter Planet Who's atmosphere. On board computers constantly monitor and make adjustments to maintain the craft's attitude and velocity during the high temperature entry.

The lander is being tracked every step of the way by Robert Tjoelker and his team in the Probe Center. The atmospheric entry goes according to plan. All that is left is for the computers of the lander and the bio-dome to coordinate to bring the craft home. Special drag mechanisms continue to decelerate the lander so that, when at the correct altitude, the buoyancy tanks will inflate and gently float the vehicle down into the bio-dome landing facility.

Robert is in the process of telling Ali, Kayla and Derek that they are home free when the lights inside the craft start to flicker. There's not much any of the three of them can do, but report this to Bob. The Probe Center team is at a loss as to what's going on and then a split second later communications with the lander goes out. Bob's team gives two scenarios that come to mind immediately. Either the main computer system and backup system have simultaneously crashed due to some software or hardware failure or the ship's electronics were taken out by some exterior phenomenon like a massive electrical storm. Whichever has happened, all they can do at this point is track the lander to where it sets down on the surface.

Inside the lander, the situation is a little more intense. Not only have they lost lighting and computer systems, but also life support. The ship will maintain environment without life support systems for a finite period of time, but unless they are able to get the power back on, the future looks pretty dire. All they can do is sit back in their seats and pray. There is a default mechanical system in place for landing the craft, but without communication between the lander and the bio-dome, there is no guidance to get the three of them to the safety of their new home.

A very long twenty minutes later, the travelers feel their transport set down on the surface. The feeling is good and bad. The landing is surprisingly soft, but this means that they might have set down in some soft, mucky substance like some areas they have all seen in the Sagan videos. Then the realization sets in. They have no idea where they are.

At a little shy of six hours into the mission, the Probe Center can see that the lander has reached the surface. Luckily, they are able to get the location and look at the radar images of the area to see what situation the landing party is in. If the lander would have set down just forty minutes later, Gaia II would have been far enough into its orbit that it couldn't have gotten this information until a day later.

Bob gets his team's attention. "Okay, people, focus. We need clear thinking right now. It has to be assumed that our friends are alive on the surface without power, which means no life support. We have about 18 hours to the next launch window. I need everybody to the planning room so we can determine our best course of action. I will notify the rest of Gaia II as to what has happened."

On the surface, there are three frightened people in the dark knowing that soon they will be losing oxygen and temperatures will start to rise. They know from the probes that the temperature outside is somewhere between 70°C and 80°C with humidity anywhere from 60% to 80% and an atmosphere with only 2% oxygen.

Derek, fortunately, has been studying the capabilities of the landing craft as well as the bio-dome. He decides to take charge. "Ali, Kayla, you need to let me run the show right now. I have been studying the lander and can give us our best chance for survival until we get help from Gaia II." They agree to this so Derek continues.

"We have about twelve hours of oxygen in the cabin, but will need to breathe out into the lifesuit helmets so that we don't put too much carbon dioxide into the air. Unfortunately, cabin temperatures will start to rise long before we run out of air. We have three lifesuits, each with an oxygen tank that also lasts about twelve hours. We might as well put on the suits now, because we want to stay as comfortable and rested as possible. It will be about 26 hours before Gaia II can send some form of aid down to us. You realize, of course, that we have not landed in the bio-dome and have no idea where it is. I will look outside, but I'm not expecting to see anything. We will probably have to stay put for the 26 hours and hope that the people above come up with something."

"It doesn't take calculus to figure out that our oxygen supply is two hours short. To complicate that, it is going to get very hot in here. Fortunately, it will be a relatively dry heat. I read on a website that, in humidity like we have outside at over 60°C, the hot water in the air would cause painful tissue damage. We can breathe without the oxygen tanks for a couple of hours at which time the heat to our faces will become unbearable. At this time, we will need to alternate between the tanks and the cabin air for five minute periods to allow our bodies to cool back down after breathing in the hot air. I mentioned that our oxygen supply is two hours short. This isn't an exact figure. If we try to stay very calm and inactive we should be able to stretch out our supply."

Ali looks at Derek with a new respect. "I'm glad you did your homework. We will do as you say and hope that Bob comes up with something."

Derek takes a look outside after putting on his lifesuit, but visibility is poor and there is no way to tell which way the bio-dome is. He re-enters the lander and the three of them begin their long wait. Breathing in the hot air is very uncomfortable, but Ali and especially Kayla are very tough for septuagenarians.

About twenty-six hours later, they are all feeling weak as oxygen is getting very low. The three of them are strictly on tank oxygen now, so at least they don't have to keep removing their helmets to breathe in that terrible hot stuff in the cabin. The cooling system of the suit is not an issue, as the thermoelectric nanocrystals should keep absorbing heat and converting it to electricity for a long time. This electricity even gives them a little light from the helmet's built in headlamp, if they want to conserve the suit's battery power.

Derek looks at his suit's information display to check the time. The electronics of the suits survived whatever killed the ship's power. It's a long shot, but he figures that, if Gaia II had sent them any aid it would be landing just about now. With great difficulty, he gets up and exits the lander. Closing the hatch as quickly as possible in his weakened state, he climbs slowly down the ladder. Even at midday here the lighting is like that of early morning or dusk on Earth. For about half an hour, he searches an ever increasing radius around the ship. He trudges along, occasionally dropping to his knees in the ankle deep hot mud. He is just about to give up, when he sees something unnatural sticking out of the surface. The finding gives him a slight boost of energy that allows him to dig it out. It's a pod sent down from the ship. He finds six tanks of oxygen, a hand held computer and a map of some kind. Gasping for air and nearly passing out, he attaches one of the tanks to his lifesuit. Taking a wonderful breath of cool oxygen, Derek looks up and says, "Thank you, Bob."

Derek then hurries back to the lander and replaces the oxygen tanks on Ali's and Kayla's suits. Kayla is doing okay, but Ali has barely survived. While Ali is reviving, Derek is planning their next action. First, he reads some instructions and signals the ship while recovering the remaining tanks from the pod. Then he downloads information from the hand-held computer to the lifesuits. Among other things, they all now have an electronic map of the area, accessible through the suit's electronics.

Derek opens up the physical contour map that was sent down in the pod, anyway. What they see is not good. The mapmakers have drawn a path of least resistance from the lander to the bio-dome, complete with intermediate and total distances. From where they are, it is 98 kilometers to the bio-dome with an increase in elevation of about 1500 meters. Kayla is in good shape for seventy years old, but Ali would never make it. Derek discusses the situation with Kayla and, when Ali becomes coherent, they tell him the plan.

Derek informs Ali using their suit-to-suit communications. "Ali, we've got six, 12-hour oxygen tanks, a map and a hand-held computer that were sent down from Gaia II in a pod. We won't need the information in the computer now since our suit's electronics are working and we've downloaded data. It does serve another purpose , however. The device will transmit a basic signal back to the ship. I have already done that to let them know that we are alive. Soon. I will take a spare oxygen tank and the map and walking to the dome. Kayla and I discussed this and decided that our best chance for survival is for me to go alone and come back for you with a hovercraft."

Ali manages a whisper. "How far?"

"It's 98 kilometers from here with a climb of about 1500 meters. If I can average 5 kilometers an hour, I can get there in twenty hours. I will use more oxygen due to physical exertion, but I should have plenty. It will take about three hours to return for you in the hovercraft, so once again we are going to need to stretch out the oxygen in case I get delayed. The time now is 8:30pm, but it's going to be daylight on the planet for a few more days. If I make it to the dome in 20 hours as planned and am able to get the hovercraft back in three hours, you should have plenty of oxygen, but conserve anyway. I should be seeing you about this time tomorrow."

"In case I don't make it, the ship will probably send another pod with more oxygen and other supplies. It should come down around 9pm tomorrow. Hopefully, you will survive until they can send down some sort of transport that can get you from here to the dome. We all have a detailed map of the area in our suits now. With assistance from the orbiting satellite I should be able to check my coordinates every four hours or so."

With that Derek doesn't waste any time. He packs the extra tank along with water and energy bars and begins his trek.

* * *

On Gaia II, the entire community is feeling the helplessness of the Probe Center team. At least they all know that Ali, Kayla and Derek have been able to recover the pod that was sent down to them and are still alive. A transport vehicle is being assembled as quickly as possible along with another lander for it to piggyback on. Best estimates say that it should be ready in about four days, with an extra day if they put it through testing. Meanwhile, the plan is to keep sending down pods every orbit. The pods essentially parachute to the surface, impacting the ground at a velocity that humans wouldn't survive if they were riding along. It wouldn't be good if a pod landed directly on the lander, but the odds are pretty slim of this happening.

Seker is spending a lot of time at home in his prayer room. He and Roya haven't told the boys about what is happening. Rachel, Jeremy, Adam and Delinda are spending most of their time watching periodic information blogs that are keeping everybody updated on the situation and what the Probe Center is doing about it.

* * *

Derek climbs down the ladder from the lander to begin his journey. He checks the time and sets his walking distance monitor to zero. He will use his electronic map and only has the physical one as a backup. There is no GPS system, except for the four hour coordinate check. The electronic map, however, does point the way using infrared imaging of surrounding terrain features. Derek starts plodding through the muck. He thinks to himself that if it's like this all the way, there is no way he can keep up a five kilometer an hour pace.

Walking through the flat featureless plain with limited visibility, Derek comes three feet away from wandering right into a deep sinkhole. It is deep enough that he would have been trapped and his journey would have been over before it had begun. He is still in communication range with Kayla and tells her to watch out for these in case she has to leave the lander.

Along the route, Derek has to detour around many obstacles, such as enormous boulders and long impassable fissures. When he reaches his first destination, which is a river, he checks out his pace and sees that the going has been even slower than he had thought. He has been trying to conserve oxygen, but he knows he has to pick up the tempo. And he hasn't even begun to climb!

The bio-dome is actually near the river he has arrived at, but upstream. The route he has been given, however, doesn't always follow the river, as there are deep canyons and high waterfalls to get past. After a short rest at the river, he continues on.

The route follows the river for a few kilometers then directs Derek up the side of a high embankment. He tries to walk up it, but for every two steps he takes, he loses a step as the ground slides downhill. He's starting to feel the extra gravity now, too. Derek weighs about 80 kilos on Gaia II, but is over 105 on

Planet Who. It's like carrying an extra 25 kilos along with the extra tank every step of the way. The embankment looks to be about 100 meters and it's just not going to happen. Derek figures that there is a good reason that the route is taking him this direction so he back tracks and takes an easier way to the top even though it costs him more precious time.

Now he is on rocky ground, but the rock is wet, so it is still treacherous, especially on higher slopes. He tries to pick up the pace anyway and winds up using more oxygen than intended. At a high spot on the route, Derek sees the reason for the detour. A majestic waterfall cascades off a cliff with a vertical drop of over 200 meters. When he reaches an intermediate destination, past the top of the waterfall, he sees that he has covered his first twenty kilometers in about five hours and has only gained 300 meters of his 1500 meter climb. He has used up about half of his original oxygen tank. Doing the math, it's not looking good.

Derek thinks back to his meditation training. He knows that if he can keep his mind in a tranquil state and control his breathing, he can use less oxygen. He pauses a moment to clear his mind and says a short recitation to himself, then begins his trip again.

He follows the river again for a distance, before he has to head away from it once more. It appears that this section of the route cuts off a wide bend that the river takes and gains another 300 meters in altitude. Derek gets to a plateau along the route and sees an awesome sight to the far left of his field of vision. Turning, he sees a geyser. The geyser sends water twice as high as any like it that he remembers seeing in holobooths as a boy. Then what he sees next changes his mind about just how amazing the site is. The superheated water spewing out of the ground is causing a steamy mudslide that crosses the route he is taking. There is no turning back now. Derek has to walk through flowing mud that sometimes gets as high as his knees. He almost gets stuck once or twice, but manages to escape the menacing suction. On the other side of the mudslide, Derek takes a short rest and checks his parameters. It's hard to tell if his meditation and controlled breathing is working since the mudslide used up a lot of energy and therefore oxygen.

When he gets to the river again, he is near the half way point. He has already switched to his back up tank and still has 900 of the 1500 meter climb to go. He soon sees the worst obstacle of his trip.

In front of Derek is a 400 meter wall rising at a slope of about 45 degrees. There's no way around this one. He closes his eyes and stays perfectly still until he reaches a state of calmness, not unlike during ruku. Once he is ready and is control of his breathing, he begins the ascent. Some areas have loose sediment and some have slippery rocks. Not one yard of the climb is as easy as a dry rock climb like this would have been on Earth. At one point, Derek grabs a rock and it gives way. He slides about 30 meters down the hill. Sharp rocks along the way slice at his suit. He feels the torrid hot moist air burning his skin in several places until the self-healing suit mends. After reentering his meditative state, he continues the climb. When he reaches the top he rests on a rock and checks his suit's altimeter. He has gained a lot of altitude, but has covered only a very short distance.

Taking another break, Derek decides to hydrate and eat an energy bar. The suits aren't designed for eating and drinking, which poses a dilemma, but he knows his body needs it. As quickly as he can, he lifts his helmet and takes a drink of warm water and puts an energy bar in his mouth. In the short time it takes him to get his helmet back on his face it is covered in burns. It takes a while for Derek to overcome the pain through meditation before he starts the next leg.

Having gotten a little energy back, he makes good time to the next intermediate checkpoint. He is able to verify his coordinates here from the satellite passing overhead and checks time, distance and oxygen level. His controlled breathing is working. About three quarters of the way through his trip now, he has a half a tank of oxygen left and about 400 meters to gain in altitude. The good news almost makes him forget the burns on his face as well as his arms and legs where his suit tore in the slide down the hill. He doesn't forget enough, however, to have any desire to take another drink of water or energy bar.

Derek encounters another steep climb along the way, but not nearly as bad as the earlier one. He is getting that extra rush of adrenaline now that mountain climbers or marathon runners experience when they are 80% of the way through their challenge. When he gets to the top, what he sees is at the same time exciting and devastating.

In the distance, he can see the bio-dome. There is much better visibility here than during the first part of his journey. What nearly makes him collapse on the ground and cry is that the dome is on the other side of the river. The river is still wide enough, deep enough and fast enough that he doesn't like his chances of swimming across in his weakened state, not to mention that he isn't a very strong swimmer. He has spent most of his life in a secluded desert environment.

What Derek decides to do is very risky and will take precious time and oxygen. He hikes to a spot upriver that he has chosen based on the curvature of its path. What he plans to do is swim at an angle downstream to cross to the other side. When he gets to where he plans on entering the river, he puts an energy bar and water container into a suit pocket and discards the pack. Of course, he still has to carry the oxygen tank on his back. In his near exhausted state, he somehow has to swim this river carrying the tank and an extra 25 kilos due to the planet's stronger gravity. He has one humorous thought that at least the swim will clean all of the grime off of his lifesuit, so that if he makes it, he will be presentable when picking up Ali and Kayla.

Into the water Derek goes. This is the hardest thing that Derek has done in his life, including the 400 meter climb earlier that day. He struggles in the water for what seems like an eternity, using every ounce of his energy and will power to keep swimming at an angle toward the far bank. When he gets near the other side he has been carried much farther down the river than he had planned. If not for his lifesuit, he probably would have drowned. Finally, he is washed up on a sandbank and just lies there, totally drained.

After about ten minutes an inner voice says, "You're not there yet." He looks at his oxygen level and sees about a tenth of a tank left or a little over one hour of air supply. He manages to look up and sees the bio-dome and estimates its distance at about one kilometer. Normally this would be easy for him, but at this point he's not sure if he can get 100 meters in an hour, let alone 1000 meters. Every muscle in his body aches and he's dehydrated. Derek decides on a final plan.

He decides to take one more drink of water and eat one more energy bar, then rest for about a half an hour before making the attempt. Against all of his instincts, he gets the water and energy bar ready, takes a good breath and raises his helmet. The pain is unimaginable as he drinks the now hot water and stuffs the energy bar into his mouth. After sealing the helmet, he wants to cry out in pain, but his mouth is full of energy bar. He makes a loud moan that only he can hear as he finishes eating. Then he passes out.

When he comes to, Derek looks at his time and oxygen displays. He has about fifteen minutes to traverse the final kilometer. The fear of the thought of running out of oxygen propels him onward. He looks like an old man on his last legs as he stumbles across the plateau to the dome. On the verge of unconsciousness, Derek thinks he sees Seker walking beside him. Seker is rambling on and on about Muslim traditions. This is so boring, he wants to sleep so badly. Then, Seker throws a scalding cup of coffee into Derek's face and he wakes up feeling his facial burns worse than ever. Unbelievably, he eventually makes it to the dome wall. Derek has to think hard to remember where the entrance is. It seems like such a long time ago that he studied the manuals on the ship. Finally, after locating a sensor, he moves his hand in front of it and enters the airlock. By the time he has normal air, temperature and pressure, so he can take off his lifesuit, his oxygen tank is in the red. He doesn't ever want to have to do that again.

After sitting a minute, Derek enters the bio-dome. He finds some cool water and something to eat. Then he locates the first aid room and finds a special cream to put on the burns on his face, hands and legs. Not wasting any time, he then goes back to grab his lifesuit and hurries to the hovercraft. He knows where to find the vehicle and gets in without putting the lifesuit on. Tossing it on the floor, he gives the voice command that initiates the hovercraft departure sequence. The craft's computers take over from there. Derek thinks, "If these computers don't work right I'm really going to be pissed." He enters in the coordinates of the lander and the hovercraft begins its three hour trip. This is as fast as this vehicle can go. Derek looks at the time and sees that it is almost 8pm.

* * *

At 8pm, 98 kilometers away, Kayla awakens to an alarm she has set for herself in her suit. Derek had estimated that he would be back around eight or eight-thirty and the pod from Gaia II is expected around 9pm. Meanwhile she and Ali have decided to sleep to conserve oxygen. When Derek hasn't shown by nine, Kayla decides to go and look for the pod. She closes the hatch quickly, because there is still a little temperature difference and definitely a humidity difference between the inside and the outside. This is critical when they raise their helmets to eat or drink.

Like Derek, she looks for about a half an hour before she sees anything. What she finds is a shock. Where the probe has impacted the ground, it has created its own sinkhole. The panels on the probe that have acted like parachutes are twenty meters down the hole with the probe. She doesn't see any possible way she can get down the hole to the supplies. It's up to Derek now.

Kayla goes back into the lander and gives Ali the bad news. A little over an hour later, when they are about to give up hope, they get a knock on the hatch. Kayla opens it and sees a man in a life suit standing on the ladder. He says, "Hi, I'm lost. I saw your place and thought I'd stop by and ask for directions."

"Very funny, help me get Ali. We're almost out of oxygen again. What happened to your face?!"

A small team of technicians in a converted room of Gaia University are preparing a handsome, dark haired Hispanic man for the daily telecast he is about to make to the people of Gaia II. Sitting to the left of the man is his co-anchor, a pretty, slightly heavy-set, very professionally dressed brunette woman. The well known twosome present the news of the previous day every morning.

A cue is given to the man and he begins. "Good evening, Gaians. Temperature in Europia is a cool 10°C and Tropicania is a balmy 18°C with a slight breeze. Our first story of the day is an update from the bio-dome on Planet Who. Here with that story is Carol Day."

"Thank you, Julio. It's been almost two and a half months now since we thought we had lost the brave crew of the bio-dome. It wasn't until we got the long awaited message, two days and nine hours after landing, from Derek Scott in the hovercraft, that we were all able to breathe a sigh of relief. Now life in the bio-dome has become routine, as they go about their day to day tasks. We were able to get an interview with Ali Zamani on our last pass over the dome. Here are some highlights of the interview."

With Ali Zamani on the viewing screen, Carol starts the interview. "We know that you have been working with Paul Drake, who has remained on the ship. How has this long distance collaboration been working out?"

"It was not necessary for Paul to come to the surface with us. We have already completed two of the five planned nanobot phases. By July, the job of the nanobots will be completed unless the temperature of the planet rises so high that they automatically reactivate. The rest of the terraforming will be done more naturally. I have enjoyed working with Paul and have always thought that he would make a great James Bond."

"What role does Derek Scott play in the bio-dome, now that he doesn't need to save your life on a daily basis anymore?"

"Derek is a fast learner. He does a lot of maintenance work around the dome and usually is the one to leave the dome when our tests require it. Kayla and I are getting older now and Derek has been invaluable when it comes to doing things that are difficult for us. One day, when we pass away, Derek will have to operate this place. We are lucky that he actually prefers a life of solitude. Who knows? He may even live to see a replacement crew arrive from Earth."

"Have you been talking to your family a lot now that it is only one week until Gaia II has to leave orbit?"

"Every day, we are growing to accept our fates. Many families on Earth had to go through the same emotional trauma when Gaia II left Earth. We will be sending and hopefully receiving messages once a week in the same way that Gaia II communicates with the Earth."

"Do you think you will ever be able to walk outside the bio-dome without a lifesuit?"

"No, if all goes according to plan, this may be possible in about one hundred years and may take as long as one thousand years."

Carol asks Ali several more questions and then talks to Kayla for a while. When she asks to talk to Derek Scott, Kayla tells her, "Sorry, Derek doesn't do interviews."

After the bio-dome interviews, the news anchor, Julio Mendes, announces the lead story of the day. "At 2am today, our probe touched down in the ocean on the day side of the terminator of the planet, Truffula, orbiting the star, Lorax. Some of you stayed up to watch this live. We can only receive communication from the probe for about a fourth of the orbit. Otherwise, the star or planet gets in the way. The Probe Center has timed a signal, commanding release of the submarine explorer, so that it will be received by the probe today at 4pm. Truffula orbits Lorax once every 16.4 days, so it will go out of communication some time tomorrow and re-emerge about twelve days later. We have to leave orbit on February 20th, so we will have to discover what the submarine has found out from our communication with the bio-dome. Ali and Kayla will be accessing the data received by the Earth Communications Satellite." During all of the newspod stories, related video and still images are shown on the site.

"In local news, preparations are being made for Carnival in Little Rio which begins Friday, February 28th and runs through Mardi Gras on March 4th. Floats and costumes are being finalized by residents for the five day celebration. Many different events are planned including music, shows and plenty of food. For a full schedule see the Little Rio website. As is our tradition, there will be a parade through all of Tropicania on Saturday and Europia on Sunday. Students living in Little Rio will be excused from school on Monday as usual."

"The years of Carnival may be numbered now. It has been decided and agreed upon by the residents of Little Rio that this Living Region will be the first to be converted to a different cultural environment. There will be a vote at the departure transition as to what the new Living Region will be. Front runners are an urban community modeled after the Southeast

Asian city of Singapore and a futuristic, high-tech city based purely on the imaginations of the residents. Catom construction will begin at the next transition to constant velocity in late 2162 and last for about a year. Meanwhile residents will live temporarily in other Living Regions."

"In more news about Departure Day on February 20th, it has been decided to have a subdued celebration since we will be leaving three of our own behind. There will be the usual food vendors and performances to pass the time, but there won't be the decoration and festivity that we had at the Arrival Celebration. This will be the first transition to constant acceleration since Gaia II left Earth, so many of us were either very young or not alive yet when Romanov School, the Webber Theater and the Zhang Health and Sciences Center were underground on the Tropicania side."

Other lesser stories of local interest are broadcast such as primary school basketball results. There are six teams, one representing each Living Region. While signing off, the newspod shows more video from the bio-dome.

Jaswinder Singh is looking at the Gaia II Mission Itinerary Summary on his monitor. He is thinking about the fifteenth entry on the page. The star is Gliese 667C. What he would give to study the life in this system while looking up at the three suns in the sky! He and Vera Greene are anxiously awaiting the delayed message from the bio-dome as are many others on Gaia II. When an image of Kayla Novac appears on the monitor, the excitement builds. Kayla tells them upfront.

"We have gotten the data that was transmitted from the probe on the planet Truffula to the Earth Communications Satellite. Gaia II may have been looking for life at the wrong star. It's not definite, but measurements of higher than expected methane and hydrogen sulfide, dissolved in the sea water, along with other by products of organic reactions, suggest that there may be some form of life on the planet. The submarine probe has been searching the ocean floor for the highest concentration of these substances. It appears that there may be some *serpentinization* in at least two places. How mantle rock has geologically recently been exposed to seawater is a mystery since we don't believe that there is plate tectonic activity here. The submarine will continue to collect samples to be examined under the surface probe's microscopic imagery to see if there is any sign of movement. If there is microscopic life on Truffula then you all know what the implications are for the abundance of life that exists in the galaxy. It would make the mystery of why there doesn't appear to be life here even more stifling. We will send you the data as we receive it so you can see for yourselves."

"This will be our last video telecast, so Ali and I would like to say goodbye to our children and grandchildren." Due to the delay this is a one-way conversation. Ali now shares the screen with Kayla. Seker's and Rachel's families are all watching together as Ali and Kayla say goodbye. There are many tears on Gaia II, not just from family members.

Ali concludes the transmission. "We love you all. Have a wonderful trip to Gliese 251. Our thoughts will be with you."

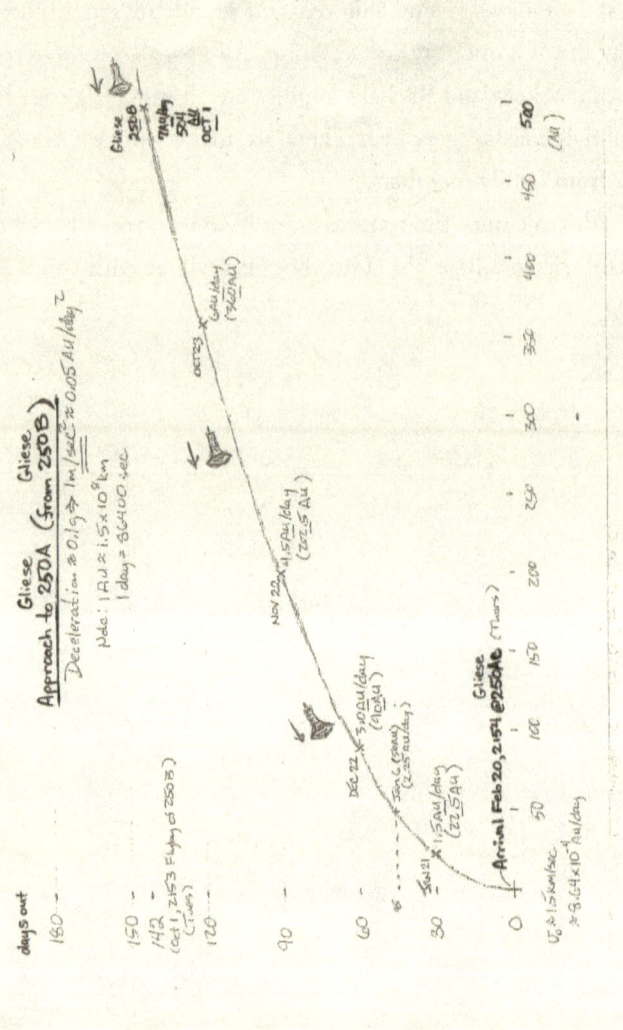

GLIESE 250 SYSTEM								

Star	Planet	Moon	Name	Dist. *	Rad. **	Mass ***	Rotation	Period (days)
250A			Zax		$0.67R_S$	$.80M_S$	15 d	
	f		Mulberry	0.12AU	$0.59R_E$	$0.2M_E$	--	33
	g		Yertle	0.18AU	$0.62R_E$	$0.2M_E$	51 d	60
	c		Who	0.30AU	$1.05R_E$	$1.2M_E$	$11^{d}9^{h}$	129
		I	Horton	4.0×10^5km	$0.7R_L$	$0.3M_L$	--	26.5
		II	Grinch	28×10^5km	$0.01R_L$	$5\times10^{-7}M_L$	--	424
	b		Sneetch	0.85AU	$1.27R_E$	$2.3M_E$	42^{h}	481
		I	One Fish	1.3×10^5km	$0.2R_L$	$8\times10^{-3}M_L$	--	3.55
		II	Two Fish	2.7×10^5km	$0.5R_L$	$0.06M_L$	--	10.6
		III	Red Fish	3.4×10^5km	$1.2R_L$	$1.4M_L$	--	15
		IV	Blue Fish	4.9×10^5km	$0.1R_L$	$3\times10^{-4}M_L$	--	26
	d		Sam	1.6AU	$1.0R_E$	$0.5M_E$	15^{h}	1035
		I	Eggs	0.7×10^5km	$0.05R_L$	$9\times10^{-5}M_L$	--	3
		II	Ham	2.2×10^5km	$0.4R_L$	$0.03M_L$	--	16.8
	e		Cat	3.5AU	$1.15R_E$	$0.7M_E$	22^{h}	2396
		I	Thing 1	1.8×10^5km	$0.5R_L$	$0.08M_L$	--	10.6
		II	Thing 2	2.3×10^5km	$1.0R_L$	$0.4M_L$	--	15.3
		III	Hat	2.9×10^5km	$0.2R_L$	$5\times10^{-3}M_L$	--	21.7
250B			Lorax		$0.5R_S$	$0.5M_S$	6 d	
	c		Truffula	0.08AU	$0.35R_E$	$0.02M_E$	--	16.4
	b		Onceler	0.12 AU	$0.73R_E$	$0.3M_E$	37 d	131
		I	Thneed	2.5×10^5km	$0.2R_L$	$0.01M_L$	--	32.1

*   distance from parent body

** R_S = Radius of Sun (Sol), R_E = Radius of Earth, R_L = Radius of Earth's moon (Luna)

*** M_S = Mass of Sol, M_E = Mass of Earth, M_L = Mass of Luna

Additional information:

Horton: Apogee 4.8×10^5km, Perigee 3.2×10^5km

Grinch: Apogee 14.9×10^5km, Perigee 41.1×10^5km, Angle of semi-major axis to that of Horton 35°, Angle of orbital plane to planetary plane 60°

Who synchronous orbit: 2.3×10^5km (Period: 11 days, 9 hours)
Gaia II orbit: 4.5×10^4km (Period: 24 hours)

Gaia II Mission Itinerary* (Launch 2112.1)
Arrival Date (Ship Time)
Nanocraft Schedule (Exobiology Results)

<u>Arrival (Yr.)</u>

2153.6   GLIESE 250AB (88 MONOCEROTIS)
K dwarf/ M dwarf binary – 28.4 LY
Planet(s) of Biological Interest: GJ250Ac (terrestrial/
rocky)/ 1.2 M(Earth))
Nanocraft Launch: 2050.1
Planned Data Return: 2120.9

2185.2   GLIESE 251 (PROXIMA GEMINORUM)
M dwarf – 18.1 LY
Planet(s) of Biological Interest: None (refueling stop)
Nanocraft Launch: 2151.8
Data Return: 2097.3 (Negative)

2224   GLIESE 475 (BETA CANUM VENATICORUM)
G dwarf – 27.5 LY
Planet(s) of Biological Interest: GJ475e (super-earth/
ocean/ 8.0 M(Earth))
Nanocraft Launch: 2051.2
Planned Data Return: 2119.8

2243   GLIESE 502 (BETA COMAE BERENICES)
G dwarf – 29.8 LY
Planet(s) of Biological Interest: GJ502d (terrestrial/
ocean/ 0.6 M(Earth))
Nanocraft Launch: 2051.1
Planned Data Return: 2125.3

2278   GLIESE 581 (HO LIBRAE)
M dwarf – 20.3 LY
Planet(s) of Biological Interest: GJ581d (terrestrial/ rocky/ 0.8 M(Earth))
Nanocraft Launch: 2050.2
Data Return: 2101.1 (Inconclusive)

2305   GLIESE 506 (61 VIRGINIS)
G dwarf – 27.7 LY
Planet(s) of Biological Interest: GJ506e (super-earth/ rocky/ 3.4 M(Earth))
Nanocraft Launch: 2050.9
Planned Data Return: 2020.9

2331   GLIESE 432AB (289 G HYDRI)
K dwarf/ M dwarf binary – 31.1 LY
Planet(s) of Biological Interest: None (circumbinary gas giants/ moons?)
Nanocraft Launch: 2051.5
Planned Data Return: 2139.7

2341   GLIESE 433
M dwarf – 29.5 LY
Planet(s) of Biological Interest: GJ433d (terrestrial/ rocky/ 1.7 M(Earth))
Nanocraft Launch: 2051.4
Planned Data Return: 2124.9

2383   **GLIESE 693**

M dwarf – 19.0 LY

Planet(s) of Biological Interest: None (establish central refueling station)

Nanocraft Launch: 2050.7

Data Return: 2098.5 (Negative)

2399   **GLIESE 780 (DELTA PAVONIS)**

G dwarf/ sub-dwarf – 19.9 LY

Planet(s) of Biological Inrterest: GJ780g (terrestrial/ rocky/ 2.0 M(Earth)

Nanocraft Launch: 2050.6

Data Return: 2100.5 (95% Positive!!)

2424   **GLIESE 17 (ZETA TUCANAE)**

F dwarf – 28.0 LY

Planet(s) of Biological Interest: Possible moon of Neptune class planet GJ17e

Nanocraft Launch: 2050.9

Planned Data Return: 2020.7

2441   **GLIESE 19 (BETA HYDRI)**

G subdwarf – 24.4 LY

Planet(s) of Biological Interest: None? (Chance to Study "Post Main Sequence Sun")

Nanocraft Launch: 2050.8

Planned Data Return: 2111.8

2461   **GLIESE 780 (DELTA PAVONIS)** Return to system en-route to next star

Chance for additional study of GJ780g

2492   GLIESE 785 (5 G CAPRICORN)
         K dwarf – 29.0 LY
         Planet(s) of Biological Interest: Possible moon of
         Neptune class planet GJ785c
         Nanocraft Launch: 2051.3
         Planned Data Return: 2123.6

2522   GLIESE 667ABC (142 G SCORPII)
         K dwarf/ K dwarf/ M dwarf trinary – 22.0 LY
         Planet(s) of Biological Interest:
         GJ667Cd (terrestrial/ ocean/ 1.5 M(Earth))
         GJ667Cc (super-earth/ rocky/ 4.5 M(Earth))
         Nanocraft Launch: 2050.1
         Data Return: 2105.2 (d – 75% Positive!!/ c –
         inconclusive)

2539   GLIESE 682
         M dwarf – 16.4 LY
         Planet(s) of Biological Interest: GJ682c (super-earth/
         rocky/ 8.7 M(Earth))
         Nanocraft Launch: 2050.5
         Data Return: 2091.9 (Inconclusive)

2548   GLIESE 674 (PROXIMA ARAE)
         M dwarf - 14.8 LY
         Planet(s) of Biological Interest: GJ674c (Mars Class/
         rocky/ .018 M(Earth))
         Nanocraft Launch: 2050.4
         Data Return: 2087.9 (Inconclusive)

2571   GLIESE 832

            M dwarf – 16.1 LY

            Planet(s) of Biological Interest: GJ832c (may be a
            double planet/ rocky/ 5.4 M(Earth))

            Nanocraft Launch: 2050.5

            Data Return: 2091.1 (Failed Mission)

            Resend: 2095.0

2594   GLIESE 876 (IL AQUARII)

            M dwarf – 15.3 LY

            Planet(s) of Biological Interest: Moons of Jupiter
            class giant GJ876b

            Nanocraft Launch: 2050.3

            Data Return: 2089.0 (GJ876c – no moons/b –
            inconclusive)

2624   RETURN TO EARTH (Earth Year 2711)

*Finalized at a Special Assembly, United Nations Building,
    Reykjavik, Iceland August 20, 2108

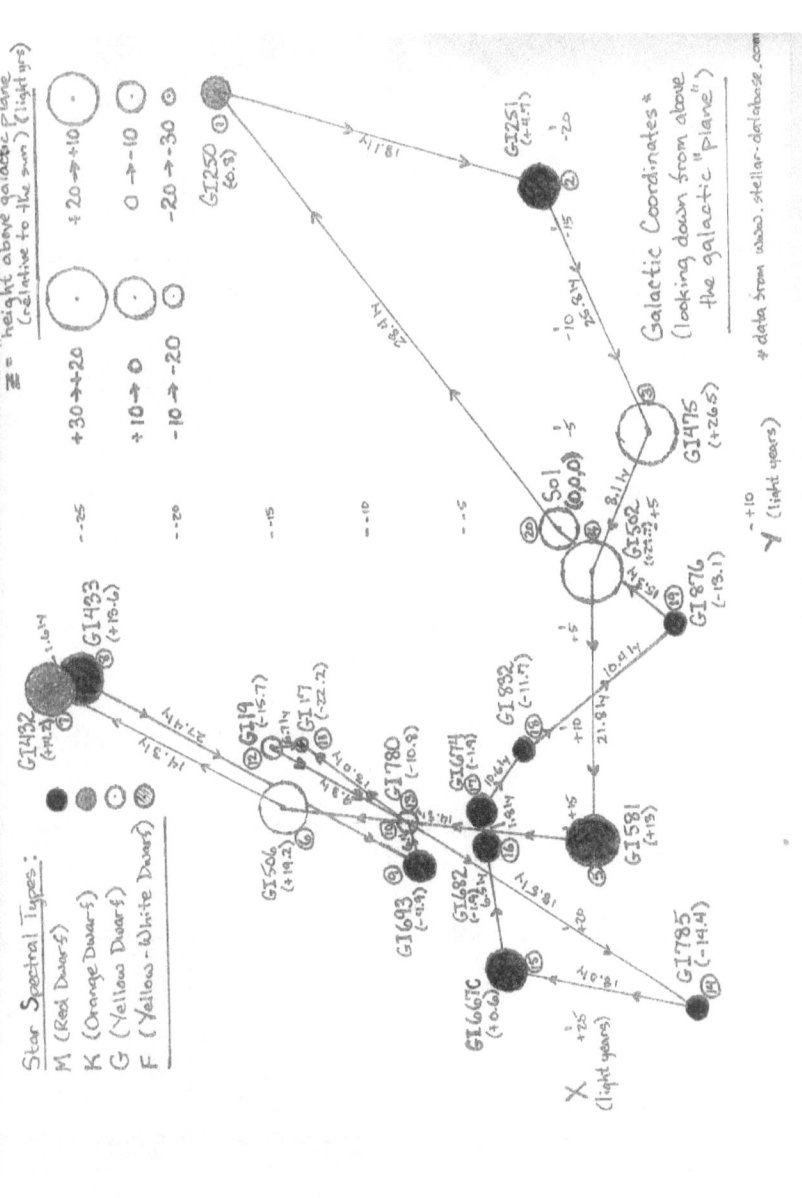

GAIA II GLOSSARY OF TERMINOLOGY
created for this writing

accretion A process where mass falls in on an object, increasing the size of the object.

Action Figures A popular musical group of 2112 that performs at the send off gala for Gaia II.

***air thrusters** In this context, they are hand-held propulsion devices to get around in the zero gravity of space hotels. They fit in a utility belt and come with replaceable compressed air canisters.

AIST (of Japan) The National Institute of Advanced Industrial Science and Technology of Japan is a federally funded research organization where the team of Akira Noda made a breakthrough discovery, in 2023, that allowed for the manufacturing of indefinitely long ribbons of carbon nanotubes, making space elevators possible.

albedo The fraction of solar energy that is reflected back into space by a celestial object.

***alien bash** What the residents of the Mars Biosphere call a party where they all dress up as sci-fi alien beings.

algorithms Step by step methods or systems of codedinstructions used to solve a problem. The same algorithm could be used in multiple applications. They are a common tool of mathematics and computer science.

****Alpenhausen*** One of the three Living Regions of the Europia Living Area on Gaia II. Designed by Disney Inc., it captures the essence of a Bavarian-Swiss alpine village.

anaerobic (life) Life existing in an oxygen free environment.

*Andrew Lloyd Webber Theater   The central gathering point of the crew of Gaia II. Designed by Pierre Montrieux to equal the grandest theaters on Earth, this venue serves the dual purpose of center of the performing arts and a safe refuge in an emergency or transition period. It is located in the Gaia II transition building with Gaia University and the nanofactory. It was named after a famous late 20th/ early 21st century musical composer.

angular diameter   The apparent size of an object as measured using the angle created by lines from the observer to opposite edges of the object.

anibots   In this text, the term refers to animal robots, which are machines created to resemble live animals in every possible way.

apogee   The farthest point an object gets from another in an elliptical orbit.

Apple II computer   One of the earliest, and most popular, versions of the desktop computer. It was first sold in June of 1977.

artificial gravity   Any force that imitates gravitational force as experienced by an object. One of the most common is centrifugal force which is caused by a centrally directed centripetal force holding an object in a circular path.

*Asimov Transfer Station   The space elevator station near the end of the tether from Santos-Dumont Station, in the Atlantic Ocean. Used for interplanetary launches and arrivals.

astrobiology   An interdisciplinary study of life as a universal phenomenon. An astrobiologist uses what is known about all forms of life as we know it along with planetary geology and climate study, paleontology and the laws of physics to model *habitable exoplanets* and the *life* they may harbor.

Astronomical Unit (AU)   The distance of the Earth from the Sun. (about 1.5×10^8 km)

Astrophysical Journal On-line   The electronic version (and only one after 2019) of the distinguished professional publishing of astronomy and astrophysics.

attitude (of an aircraft)   The orientation of an aircraft with respect to the horizon.

***Austin Healey Pegasus**   A make of car, made by the "reborn" company Austin-Healey in the late 21st and early 22nd century, that converts into a personal aircraft.

autogenics   A combination of self hypnosis and biofeedback used to calm oneself and to control what would otherwise be involuntary bodily functions.

avatar   In this use, an animated representation of a person used for entertainment value when communicating on comm-devices.

backdoor   As a computer programming term, it is a password that a programmer uses in order to easily access his/her own program, bypassing encrypted barriers.

Barrymore, John (the ninth)   An actor in a long line of famous acting Barrymores dating back to the early twentieth century.

***Bazaar**   A musical written by John Diallo on Gaia II and performed by the Romanov Primary School Drama Club directed by Chakori Singh.

bio-dome   In this book, this is a habitat with life support in a location where humans cannot survive unprotected, but is not completely self-contained like a CELSS or biosphere.

biosignatures   The remote detection of certain molecules or combinations of molecules, such as ozone or oxygen together with methane, in a planetary atmosphere may be a strong indicator that there is life on the planet. Such a "signature" would be detected using spectroscopy.

biosphere   In this text, the term is used to mean a CELSS; a totally contained, self maintaining ecosystem that can support life indefinitely, with the only external input being energy. Heat is released to the environment.

blackbody radiation   The energy an object emits in the form of radiation in order to maintain thermal equilibrium. The object would otherwise continue to increase in temperature due to incoming absorbed radiation. Planets tend to emit in the infrared part of the spectrum.

*Bose Crater Lunar Observatory   The southernmost of the three radio telescope arrays on the far side of the moon. In Bose crater, it is at lunar latitude 53.5° S and long. 170° W.

*Bradford Transfer Station   The space elevator station near the far end of the tether of the Mars Space Elevator, which extends down to Sagan Crater at the surface. It is used for interplanetary arrival and departure.

BrainGate ™   Developed in its infancy at Brown University in the early 21st century by John Donaghue, this is a chip implanted near the motor cortex of the brain that allows direct communication from the brain to a machine. Originally an aide for patients with brain injuries to control body movements, by the end of the 21st century it begins to see its full potential when it is used for virtual entertainment and many other functions.

bucky-ball   A slang name for a molecule discovered by Buckminister Fuller that looks like a tiny soccer ball with 20 hexagons and 12 pentagons with a carbon atom at each vertex.

Bussard ramjet   A proposed solution to interstellar travel by Robert Bussard in 1960. The design scoops up and compresses interstellar hydrogen until fusion occurs with resulting energy directed out of the ship as propulsion.

Caladan   A fictional planet in the classic science fiction novels of *Dune*, by Frank Herbert. It is placed in orbit about the star Delta Pavonis.

CNO cycle   A fusion process, using carbon as a catalyst, to convert 4 ^1H atoms into a ^4He atom, 2 positrons, 2 neutrinos, 3 photons and 26.8 MeV of energy. It occurs in hot stars.

carbon nanotube   A carbon molecule with carbon atoms arranged in cylindrical form with a one atom thick wall. The bonds are stronger than carbon bonds in diamond.

carbon nanotube ribbon   A long *cable* made of carbon nanotubes. When a breakthrough allows ribbons long enough to be made, their incredible strength, flexibility and conductivity makes the construction of a space elevator possible.

Casimir (effect)   A demonstration that a zero-point energy (or vacuum energy) exists. It is manifested by the creation of short lived particle pairs, which create a pressure difference between the inside of two plates, micrometers apart, and the outside of the plates.

Catom Control Center   The monitoring center for the construction and morphing processes involving catoms on Gaia II. It is located in a transition building below Gaia University.

CELSS   Controlled Ecological Life Support System. Casually called a biosphere, it is a fully self maintaining, closed habitat that can support life indefinitely with the only external input being solar or some other form of energy. Some biospheres such as the one on Mars may get some materials (such as water) from the environment, also.

centrifugal force   A false force that feels like it is pushing an object away from the center of a spinning system due to the natural tendency of an object to travel in a straight line.

centripetal force   A true force pulling an object toward the center of a spinning system to keep it circling about the center.

CERN   A famous lab near Geneva, Switzerland. It is the home of the Large Hadron Collider that proved the existence of the Higgs boson. Among other roles, it is also a major developmental location of advanced computer technology in the late 21st century.

Chemoautotrophs   Organisms that get energy from oxidation of inorganic compounds using carbon dioxide. They are found near thermal vents on the seafloor and are thought to be the precursor on Earth to oxygen-breathing organisms.

Chemosynthesis   An alternative to photosynthesis where life forms get energy from inorganic compounds without the need of sunlight.

*__*Chianti Villas__   One of three Living Regions of the Living Area Europia on Gaia II, it creates the feel of rural living in Tuscany, as was the goal of designers, Disney Inc.

(Le) Chocolatier Suisse   The re-creation on Gaia II of an actual Swiss chocolate shop.

chondrules   Tiny spheres on the order of one millimeter in diameter found in most meteorites on Earth. It is thought that they were tiny molten droplets formed in space when a supernova exploded in the solar neighborhood at the time the solar system was forming. These "droplets" were then accreted by asteroids.

*__*Clarke Island__   One of the three space elevator stations on Earth in the 21st century. Located off the coast of Australia in the Indian Ocean, its original members were China, India, Indonesia and Australia.

claytronic atoms (catoms)   A creation of the early 21st century where molecular sized *building blocks* are *programmed*, using tiny wires with charged ends, to self-assemble into macroscopic structures. In practice, catoms the size of a plant cell are used.

*__*comm-device__   Any of a variety of different types of communications devices used in the time period of the text.

*comm-goggles   A preferred method of communication in the late 21st/ early 22nd centuries. This lightweight product that covers the eyes, with ear receivers, that allows the user hands free communication and internet use with holographic imaging. They fold away compactly into a utility belt.

*Computer Center   The main hub for monitoring the computer operations on Gaia II. Occupying Levels J to C of the transition building below the primary school, it is the home of the vast digital library of the accumulated knowledge of the human race. It is also where the development of the new quantum computer system for Gaia II is being done.

conservation of energy   The physical law that energy can neither be created nor destroyed, only changed. Must keep in mind the mass-energy equivalence (classically $E = mc^2$).

constant acceleration starship   As of 2112, this is the only way for a spacecraft to achieve high enough velocities to travel interstellar distances in a lifetime. Continuous propulsion, which in text is provided by a QFT ramjet system, also creates an artificial gravity.

coriolis effect   When the observers *frame of reference* is rotating, this is an effect where a *falling* object will *curve* in the opposite direction of rotation due to inertia. This can be seen on Earth when water goes down a drain or in weather patterns.

cryogenics   A concept, commonly used in science fiction, that a life form, usually human, can be *flash* frozen and stored for a very long period of time, then later revived and brought back to life completely unharmed.

cyanobacteria (blue-green algae)   A class of bacteria that gets energy through photosynthesis. They are responsible for all photosynthesis on Earth.

cyberfunction library   A vast collection of programs, subprograms and algorithms that each do a specific function in a computer program and so may be reused in future programs avoiding the timely effort of rewriting them.

cyberspace The concept of an imaginary domain consisting of all of the data and applications of a connected computer system, accessible by any terminal in the network.

*Daedalus Equatorial Lunar Array The first and largest radio telescope array on the far side of the moon. Located in Daedalus crater, at lunar latitude 6°S near the middle of the far side, its telescope dishes extend in three radial lines in the 93 km diameter crater.

Def Leppard A musical group popular in the 1980s. It was considered one of the *big hair* bands.

*De Grassi Park Public Airfield One of many small public airfields, created in the mid 21st century, that are free to be used by people with cars that convert to planes. This one is the closest of its kind to CERN near Geneva, Switzerland.

decreases linearly The statement that over any equal interval (usually of time or distance) that a measured quantity decreases by the same amount.

Deep Space Industries An American company formally announced in 2013 with plans to offer resources to other space industries by mining asteroids.

Deimos The smallest of Mars' two moons. It has an equatorial, nearly circular, orbit about 23000 km above the surface.

Delta Pavonis Fourth brightest star in the constellation Pavo. It is a sun-like star in the process of becoming a red giant. About 20 light years from Earth, in text, it is where the first extraterrestrial life is discovered. (to a very high probability)

*Delta Pavonis g The sixth planet to be confirmed in orbit about star Delta Pavonis. This is where nanocraft detect an ozone line in

the atmosphere inferring oxygen in abundance so high as to probably be caused by photosynthesis.

delta-v   Essentially just a change in velocity. This is the popular term used when a rocket burn causes the velocity change in order to move into a different orbit.

deuterium   An isotope of hydrogen with one proton and one neutron, found in the ratio of one ^{2}H atom for every 6400 ^{1}H atoms in natural water. It is commonly used in fusion reactions.

deuterium-helium3 fusion   The fusion reaction used on Gaia II when traveling less that 13% of the speed of light. The product of the reaction is ^{4}He, a positron and 18.4 MeV of energy. Not commonly used on Earth because of higher temperature requirements and the difficulty of acquiring ^{3}He. The reaction is ideal in space since there is no neutron by-product and ^{3}He can be easily acquired from the moon.

deuterium- tritium fusion   The fusion reaction most commonly used in early fusion reactors since lower temperatures are required and both reactants are easily found in sea water. The reaction formula is ^{2}H + ^{3}H = ^{4}He + n + 17.6 MeV energy, where n is a neutron.

*_diggers_   The slang term used in this text for a mining probe that lands on the surface of a moon, asteroid or comet to harvest resources.

*disposable ear receivers   Similar to disposable ear plugs of old. They have inexpensive wireless receivers for listening to any audio transmission they are tuned to. Most tune automatically to the nearest transmission.

dissociation   A process in which ionic compounds are split into parts. In this text, it is photo-dissociation of water vapor into hydrogen and oxygen by UV light.

*_Dixon, Jackie_   This early 21st century astrobiologist was the lead scientist of the team to first create self-replicating, evolving and metabolizing synthetic life. Awarded the Nobel Prize in Biology in 2132, she became a world-wide celebrity.

DNA Computer A type of molecular computer using DNA strands to store and process data. As with other molecular computers they have the advantage that many simultaneous calculations can be done on many DNA molecules.

Doppler Shift A well known effect where a wavelength of light (or sound) is *compressed* if two objects are moving toward each other and *stretched* if they are moving away.

dormant life Life forms that stay in a "hibernated state" for extended periods of time, only to be "awoken" by some environmental phenomenon.

***Drake Enterprisies** A multi-billion dollar robotic industry founded by Paul Drake with primary location in Central England. The company uses state of the art nano-technology to produce both microscopic and macroscopic programmable machines.

***Dual Propulsion Ion Thrust Ship** An interplanetary craft used in the mid 21st century that can accelerate very slowly, but for long periods of time, to cover planetary distances in a short duration. It also has a faster, higher velocity change capability. Using this craft, travel to Mars is possible in 39 days.

***Earth Awareness Period** A program established at Romanov Primary School on Gaia II after a crisis on the ship is caused by a few students longing to return to Earth.

eccentricity A measure of how elliptical an orbit is defined by the formula: $e = (r_a - r_p)/(r_a + r_p)$, where r_a is the farthest the orbiting object is from the center of gravity of the system and r_p is the closest.

***Egyptian Biosphere** The first successful CELSS on Earth thanks to innovations by Seker Fayed who lived there for 40 years. It leads the way to establishing the Mars Biosphere and Gaia II.

electron donors   Chemical compounds that can supply energy in a reaction by losing an electron.

Emden Northern Lunar Array   The smallest of three arrays of radio telescopes near the center of the far side of the moon, longitudinally. It is located in Emden crater at about 60° North lunar latitude.

encryption   In this text, essentially a set of coded instructions needed in order to enter a   computer program to access or change data or cyber-commands.

Enhanced Resolution Systems   ERS telescopes use evolving computer technology to obtain better "seeing" of an object than would be possible otherwise. Adaptive Optics technology is a type of ERS that cancels out atmospheric distortion effects.

entropy   The *state of disorder* of a closed system. A law of nature is that the universe or any closed system will always increase in entropy or become more disordered. (Closely tied with the *arrow* of time)

equatorial orbit   An orbit above the equator of a celestial body or the imaginary line around the body which is equidistant from the poles of the spin axis.

***Europia* (Living Area I)**   One of the two Living Areas of Gaia II designed by Disney Inc.. It fills the inner surface of a cylinder one kilometer long and one kilometer radius and contains the Living Regions of Alpenhausen, Wicklesby and Chianti Villas.

exobiology   In this text, it is anything that we define as life, which has an origin somewhere other than Earth.

Fayed, Seker   A legendary scientist who lived in the Egyptian Biosphere for over 40 years perfecting the CELSS and thus making the Mars Biosphere and Gaia II possible.

feedback mechanism   Any cyclic process in which the result effects the next cycle of the process in a   positive or negative way.

Final Fantasy *B.G. II (TM)   Based on the popular video game of the early 21st century, this version uses a BrainGate^{TM} Helmet to become totally immersed in the virtual world.

fermentation   A metabolic process converting sugars to acids, gasses and alcohol. This is a weak method of creating ATP, which is the product used for energy by all life on Earth.

food replicator   This device takes organic material (proteins, plant cells, etc.) and re-creates, with programmed nanomachines, common food items or dishes as closely as possible. Technically this is a fabricator, not a replicator.

four dimensional (4D) space-time   By looking at time as the fourth dimension, many realities of nature can be more simply explained mathematically.

fusion energy reactor   An energy power plant using one or more of many possible reactions using the fact that, when very stable ^{4}He is a final product of a reaction, excess energy is released.

g force   The force on an object due to acceleration as expressed in terms of multiples of the force of gravity at the Earth's surface.

*Gaia II   This constant acceleration starship propelled by QFT technology is the first manned vessel to leave the solar system. Launched on January 28, 2112, the initial crew was 750 residents. The mission is planned to last over 600 years and visit 18 stars.

*Gaia University   The higher learning institute on Gaia II that shares the transition building between Alpenhausen and Hanalei Village with the Theater, Nanofactory, Catom Control Center and Raw Material Storage.

galactic civilization   In this text, this refers to a race of beings capable of colonizing an entire galaxy.

Gasthaus Rauch   A cozy Bavarian style bed and breakfast with a beer garden. Run by Herbert and Ilsa Rauch, who also provide musical entertainment, it is modeled after one in Germany of the same name.

geo-political   Events effecting a nation or region influenced by geography and politics.

geostation   A term used for a space elevator station at the altitude of geosynchronous orbit. This is the location for space hotels and support stations for space laboratories, industries, communications satellites and even living habitats.

geostationary orbit   An orbit at an altitude where orbital period is the same as the rotation of the Earth and thus maintains the same location above the Earth's surface.

Geosynchronous   Essentially the same as geostationary. Orbital speed matches Earth rotation.

Gliese 250   The first destination of Gaia II, this is a double star system. Four planets orbiting the primary and two around the companion had been confirmed at time of Gaia II launch. The innermost confirmed planet is the most Earth-like planet found within a 50 light year radius from Earth and is one reason this star is chosen as the first destination.

Gliese 667C   This red dwarf star is the smallest of a triple star group about 22 light years from the sun. This star created excitement in the early twenty first century when four, possibly habitable, super-earths were thought to have been discovered.

*Gliese 667Cd   This was a "rediscovered" planet about 50% more massive than the Earth. In March 2105, nanocraft data showed this to be an ocean planet with a 75% chance of life.

Google Earth *2050   The project beginning in 2050 to totally rework the famous web site with holographic technology to be able to view the planet in 3 dimensions at any altitude.

Gran Polley's Tea Room A quaint English café in Wicklesby on Gaia II ran by Betty Jones.

graphene A one atom thick carbon molecule "sheet" with bonds stronger than the carbon bonds in diamonds. It has many revolutionary applications and properties.

gravity assist velocity boost Commonly called the "slingshot effect", if a spacecraft can have a parabolic orbital encounter with a celestial body it can take advantage of that body's motion to essentially "bounce off" the object, increasing its speed by up to double the relative velocity of the object. The effect can be used to slow a spacecraft, also.

Great Oxidation Event The time in the Earth's history when cyanobacteria converted the atmosphere from a reducing one to an oxidizing one by means of photosynthesis. This caused a great extinction of oxygen intolerant organisms.

gyroscope A spinning device used to maintain orientation of an object using the principals of angular momentum. As in a top or yoyo, the direction of the spin axis is maintained.

habitable zone At this time, it is defined as the distance range from a star where liquid water can exist on the surface of a planet.

Hanalei Village One of three Living Regions of the Living Area Tropicania on Gaia II. Modeled after the town of Hanalei, Hawaii, names of some places and roads were copied.

handedness of a molecule A chiral molecule is one where its mirror image is not the same as the original due to asymmetry along the z-axis. The resulting pair are designated "left hand" and "right hand".

Harrison, Scott A musician very popular in the early 22nd century. He is playing in a lounge at the Space Hilton when Paul and Renata pass through.

Helium3 ^{3}He is an isotope of helium with two protons and one neutron. It reacts with ^{2}H (deuterium) or with itself in aneutronic fusion reactions. Hard to come by on Earth, it is mined from lunar regolith for use in fusion reactors.

Helium4 ^{4}He is the very stable (low energy) isotope of helium with two protons and two neutrons. It is the end product of fusion reactions along with the excess energy remaining from the reaction and sometimes "left over" particles such as neutrons, neutrinos, positrons or photons.

hermetically sealed   An opening is hermetically sealed when a chemically created substance prevents the escape (or entry) of gasses.

Higgs Boson   An elementary particle theorized in 1964 by Peter Higgs, first seen in 2012, then confirmed in 2014. The last confirmed particle of the Standard Model of Particle Physics, it is thought to be the "messenger" particle that gives other particles and itself mass from a Higgs field that is believed to exist throughout all of space.

Hohmann orbit phase transition   The lowest energy method for changing location in an orbit. A "delta v" enters a craft into an elliptical orbit then an equal but opposite "delta v" returns the craft to the original orbit at a different phase in the orbit since the elliptical orbit has a different period than the original orbit.

Holland, Jon (Space Dance)   A popular late 21st century composer with "Space Dance" being one of his most popular works.

holo-blog   A "blog" (idea or information put out on the internet in an interactive format) using holographic technology.

holobooth   Early in this text, this is a booth used by clothing retailers. The customer enters the booth to have a three dimensional scan, then a "fashion show" can be watched by the buyer seeing him or herself in any of the retailers e-catalog of styles. The purchased software is then taken to a fabricator to create the clothing which is perfectly tailored to the buyer. The name is used later in text for a virtual reality structure that a person enters in order to be immersed in a 3D environment.

hovercraft Any vehicle that is capable of traveling over a terrain using a cushion of low pressure, high volume air between the vehicle and the surface below.

hybrid rocket engine Generally, any rocket engine using more than one means of propulsion. In text, the vehicle is an orbital shuttle using chemical fuels for high velocity quick burns and different propulsion method for longer lasting low velocity burns.

hydroponic high yield plants A soil-less method of growing vegetation in water with nutrients dissolved in solution. The plants are grown in a three-dimensional array making the best use of limited space.

inflation theory A theory about the beginning of our universe that has been very good at explaining observation, such as the distribution of the background radiation left over from the "Big Bang". The idea is that in a tiny fraction of a second (10^{-36}) after the beginning, lasting a very short duration (about 10^{-30} seconds), the universe went through an immense expansion (10^{78} times in volume).

initial conditions A term, commonly used in science, which refers to the state of a system at the beginning of an observation or action that causes a change in the system.

interface A "bridge" between two otherwise incompatible items. In text, it is the electronic equipment needed to connect the new quantum computer to the molecular system.

interstellar hydrogen Hydrogen atoms (one proton with an electron) that fill the space between the stars in a galaxy. (Densities: galactic average: 0.5 atoms/cm^3, Local Bubble: 0.05 atoms/cm^3, Local Cloud: 0.3 atoms/cm^3)

Island Fever syndrome   A psychological ailment something like claustrophobia that comes from living in a spatially limited area for a long duration.

isotopes   Varying forms of an element determined by the number of neutrons in the atom.

Jet Propulsion Labs (JPL)   A facility, in Pasadena, California, famous in the late 20th/ early 21st century for operating robotic spacecraft visiting other planets and moons.

__Kalons (Galactic Civilizations)__   A fictional science fiction race of beings in the web series "Galactic Civilizations" that was popular in the 2090's.

kinetic energy   In a given frame of reference, this is the energy associated with the motion of an object. At low speeds this is approximately ½ of the mass of an object times the square of its velocity. It is the amount of work required to bring the object to rest in the frame.

lederhosen   German "leather pants", with support straps, that are traditional attire worn at cultural celebrations and events.

__Level System__ **of schooling**   A process of education in which students advance at their own pace to higher and higher levels in selected disciplines with a minimum level in all disciplines required for graduation.

lunar latitude/longitude   Since the same side of the moon always faces the Earth, imaginary vertical and horizontal lines are drawn through its center as the moon crosses the projected equator of the Earth. These are labeled as 0° latitude and 0° longitude with west to the left, east to the   right, north up and south down as seen from Earth.

lifesuit   The term used in this book for the modern spacesuit, which is used in space and on a planetary surface to provide full life support. It has special technology which allows it to be skintight and very flexible and mobile along with having other features such as self-healing capability and enhanced vision.

Life Support Area A section of Gaia II which along with hydroponic food production is the home of genetically enhanced algae and other mechanisms used to create a cycle on the ship that keeps the air mixture and other elements at the right levels to support life.

light sails (solar sails) A method of propelling spacecraft using radiation pressure pushing large, ultra-thin mirrors. This is how nanocraft are propelled.

Little Rio One of three Living Regions of the Living Area Tropicania on Gaia II. It was designed by Disney Inc. to capture the best aspects of the city of Rio de Janeiro, Brazil.

Living Area One of two kilometer long sections of the rotating, cylindrical starship Gaia II. The inner surface of the cylinder has been made livable by adding water, substructure materials, with catom containing soils and objects to mimic Earth environments.

Living Region Each Living Area of Gaia II is divided into three very different habitats. The original regions are designed to re-create six very desirable, culturally different and ecologically different places on Earth.

Local Bubble The result of a supernova that exploded 10-20 million years ago, this is a "bubble" of hot disperse gas that has only about 10% of the average interstellar hydrogen density of the rest of the galaxy. It is irregular and is about 300 light years across.

Local Interstellar Cloud A region within the Local Bubble that has an interstellar hydrogen density of about 60% of the average in the galaxy. The sun entered this cloud 44000 to 150000 years ago and should be in it for another 10000 to 20000 years as it moves into the neighboring "G Cloud". The Local Cloud is about 30 light years across extending toward the star Altair.

Lovelock, James   A revolutionary thinker who, in the latter part of the 20th century, saw the Earth as one, large, self-regulating, emergent system. He described how biological and geophysical processes work together to optimize conditions for life on the planet. He named this "living organism" after the Greek goddess Gaia.

*low g basketball (b-ball)   A game invented by the residents of the Mars Biosphere that slightly modifies the rules of normal basketball to suit Martian gravity (30% of Earth's).

*Low-g Games   A group of contests, competed in annually, that are specifically suited for the lower gravity environment in the *Low-g Park* on Gaia II.

*Low-g Park   A recreational area created in the *Sky Cylinder* on Gaia II that takes advantage of its lower artificial gravity, (one-tenth of that on the living surface).

luminosity (of a star)   The star's brightness. Actually, its total energy output per unit time.

*Lunar Cyclotron   A particle accelerator on the moon which is an advanced laboratory to study particle physics. Among other projects, it is used to produce anti-matter.

macro-scale robotics   Intelligent machines that become more and more dominant in industry, household use, the workplace and many other facets of everyday society in the 20th and 21st century.

magnetic levitation (maglev)   A system of transportation in which a vehicle is suspended above a track, guided and propelled by magnetism.

magnetic linear motors   Electric motors aligned to produce a linear force along their length. They are used to accelerate a vehicle in a magnetic levitation system.

Marriot Space Hotel   The second hotel to be constructed at a geostation on a space elevator, after the Space Hilton. It is part of Noda Geostation, accessed from Tsiolkovsky Station in the Pacific Ocean.

Mars synchronous orbit   An equatorial orbit of Mars at an altitude where orbital velocity matches rotation of Mars so that the orbiting object stays above the same location on the planet.

mass driver   A method of non-rocket space launch using magnetic linear motors to accelerate and catapult payloads into orbit.

maximum cratering threshold   The density of the number of craters on the surface of a planet or moon reaches a maximum when new craters just replace old ones.

Mealmaker   A special kind of food fabricator that produces select individual meals.

mechanical counterpressure system   A lifesuit system that uses mechanical pressure rather than air pressure and thus uses a skin tight garment that allows greater mobility.

metallicity (of a star)   The proportion of a star's matter that is made up of elements other than hydrogen or helium.

metamaterials   Artificial materials engineered to have properties not found in nature. In the text, one metamaterial used is the "skin" of a plasma jet, which is super strong, temperature resistant and essentially frictionless.

Mildenhall Central England Public Airfield   A free public park with air strips for personal vehicles which are cars that transform into planes. It was the site of an Air Force Base in the 20th century. The site has a shop where a traveler can purchase a battery exchange.

miners **(nanomachines)**   The slang term used in this book for nanomachines that are sent down a hollow drill from a mining probe to break up regolith so it can be drawn back up to for processing.

molecular computer   A category of both organic and inorganic computers that do simultaneous calculations on molecules, mimicking the parallel processing capabilities of the brain.

*__*Montrieux, Pierre__*   A famous French architect of the late 21st century who, among many other accomplishments, designed the state of the art theater on Gaia II, that is the equal of the grandest theaters on Earth in New York, London, Paris, Moscow and Beijing.

__*morphing of the living areas__   A shifting of the catoms making up the landscape and large structures in the Living Areas of Gaia II. This shifting coincides with the change in the direction of the artificial gravity when transitioning between constant velocity and constant acceleration or deceleration (which on Gaia II is 1 meter/sec^2 or about .1g)

__Mos Eisley Cantina Bar__   A lounge at the Space Hilton Hotel that was modeled after an alien bar in the movie series "Star Wars".

nanobatteries   A far superior battery to the old lithium-ion type, in which microscopic size particles coat the electrode to allow more current flow and thus a more powerful battery with quicker charging time. Other "nanoparticles" block the liquid in the batteries from the electrodes to prevent discharging for a longer lasting battery.

nanobots   A slang name for microscopic machines that are programmed to perform a specific function. The ultimate nanobot is a "Turing Machine" that can replicate itself.

Nanofabricator   Usually just called a fabricator, this is a machine that feeds an exact amount of raw materials into a processor in which tiny machines assemble whatever product the fabricator is programmed to create.

nanofactory   An assembly plant based on nano-technology where basic components of products are made in fabricators and then are assembled into larger products using robotics.

nanocraft   Tiny robotic space ships, with light sails, that were slowly accelerated to high velocities (80% speed of light) by a powerful laser satellite. First sent to selected nearby star systems in the 2050's, they were sent out in very high numbers so that the desired amount of data would be transmitted back to Earth. Toward the end of the 21st century, nanocraft were developed that could make use of QFT propulsion technology and thus accelerate and decelerate without sails.

nanoprobe (medical)   Tiny machines that are swallowed or injected into a patient to perform a certain medical task or diagnosis. They are so small that there is no antibody response from the immune system.

nano-recycler   A processing machine that breaks waste products down to basic microscopic constituents using nano-machines. The basic elements are separated and transferred to a location where new products can be produced.

nanotechnology (nano-tech)   A multifaceted technological field made possible by the capability to construct microscopic machines and materials in large numbers inexpensively.

*New Instrument Classical Revival Era   With the invention of new musical instruments, using new technologies (ie. nano-tech), there is a resurgence of classically composed music, taking advantage of the new instruments.

Newton's third law   For every action there is an equal, but opposite, reaction. In the text, this is an important concept to remember when weightless. (If you push on something of equivalent weight to yourself, you will move "backward" as fast as what you push moves "forward")

*NGIRI   New Generation Infrared Interferometer. In 2032, NASA/ESA finally were able to get a long sought after, high precision infrared interferometer launched and established at Lagrangian Point 2 (L2). This multi-spacecraft endeavor took advantage and improved upon the research accomplished by earlier canceled missions such as SIM (Space Interferometry Mission), TPF (Terrestrial Planet Finder) and Darwin.

Noda, Akira The lead scientist of the team at AIST of Japan who makes the technological breakthrough in carbon nanotube ribbon production that allows for the construction of space elevators. The discovery in 2023 led to a Nobel Prize in 2029.

Noda Geostation The space elevator station at geosynchronous orbit named after Akira Noda. It is part of the first space elevator built, originating at Tsiolkovsky Station in the Pacific Ocean and extending to Edwards Transfer Station at the end of the 100km tether.

Nova website An internet site continuing the tradition of the old PBS science series. The *Man on the Moon* special aired in 2100 documenting man's increasing presence on the moon in the 21st century culminating in the discovery of extraterrestrial life in the early morning hours of July 11, 2100 at the Bose Crater Lunar Observatory

O'Neill, Gerard A professor at Princeton University in the late 20th century, he was way ahead of his time in not only predicting but designing space habitats and orbiting solar energy stations. *The High Frontier* was his classic publishing.

orbital plane inclination The angle between the plane defined by the orbit of an astronomical body and the plane of the majority of objects orbiting the parent star or planet.

outgassing The release of gasses that get trapped in the interior of a planet or moon when it is formed in a solar nebula.

ozone absorption line If a spectrograph is taken in the infrared part of the spectrum, the presence of ozone in a planetary atmosphere can be determined by dark lines caused by the absence of light at a signature frequency band due to absorption of photons of this frequency by the molecule. Ozone (O_3) is a molecule of three oxygen atoms that only is found due to ultraviolet light acting on free oxygen (O_2).

parallel processing   A computing method doing many calculations at the same time rather than one at a time in series, as in early computers. Makes solving certain kinds of problems much faster and is how the brain works.

particle accelerator   A research tool in the shape of a large donut that uses electricity to propel charged particles to very high speeds. When two particles going near light speeds in opposite directions collide, one can study their component parts.

particle-antiparticle pair   Most particles in nature have an "antiparticle" of same mass, but opposite charge. When two of these particles collide (i.e. an electron and a positron) they totally annihilate each other leaving nothing but energy in the form of gamma rays. Quantum fluctuations produce virtual pairs of these particles, from the vacuum energy of space. They are produced, then combine to annihilate each other, in a time period so short as to be impossible to observe. The energy then returns to the vacuum field.

Phobos   The irregularly shaped, innermost moon of Mars. It orbits Mars faster than the planet's rotation speed and thus rises in the west and sets in the east.

planetary civilization   In some writings this means an intelligent life form that harnesses the entire energy of a planet. Here it refers to a population of a planet with common language, communication, shared intelligence and global awareness that has begun to occupy the entire solar system of a star.

planetary migration   The theory developed to explain Hot Jupiters and Ocean Planets that were formed in the outer regions of a planetary disc, but were surprisingly found close to host stars.

Planetary Resources   An American company formed in 2010 with the stated goal of expanding the Earth's natural resource supplies by developing and using technology to mine asteroids.

plasma jet   An aircraft in which powerful nanobatteries supply the power to compress air into a supersonic, superheated plasma, which then expands through an exhaust turbine to propel the plane.

plate tectonics   The motion of segments of a planet's crust and upper mantle over time scales of thousands of years or greater.

positron   The antiparticle of the electron, it has the same mass but opposite charge. It can be a shortly lived by-product of a fusion reaction since a positron is combined with a neutron in a proton, giving the proton its positive charge.

potential energy   A "stored" energy in an object usually determined by the amount of work done to get an object or system of particles to a certain position.

proton-proton fusion   This is the main fusion process that takes place in lower temperature stars like our sun. The reaction is $^1H + {}^1H > D (+ e^+ + v)$, $D + {}^1H > {}^3He$, $^3He + {}^3He > {}^4He + 2\,{}^1H$. A cubic meter of the center of the sun only emits about 276 Watts of energy, but it is continuous and the immense size of the sun accounts for the large radiation output.

protoplanetary disc   Debris orbiting a newly born star that will eventually form planets and other objects in a new solar system.

prototype   The first of its kind, possibly a test model.

*quantene   A special sheet molecule discovered by Petr Romanov in 2088 with the fantastic quality that when it is used in layers with graphene, virtual particles from quantum fluctuations in space can be captured for long enough to harness their energy. Also, these same quantene-graphene sheets are used in a working model of the quantum computer.

quantum computer (QC)   A computer working at the quantum level using particle spin to store and process data. The QC can do calculations never before possible since the parallel processing power is orders of magnitude better even than the molecular computer. It is particularly useful in modeling quantum systems such as weather models.

quantum fluctuations   Due to the vacuum energy that permeates all of space, quantum effects cause the creation of virtual particle-antiparticle pairs. They quickly annihilate each other in a time period so short that they are never seen   due   to   the uncertainty principal.

***QFT* ramjet**   Quantum Fluctuation Temporizer. A new propulsion mechanism used for Gaia II made possible by the discovery of quantene and its properties when used in sheets with graphene. Particle-antiparticle pairs created by quantum fluctuations are "captured" for a long enough time to use their energy to propel the ship. The energy available in "empty" space is large enough that large interstellar craft can be accelerated for long periods of time to achieve high velocities.

radio telescope array   Rows of radio antenna dishes, often three radial arms, that work together to form an effective receiver of radius equal to the length of the arms. Three of these were put in craters near the center of the far side of the moon in the mid 21st century.

Real Earth Society   In the text, this was a group secretly formed by 16 year old Derek Scott to learn about the Earth and to vent anger toward parents for taking them away.

rendezvous   A meeting of parties, this term is commonly used when spacecraft are doing the   necessary   velocity   changes   and maneuvers in order to come together.

replicator   A machine that can assemble any object, that it is programmed for, if given adequate quantity of the object's fundamental elements. Unlike a fabricator, this machine assembles from the molecular level up and in text requires a quantum computer and Turing machines to deal with the immense quantity of particles.

retro velocity change A rocket burn in the opposite direction of that being traveled to slow a spacecraft and thus change its orbit.

Role Playing Game (RPG) A video game or virtual game in which players assume the roles of characters in the game.

***Romanov Primary School** The pre-university school on Gaia II named after Nobel prize winner Petr Romanov. It is located in the transition building between Little Rio and Chianti Villas with the Computer Center and Data Storage Library.

***Sagan Crater Research Center/ Biosphere** The manned research station on Mars at the base of the Mars Space Elevator. It was expanded from a small research station to a self sustaining biosphere when a fusion reactor on site went on-line. Sagan Crater was chosen due to location, close but not too close to the equator, and the shallow depth of the permafrost at the site, among other reasons.

***Santos-Dumont Station** The second space elevator to be built was anchored to Earth by this station in the South Atlantic Ocean. Original partners were the European Union, South Africa and Brazil. Since construction costs were reduced significantly by the existence of the first elevator, much more attention to aesthetics was given to this station.

self regulatory system A closed system that adjusts itself to maintain an ideal environment. A simple example would be a thermostat. In text, this term is used to describe the entire biosphere of the Earth.

self replicating nanobots *Turing* machines. Microscopic machines that are so sophisticated that they can produce exact replicas of themselves using materials from the environment, which in turn can produce others.

Serpentinization   The process where high-temperature rock from a planet's mantle comes in contact with low temperature seawater. The water acts as a catalyst to convert the iron and magnesium rich rock into "serpentine group" minerals. The excess energy from this reaction supports bio-systems at deep ocean locations.

Shangri La   A musical performance originally presented by the Chinese Opera in Beijing, China, it quickly became popular worldwide. In 2110, it became the highest grossing stage show of all time and was chosen as one of the performances for the send off gala for Gaia II.

Ship Control Center   Located in the ring at the rear (or west end) of Gaia II, this is the location where ship   propulsion   and energy systems are monitored and controlled.

sifters **(nanomachines)**   The slang term used in this text referring to the nanomachines that separate a desired substance from regolith in a mining probe, so it can be stored in a pod which is transported back to a mining company or spacecraft.

silica nanoskeletons   Basic microstructures, on which polymers are coated, that give a lifesuit good insulation with excellent elasticity and flexibility.

silicon-based life   An alternative to the type of life found on Earth, which is based on carbon. Silicon is chemically similar to carbon and forms similar compounds.

Sky Cylinder   A hundred meter radius cylinder with the same rotation axis as rest of the ship, it runs the entire length of the two Living Areas of Gaia II. Three special light fixtures on a track mimic the sun and moon, lighting each area through the transparent cylinder, with the illusion of blue sky and clouds on the surface.

smart **chair**   A special chair that totally conforms to the person who is sitting in it. The chair uses small sensors built into the chairs that can make tiny adjustments to relieve pressure points while still giving necessary support.

smart **shoes**   Like the smart chair, smart shoes use tiny sensors to mold a shoe for ultimate comfort and support for the wearer.

Sonora   One of the three Living Regions of Tropicania on Gaia II. This environment is inspired by the desert southwest of the United States, including special desert homes that blend with the surroundings.

space elevator   This concept, dating back to 1895 (Konstantin Tsiolkovski), became a reality when a tether could be made strong enough and flexible enough to extend from a floating station on Earth to a counterweight 100km above the surface. High powered lasers transmit energy to transports climbing the tether until they reach an altitude at which solar energy can take over. This method of escaping the gravity well of the Earth was so much less expensive than chemical rockets that, once constructed, space travel, industry, research, tourism, solar energy satellites and even space habitats boomed.

space elevator tether   A large number of carbon nanotube ribbons woven together to create a cable strong enough and flexible enough to handle the stress of a space elevator system extending 100km into space from a floating station on Earth.

space elevator transport   This "car" that carries cargo and passengers up a space elevator tether is initially powered by high energy lasers and then with solar energy. The transports take a 40 hour trip to a geostation at geosynchronous orbit and back. Different transports take the 4 day trip to a transfer station for interplanetary launch and arrival.

Space Hilton Hotel   The first true space hotel, it was constructed as part of the space elevator connecting Santos-Dumont Station, in the Atlantic Ocean, to Asimov Transfer Station 100km above. It is part of Sumio Geostation at geosynchronous earth orbit.

spectrograph   A data gathering instrument that uses a prism or similar concept to separate light into its component frequencies. One can get information about the composition of the emitting object or the material that the light passes through by examining bright and dark lines in the spectra.

Standard Model of Particle Physics   The theory organizing all of the particles found in nature, or produced in collisions, by properties such as spin, generation and function, it was completed in   the early 21st century when the Higgs Boson, that was predicted by the model , was found then confirmed.

Stargate   A popular movie and TV series at the turn of the 21st century. It is about a team finding and using a portal found on the Earth through which a person can travel to distant worlds.

stellar braking   In this text, it refers to the use of a star's extended atmosphere to decelerate a spacecraft. Magnetic sails and super temperature resistant materials are used by the vessel.

*Straub, Gerhardt   A German quantum physicist and computer scientist who uses the newly discovered quantene and its unique properties in sheets with graphene to develop the first practical quantum computers.

String Theory   The concept that the smallest indivisible components of matter are tiny strings. It explains that the variety of particles found in nature is due to vibration modes of the strings in an 11 dimensional universe.

subduction   The process in which one tectonic plate moves under another one, taking deposited materials with it into the crust and upper mantle of a planet.

*Sumio Geostation   The space elevator station at the altitude of geosynchronous orbit constructed as part of the 100km space elevator stretching from Santos-Dumont Station in the Atlantic Ocean to Asimov Transfer Station. It is home of the Space Hilton Hotel.

*Super Low-g Aerial Staging Facility   A structure built in the Low-g Park on Gaia II that is even closer to the axis for special extreme sports such as low-g aerials.

superluminal (warp) speed   A science fiction concept of faster than light speed. In this text, it is not possible and may never be.

Tahiti Nui Café   In the text, this is a small diner in Hanalei Village on Gaia II that is modeled after one of the same name in Hanalei, Hawaii on the island of Kaua'i.

*Tech City, West Antarctica   Conceived at a First World conference in 2048, the decision was made to create an isolated location to continue technological advance during times of world conflict and turmoil. The chosen site in West Antarctica was made possible by the success of the first operational fusion energy plant which had been secretly constructed and tested at the site. The nature of the city and high education of the populous made certain social experiments possible, such as eliminating personal vehicles and the absence of exchange currency.

teleportation   A science fiction process in which an object (usually a human) is broken down into energy then *beamed* to a distant location where it reassembles into the original object unharmed. In this text, it is not considered possible other than for particles in the quantum realm.

termination shock   The shock wave where a star's "stellar wind" is slowed down to a speed below the   speed   of   sound   by interaction with the interstellar medium.

terminator (of a planet)   The imaginary line separating the day side from the night side of a planet that is "tidally locked" in orbit of its host star.

terraforming   In general, this is the process of transforming an alien planet into one like Earth where humans can live without protective apparatus.

tidal heating (of a planet or moon) The heating of the interior of a planet or moon due to gravitational "stretching" due to an elliptical orbit about the parent body.

tidally locked A gravitational effect when an object such as a planet or moon is so close to a massive object that it's same side always faces that object (i.e. the Moon facing the Earth).

theoretical construct A concept of something that just exists in the mind as opposed to a *real* object that exists in the absence of a mind.

thermoelectric nanocrystals Tiny crystals which have the property of absorbing heat and converting it into electricity. They are used as a cooling mechanism in lifesuits.

transit (of a celestial object) The period of time when an object such as a planet or companion star comes between a star and the observer.

***transition buildings** Three major constructions connect the two Living Areas of Gaia II. The building between regions Little Rio and Chianti Villas contains Romanov Primary School, the Computer Center and Data Storage Library. The building between regions Alpenhausen and Hanalei Village contains the theater, university, the nanofactory and Catom Control Center. The third building, between the regions Sonora and Wicklesby, is the home of the Zhang Health and Sciences Center.

tritium ^{3}H is a radioactive isotope of hydrogen that is used along with ^{2}H (deuterium) in early fusion reactors on Earth. A tritium atom consists of one proton and two neutrons.

***Tropicania* (Living Area II)** One of two Living Areas of Gaia II, it is a catom creation by Disney Inc. on the inner surface of a rotating cylinder. Tropicania is divided into three Living Regions that are chosen to duplicate very desirable, warmer climate regions of the Earth. The three original Living Regions of Tropicania are Little Rio, Sonora and Hanalei Village.

*Tsiolkovski Station   This, Pacific Ocean based, beginning of the world's first space elevator was named after the early 20th century scientist Konstantin Tsiolkovsky, who first conceived the idea. It initially consisted of three floating platforms, two that anchored elevator tethers to the Earth and a third that supported a high energy laser. Two more islands were later added with additional tethers to accommodate the large demand for inexpensive access to space.

ultraviolet flare   A sudden burst of radiation from a star due to the release of magnetic energy stored in the corona. Young red dwarf stars have these frequently.

uncertainty principal   A well tested concept, first proposed by Werner Heisenburg, that there is a property of nature that limits how accurately certain parameters can be measured. In particular, the position of a particle can only be known to an accuracy of $h/2\pi$ multiplied by its momentum (where h is the Planck constant)

*Uncle Albert's Tea Room   A small eating place in the Marriot Space Hotel at Noda Geostation. It was inspired by a scene in the movie *Mary Poppins*.

underground permafrost   A layer of the crust of a planet, beneath surface dust and rock, that contains permanently frozen water mixed with other elements. Martian bases depend on this layer and are located where it is not too far beneath the surface.

utility belt   In the text, this is a hands free method of carrying comm-devices, ear receivers, currency, flash drives or any other item convenient to have on one's person.

vacuum energy (zero-point energy)   A proposal of inflation theory that there is a non-zero energy field that permeates all of space. One experiment that gave credibility to this idea was the Casimir Effect demonstrating the reality of quantum fluctuations created by this field. The idea was universally accepted when the discovery of quantene, and its properties when used with graphene, allowed this energy to be used to propel interplanetary spacecraft.

Valley Marineris Standard Time   With Mars having a rotation period similar to that of the Earth, it is also divided into time zones. Sagan Crater Research Center is located in this time zone that also includes a large part of Valley Marineris (a vast canyon on Mars).

Van Halen (Eddie)   A popular rock band of the late 20th century, it was named after two of the founding members, Alex and Eddie. Eddie Van Halen was known for his unique guitar playing, but also designed his own guitar bodies, often a variation of his *signature* red with random black and white crossing lines.

velocity vector   A value assigned to both the magnitude of relative speed and direction of motion of an object.

Vertical Take-off Plane (VTO)   Any plane that can use its propulsion to rise straight up from its landing pad and then convert to horizontal propulsion to travel to its destination, then land the same way. Helicopters are not usually listed in this category.

Viking probes   Two very successful probes controlled by the Jet Propulsion Labs in Pasadena, California, that landed on Mars and conducted experiments with robotic equipment in the 1970s.

Villa Dievole   A hotel and Italian restaurant near the east wall of the Chianti Villas Region of Gaia II. It is on a hill overlooking the region. The facility is operated by Dario Russo.

Virtual Entertainment Center   Occupying Levels A and B above the Computer Center and below the primary school on Gaia II, this recreational area has rooms, booths and stations for enjoying virtual games or experiences (where one is immersed in a 3D imaginary environment).

Viva La Vida *musical*   A very successful musical of the late 21st century that was based on the music of Coldplay, a very popular musical group earlier in the century. It was performed for the send off gala for Gaia II.

Wailea Park Condos   Inspired by condominiums in Hanalei, Hawaii, it is where main characters Barry Donaldson and Mei Sun live on Gaia II.

web channel   During the 2020's, television became obsolete as the internet took over as the vehicle for entertainment as well as information and communication. A web channel is a website carrying a specific theme of entertainment (in text, the Discovery Web Channel)

Wicklesby   A small town in the center of a Living Region of Gaia II of the same name, the region captures the feeling of the English countryside and the town of Wicklesby is the attempt of designer, Disney Inc., to re-create a quaint, charming little town centered by a large church of Roman Gothic style.

Wicksteed Park   A community gathering and recreational place in the town of Wicklesby on Gaia II. It is modeled after a park of the same name in Kettering, England.

Wikipedia *2100   The most complete and accurate collection of knowledge ever by a single media source. Modeled after multi-volume reference books called encyclopedias, Wikipedia kept adding and improving throughout the 21st century.

wormhole   A commonly used science fiction phenomenon, it allows travel from one part of space to another far away through an irregularity in the fabric of space-time.

You Tube *2100   When the *You Tube* website did away with its ten minute limitation, entire old and new drama, comedy and educational programs were presented on the site. This was the beginning of the end of the television media that dominated the 20th century. *You Tube* 2100 is the latest version.

zero g   Thought of as the absence of gravitational force, it is more common that gravity is offset by a different force (i.e. centrifugal) leaving a   *net* force of zero on an object.

zero g laser tag   A game, usually played by groups of players, where opponents beam lasers at each other that are detected by a sensor if a player is *hit*. Special rules and obstacles are used when playing in zero g (i.e. at a space hotel).

zero g toilet   A special bathroom fixture that facilitates the difficulties of zero gravity, it usually uses air pressure. The device was perfected in the late 20th century.

zero g shower   A personal washing facility with devices for spraying and collecting water specially designed for zero gravity.

zero g volleyball   A version of the popular game with special rules and devices for play in zero gravity.

Zhang Health and Sciences Center   This transition building, located between Wicklesby and Sonora, houses the medical facilities of Gaia II, the physical fitness center, astrobiology labs, other research labs and the Conference Auditorium. It was named after Feng Zhang, the inventor of the CRISPR process, which has been considered the birth of the revolution in curing disease through gene therapy.

*Most of the information and, in some cases, entire definitions for this glossary are from the Wikipedia website. Please donate to it if you can.

Islamic Terminology

Allah God of Islam

Quran holy book of Islam

Muhammad holiest prophet of Islam

Muslim follower of the religion of Islam

salat prayer

ruku action of getting into a kneeling position with hands on knees until attaining calmness

takbir prayer action where one raises hands to ears and says "Allahu akbar." (God is great.)

Hijri calendar Islamic calendar with 354 days in a year based on the lunar cycle

Ramadan fasting month of the Hijri calendar

suhoor pre-fast meal (before dawn)

iftar fast breaking meal (after sunset)

salah of isha evening prayer before iftar consisting of four raka'at

raka'at units of prescribed actions and words to be repeated

Tarawih prayers recitation of verses of the Quran after isha (attempt khatm over 30 days of Ramadan)

khatm complete recitation of the Quran

Laylat al-Qadr* holiest day of Islam when Muhammad received first verses of the Quran

Eid ul-Fitr end of fasting ceremony and celebration on 1 Shawwal

Shawwal Islamic month after Ramadan

*Observed in this text on 27 Ramadan

SOURCES

NON-FICTION BOOK SOURCES:

"Exoplanets" Sara Seager ed. (2010)

"Life As We Do Not Know It" Peter Ward (2005)

"Astrobiology: A Very Short Introduction" David C.
       Catling (2013)

"Physics of the Future" Michio Kaku (2012)

"Nanotechnology For Dummies" Richard Booker and
Earl Boysen (2011)

"Leaving the Planet by Space Elevator" Bradley
       Edwards & Philip Ragan (2006)

"The Crowded Universe: The Race to Find Life Beyond
       Earth" Alan Boss (2010)

"The High Frontier: Human Colonies in Space" Gerard
       K. O'Neill (3rd ed. 2000)

"Gaia/ Series of Books" James Lovelock (1979-2009)

"Signatures of Life: Science Searches the Universe"
Edward Ashpole (2013)

SCIENCE DOCUMENTARY SOURCES:

Alien Planet (Documentary) – The Discovery Channel

The Universe (Series) – The History Channel

Cosmos (Series) – Original Series: PBS/ New Series: Fox (Carl
Sagan/ Neil Degrasse Tyson)

WEBSITE SOURCES (http://)

General Information:
> en.wikipedia.org/
> www.nasa.gov/
> adswww.harvard.edu/

Star Data:
> en.wikipedia.org/
> www.stellar-database.com/
> www.solstation.com/
> www.projectrho.com/
> www.astrostudio.org/data.html
> simbad.u-strasbg.fr/simbad/

Organizations:
> www.seti.org/
> 100yss.org/
> www.icarusinterstellar.org/
> www.marssociety.org/

Asteroid Mining Companies:
> www.planetaryresources.com/
> deepspaceindustries.com/

Space Math (Distance between stars/ relativistic time):
www.neoprogrammics.com/distance_between_two_stars/
math.ucr.edu/home/baez/physics/Relativity/SR/rocket.html
> www.cthreepo.com/lab/math1/

Looking Back at Earth from Gliese 250:
  www.bdm.id.au/localspace/systems/250.html

Local Solar Environment:
  science.nasa.gov/science-news/science-at-
  nasa/2009/23dec_voyager/

Habitable Star Selection:
  www.seti.org/
  arxiv.org/abs/astro-ph/0210675
www.nasa.gov/vision/universe/newworlds/HabStars.html
en.wikipedia.org/wiki/Habitability_of_red_dwarf_systems

Astrobiology/ Exoplanets:
  www.solstation.com/planets/water-worlds.htm
  www.astrobio.net/
  epod.usra.edu/blog/2009/02/sky-colors-for-
  exoearths.html
  www.solstation.com/life/a-plants.htm

Planetary Atmospheres (Evolution/ Life)   :
  science.nasa.gov/science-news/science-at-
        nasa/2002/10jan_exo-atmospheres/
  cips.berkeley.edu/events/planets-life-
  seminar/kaltenegger07.pdf

Biospheres (CELSS):
  www.permanent.com/space-colonization-nasa-
  celss.html

Nanocraft:

ntrs.nasa.gov/archive/nasa/casi.ntrs.nasa.gov/20100036571_
   2010034507.pdf   www.iase.cc/launcher.htm

Future Predictions:

   www.futuretimeline.net/
   www.spacefuture.com/archive/space_tourism
   www.futuretechnology500.com/index.php/future-airplanes/
   www.popsci.com/technology/article/...-10/deep-space-
   suit?single-page-view=true

Propulsion/ Orbital Transfer:

www.greenstone.org/greenstone3/...=&et=&p.a=b&p.s=Class
   ifierBrowse&p.sa=
   en.wikipedia.org/wiki/Spacecraft_propulsion
www.faa.gov/other_visti/aviation...II.4.1.5%20Maneuvering
   %20in%20Space.pdf
   www.gsjournal.net/old/weuro/turtur2e.pdf

Zero Point Energy:

www.bibliotecapleyades.net/ciencia/ciencia_zeropointenergy
   05.htm

Interstellar Communications (twisted optical lasers):

   www.coseti.org/opticals.htm

MAPS

Pubs.usgs.gov/imap/i2782/i2782_sh1.pdf

www.antarctica.ac.uk/met/SCAR_ssg_ps/ACCE_25_Nov_2009.pdf

Hajri to Western Calendar Conversion:

www.iranchamber.com/calendar/converter/iranian_calendar_converter.p
hp

The Constellation "The Phoenix"
From Gliese 250 (Zax / Lorax)
Drawn by: Ali Zamani

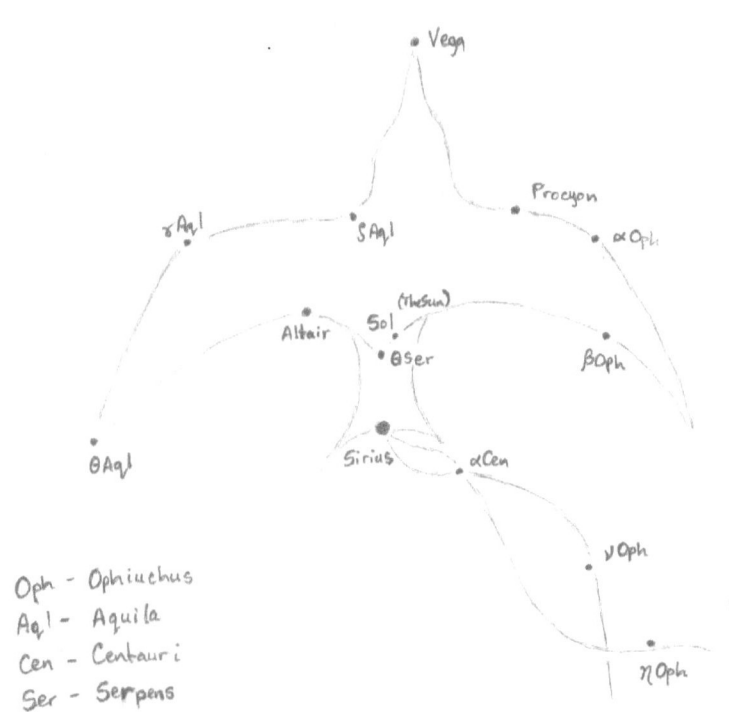

• Vega

Procyon

γ Aql   S Aql   α Oph

(The Sun)
Altair   Sol   Sol
• θ Ser   β Oph

θ Aql   Sirius   α Cen

ν Oph

Oph - Ophiuchus
Aql - Aquila
Cen - Centauri
Ser - Serpens

η Oph

Reference:
www. bdm. id. au / localspace / systems / 250. html